"YOU WANT TO KISS ME."

Her whispered words brushed by him, setting his pulse thrumming. Damn it, yes, he wanted to kiss her. *Needed* to . . .

Giving in to a craving he couldn't explain or fight any longer, he leaned forward. He moved closer, until only inches separated them. The scent of lilacs filled his head. "Have you ever been kissed?"

"Of course. Thousands of times."

"I meant by a man."

"Oh. In that case . . . once."

Unexpected irritation rippled through him. "Indeed? And did you enjoy it?"

"Actually, no. It was rather . . . dry."

"Ah. Then you were not *properly* kissed."

"And you wish to kiss me properly?"

"No." He leaned forward and whispered in her ear, "I intend to kiss you most *im*properly."

He pulled her closer, until her long, lush body was pressed tightly against him.

His common sense roused itself and demanded he stop, but he couldn't. Damn it, he should have been appalled at himself for kissing her. . . . Instead, he was fascinated, aching, and aroused.

Summoning his last ounce of self-control, he ended their kiss.

Her eyes opened slowly. "Oh my."

Oh my, indeed. He didn't know what he'd expected, but he certainly hadn't anticipated this woman unleashing the flood of lust clutching him in a stranglehold. . . .

PRAISE FOR JACQUIE D'ALESSANDRO'S
PREVIOUS NOVEL

RED ROSES MEAN LOVE

"A romance filled with warmth, charm, and a wonderful
freshness that is sure to captivate readers.
Ms. D'Alessandro brings new verve to the genre."
—*Romantic Times*

"Ms. D'Alessandro has written one of the most
humorous, heartwarming, loving books that it has been
my pleasure to read. Every minute spent with this family
is enjoyable. Well written characters and excellent
plotting. Thus marks Ms. D'Alessandro's writing debut.
Her first outing is a triumph!"—*Rendezvous*

"What lifts this book above the ordinary is the humor
flowing throughout the story. Small scenes here and there
will have readers laughing out loud. . . . The climax is as
heart-tugging as any reader could wish. The sexual tension
sizzles. . . . Nothing about *Red Roses Mean Love* suggests
it's a first novel. Witty, stylish, and endearing, it's one of
the best books I've read this year."
—*The Romance Reader*

"Regency romance fans will simply love *Red Roses Mean
Love* because the jocular story line smoothly blends an
entertaining mystery within a warm romance. . . . A
prediction: In the years to come Jacquie D'Alessandro
will become a household name for lovers of
the romance genre."
—Harriet Klausner

Also by Jacquie D'Alessandro

RED ROSES MEAN LOVE

Whirlwind
Wedding

Jacquie D'Alessandro

A Dell Book

Published by
Dell Publishing
a division of
Random House, Inc.
1540 Broadway
New York, New York 10036

This book is a work of fiction. Although certain historical figures, events, and locales are portrayed, they are used fictitiously to give the story a proper historical context. All other characters and events, however, are the product of the author's imagination, and any resemblance to persons living or dead is entirely coincidental.

ISBN: 0-440-23551-0

Printed in the United States of America

Published simultaneously in Canada

September 2000

10 9 8 7 6 5 4 3 2 1

OPM

This book is dedicated with love and my heartfelt gratitude to Deborah Smith, Sandra Chastain, Anne Bushyhead, and Ann Howard White for throwing me a lifeline when I was adrift at sea and sinking fast.

And to my critique partners Donna Fejes, Susan Goggins, and Carina Rock for smoothing the rough waters and pulling me back onboard every time I was ready to jump ship.

And, as always, to my incredible, wonderful, and supportive husband Joe—the Captain of my Heart; and my terrific, makes-me-so-proud son Christopher, aka Captain Junior.

Acknowledgments

I would like to acknowledge the following people for their help and support.

My editor, Maggie Crawford, for her encouragement and guidance.

Editorial assistant Caroline Sincerbeaux, for her patience and help.

My agent, Damaris Rowland, for her faith and wisdom.

My mom and dad, Kay and Jim Johnson, for a lifetime of love and support—and for bragging about me.

My sister, Kathy Guse, for all the laughs and good times—and for bragging about me.

My in-laws, Lea and Art D'Alessandro, for the precious gift of their son—and for bragging about me.

My uncle Bill and aunt Gwen Johnston, and my aunt Eve Johnson, for their cards and letters—and for bragging about me.

(If you meet any of these "bragging" people—prepare yourself!)

I would also like to thank all the wonderful people at Bantam/Dell, most especially Amy Farley, Kara Cesare, Marietta Anastassatos, and Adrian Wood.

Thanks also to all the members of Georgia Romance Writers, especially Martha Kirkland, who is my best research resource.

And a very special thank-you to Wendy Etherington, Jenni Grizzle, Shari Griffin, Deborah Dahlmann, Steve and Michelle Grossman, Jeannie and Ken Pierannunzi, Cherie Imam, Sheryl Brothers, Christine McGinty, and to all my wonderful friends and neighbors for their incredible support.

Last, thank you to all the readers who have taken the time to write or e-mail me. I love hearing from you and your support means the world to me. Stop by and visit me at www.JacquieD.com
or say "hi!" at
JacquieD@MCIWorld.com.

Chapter 1

England, 1816

Austin Randolph Jamison, ninth Duke of Bradford, stood
in a shadowed alcove and surveyed his guests. Couples
swirled on the dance floor, a colorful rainbow of expen-
sively gowned and jeweled women escorted by perfectly
turned out gentlemen. Hundreds of beeswax candles twinkled in the overhead chandeliers, casting a warm glow
over the festivities. Over two hundred of Society's elite
had gathered in his home, and he had only to reach out his
hand to touch any one of a dozen people.

He'd never felt so alone in his life.

Emerging from the shadows, he plucked a brandy from
a passing footman's silver tray and raised the snifter to his
lips.

"There you are, Bradford. Been looking for you everywhere."

Austin froze, smothering a vicious oath. He wasn't sure
who the speaker was, but it didn't matter. He knew *why*
whoever stood behind him had been looking for him, and
his stomach tightened into a knot. Well, there was no

escaping now. Tossing back half his brandy, he braced himself, then turned around.

Lord Digby stood before him. "I just visited the gallery, Bradford," Digby said. "The new portrait of William in his military uniform is magnificent. A fitting tribute." His round face collapsed into a frown and he shook his head. "Deuced tragedy, passing on during his final mission."

Austin forced himself to nod politely. "I agree."

"Still, it's an honor to die a war hero."

Pressure built in Austin's chest. War hero. If only that were true. But the letter locked in his desk drawer confirmed his suspicions that it was not.

A vivid picture of William flashed through his mind—that last gut-wrenching image that nothing could erase. Guilt and regret slammed into him, and his fist tightened around his brandy snifter.

Air. He desperately needed air to clear his mind. Excusing himself, he headed toward the French windows.

Caroline caught sight of him and smiled, and he forced himself to smile at his sister in response. As much as he dreaded social functions, he was pleased to see Caroline looking so happy. It had been too long since that gleam of carefree joy had lit her lovely face, and if hosting this damn ball was what was necessary to make her happy, then host it he would. Still, he wished Robert were here instead of traveling on the Continent. His jovial younger brother was much more at ease in the role of host.

Ignoring the curious gazes cast in his direction, Austin exited the ballroom and made his way to the gardens. Neither the sweet fragrant roses scenting the warm summer air nor the full moon casting a silvery luster over the landscape improved his mood or relaxed the tension clenching his muscles. Couples strolled together, talking quietly, but Austin ignored them, determined to find a few minutes of peace.

But even as he struck out along a well-manicured path, he knew in his heart that peace was too much to ask for.

Would anyone guess the truth? No, he decided. Everyone—Caroline, Robert, his mother, the entire bloody country—all believed William died a hero, and it was an illusion Austin would pay any price to maintain. Anything to keep his family and his brother's memory safe from ruin.

He soon arrived at his destination, a private area surrounded by tall hedges at the perimeter of the gardens. The unoccupied curved stone bench was the most welcome sight he'd beheld all evening. *Sanctuary.*

Heaving a sigh of relief, he sat on the bench and stretched out his legs, ready to enjoy this peaceful haven. He reached into his pocket to extract his gold cigar case, but paused when he heard a rustling in the hedges.

The bushes parted and a young woman attempted to scramble through them. Panting and muttering under her breath, she tried unsuccessfully to free herself from the branches tearing at her hair and pulling at her gown.

Austin gritted his teeth and stifled an obscenity. He knew it was pointless to pray for her to go away. His prayers hadn't been answered very often lately.

The thrashing and muttering in the bushes continued. No doubt some chit sneaking about to indulge in a clandestine meeting with a lover. Or perhaps she was but yet another senseless female in search of a title and hoping to trap him into marriage. For all he knew, she might have followed him into the garden. Frustration shot through him and he arose to leave.

"Damnation!"

The exasperated cry exploded from the young woman's lips. She tugged impatiently on her gown to free it from the thicket, but it refused to budge. Grabbing her skirt with both hands, she gave a mighty heave. The unmistakable sound of fabric tearing cut the air.

Suddenly freed from the constraining hold of the bushes, she pitched forward, landing facedown in the damp grass. The air rushed from her lungs in a loud *whoosh*.

"Blasted ball gowns," she mumbled, shaking her head as if to clear her vision. "They're going to be the absolute death of me."

Austin clenched his hands. His first instinct was to escape before she caught sight of him, but as she remained lying there, motionless, he hesitated. Perhaps she was injured. He couldn't very well leave the foolish baggage here to rot, tempting though the idea was. If Caroline were injured, he'd want someone to help her—not that his sister would ever find herself in such a ridiculous situation.

Cursing his inability to simply walk away, he asked, "Are you all right?"

She gasped and jerked her head up. Her gaze locked on his black formal breeches for several seconds, then she lowered her head back onto the grass. "Why, oh *why* did someone have to see this?"

"Are you all right?" he repeated, fighting his growing impatience.

"Yes, of course I am. My health has always been of a most robust nature. Thank you for inquiring."

"May I offer you some assistance?"

"No, thank you. Pride demands I extricate myself from this, my latest in an endless series of embarrassments." She didn't move. A heavy pause filled the air.

"Are you going to get up?"

"No, I don't think I shall. But thank you again for asking."

Austin clenched his teeth until his jaw ached, and he wondered how much champagne the chit had swallowed. "Are you foxed?"

She raised her head several inches. "I don't know. I suppose it is possible. What does foxed mean?"

Her distinctive accent pierced through his annoyance. Closing his eyes, he barely suppressed a groan. "American?"

"Oh, for the love of heaven! I swear if one more person asks me that—" She broke off and glared at his knees. "*Obviously* I'm American. Everyone knows that an *Englishwoman* would never be caught dead sprawled on the grass in such an undignified fashion. Heaven forbid."

"Actually it wasn't your present position on the lawn, but your accent that gave you away," Austin said, staring down at the top of her head, surprise mingling with his annoyance. The chit was impertinent as hell. "For those unacquainted with English cant, *foxed* means to have overindulged in strong spirits."

"Overindulged?" she echoed, sounding outraged. Employing a series of unladylike but nonetheless effective movements, she scrambled to her feet. Planting her hands on her hips, she jutted out her chin at an unmistakably belligerent angle. "I have not indulged, over or otherwise, sir. I merely tripped."

Any response he may have considered making died on his lips as he took in her appearance.

She was remarkably attractive.

And an utter mess.

Her coiffure, which he surmised had started out as a topknot, now listed precariously to the left. Leaves and twigs clung to the shiny auburn strands and several curls stuck up at odd angles. The entire affair resembled a lopsided bird's nest.

A slash of dirt marred her chin, and a blade of grass clung to her lower lip—a very lush lower lip, he noted. His gaze traveled slowly downward, observing that her pastel gown bore an unfortunate mass of wrinkles and grass stains, and was further decorated with clumps of dirt. The ruffled flounce around her hem drooped in the back, clearly the result of the tearing noise. And it appeared she was missing a shoe.

He wasn't sure if he was more shocked or amused by her appearance. Who on earth was this disheveled woman, and how had she come to be a guest in his home? Caroline and his mother had made up the guest list for the party, so clearly they knew her. Why didn't he?

And as she'd called him "sir," it appeared she didn't know him either, a fact that stunned him. It seemed as if every breathing female in England dogged his steps, intent upon gaining his favor.

But apparently not this woman. She was spearing him with an expression that clearly stated *I wish you'd go away*, which both irritated him and piqued his interest.

"Perhaps you'd care to tell me why you were lurking in the bushes, Miss . . . ?" he asked, still suspicious of her sudden arrival. Were her mother and a posse of outraged chaperones about to leap from the hedges and claim he'd ruined her?

"Matthews. Elizabeth Matthews." She performed an awkward curtsy that dislodged several clumps of dirt from her gown. "I wasn't lurking. I was walking and heard a kitten meowing. The poor little fellow was caught in the bushes. I managed to rescue him, only to find myself entangled in the very same hedge."

"Where is your chaperone?"

Her expression turned sheepish. "I, um, managed to escape while she was dancing."

"She isn't lurking in the bushes?"

She appeared so amazed by his question, Austin knew she was either alone or the finest actress he'd ever encountered. And he suspected she was a poor actress. Her eyes were too expressive.

"Do you question if everyone lurks in the bushes? My aunt is a lady and does not lurk." She squinted at him. "Oh, dear. I really must look a fright. You have a most peculiar expression on your face. As if you just tasted something sour."

"You look . . . fine."

She burst out laughing. "You, sir, are either incredibly gallant or extremely shortsighted. Perhaps a bit of both. While I appreciate your effort to spare my feelings, I assure you it's not necessary. After spending three months on a wind-tossed ship sailing to England, I'm quite accustomed to looking frightful."

She leaned toward him, as if she were about to impart a great secret, and her scent assailed his senses. She smelled like lilacs, a fragrance he knew well for the gardens abounded with the purple flowers. "An Englishwoman traveling on board the ship was fond of muttering about 'Colonial Upstarts.' Thank goodness she isn't here to witness *this* debacle." Sticking out her foot, she examined her one remaining grass-stained slipper and heaved a sigh. "Good heavens. I am indeed a spectacle. I—"

A mewling sound cut off her words. Looking down, Austin watched a tiny gray kitten pounce from beneath the hedges and attack the flounce trailing from Miss Matthews's gown.

"There you are!" She scooped up the furry bundle and scratched behind its ears. The kitten immediately set up a loud purr. "Did you perhaps see my shoe in your travels, you little devil?" she murmured to the furball. "I believe it's stuck somewhere in those bushes." She turned to Austin. "Would you mind terribly taking a look?"

He stared at her, trying to hide his astonishment. If anyone had told him that his quest for solitude would turn into a rescue mission for a madwoman's slipper, he would not have believed it. A madwoman who had asked him to fetch her shoe as if he were a lowly footman. He should be out-raged. And as soon as this inexplicable urge to laugh left him, he was sure he would be. Crouching down, he peered into the hedge from which Miss Matthews had sprung.

Spying the missing shoe, he plucked it from the bushes, stood, then handed it to her. "Here you are."

"Thank you, sir."

Raising her skirts several inches, she slid her stockinged foot into the slipper. She had lovely, slim ankles and surprisingly small feet for a woman whom he judged stood about five feet seven. Taller than fashion dictated, but a very nice height, he decided. His gaze roamed upward to her face. Her head would nestle perfectly on his shoulder, and he'd have easy access to that incredibly lush mouth—

Heat rushed through him. Bloody hell, had he taken leave of his senses? One peek at her ankle and he'd lost his mind. He forced his gaze away from her lips and settled it on the contented kitten nestled in the crook of her arm. The animal opened its tiny mouth in a huge yawn.

"It appears Gadzooks is ready for a nap," he said.

"Gadzooks?"

"Yes. One of the tabbies gave birth ten weeks ago. When Mortlin, the groom, found the brood living in the stables, he said, 'Gadzooks, look at all those kittens!'" Despite himself, a smile tugged at his lips. "Actually, we should consider ourselves fortunate. The last litter was born in Mortlin's bed and the names he christened the beasts were much more, er, colorful."

Twin dimples appeared on either side of her mouth. "Goodness. It appears the tabby is quite busy."

"Indeed he is."

"You seem to know all about Gadzooks and his mama. Do you live nearby?"

Austin stared at her, nonplussed. She had to be the only

woman in the bloody kingdom who didn't know who he was. "Ah, yes, I do live nearby."

"How nice for you. It's lovely here." She settled Gadzooks more comfortably in her arms. "Well, as much as I've enjoyed speaking with you, I really must be going. Could you possibly direct me to the stables?"

"The stables?"

"Yes." Her eyes twinkled at him. "For those unfamiliar with American cant, it means 'a place where the horses are kept.' Since Gadzooks lives there, his mama is no doubt looking for him."

Amused, he asked, "Perhaps you'd permit me to escort you?"

Surprise flitted across her face and she hesitated. "That is very kind, sir, but unnecessary. Surely you wish to remain and enjoy your solitude."

Yes, surely he wished to do that. Didn't he? But the idea of being alone with his thoughts suddenly held no appeal.

When he didn't answer, she added, "Or perhaps you'd rather return to the party?"

He suppressed a shudder. "As I escaped the party only a short time ago, I'm not anxious to return just yet."

"Indeed? Were you not enjoying the festivities?"

He considered telling a polite lie, but decided not to. "In truth, no. I detest these soirees."

She gaped at him. "Heavens, I thought it was only me."

He couldn't hide his surprise. Every female he knew *lived* for balls. "You weren't enjoying yourself?"

A pained look settled in her eyes, and she dropped her gaze. "No, I'm afraid not."

It seemed clear that someone had treated this young woman unkindly—someone in his home, attending his foolish ball. He could well imagine the belles of Society twittering behind their fans about the "Colonial Upstart."

Polite manners dictated that he return to the house and

act as host, but he had no desire to do so. He suspected his mother was at this very moment sending exasperated glances in every direction, wondering where he was and how long he planned to remain in hiding. Knowing there were at least two dozen marriageable women his matchmaking mother hoped to throw in his path made him more determined to avoid the ballroom.

"Clearly we both needed some fresh air," he said with a smile. "Come. I shall show you to the stables and you can tell me about your adventures with Gadzooks."

Elizabeth hesitated. If Aunt Joanna knew she was alone in the garden with a gentleman, she knew she'd be on the receiving end of a lecture. But returning to the party was simply impossible considering the current state of her appearance. Besides, she'd suffered enough for one evening.

She was tired of being stared at and whispered about because she enjoyed conversing on topics other than fashion and the weather. And she could not help it if she was a miserable dancer and taller than deemed appropriate. If this gentleman was aware of the mockery circulating about her nationality and personality, he was polite enough not to show it.

"I realize you are without a chaperone," he said, his tone amused, "but you have my word I shall not abscond with you."

Assuring herself there was no harm in accepting his offer of escort, Elizabeth said, "By all means, let us walk."

Strolling beside him down the path, her flounce dragging behind her, she cuddled Gadzooks in her arms and cast a surreptitious glance at her companion. Thank goodness she wasn't prone to heaving dreamy, romantic sighs, for this was certainly a man who could induce them. Thick ebony hair framed a strikingly handsome face made all the more intriguing by the play of shadows from the moonlight. His eyes were steady and intense, and when he'd gazed at her a moment ago her toes had involuntarily curled inside her slippers. High cheekbones, nose straight as a blade, and a full, firm mouth that she knew could quirk with amusement and she imagined would look fierce in anger.

In truth, everything about him was attractive. But there was no point in finding this stranger intriguing. As soon as he realized what a social disaster she was, he would surely rebuff her, just as so many others had.

"Tell me, Miss Matthews, with whom are you attending this ball?"

"I came with my aunt, Countess Penbroke."

Speculation filled his gaze. "Indeed? I knew her late husband, however I was not aware they had an American niece."

"My mother and Aunt Joanna were sisters. My mother settled in America when she married my father, an American physician." She shot him a sidelong glance. "My mother was born and raised in England. Thus, I am half English."

A smile touched his lips. "So you are, then, only half an Upstart."

She laughed. "Oh, no. I fear I'm still an Upstart through and through."

"Is this your first visit to England?"

"Yes." There was no point in telling him this was more than a visit—that she would never return to her hometown.

"And are you enjoying it?"

She hesitated, but decided to tell him the unvarnished truth. "I like your country, but I find English society and all its rules restricting. I grew up in a rural area and had much more freedom. It is not easy adjusting."

He glanced at her clothing. "Clearly you're experiencing difficulty giving up the American custom of crawling about in the bushes in your evening clothes."

A giggle erupted from between her lips. "Yes, it appears so."

The stables loomed ahead. As they approached, a tremendously plump cat emerged from the doorway and let out a loud meow.

The gentleman bent to stroke the animal. "Hello there, George. How's my girl tonight? Are you missing your baby?"

Elizabeth lowered Gadzooks to the ground and the kitten immediately pounced on George. "Gadzooks's mother is named *George*?"

He looked up at her from his crouched position and smiled. "Yes. As in 'By George, that cat must be a female because look there—she's having kittens!' My groom named her. Mortlin knows everything about horses, but little, I'm afraid, about cats."

Her answering smile faded as the significance of his words hit her. "*Your* groom? Are these *your* cats?"

Austin rose slowly to his feet, inwardly cursing his carelessness. His pleasant interlude was about to come to an end. "Yes, the cats are mine."

Her eyes widened. "Oh, dear. Then this is your home?"

Austin cast a quick glance toward the mansion in the distance. It was where he lived, but it hadn't felt like a home in over a year.

"Yes, Bradford Hall belongs to me."

"Then you must be . . ." She swept downward into an awkward curtsy. "Forgive me, your grace. I didn't realize who you were. You must think me incredibly rude."

He watched her arise from her curtsy, waiting to see her eyes narrow with speculation, flicker with avarice, sparkle with anticipation of how to best put her unexpected meeting with "England's Most Eligible Bachelor" to her advantage.

He saw none of it.

Instead, she seemed genuinely distressed. And anxious to get away from him.

How very interesting.

"I'm so sorry I said I wasn't enjoying your party," she said, taking several steps backward. "It's a delightful party. Delightful. The food, the music, the guests, they are all . . ."

"Delightful?" he supplied helpfully.

She nodded and retreated several more steps.

His gaze never left her face. Emotions streaked through her expressive eyes—embarrassment, dismay, surprise, but not once did he discern a hint of coyness or speculation. Nor did she seem particularly impressed with his lofty title. But it was the complete lack of something else that utterly fascinated him.

She wasn't flirting with him.

She hadn't flirted earlier, before she'd known who he was, but now . . .

How *incredibly* interesting.

"Thank you for escorting me, your grace. I believe I shall return to the house now." She took several more steps backward.

"What about your gown, Miss Matthews? Not even a Colonial Upstart would dare enter the ballroom in your present condition."

Halting, she looked down at herself. "I don't suppose there's any hope that no one would notice."

"No hope at all. Are you and your aunt spending the night?"

"Yes. In fact, we're staying on here at Bradford Hall for several weeks as guests of the dowager duchess . . ." Understanding dawned in her eyes. "Who is your mother."

"Indeed she is." Austin briefly wondered if his mother had arranged for the visit with the hopes of making a match, but he immediately discarded the idea. He couldn't imagine that his very proper mother would deem an American to be a suitable duchess. No, he knew all too well that she had her matchmaking eye set on several young women of impeccable British lineage. "As long as you're staying here, I believe I can solve your problem. I'll show you to a little-used side entrance that leads directly up to the guest chambers."

There was no mistaking the gratitude in her eyes. "That would certainly avert the social disaster I fear looms on the horizon."

"Then let us be off."

As they walked toward the mansion, Elizabeth asked, "I hate to further impose upon your kindness, your grace, but would you mind giving my excuses to my aunt when you return to the ballroom?"

"Of course."

She cleared her throat. "Ah, what excuse shall you use?"

"Excuse? Oh, I suppose I'll say you suffered from a fit of the vapors."

"Vapors!" She sounded outraged. "Nonsense! I would never fall victim to such a frivolous thing. Besides, Aunt Joanna would not believe it. She knows I am of a most robust nature. You must think of something else."

"All right. How about the headache?"

"I never get them."

"Dyspepsia?"

"My stomach never causes me discomfort."

Austin fought the urge to roll his eyes heavenward. "Do you *ever* suffer from any malady?"

She shook her head. "You keep forgetting that I am—"

"Most robust. Yes, I'm beginning to see that. But I fear that any other excuse, such as a fever, would unduly alarm your aunt."

"Hmmm. I suppose you're right. I don't wish to

frighten her. Actually, a headache is not far from the truth. The mere thought of returning to the ballroom sets my temples to pounding. Very well," she said with a nod, her tone crisp. "You may say I've succumbed to the headache."

Austin's lips twitched. "Thank you."

She beamed at him. "You're quite welcome."

They arrived at the mansion several minutes later and Austin led her through the shadows to a side door almost entirely obscured with ivy. He felt for the knob and pulled the door open. "There you are. The guest chambers are at the top of the stairs. Be careful on the steps."

"I shall. Thank you again for your kindness."

"My pleasure."

His gaze searched her face in the dim light. Even completely disheveled, she was lovely. And amusing. He could not recall the last time he'd felt so lighthearted. Pressing concerns awaited him once he returned to the house, yet he couldn't resist prolonging this pleasant interlude for a few moments longer. Reaching out, he gently grasped her hand and lifted it to his lips. Her hand was warm and soft, her fingers long and slender. The subtle scent of lilacs again assailed him.

Their eyes met and his breath stalled. Damn it, she looked so delightfully mussed . . . as if a man's hands had disarranged her hair and clothing. His gaze dropped to her mouth . . . her full, incredibly tempting mouth, and he wondered what she would taste like. He imagined leaning forward, brushing his lips over hers, once, twice, then deepening the kiss, sliding his tongue into the luscious warmth of her mouth. She tasted delicious, like—

"Oh my."

Her fingers tightened on his hand and she regarded him with wide eyes. Her gaze rested on his lips for several seconds, then she looked away, clearly flustered. Warmth crept through him, surprising him. If he didn't know better, he'd swear she'd read his thoughts.

He was about to release her hand when she gasped. Their eyes met and he noted she appeared suddenly pale. He tried to extricate his hand from hers, but she only tightened her grip.

"What's wrong?" he asked, alarmed at her pallor, unnerved by her concentrated stare. "You look as if you've seen a ghost."

"William."

He froze. "Excuse me?"

Her eyes desperately searched his. "Do you know someone named William?"

Every muscle in his body tensed. "What game are you playing here?"

Instead of answering, she squeezed his hand between her palms and closed her eyes. "He's your brother," she whispered. "You've been told he died while serving his country." She opened her eyes and the look she leveled at him gave him the eerie sensation she could see right into his soul. "It's not true."

His blood turned to ice. He pulled his hand from hers and stepped back, shocked by her words. By God did this woman know his darkest secret? And if she did, *how* did she know?

The images he'd spent the last year trying to erase crashed through his mind. A dark alley. William meeting with a Frenchman named Gaspard. Crates of weapons. An exchange of money. Haunting questions. A bitter confrontation between brothers. Then, only weeks later, the news that William had died at Waterloo—a war hero.

His heart beat heavily in his chest as he fought to remain calm. Could this woman be more than she appeared? Could she know something about the letter he'd recently received or the activities William had conducted with the

French? Could she be the clue he'd spent the last year searching for?

His eyes narrowed on her pale face and he uttered the lie he'd told countless times before. "William died fighting for his country. He is a hero."

"No, your grace."

"Are you saying my brother wasn't a hero?"

"No. I'm saying that he didn't die. Your brother William is alive."

Chapter 2

Elizabeth felt the onset of the numbing fatigue that sometimes followed a vision. She wanted desperately to sit down, but the suspicion blazing from the duke's eyes held her pinned in place.

"You will tell me everything you know that makes you claim my brother is alive," he commanded in an icy tone. "Immediately."

Dear God, why did I say anything? But even as she asked herself, Elizabeth knew the answer. A young woman's face flashed in her mind . . . the beloved friend she'd never see again . . . all because Elizabeth remained silent about a premonition. It was a mistake she'd vowed never to make again.

And the fact that this William was alive—surely that was joyous news? But the hostility and distrust in the duke's eyes indicated she'd spoken too hastily. Yet surely she could convince him she spoke the truth.

"I know your brother is alive because I saw him—"

"Where did you see him? When?"

"Just now." Her voice dropped to a whisper. "In my mind."

His eyes narrowed to slits. "In your *mind*? What rubbish is this? Are you daft?"

"No, your grace. I . . . I am able to see things. In my mind. I suppose some might call it a second sight. I'm afraid I cannot really explain it."

"And you're saying you saw my brother. Alive."

"Yes."

"If that is true, where is he?"

A frown puckered her brow. "I do not know. My visions are most often vague. I only know he did not die as everyone believes."

"And you expect me to believe this?"

The icy disbelief in his tone chilled her. "I understand your doubts. That which cannot be explained scientifically is easy to dismiss as fiction. I can only assure you that what I am telling you is true."

"What did this man you claim was my brother look like?"

Closing her eyes, she inhaled deeply, forcing her mind to empty then focus on what she'd seen. "Tall. Broad shouldered. Dark hair."

"How convenient. You've just described half the men in England, including the Regent himself, who, as I'm sure you know, is very much alive. And it would not be difficult to describe my brother when there is a large portrait of him hanging in the gallery."

Opening her eyes, she said, "I have not seen a portrait. The man I saw looked like you, and he had a scar."

He stilled and she sensed his sudden tension. "Scar? Where?"

"On his upper right arm."

"Many men bear scars." A muscle in his jaw ticked. "If you think to convince me that you possess some sort of magical powers, you've picked the wrong man to ply with your schemes. Gypsy thieves have roamed Europe for centuries, claiming such powers, lying, hoping to trick foolish people into parting with their gold, and stealing it if they failed."

Anger shot through her. "I am not a gypsy, a schemer, a thief, or a liar."

"Indeed? I suppose next you'll tell me you can read minds."

"Only occasionally." Her gaze dropped to his mouth, which was set in a disdainful line. "I read your thoughts when you touched my hand."

"Did you? And what was I thinking?"

"You . . . wished to kiss me."

He merely raised his brows. "It would not require any special powers to hazard such a guess. My attention was momentarily fixed on your mouth."

In spite of his casual reply, however, she could feel his tension, his wariness and suspicion—feelings she was well used to discerning. But underneath those, she felt something else that, in spite of her anger, called out to her.

Loneliness.

Sadness.

Guilt.

They surrounded him like a dark cloak and her heart pinched in sympathy. She knew those feelings all too well, how much they hurt the spirit, ate at the soul.

She, too, had regrets she wished to atone for. Could she, perhaps, help him? Would that ease her own guilt?

Determined to convince him she wasn't crazy and that he had truly desired her for a moment, she whispered, "You wanted to kiss me. You wondered what I would taste like. You imagined leaning forward, brushing your lips over mine, once, twice. Then you deepened the kiss . . ."

His eyes flickered, his gaze darkening then dropping to her mouth. "Go on."

Heat curled through her when she imagined what he'd thought next . . . his tongue caressing hers. "I believe I've proven my point."

"Do you?" Austin regarded her through narrowed eyes. It was one thing to hazard a guess that he'd thought about kissing her, but it was damned odd that her words had so exactly mirrored his thoughts.

Jesus, what if she were right? What if William was alive? Impossible, illogical hope rushed forward with such force he nearly staggered, but sanity quickly returned. Several soldiers had witnessed William going down in battle. Even though the gunshot wound had destroyed his face, he'd been positively identified by the engraved timepiece found under his body.

There was no mistake. William was dead. If he wasn't, he would have contacted his family and come home.

Unless he were a traitor to the crown.

His mind reeled. It was damned suspicious that Miss Matthews made this claim on the heels of the disturbing note he'd received a fortnight ago, a note that confirmed his worst fears regarding William's loyalty to the crown. Could she know something about that letter or William's war activities? Might she know something about the Frenchman he'd seen with William?

How had she known about the scar? William had a small scar on his upper right arm, a trophy from a childhood riding mishap. Could she have known William? Intimately enough to know his body?

Softly illuminated in the moonlight, her disarranged hair teased by the summer breeze, she certainly did not look like a spy, a murderess, or a seductress, but he well knew that looks were deceiving. Some of the most beautiful women he knew were vicious, conniving, and heartless. What sort of person lay beneath her innocent facade? He didn't know what game she was playing, but he was determined to find out. And if it was necessary to play along with her "visions" ploy, he would.

He opened his mouth to speak, but before he could utter a word, she said, "I'm not playing games, your grace. I want to help you."

Damn. He was going to have to be very careful around this woman. While he discarded her claims of visions—what sane man wouldn't?—she was uncannily, eerily perceptive.

If he didn't watch his step, he suspected she might somehow learn his secrets—secrets that could ruin his family.

"Tell me what you know about my brother," he said.

"I don't know anything about him, your grace. Until I touched your hands, I hadn't known he existed."

"Indeed? How long have you been in England?"

"Six months."

"And you expect me to believe that in all that time, no one has mentioned my brother?" A mirthless laugh escaped him.

She hesitated, then said in a quiet voice, "I'm afraid I haven't been what one would call the social success of the Season. I find I am most often talked *about* rather than talked *to*."

"Surely your aunt keeps you abreast of the latest *on dit*."

A wry, half smile curved her lips. "To be perfectly honest, your grace, my aunt speaks of little else but the comings and goings of London's finest. I love her dearly, but after five minutes of such conversation, I fear I develop a bit of a deaf ear."

"I see. Tell me more about this, er, vision you had of William."

"I saw a young man wearing a military uniform. He was injured, but alive. I only know his name was William, and he was important to you." She turned troubled eyes to him. "You believe he is dead, but he is not. I'm sure of it."

"You make this outlandish claim, yet you offer no proof."

"No . . . at least not yet."

"Meaning?"

"If we spend some time together, I might be able to tell you more. My visions are erratic and usually nothing more than flashes, but they normally occur when I'm touching something, most often a person's hands."

He raised his brows. "So you're saying that if we sit about holding hands, you might be able to see something more."

Her eyes clouded at his sarcastic remark. "I understand your skepticism, and for that reason I normally do not reveal my premonitions."

"Yet you revealed this one."

"Yes. Because the last time I remained silent it cost me dearly." She frowned. "Are you not pleased to know your brother is alive?"

"What I *know* is that my brother is dead. And I won't have you mentioning this vision nonsense to anyone else, most especially my mother or sister. It would be unspeakably cruel to offer them hope where none exists. Do you understand?"

She gazed at him steadily for several heartbeats. There was no mistaking the steely menace in his tone. "I shall respect your wishes, your grace. As you know, my aunt and I will be your houseguests for the next several weeks. If you change your mind and would like me to try to help you, I will not be hard to find. I'm very tired and wish to retire now. Good night, your grace."

He watched her climb the steps to the guest chambers.

Oh, you'll help me, Miss Matthews. If you know anything about William, you won't have a choice.

It took Austin several minutes to locate Miles Avery in the crowded ballroom. When he finally spotted his friend, he wasn't surprised to see the dashing earl surrounded by a bevy of ladies. Damn it, he hoped he wouldn't have to drag Miles by the hair to wrest him away from his adoring audience.

He was saved from that unpleasantness, however, when Miles spotted Austin bearing down on him. Leveling a pointed look at his friend, Austin jerked his head toward the corridor leading to his private study, then made his way to the room, confident Miles would arrive close behind him. After more than two decades of friendship, they understood each other well.

He'd barely finished pouring two brandies when a discreet knock sounded on the door.

"Come in."

Miles entered the room, closing the door behind him. A crooked smile curved his lips. "It's about time you resurfaced. I've been looking for you everywhere. Where were you hiding yourself?"

"I took a stroll in the garden."

"Oh? Were you admiring the flowers?" Miles's eyes danced with mischief. "Or were you perhaps partaking of nature's delights in some other . . . oh, shall we say, *lusty* way?"

"Neither. I simply took myself off in search of some peace and quiet."

"And was your search successful?"

An image of Miss Matthews flashed in his mind. "I'm afraid not. Why were you looking for me?"

The teasing gleam lighting Miles's eyes grew more pronounced. "To give you a piece of my mind. What sort of friend are you, deserting me in such a manner? You hardly ever attend parties and suffer your portion of the wedding-minded virgins who pursue us, and even when the ball is in your own home, you're nowhere to be found. Lady Digby and her numerous daughters trapped me behind a potted palm. Thanks to your departure, she foisted the chits on me. They're all cabbage-headed nincompoops and horrid dancers as well. My poor abused toes will never be the same."

With a perfectly straight face, Miles went on, "Of course that group you summoned me away from just now appeared much more promising. The ladies were all but hanging on my every word. Do you see the pearls of wisdom dripping from my lips?"

Austin regarded him over the rim of his snifter. "I cannot fathom why you find the false adoration of brainless twits so diverting. Don't you ever grow tired of it?"

"Of course. You know how I utterly detest it when beautiful, nubile females with ripe, lush curves throw themselves at me. I shudder with horror every time." Miles was about to sip his brandy, but his hand arrested halfway to his lips. "I say, Austin. Are you all right? You look, well, rather peaked."

"Thank you, Miles. Your kind words never fail to warm my heart." He took a long swallow of brandy, searching for the right words. "To answer your question, I'm a bit unsettled. Something has happened and I need a favor."

The humor instantly vanished from Miles's eyes. "You know you have only to ask."

A pent-up breath he hadn't realized he held escaped Austin. Of course he could count on Miles, just as he'd always been able to. The fact that he kept secrets from this man who'd been his closest friend since childhood filled him with guilt. *It's for his own good and protection that he not know the circumstances surrounding William's war activities.* "I need some discreet inquiries made."

Interest kindled in Miles's intelligent ebony eyes. "Regarding what?"

"A certain young woman."

"Ah. I see. Looking to hang yourself in the matrimonial noose?" Before Austin could correct him, Miles plunged on. "Can't say I envy you. There's not a woman alive I'd care to see across the dinner table every day. The very words *Till death do you part* send chills of horror down my spine. But I suppose you must do your duty to the title and you're not getting any younger. I thank God every day my cousin Gerald can inherit the earldom from me. Of course, Robert can inherit the dukedom, but we both know your younger brother wants the title as much as he'd relish the pox. In fact—"

"Miles." The single brusque syllable halted the flow of words.

"Yes?"

"Not that sort of young lady."

A knowing grin touched Miles's lips. "A*ha.* Say no more. You need information regarding someone who is . . . less than suitable. I understand." He tossed a broad wink at Austin. "Those are the most fun."

Frustration welled up and Austin fought to keep his temper in check. "The young lady I wish to know about is a Miss Elizabeth Matthews."

Miles's brows rose. "Lady Penbroke's American niece?"

Austin schooled his features into a blandness he did not feel. "You've met her?"

"On several occasions. Unlike *some* unsociable sorts

we know, *I* attended dozens of balls this Season—balls Lady Penbroke and Miss Matthews attended. In fact, Miss Matthews is here this evening. Do you wish me to introduce you?"

"We met, earlier, in the garden."

"I see." Although a dozen questions clearly flashed in Miles's eyes, he merely asked, "What do you want to know about her?"

Everything. "As you've met her, tell me your impressions."

Miles took his time before answering, settling himself in an overstuffed wing chair by the fireplace, then swirling his brandy in his snifter with a leisure that had Austin gritting his teeth with impatience.

"I think," Miles finally said, "that she is a fine young woman, intelligent, with a clever wit. Unfortunately, she's somewhat awkward in social situations, tongue-tied and shy one moment, outspoken the next. In truth I thought her rather a breath of fresh air, but based on the gossip I hear, I possibly stand alone in that opinion."

"What gossip? Anything scandalous?"

Miles waved his hand in dismissal. "No, nothing of that sort. Indeed, I don't see how the woman could find herself caught in a scandal when nearly everyone shuns her."

An image of a disheveled, smiling woman flashed in Austin's mind. "Why is she shunned?"

Miles shrugged. "Who can say how these things start? The women twitter behind their fans at her awkwardness on the dance floor and her lack of conversation. Several branded her a bluestocking after she engaged a group of lords in a discussion regarding the benefits of herbal healing. The instant *one* person labels her unacceptable, the rest follow."

"Doesn't Lady Penbroke lend her niece support?"

"I haven't paid particular attention, but no doubt the

worst snubs are conducted away from the countess's sharp eyes. But even her formidable support cannot singlehandedly ensure gaining the *ton*'s favor."

"Do you know how long she's been in England?"

Miles stroked his chin. "I believe she arrived soon after Boxing Day, so she'd be here about six months."

"I'd like you to find out exactly when she arrived and on what ship. I also want to know if this is her first trip to England."

"Why don't you simply ask her?"

"I did. She claims she arrived six months ago and that this is her first visit here."

Miles's eyes sharpened with interest. "And you don't believe her? May I ask why?"

Forcing nonchalance into his voice, Austin said, "It's possible she may have been acquainted with William. I want to know for certain. If she was, I want to know how, when, and where they met."

"Again, why don't you simply ask her?"

Austin suppressed the urge to rake his hands through his hair in frustration. "I cannot say until I know more. I also want to know about her past. Why she left America. Her financial situation. Her family status. Anything you can find."

"Perhaps you should hire a Bow Street Runner. They—"

"No." The razor-sharp word sliced off Miles's suggestion. He'd already engaged a Runner a fortnight ago to locate the Frenchman named Gaspard—the man he'd seen with William that last time . . . the man Austin suspected knew something about the letter now locked in his desk. He had no wish to involve Bow Street in this matter. "I need complete discretion from someone I trust. Now, will you make the necessary inquiries? You'll most likely need to travel to London."

Miles studied him for several long seconds. "This is important to you."

An image of William rose in his mind. "Yes."

A silent look passed between them, a look born of years of friendship. "I'll leave in the morning," Miles said. "In the meantime, I'll begin investigating immediately by feeling out some of the party guests about the lady in question."

"An excellent idea. Needless to say, I want any and all information as soon as possible."

"Understood." Miles finished his brandy and stood. "I suppose you know that Miss Matthews and Lady Penbroke are staying here for the next several weeks as your mother's guests."

"Yes. By sending *you* to London, I am able to remain here and keep my eye on Miss Matthews."

Miles quirked a brow. "Is that what you intend to keep on her? Only your eye?"

Austin chilled his already frosty expression to a narrow-eyed iciness. "Are you quite finished?"

Miles wisely took note of the suddenly arctic air. "Very finished." His expression sobered and he placed a comforting hand on Austin's shoulder. "Don't worry, my friend. Between the two of us, we'll find out everything there is to know about Miss Elizabeth Matthews."

After the door closed behind Miles, Austin slipped a silver key from his waistcoat pocket and unlocked the bottom drawer of his desk. He withdrew the letter he'd received two weeks ago and reread the words that were already burned in his brain.

Your brother William was a traitor to England. I have the proof, signed by his own hand. I will remain silent, but it will cost you. You will go to London by July first. You will receive further instructions there.

Chapter 3

Just before dawn the next morning, Elizabeth tiptoed from her room carrying her knapsack.

"Where are you off to so early, Elizabeth?"

Elizabeth nearly jumped out of her skin. "Good heavens, Aunt Joanna, you startled me." She smiled at the woman who had opened her heart and her home to her without question. "I thought I'd walk the grounds and do some sketching. Would you care to join me?"

A horrified expression crossed her aunt's plump face. "Thank you, dear, but no. The early morning dew would completely wilt my feathers." She lovingly patted the long ostrich plumes protruding from her chartreuse turban. "I'm going to read in the library until breakfast." Aunt Joanna cocked her head to one side and Elizabeth leaned back to avoid the feathers. "Are you feeling better?"

"I beg your pardon?"

"His grace informed me last evening that you'd retired due to the headache."

Warmth crept up Elizabeth's neck. "Oh! Yes, I'm feeling much improved."

Her aunt eyed her with open curiosity. "Obviously you had an opportunity to speak with the duke. What did you think of him?"

He is devastatingly attractive. And lonely. And he thinks I'm a liar. "He was very . . . charming. Did you enjoy the party, Aunt Joanna?"

An unladylike snort erupted from between her aunt's lips. "I was having a merry time until Lady Digby and her dreadful daughters surrounded me and I couldn't escape. Never in my life have I encountered such a gaggle of twittering fools. I'll be stunned if she manages to marry off even one of those buttertoothed harpies." She reached out and patted Elizabeth's cheek. "She is green with envy that my niece is so lovely. We won't have any trouble finding you a husband."

"In case you haven't noticed, Aunt Joanna, we can barely find me a gentleman to dance with."

Her aunt waved a dismissive hand. "Pish posh. You're simply unknown. No doubt some gentlemen are put off because you're American, what with last century's Rebellion and this most recent series of skirmishes. But things have settled down again, so it's only a matter of time."

"A matter of time for what?"

"Why, until some nice young man takes notice of you."

Elizabeth refrained from pointing out that so far nearly everyone who had taken notice of her had found her lacking. Holding her bag aloft, she said, "I've packed a snack, so I'll see you after breakfast."

A frown puckered her aunt's brow. "Perhaps I should ask a footman to accompany you." Before Elizabeth could protest, her aunt rushed on, "Oh, I suppose it's not necessary. You go along, dear, and enjoy yourself. After all, no one except us is even awake. Who on earth would you meet at this ungodly hour?"

Elizabeth strolled along, relishing the quiet that was broken only by the rustle of leaves and the ravens' caws. She chose paths at random, not particularly caring where she went, just happy to be outdoors. After a while, the forest thinned out to a wide meadow where bees hummed, hovering around sweet-smelling honeysuckle. Colorful butterflies flitted over clumps of red and yellow wildflowers.

She soon reached a picturesque lake. Pale shafts of hesitant gold light peeped down between leafy tree branches, offering a dawn-kissed, shady retreat. Removing her sketch pad from her knapsack, she sank down on the grass and propped her back against the trunk of a huge oak tree.

A frisky squirrel peeked at her from a nearby tree branch and she quickly sketched him. A family of timid rabbits made another subject before they hopped away to the safety of the tall grass. She drew a detailed picture of Patch, her heart pinching as she thought of her beloved dog. She'd wanted desperately to bring him to England, but he was old and infirm and she knew he wouldn't have survived the rigorous ocean journey. She'd left him behind, along with a piece of her heart, with people who loved him almost as much as she did.

Forcing aside the melancholy that thoughts of Patch evoked, she drew a likeness of Gadzooks. When she finished, however, she quickly banished the kitten from her mind. If she thought about the furry beast, she'd recall the rest of her time in the garden . . . and the man she'd met there. The man whose hidden sadness and loneliness had touched her heart, a man she knew had secrets that tore at his soul.

She'd offered to help him, but she'd spent half the night

wondering if she'd been too hasty. The Duke of Bradford obviously did not believe in her second sight.

Could she somehow convince him? After last evening, it did not appear so, but she wanted, needed, to help him. Wanted to erase the shadows she'd felt darkening his happiness. And needed, for herself, to try and make up for the havoc she'd caused in America. Surely her guilt would ease if she could somehow reunite the duke with the brother he believed dead.

No, she had not been too hasty in offering to help him. In fact, she was determined to do so, whether he wanted her to or not. All she needed to do was provide some sort of definite proof that his brother was indeed alive. To do that, however, she'd need to touch him again.

Heat shot through her at the thought. He'd haunted her sleep, his handsome face, his intense eyes, his strong body. He'd made her wish, for one useless instant, that she'd looked beautiful and elegant, and that a man like him might actually be interested in her for more than a fleeting moment.

And he had been interested, as she'd discovered when he'd touched her hand.

He had wanted to kiss her.

His thoughts had come to her so clearly, so unexpectedly. Her breath caught at the thought of his lips caressing hers, his strong arms pulling her close, pressing her against his body. What would it feel like to be kissed by such a man? Touched and held by him? *Heaven . . . It would feel like heaven.*

A sigh escaped her, the sort of feminine sigh she'd thought herself incapable of. Shifting herself to a more comfortable position, she gave in to her longing, closed her eyes, and imagined what his kiss would feel like.

*   *   *

Austin caught sight of a yellow skirt fluttering in the breeze and reined Myst to a halt. Bloody hell, was he *never* to find himself alone?

He would have turned back, but he'd ridden Myst hard for the last hour and the gelding needed a rest and a drink.

Resigned to making idle conversation for a few moments with one of his mother's houseguests, he approached the lake. As he rounded the huge oak tree, he drew up short.

It was her. The woman who had disrupted his sleep and invaded his every thought since he awoke. The woman he needed to find out more about. She sat beneath the shady tree, her eyes closed, a half smile touching her lips.

He dismounted and walked quietly toward her, studying her all the while. Shiny auburn curls surrounded her face in windblown disarray. He scrutinized her in an unhurried fashion, taking in her porcelain skin, long lashes, and those remarkable, tempting lips.

His gaze continued downward, drawn to her slender throat and the creamy skin that glowed above her modest bodice. Her legs appeared impossibly long under her muslin gown.

The breeze dislodged another curl from her somewhat haphazard chignon, and it brushed across her mouth. Her lips twitched several times and her eyes peeked open a crack as she flicked the bothersome lock aside.

Austin knew the exact instant she saw his black riding boots in front of her. She stiffened and blinked. Then her gaze traveled upward and she gasped.

"Your grace!" She bounded to her feet and performed a curtsy that most would have labeled graceless, but that he found utterly charming.

"Good morning, Miss Matthews. It seems you were correct when you predicted you would not be hard to find. I seem to run into you everywhere I go."

Heat flashed in Elizabeth's cheeks. How disconcerting to be daydreaming of a man kissing you breathless only to open your eyes and find that very man watching you. And good heavens, what a wildly attractive man he was.

The filtered light from the rising sun shimmered on his raven hair. A single, windblown lock fell across his forehead, lending him an almost boyish appeal completely at odds with the compelling intensity of his gray eyes. Aristocratic bearing and masculine strength all but oozed from his tall, rugged frame.

A stark white shirt covered his broad shoulders. He wore no neckcloth and the strong tanned column of his neck rose from the opening in the fine lawn. Her heart sped up at the sight of a few dark hairs peeping up from that intriguing opening before his shirt thwarted her view.

His wide chest tapered in a perfect V to narrow hips, and his long, muscular legs were covered in buff breeches that disappeared into shiny black leather riding boots. She imagined a string of broken-hearted females littered the streets of London. He'd certainly make a wonderful subject to sketch.

"Do I pass inspection?" he asked in an amused drawl.

"Inspection?"

"Yes." A half grin touched his lips. "It's an English word meaning 'to examine thoroughly.'"

Although he was clearly teasing, hot chagrin flooded her. Good heavens, she was indeed staring at him as if she was starving and he was a banquet. But at least he no longer seemed upset with her.

"Forgive me, your grace. I'm simply surprised to see you here." Her eyes narrowed on a mark on his cheek. "Did you injure yourself?"

He gingerly touched the spot. "A branch caught me. 'Tis only a scratch."

A soft nickering claimed her attention and she glanced

at the magnificent black gelding drinking from the lake. "Are you enjoying your ride?"

"Very much." He looked around. "Where is your mount?"

"I walked. It's a lovely morn—" An image flashed in her mind, cutting off her words. A horse rearing, a black horse very much like the one drinking from the lake.

"Are you all right, Miss Matthews?"

The image vanished and she dismissed the vague impression. "Yes, I'm fine. Actually, I'm—"

"Most robust."

She grinned. "Yes, I am, but I was going to say I'm hungry. Would you care to join me in something to eat? I brought more than enough." She dropped to her knees and began unloading food from her knapsack.

"You packed breakfast?"

"Well, not exactly breakfast. Just some raw carrots, apples, bread, and cheese."

Austin watched her, intrigued. He'd never been invited to such an informal picnic. Here was a perfect opportunity to spend some time with her. What better way to ferret out her secrets and determine exactly what she knew about William and the blackmail letter? Settling himself on the ground next to her, he accepted a slice of bread and a chunk of cheese. "Who packed your picnic?"

"I did. Yesterday morning, before leaving London, I helped Aunt Joanna's cook with a problem. In gratitude, Cook told me I could help myself." She polished an apple on her skirt.

Austin bit into the cheese, surprised that something so simple could taste so good. No fancy sauces, no muted clink of silverware, no servants hovering. "What did you do to help Cook?"

"She cut her finger and suffered a wound that required several stitches. I was in the kitchen searching for some cider when the accident occurred. Naturally, I offered to help."

"You sent for a doctor?"

She raised her brows, amusement lurking in her eyes. "I treated the injury and then stitched her up myself."

Austin nearly choked on his cheese. "*You* stitched her wound?"

"Yes. There was no need to bother a doctor when I was perfectly capable of taking care of her. I believe I mentioned last evening that my father was a physician. I often helped him."

"You actually performed, er, *duties*?"

"Oh, yes. Papa was a very good teacher. I assure you, Cook was well taken care of." She offered him a smile, then bit into her apple.

Austin's gaze was drawn to her full lips, glistening with apple juice. Her mouth looked moist and sweet. And incredibly tempting. Not that he believed she could actually read his thoughts, but in light of her odd perceptiveness, he jerked his attention away from her lips.

"It is such a lovely morning," she said. "I wish I could capture the colors of the sunrise, but I have no talent for watercolors. Only charcoals, and I'm afraid they only come in one color."

Austin cocked his head toward the sketch pad next to her. "May I?"

She handed him the tablet. "Of course."

He examined each drawing and could tell at once that she was very talented. Her bold strokes rendered images so vivid, so startling, they appeared to leap off the page.

"Did you recognize Gadzooks?" she asked, looking over his shoulder.

The gentle scent of lilacs surrounded him. "Yes. It's an exact likeness of the little devil." Glancing up from the sketch, his attention was captured by the intriguing gold

flecks in her eyes. Huge, golden brown eyes, the color of
fine brandy. Her steady gaze met his and held him captive
for a long moment. A spark ran through him, igniting his
pulse. Although he sat on the ground, he suddenly felt as if
he'd run a mile. This woman had the oddest effect on his
senses. And his breathing.

He cleared his throat. "Have you had the opportunity to
meet Gadzooks's family?"

"Only his mother, George, last evening."

"Then you must stop by the stables and meet By Jingo,
By Jove, By Jupiter, and the rest of them."

Laughter bubbled from her. "You're making up those
names, your grace."

"I'm not. Mortlin named the beasts as they were
born . . . and born . . . and born. There were ten in all in
this last litter and the names grew more, er, *inventive* as
the births continued. Decency prevents me from saying
some of them." With an effort he forced his gaze back to
the tablet. "Whose dog is this?"

The merriment faded from her gaze. "That's my dog.
Patch."

The sad longing with which she looked at the picture
tugged at him, prompting him to ask, "Where is Patch?"

"He was too old to make the journey to England. I left
him with people who love him." Reaching out, she ran a
gentle fingertip over the drawing. "I was five when my parents gave him to me. Patch was so tiny, but within several
months he'd grown bigger than me." Slowly pulling her
hand away, she said, "I miss him terribly. Although he'd be
impossible to replace, I hope to someday have another
dog."

He handed her back the tablet. "These are very good,
Miss Matthews."

"Thank you." She cocked her head to one side. "You
know, your grace, you would make an interesting subject."

"Me?"

"Yes indeed. Your face is . . ." She paused and studied him for a long moment, tilting her head from left to right.

"That bad?" he asked in mock horror.

"Goodness, no," she assured him. "Your face is most interesting. Filled with character. You wouldn't mind if I sketched you?"

"Not at all." *Most interesting? Filled with character?* He wasn't sure if that was good or bad, but one thing was certain. Those weren't the flirtatious words the women of the *ton* would use to describe him. It seemed, at least as far as men were concerned, Miss Matthews was artless and without guile. *Unbelievable. And damned unlikely. But I'll discover whatever game she's up to soon enough.*

"Perhaps you'd sit under the tree?" she asked, scanning the immediate area. "Prop your back against the trunk and make yourself comfortable." She gathered her supplies, and in spite of feeling rather foolish, Austin did as he was bid.

"How's this?" he asked once he found a comfortable spot.

She knelt in front of him. "You look tense, your grace. Try to relax. This won't hurt a bit, I promise."

Austin adjusted his position and drew a deep breath.

"That's much better." Her eyes roamed his face. "Now, I'd like you to reminisce for me."

"Reminisce?"

Amusement sparkled in the eyes. "Yes. It's an American word that means 'to recall past events.'"

Suspicion pricked at him. Was she trying to glean information from him? Keeping his expression carefully blank he asked, "What do you want to know?"

"Why, nothing, your grace. Just think of one of your fondest memories while I sketch. It will help me to capture your expression correctly."

"I see." But he didn't see at all. Fond memory? Of what? He'd sat for several portraits, all of which hung in the gallery at Bradford Hall, and he'd had to do nothing save sit immobile for interminable lengths of time. He searched his mind and came up totally blank.

"Surely you have *one* fond thought lurking in there somewhere, your grace."

Not bloody likely. But he wasn't about to let her know that. Determined to dig up a happy thought, Austin concentrated while she continued to watch him.

"Just let your mind wander . . . and relax," she said softly.

His gaze moved past her and settled on Myst grazing nearby. An image of William popped into his mind . . . William, at thirteen, running to the stables behind Austin, and Robert close behind his older brothers . . .

"You're sporting a most intriguing smile," she said. "Will you share your thoughts with me?"

He considered refusing, but decided no harm could come in telling her. "I'm thinking about a grand adventure I shared with my brothers." Warmth spread through him as he recalled the day in vivid detail. "We were forced to flee to the stables after we'd schemed to force Caroline's sour-faced governess to resign her post. We'd rigged a barrel of flour and a bucket of water over the woman's bedchamber door. When she opened the door, her outraged screams shook the rafters. We hid in the hayloft and howled with laughter until we could barely breathe."

"How old were you?"

"I was fourteen. William was thirteen and Robert ten."

The memory faded slowly, like a plume of smoke wafting on a gentle breeze.

"What other mischief did you boys get into?"

Another image immediately popped into his mind and a chuckle worked its way up his throat. "One day, that same summer, the three of us were walking by the lake when Robert, who's been a devil since the day he was born, dared William to shuck his clothes and jump in, an activity that our father strictly forbade. Not to be outdone, I immediately dared him to do the same. Within moments, we were all stripped bare, splashing and diving, enjoying the time of our lives. But we suddenly realized we weren't alone."

"Oh, dear. Did your father come upon you?"

"No, although that might have been better. It was our friend Miles, now the Earl of Eddington. He stood on the shore, his arms laden with our clothes and an unmistakable look in his eyes. We raced off in hot pursuit, but Miles was too fast. We were forced to sneak into the house, without a stitch on, through the kitchen." He shook his head and laughed. "We managed to avoid Father, but the kitchen staff had fodder for their gossip mill for months."

His laughter faded and a rapid succession of memories flashed through his mind: he and William swimming together, fishing together; explaining to William the intricacies of where babies come from, then laughing uproariously at the expression of horror on his face. Then, years later, sharing a meal at their club, or a laugh at the faro table, or a race on horseback. So many moments shared . . . moments that were gone forever. *God, how I miss you, William.*

"I'm finished."

The soft words broke through Austin's reverie. "I beg your pardon?"

"I said I'm finished with your sketch." She held the tablet out to him. "Would you like to see it?"

Austin took the sketch and studied the picture intently. It depicted him as he was not used to seeing himself. The man in the picture appeared completely relaxed, leaning back against the tree trunk, one leg drawn up, his fingers casually linked around his raised knee. His eyes held a mischievous gleam, and a small smile played around the corners of his lips, as if he were thinking of something amusing and happy.

"Do you like it?" she asked, leaning over his shoulder to study her handiwork.

Her light lilac fragrance again assailed his senses. Shiny hair lay in wild disarray around her lovely face. One long auburn curl brushed his upper arm and he stared at it, a slash of dark red against his white sleeve, and he fought the almost irresistible urge to reach out and touch it.

He cleared his throat. "Yes. I like it very much. You captured my mood perfectly."

"You mentioned a younger brother named Robert."

"Yes. He's away, traveling on the Continent."

She studied him intently. "And William—you love him very much."

A lump lodged in his throat. "Yes."

He didn't comment on her use of the present tense. God, yes, he'd loved William. Even at the end, when he'd claimed he didn't . . . when he'd witnessed with his own disbelieving ears and eyes his brother's unthinkable treason.

"Yes. I loved him." He handed her back the tablet.

Her gaze riveted on his cheek. "Does your injury pain you?"

"It stings a bit."

"Then I insist on preparing you a salve." She pulled a satchel from her knapsack.

"What is that you have?"

"My medical bag."

"You brought a medical bag on a walk?"

She nodded. "Whenever I walk or ride. As a child, I constantly skinned my elbows and knees." A teasing gleam entered her eyes. "As you already know my fondness for crawling about in the bushes, I'm sure this doesn't surprise you. Papa finally fashioned a bag for me to bring along whenever I left the house. I've pared the supplies down to the bare minimum and the bag isn't heavy."

"How did you manage to skin your knees? Didn't your skirts protect you?"

A blush washed over her cheeks. "I'm afraid I tended to, er, hike my skirts up a bit." His surprise obviously showed because she quickly added, "But only when I climbed trees."

"Climbed trees?" A picture of her, long limbed and laughing, her skirts hiked up to her thighs, flashed in his mind, leaving a trail of heat in its wake.

She shot him a teasing smile. "Have no fear, your grace. I stopped climbing trees several weeks ago. But I still bring my bag with me. You never know when you may run across a handsome gentleman in need of medical aid. I find it best to always be prepared."

"I suppose that's true," Austin murmured, oddly pleased she thought him handsome, yet surprised that her words did not strike him as flirtatious—merely friendly.

He watched with interest as she removed several pouches and small wooden bowls from the satchel. Excusing herself, she walked to the lake, returning with a container of water. After setting her supplies around her, she set to work, her face a study in concentration.

"What are you mixing?" Austin asked, fascinated by her unusual actions.

"Nothing more than dried herbs, roots, and water."

He didn't see how a few herbs and water could help his stinging cheek, but he remained silent and simply watched her, reminding himself that the more he observed her, the more he would learn about her.

When she finished, she knelt in front of him, then

dipped her fingers into the bowl of salve. "This may sting a bit at first, but only for a moment."

He eyed the creamy concoction dubiously. "What possible good can that do?"

"You'll see. May I proceed?"

When he hesitated, she raised her brows, her eyes dancing with mischief. "Surely you're not afraid of a bit of salve, your grace."

"Of course not," he all but huffed, irked that she would suggest such a thing, even in jest. "By all means, apply the salve."

She leaned forward and gently rubbed her cream into his injured cheek. It stung like the very devil and he forced himself not to pull away and wipe off her ridiculous remedy.

In an effort to distract himself from his fiery skin, he turned his attention to her. An expression of concern puckered her brow as she dabbed on more of the salve. Streaks of early morning sunlight dappled through the trees, shooting her hair with red and gold highlights. For the first time he noticed the smattering of tiny freckles on her nose.

"Just a bit more, your grace. I'm nearly done."

Her warm breath touched his face. His gaze dropped to her mouth, and his throat tightened. Damn it, she possessed the most incredible mouth he'd ever seen. He suddenly realized that not only did his cheek no longer sting, but her gentle touch was sending ripples of pleasure streaking through him.

His entire body pulsed to life. The desire to kiss her, to feel those amazing lips crushed beneath his own, to touch his tongue to hers, slammed into him, overwhelming him. If he leaned forward just a tiny bit . . .

She abruptly leaned back. "Does it still sting?"

He blinked, feeling dazed. And unkissed. "Ah, no. Why do you ask?"

"You moaned. Or perhaps it was more like a groan."

Annoyance, at both her and himself, surged through him. Here he was, fantasizing about kissing her, his trousers growing increasingly uncomfortable, moaning—or was it groaning?—and she wanted to know if she was hurting him.

She was damn near killing him.

He was truly losing his mind. He needed to focus on the matters at hand, but it was damn hard to do with her so tantalizingly close. *Concentrate on William. The blackmail note. What she might know about them.*

"Thank you, Miss Matthews. It feels much better. Are you finished?"

She frowned, then nodded while wiping her fingers on a square of cloth. He wondered what she was thinking, his curiosity aroused by her silence and troubled expression.

"Is something wrong, Miss Matthews?"

"I'm not certain. May I . . . touch your hand?"

Heat snaked down his spine at her request. Without a word, he lifted his hand.

She pressed it tightly between her palms and closed her eyes. After what seemed like an eternity, her eyes slowly opened. There was no mistaking the fear and concern shadowing them.

"Is something amiss?"

"I'm afraid so, your grace."

"Did you, er, *see* William again?"

"No. I saw . . . you."

"Me?"

She nodded, looking worried. "I saw you. I felt it."

"What did you feel?"

"Danger, your grace. I fear you're in grave danger."

Chapter 4

Austin stared at her. Clearly she was suffering from delusions, but the fearful expression in her eyes chilled him. *Hell, if I don't take care, she'll have me convinced goblins lurk behind every tree.* He tried gently to extricate his hand, but she clasped it tightly between her own.

"Soon," she whispered. "I see trees, moonlight. You're on horseback, in a forest. Rain is on the way. I wish I knew more, but that's all I saw. I cannot tell you what form this danger will take, but I swear the threat to you is genuine. And imminent." Her voice turned into a desperate plea. "You must not ride in the forest after dark, in the rain."

Disgusted with himself for feeling slightly unnerved, Austin pulled his hand from between hers. "I am perfectly capable of taking care of myself, Miss Matthews. Do not concern yourself."

Frustration flickered in her eyes. "I *am* concerned, your grace, and you should be as well. While I can understand your skepticism, I assure you what I say is true. What possible reason could I have to lie to you?"

"I have asked myself that very question, Miss Matthews. And I'm very interested in the answer."

"There is no answer. I am *not* lying. Good heavens, are you *always* this pigheaded?" Her eyes narrowed on his face. "Or are you perhaps beavered?"

Had she just called him pigheaded? And what the hell was—*"Beavered?"*

"Yes. Have you overindulged in strong spirits?"

He glared at her. "*Foxed*. You mean foxed. And no, of course I'm not. Good God, it's barely seven in the morning." He leaned closer to her and his annoyance peaked when she stood her ground and glared right back at him. "Nor am I pigheaded."

An unladylike snort that sounded suspiciously like an *oink* escaped her lips. "I'm certain you enjoy thinking you're not." She gathered up her supplies, then rose. "I must go. Aunt Joanna will wonder what's become of me." Without another word, she turned and headed swiftly down the path leading back to the house.

Austin watched her disappearing form and reined in his irritation. Damn impertinent woman. God help the poor bastard who leg-shackled himself to that ill-mannered American.

Once his anger cooled, however, her disturbing words replayed in his mind. *Danger.*

An uneasy sensation slithered through him, but he resolutely shook it off. He was on his own private estate, miles away from anything except nature. What could possibly endanger him here? A hungry squirrel biting his leg? A goat butting his arse? He inwardly chuckled at the thought of being chased about the grounds by furry animals.

His amusement abruptly died as he thought of the blackmail letter. Could the blackmailer mean to harm him? He shook his head, dismissing the thought. The blackmailer wanted money—he wouldn't get it if he harmed the source.

Still, what were her intentions in warning him about danger? Could she be in cahoots with the blackmailer? Was she trying to make him worry about the blackmailer so he'd pay the bastard? Or was she perhaps another of the blackmailer's victims and merely trying to help him? Or was she simply daft?

He didn't know, but he put no credence in this visions nonsense.

No, he was not in danger.

Absolutely not.

And he wasn't pigheaded, either.

Two hours later, Austin walked into the dining room, hoping for a peaceful cup of coffee, and nearly groaned. Two dozen pairs of eyes looked at him. Damn. He'd forgotten about his mother's remaining guests who were actually *his* guests.

"Good morning, Austin," his mother said in a tone he recognized all too well. It was her thank-heavens-you've-shown-up-because-someone-is-boring-us-all-to-tears voice. "Lord Digby was just expounding on the virtues of the latest irrigation systems. I believe that is a pet subject of yours."

He nearly laughed out loud at the desperate look she sent him—a look even the most heartless man could not ignore. Knowing she wanted him to occupy Lord Digby's attention, he eased into his chair at the head of the table and gave the man an encouraging nod. "Irrigation systems? Fascinating stuff." Conversation resumed, and after accepting coffee from a footman, he pretended to listen to Lord Digby while his gaze drifted down the table.

Caroline smiled at him, then after a surreptitious peek

left and right, she rolled her eyes toward the ceiling. He winked back, pleased that she looked so happy and had somehow managed to retain her sense of humor through what was rapidly promising to be a deadly boring meal.

His eyes skimmed over the other guests while he absently nodded in response to Lord Digby's harangue. Lady Digby sat surrounded by her numerous daughters. Good God, how many were there again? Taking a quick inventory, he counted five, all of whom were currently fluttering their eyelashes at him.

He barely suppressed a shudder. What had Miles called the chits? Oh yes. Cabbage-headed nincompoops. He made a mental note to take Miles at his word and stay as far away from the Digby daughters as possible. No doubt if he paid them the slightest attention, Lady Digby would immediately summon the vicar.

Countess Penbroke sat next to his mother, and the two women were engaged in an animated conversation Austin could not hear. Lady Penbroke wore but yet another sample from her seemingly endless supply of outlandish headgear. Austin watched, strangely fascinated, as a footman nimbly dodged the long ostrich feathers protruding from her chartreuse turban that threatened to poke out eyes every time she moved her head.

He nearly choked on his coffee when he observed Lady Penbroke carelessly toss her feather boa, another favorite accessory, over her shoulder. Instead of settling about her plump shoulders, the trail of feathers landed squarely in a Digby daughter's plate. The chit, engrossed in smiling insipidly at him, unknowingly speared the boa on her fork. Before Austin could issue a warning, the same quick-moving footman who'd avoided Lady Penbroke's plumes reached out, plucked the boa from the fork, settled it about Lady Penbroke with an expert flick of the wrist, then continued around the table without batting an eye.

Impressed, Austin made a mental note to increase the man's wages.

Leaning back, he continued his perusal down the table. His mother, he noted, looked happy, composed, and surprisingly refreshed considering she probably hadn't retired until close to dawn. Her golden hair was arranged in a becoming chignon, and her midnight blue gown exactly matched her eyes. She and Caroline looked so much alike, he knew exactly what his sister would look like in twenty-five years—absolutely beautiful.

Austin's gaze continued moving along the guests and he raised his brows when Miles nodded to him over the rim of his coffee cup. Could the fact that his friend hadn't yet departed for London indicate that he might already have something to report about Miss Matthews?

A frown pinched his brow and his gaze swept over the guests once again. And just where was Miss Matthews? One chair at the table remained conspicuously vacant.

Not that he was anxious to see the damn impertinent piece. No indeed. In fact, if he didn't need to find out what possible connection she could have to William, he'd dismiss her from his thoughts entirely.

Yes, he'd dismiss her big golden brown eyes that could change from smiling to serious in a heartbeat, and that thick, curling auburn hair that begged to have a man's fingers sift through its luxurious length. He wouldn't give her mouth another thought. Hmmm . . . her mouth. Those delectable, full, pouty lips—

"By cracky, your grace, are you feeling all right?"

Lord Digby's voice yanked Austin's attention back to reality. "I beg your pardon?"

"I inquired about your health. You groaned."

"I did?" Bloody hell! The woman was a nuisance even when she was absent.

"Yes. Kippers affect me that way, too. Onions as well."

Lord Digby leaned closer and lowered his voice. "Lady Digby can always tell if I've indulged myself at dinner. Blasted woman knows every morsel I put in my mouth and locks her bedchamber door if I've sneaked so much as one bite of onion." He cast a pointed look down the table at his five daughters. "Something you might want to keep in mind when *you're* ready to choose a wife."

Good God. The thought of being leg-shackled to a Digby daughter chased away his remaining appetite. Throwing a meaningful look at Miles, Austin excused himself to Lord Digby and rose.

"Where are you off to?" his mother asked.

Walking over to stand behind her, Austin dropped a quick kiss on her temple. "I have some business with Miles."

She turned, her concerned gaze searching his face, no doubt looking for the telltale signs of fatigue that he knew often shadowed his eyes. Knowing she worried about him, he forced a smile and made her a formal bow. "You look lovely this morning, Mother. As always."

"Thank you. You look"—her voice dropped to a confidential pitch—"distracted. Is something amiss?"

"Not at all. In fact, I'll make it a point to join you this afternoon for tea."

Surprise sparkled in her eyes. "Now I *know* something is wrong."

Chuckling, he excused himself, then made his way to his private study to await Miles.

Austin leaned his hips against his mahogany desk and regarded Miles, who lounged in Austin's favorite maroon leather wing chair. "You're absolutely certain she's never been in England before she arrived six months ago?" Austin asked.

"As certain as I can be without actually looking through mountains of ships' passenger logs." When Austin frowned, Miles quickly added, "Which is exactly what I shall do once I reach London. But until then, I can only relate what Countess Penbroke told me. We engaged in a lengthy chat last evening, one that nearly resulted in my losing an eye to the hazard she'd dressed her head with. Look here." He pointed to a small scratch on his temple. "I'm probably scarred for life."

"I never said this mission wasn't without certain dangers," Austin said blandly.

"Downright fraught with danger if you ask me," Miles muttered. "But while I fetched Lady Penbroke numerous cups of punch and dodged her feathers, she told me, quite emphatically, that this is her niece's first visit to England. I believe Lady Penbroke's exact words were 'And it's about damn time.'"

"Do you know how long Miss Matthews is planning to stay?"

"When I asked Lady Penbroke, she fixed a steely look on me and informed me that as the gel had barely just arrived, she'd not made any plans to send her back to America."

"What about her family?"

"Her parents are both deceased. Her mother, Lady Penbroke's sister, died eight years ago. The father passed away two years ago."

"Any brothers or sisters?"

"No."

Austin raised his brows. "What did she do after her father died? She can't be much older than twenty. Surely she didn't live alone."

"She is two and twenty. I came away with the impression that Miss Matthews's father left her comfortable, but far from wealthy. She settled her father's affairs, then moved in with distant relations on her father's side who lived in the same town. Apparently these relatives have a daughter close in age to Miss Matthews and they're great friends."

"Did you find out anything else?"

Miles nodded. "When Miss Matthews sailed to England, she arrived with a hired traveling companion named Mrs. Loretta Thomkins. They parted company when the ship docked. Lady Penbroke understood that Mrs. Thomkins planned to remain in London with family. If that is the case, she won't be difficult to locate."

"Excellent. Thank you, Miles."

"You're welcome, but you owe me a boon. Several, in fact."

"Based on your tone, I'm not sure I want to know why."

"I asked so many questions about her niece, I believe Lady Penbroke entertains the notion that I fancy the chit."

Austin stilled. "Indeed? I imagine you promptly disabused her of that notion."

Miles shrugged and flicked a bit of lint from his sleeve. "Not exactly. Before speaking to Lady Penbroke, I brought up Miss Matthews to several well-connected ladies. The mere mention of her name induced giggles, twitters, and eye rolling. If Lady Penbroke spreads the word that I've shown interest in her niece, perhaps some of the twittering will stop. Miss Matthews strikes me as a nice young woman who does not deserve to be cast out. In fact, now that I think of it, she's really quite lovely, don't you agree?"

"I hadn't particularly noticed."

Miles's brows almost disappeared into his hairline. "*You?* Not notice an attractive female? Are you ill? Feverish?"

"No." Damn it, when did Miles become such a blasted pest?

"Well, allow me to enlighten you. What Miss Matthews lacks in social graces, she more than makes up for with her lovely face, smooth complexion, and dimpling smile. Her beauty is quiet, understated, requiring a second look before it can be fully appreciated. While fashionable society decrees her height *un*fashionable, I find it fascinating." He tapped his chin with two fingers, his expression thoughtful. "I wonder what it would be like to kiss such a tall woman . . . especially one with a lush mouth like Miss Matthews possesses. Her lips are really quite extraordinary—"

"Miles."

"Yes?"

Austin ordered his clenched muscles to relax. "You've wandered off the subject."

Miles's face bore a mask of pure innocence. "I thought we were discussing Miss Matthews."

"We were. It's simply not necessary to mention her . . . attributes."

A gleam sparkled in Miles's eyes. "Ah. So you *did* notice."

"Notice what?"

"Her . . . attributes."

Determined to put an end to this conversation, Austin said, "I'm not blind, Miles. Miss Matthews is, as you say, lovely. I do not intend to let that sway or influence me in my search for information." He fixed a penetrating stare on his friend. "I trust you will not allow it to, either."

"Certainly not. *I* am not the one who is interested in the woman."

"I am not *interested* in her."

"Indeed?" Chuckling, Miles rose, crossed the Axminster rug, then laid a hand on Austin's shoulder. "You have me traipsing about the kingdom gathering information about her for reasons that you've yet to share with me

although you must realize I'm burning with curiosity, and
you looked positively grim when I waxed poetic about her
remarkable lips."

"I'm sure I looked nothing of the sort."

"Grim," Miles repeated, "and ready to toss me out on
my very elegantly attired posterior."

To Austin's annoyance, heat crept up his neck. Before
he could reply, Miles said, "You look like a volcano on the
verge of eruption. How very . . . interesting. And on that
note, I shall depart for London. I'll report back as soon as
I've discovered anything of interest." He crossed the room,
but paused at the door. "Good luck with Miss Matthews,
Austin. I've a feeling you're going to need it."

Chapter 5

Austin spent most of the afternoon ensconced in his study, going over the accounts of his Cornwall estate. Unfortunately, his mind was not focused on the task and the rows of numbers kept running together, refusing to add up properly. His brain churned with questions. Was it possible that the blackmailer had some connection to the Frenchman Gaspard? Or perhaps the blackmailer *was* Gaspard. He strongly suspected so, and if so, he was most likely in England, in which case Austin hoped his Bow Street Runner would locate him. *Contact me again, you bastard. I look forward to finding you. You plan to write me again in London after July first—but perhaps I'll find you first.* He wanted this settled and the threat to his family over. And he needed to figure out how Miss Matthews fit into the equation.

In need of a reprieve, he stretched and walked to the windows. Gazing down on the lawns, he saw Caroline and Miss Matthews frolicking with Gadzooks and three other kittens whom he believed were Egad, Balderdash, and

Fiddlesticks—although it was sometimes difficult to tell the beasts apart. It was quite possible they were Damn It All, Bloody Hell, and Blow My Dickey.

Shaking his head, he realized that if Miss Matthews and Caroline were going to entertain themselves with the cats, he'd have to warn Mortlin to adjust the beasts' names.

He opened the window a crack, and feminine giggles drifted up to him. Tenderness seeped through him at Caroline's sweet laughter. It was a sound he had missed for many months after William's death. His gaze settled on Miss Matthews and his heart seemed to skip a beat. A dimpling smile wreathed her face and bright sunlight shimmered on her glorious hair. She looked young, carefree, innocent, and impossibly lovely.

And she'd made his sister laugh.

A rush of gratitude warmed him, catching him off guard. He needed to remember that Miss Matthews was obviously more than she appeared. Yes, she'd amused Caroline, but what else might she be telling his sister? Hopefully she wasn't spreading tales of William being alive or spouting nonsense about visions.

Still, if Caroline befriended her, perhaps his sister could offer him some insights into Miss Matthews's character. Yes, he definitely needed to speak with Caroline.

As soon as possible.

Austin's first opportunity to have a private word with Caroline was in the drawing room before dinner that evening. Maneuvering her aside, he remarked in a casual tone, "It appears you've made a new friend."

Caroline accepted a glass of sherry from a footman. "You mean Elizabeth?" At Austin's nod, she said, "We spent most of the day together. I like her very much. She's unlike anyone I've ever met."

"Indeed? What is so unusual about her?"

"Everything," Caroline said without hesitation. "Her knowledge of medicine, her love of animals. She's amusing, but her humor is not at the expense of others. She did not utter an unkind word about anyone the entire day."

"That isn't unusual," Austin muttered, relieved that Miss Matthews had clearly said nothing to upset Caroline. "That's a miracle." Especially given the way the members of the *ton* had treated her.

"Exactly. She possesses an interesting combination of shy awkwardness and bold intelligence, yet I sensed a sadness about her. She misses her home."

"Had you met her before last evening?"

"We were introduced, but I hadn't had the opportunity to speak with her at great length."

"Have you heard any gossip about her?"

"Only that she is a poor dancer and considered somewhat of a bluestocking. I noticed that most of the gentlemen ignore her, but I believe I may have fixed that."

He stilled. "What do you mean?"

Caroline waved her hand in a breezy manner. "I simply shared a few fashion ideas with her, then sent my abigail to her this evening to style her hair." Her blue eyes sparkled with sudden interest. "Why do you ask about Elizabeth?"

"Just curious. I observed you with her today, playing with the kittens." He smiled at her. "It was good to hear you laughing."

"I cannot recall the last time I enjoyed myself so much. I believe Elizabeth and I will be the best of friends. Have you had the chance to speak with her?"

He arranged his features into a bland mask. "Yes."

"And what did you think of her?"

"I thought she was . . ." His words drifted off as he caught sight of her entering the drawing room. *Exquisite.*

Surely *this* ravishing creature wasn't the same woman whom the gentlemen of the *ton* ignored. How could any man who saw her not want her? Dressed in a simple gown of ivory silk, a long, unadorned fluid column of alabaster, she rendered most of the other women in the room over-dressed and garish in comparison.

Her auburn tresses were caught up in an elegant top-knot. A single thick curl cascaded over her shoulder, ending just below her waist, an enticing streak of shimmering color against a pale background. He'd had no idea her hair was so long, and he wondered what she would look like with it unbound, falling down her back. *Exquisite.*

She hesitated in the doorway, her eyes anxiously searching the guests until they lit on Caroline. A smile warmed her golden brown eyes, a look that he noticed faltered when she caught sight of him standing next to Caroline.

"Doesn't she look marvelous!" Caroline enthused. "I *knew* with the correct dress and coiffure she'd be stunning. Why, I've transformed her into a swan!" Caroline glanced at him, then whispered, "Stop frowning, Austin. I told Elizabeth to meet me here by the fireplace and you'll frighten her away."

"I'm not frowning."

Caroline sent him an arch look. "Your countenance resembles a thundercloud. Shall I fetch you a mirror?"

He forced his facial muscles to relax. "No."

"That's better. You never finished telling me your impression of Elizabeth."

Austin watched her making her way across the room, pausing to chat with her aunt. His hands clenched when he noticed that every damn man in the room was watching her as well. She glanced in his direction and their eyes met for several heartbeats before she raised her chin a notch, then turned away.

Warmth crept up his neck at her obvious dismissal. With his gaze still fixed upon her, he said, "Miss Matthews struck me as unusual, no doubt because of her colonial upbringing."

"Unusual?" Caroline repeated softly. "Yes, I suppose that would explain it."

"Explain what?"

"Why you haven't been able to take your eyes off her since she appeared in the doorway."

He snapped his head around and encountered Caroline's amused blue gaze. Leveling his best frigid glare on her, he said, "I beg your pardon?"

Reaching up, she gently patted his cheek. "Austin, darling. You know that icy stare doesn't scare me. Now, if you'll excuse me, I believe I'll join Elizabeth and Lady Penbroke."

She sauntered off, and Austin tossed back his champagne in a single gulp. His gaze again settled on Miss Matthews as she greeted Caroline with an inviting smile curving her lips, and he wondered how it would feel to have her greet *him* in such a warm manner. The very thought sent a tingle through him, thoroughly annoying him.

Caroline's words echoed in his mind. *You haven't been able to take your eyes off her since she appeared in the doorway.* Couldn't take his eyes off her? Ridiculous! Of course he could. And he would. As soon as she turned away and he could no longer see her smile. Or her mouth. Or that fascinating single curl flowing down her dress.

Until then, he needed to watch her, to observe her, to find out all he could about her.

For investigative purposes only, of course.

*   *   *

At dinner, Elizabeth sat between her aunt and Lord Digby. To her surprise, Lord Digby conversed with her at length, engaging her in conversation about American farming techniques. She knew next to nothing about the subject, but listened politely, nodding encouragingly, while she enjoyed the sumptuous ten-course meal and dodged her aunt's peacock feathers.

While Lord Digby waxed poetic about sheep-shearing procedures, her attention wandered to the head of the table where the duke sat. Resplendent in black evening wear, he all but took her breath away, a fact that irritated her to no end. She did *not* want to find that pigheaded man attractive.

He chatted easily with the guests seated around him, but she noticed that he rarely smiled, a fact that pushed her irritation aside and tugged at her heart.

A troubled soul lurked beneath his polished exterior, but he hid it well. If she hadn't touched him, she would have seen only what he presented. She wouldn't have known his sadness or loneliness or guilt. Or sensed the danger threatening him.

She hadn't realized she was staring at him until their eyes met. His silvery gaze locked onto hers and her skin tingled under his intense look. Heat suffused her, and she knew she should look away, but she couldn't. She wanted so much to help him. If only he would listen to her.

Dear God, she wished she'd been able to see more, to know what menace threatened him, and when. Would harm befall him this very night? If so, what could she do to prevent it?

His gaze penetrated her, heating her as if he'd touched her. She forced her attention away from that disturbing stare, back to Lord Digby, but she'd already made a decision.

She would do whatever was necessary to see that the duke remained safe.

Austin approached the stables a little after midnight, restless, unsettled, wanting only to ride Myst and work this annoying, unnamed frustration out of his system.

It had started the moment he'd seen her in the drawing room doorway, looking achingly beautiful, smiling at everyone . . . everyone except him. As much as it irked him to admit it, he hadn't been able to keep his eyes off her all evening. Even when he'd managed to focus his attention elsewhere, he'd been aware of her every minute, knew whom she was speaking to, what she ate. And when their eyes had met across the length of the dinner table, he'd felt as if someone had punched him in the heart.

Her presence had distracted him all evening, and he'd breathed a sigh of relief when she'd retired shortly before eleven. But his relief was short lived because he couldn't get the damn woman—her eyes, her smile, her luscious mouth—out of his mind. It galled him that he had to keep reminding himself that she knew things she shouldn't know, couldn't know, without a reason other than the "visions" explanation she'd given him.

But every time he tried to convince himself she was up to something with her talk of visions, that she might be involved with the blackmail scheme and couldn't be trusted, all his instincts rebelled. There was a kindness, an innocence, and, damn it, a trustworthiness about her that kept trying to stomp down his suspicions every time they cropped up.

Was it possible that she was merely placing too much credence in her own undeniable intuitiveness, calling it "visions"? Could her words and actions truly be no more than what she claimed—an attempt to help him?

He entered the stables, making his way toward Myst's stall, but halted when a subtle scent wafted to him, a scent out of place with the smell of leather and horse. Lilacs.

Before he could react, she emerged from the shadows and stepped into a shaft of moonlight. "Good evening, your grace."

Much to his annoyance, anticipation skittered down his spine. She still wore the cream silk gown she'd worn to dinner, and that same long, tempting auburn curl drew his gaze. "We meet again, Miss Matthews."

She stepped closer to him, and he noticed her expression. She appeared distinctly annoyed.

"Why are you here, your grace?"

"I might ask the same of you, Miss Matthews."

"I am here because of you."

And I am here because of you . . . because I cannot stop thinking about you. Crossing his arms over his chest, he contemplated her with studied detachment. Damn it, he wished he knew what to make of this woman. "What about me draws you to the stables at such an hour?"

"I suspected you might plan to ride." She raised her chin a notch. "I'm here to stop you."

He couldn't contain his bark of disbelief. "Indeed? And how do you intend to do that?"

Her eyes narrowed. "I don't know. I suppose I was hoping you'd be intelligent enough to heed my warning about danger befalling you should you choose to ride at night. Clearly I was mistaken."

Bloody hell, who did this woman think she was? Approaching her slowly, he didn't stop until only two feet separated them. She didn't retreat so much as an inch, just stood her ground, watching him with a single raised brow that irked him further.

"I don't believe anyone has ever dared question my intelligence, Miss Matthews."

"Indeed? Then perhaps you weren't listening, your grace, because I just did that very thing."

Full-blown anger struck him like a slap. He'd had more than enough of this damn woman. Before he could give her the scathing set down she deserved, however, she reached out and pressed his hand between both of hers.

A tingle sizzled right up his arm, effectively cutting off his angry words.

"I still see it," she whispered, her eyes huge, trained on his. "Danger. You hurt." Releasing his hand, she laid her palm against his cheek. "Please. Please do not ride tonight."

Her soft hand lying against his face ignited his skin, overwhelming him with the desire to turn his head and brush his lips over her palm. Instead, he grasped her wrist and pushed her hand away from him.

"I do not know what game you're playing—"

"I am not toying with you! What can I do, what can I say, to convince you?"

"Let's start by you telling me what you know about my brother and how you know it. Where did you meet him?"

"I never met him."

"Yet you knew about his scar." He allowed his gaze to roam over her in an unmistakably insulting fashion. "Were you his lover?"

Her eyes widened with shock too real to be forced. Relief swept through him, a reaction he did not care to examine.

"*Lovers?* Are you mad? I had a *vision* about him. I—"

"Yes, yes, so you've said. And you can read minds as well. Tell me, Miss Matthews, what am I thinking right now?"

She hesitated, her eyes searching his face. "I am not always able to tell. And I'd need to . . . touch you."

He held out his hand. "Touch me. Convince me."

She stared at his hand for several heartbeats, then nodded. "I'll try."

When his hand was firmly pressed between her palms, he closed his eyes and purposely focused his thoughts on something provocative. He imagined her in his bedchamber, backlit by the golden flames dancing in the hearth. Reaching out, he flicked open the pearl-encrusted clip holding her hair in place. Silky tendrils tumbled down into his hands, falling over her shoulders, down, down—

"You're thinking about my hair. You want to touch it."

Heat stung him and his eyes popped open. The first thing he saw was her mouth . . . that incredible, kissable mouth. If he leaned forward just a bit, he could taste it—

She released his hand. "You want to kiss me."

Her whispered words brushed by him, setting his pulse thrumming. Damn it, yes, he wanted to kiss her. Needed to. *Had* to. Surely one kiss would satisfy this inexplicable hunger to taste her.

Giving in to a craving he couldn't explain or fight any longer, he leaned forward.

She stepped back.

He closed the distance between them, but again she retreated, her expressive eyes filled with uncertainty. Hell, the woman hadn't backed down before him once—not in the face of his anger, his sarcasm, or suspicions. But the thought of his kiss sent her into retreat.

"Is something amiss?" he asked softly, stepping closer.

"Amiss?" She backed up and nearly tripped on her hem.

"Yes. It's an English word meaning 'wrong.' You seem . . . nervous."

"Certainly not," she retorted, inching backward until the wooden wall stopped her. "I'm merely, er, warm."

"Yes, it's quite warm in here." Two long, unhurried strides brought him directly in front of her. He braced his hands on the wall on either side of her shoulders, bracketing her in.

Raising her chin a notch, she stared at him with what he had to admit was a fine show of bravado, but her rapid breathing spoiled the effect.

"If you're trying to frighten me, your grace—"

"I'm trying to kiss you, which will be much easier now that you've stopped moving about."

"I don't want you to kiss me."

"Yes, you do." He moved closer, until only inches separated them. The scent of lilacs filled his head. "Have you ever been kissed?"

"Of course. Thousands of times."

Recalling her stunned reaction when he'd asked if she'd been William's lover, he raised a brow. "I meant by a man."

"Oh. Well, then, hundreds of times."

"By a man other than your father."

"Oh. In that case . . . once."

Unexpected irritation rippled through him. "Indeed? And did you enjoy it?"

"Actually, no. It was rather . . . dry."

"Ah. Then you were not *properly* kissed."

"And you wish to kiss me properly?"

"No." He leaned forward and whispered in her ear, "I intend to kiss you most *im*properly."

Drawing her into his arms, he covered her lips with his. God help him, she felt exquisite. Soft and round, warm and delicious.

When he ran his tongue along the seam of her lips, she gasped, effectively parting her lips, and he slipped his tongue into the luscious warmth of her mouth. Strawberries. She tasted like strawberries. Sweet, delicious, seductive.

He pulled her closer, until her long, lush body was

pressed tightly against him, and he marveled at the unique sensation of kissing such a tall woman.

His common sense roused itself and demanded he stop, but he couldn't. Damn it, he should have been appalled at himself for kissing her, uninterested in the naive chit, bored with her innocence.

Instead, he was fascinated, aching, and aroused. When she shyly touched her tongue to his, a groan rumbled deep in his throat, and he delved deeper, slanting his mouth over hers, tasting, thrusting, swallowing her breathy moans. He lost all sense of time and place, could think only of the woman in his arms, the warm, soft feel of her, the sweet, drugging taste of her, the gentle floral scent of her.

His arousal ached with a need that grew so intense, it finally dragged him from his sensuous haze. He had to stop. Now. Or he'd lay her down right here in the stable.

Summoning his last ounce of self-control, he ended their kiss.

Her eyes opened slowly. "Oh my."

Oh my, indeed. He didn't know what he'd expected, but he certainly hadn't anticipated this woman unleashing the flood of lust clutching him in a stranglehold. His heart slapped against his ribs, and his damn hands were shaking. Instead of satisfying his curiosity, her kiss had only whetted his appetite, a hunger that threatened to consume him whole—right after it burned him alive.

Her soft breasts were crushed against his chest, igniting fires on his skin. His arousal throbbed painfully and only a lifetime of keeping himself in strict control afforded him the ability to lower his arms and step away from her.

She drew a long, shuddering breath, and he grimly noted that she was obviously as shaken as he.

"Goodness," she said in an unsteady voice. "I had no idea that kissing *im*properly was so . . ."

"So . . . what?"

"So . . . *not* dry." She inhaled several more times, then cleared her throat. "*Now* do you believe that I read your thoughts?"

"No."

Color stained her cheeks and temper flashed in her eyes. "Are you denying you wanted to kiss me?"

His gaze dropped briefly to her mouth. "No. But any man would want to kiss you." And damn it, he felt like he'd kill any man who did.

"Do you still intend to ride tonight?"

"That is none of your concern."

She simply stared at him for several heartbeats, then shook her head. "In that case, I can only hope that you'll reconsider and heed my warning. And pray that no harm comes to you. At least it isn't raining as it was in my vision, so perhaps you'll be safe. This time. Good night, your grace. I won't bother you with my visions again."

Austin watched her disappear into the darkness, forcing himself not to go after her. Something in her voice as she'd uttered those last words scraped at his insides. He raked his hands through his hair and paced. Damn it all, how could she expect him, expect *anyone*, to seriously credit her claims of visions and mind reading? It was simply too far-fetched, too illogical, to consider.

But no matter how much it chafed him to admit it, she was right about one thing. He had wanted to kiss her. With an intensity that stunned him. And now that he'd tasted her, he wanted to do it again.

And again.

Chapter 6

Elizabeth approached the stables early the next morning, anxious to get out of the house after a restless night spent trying to forget her disturbing encounter with the duke. Had he gone riding? She'd lain awake half the night, listening for rain, but the weather had thankfully remained fair. Hopefully some fresh air and a brisk ride would obliterate her worry and concern, not to mention the disappointment and hurt, aching inside at the realization that she'd never convince him about her visions.

Yet she knew mere exercise would never erase the memory of that kiss. That incredible, soul-stirring, unforgettable kiss that had touched her deep inside and awakened a sleeping passion she hadn't known existed. And kindled feelings . . . yearnings . . . she was afraid to examine too closely.

She desperately wanted, *needed*, to forget the exquisite feel of him, the heavenly taste of him, but her heart was simply not cooperating.

She entered the stables and Mortlin greeted her with a

smile. "Come to visit the cats, Miss Matthews? Or do ye wish to ride?"

Forcing aside her turmoil, she returned the groom's smile, then bent down to scratch George behind her ears. "Both. How about I visit with the kittens while you saddle a mount for me?"

"Fine idea," Mortlin said. "Look, there's two 'idin' by that 'ay stack that ye 'aven't met."

Spying the two frisky calico furballs, she said, "They're adorable. What are their names?" She sent him an arch look. "Or should I not ask?"

Color seeped into Mortlin's thin cheeks and he shuffled his feet. "Well, the bigger one's named Zounds—"

"That isn't so terrible."

"And the other one is, er . . ." He flushed to the tips of his protruding ears. "I can't say it in front of a lady."

Pressing her lips together to contain her amusement, she said, "I see."

"Guess I've got to change the wee beastie's name, but 'twas the first thing what popped out of me mouth when it was born." He shook his head, clearly bemused. "Them kittens just kept comin' and comin'. No stoppin' them, there was. Gave me quite a turn, it did."

"Yes, I imagine so." She ran her hands over George's warm belly, then stilled. After gently pressing the furry tummy several more times, she hid a smile. "The gestation period for a cat is about sixty days. I'm afraid I won't still be here when George gives birth to her next litter, or I'd offer to assist you. I'm quite capable in these matters."

"I'm sure ye are, but . . ." His voice trailed off and his eyes widened to saucers. "*Next* litter?"

"Yes. I predict George will be a mama again in about a month."

Mortlin's widened eyes bugged out. "Surely the beast is

just fat! The kittens aren't even three months old! 'Ow the blazes did this 'appen?"

She had to bite the inside of her cheek to keep from laughing at the groom's dumbfounded expression. "In the usual way, I suspect." Giving George's tummy one last rub, Elizabeth stood, then patted the man's arm. "Do not worry yourself, Mortlin. George will be fine, and you'll have a new group of mice catchers."

"Got more mice catchers underfoot now than I need," he grumbled. "Stubble it, this is *supposed* to be a stable. I'm a *groom*, not a cat doctor. I'd best saddle yer mount now—before the blasted feline starts spewin' out babes again."

Suppressing her amusement, Elizabeth entertained herself with the kittens while Mortlin went about his tasks. He soon presented her with a lovely brown mare named Rosamunde and offered her a hand up. She landed in the sidesaddle with a bone-jarring *plop* that shook her teeth. At home she'd often ridden astride on her solitary rides, but she dared not do so here even though she disliked sidesaddle. The fussy riding ensemble English fashion dictated she wear also irritated her. So many yards of material and poufs and flounces. She thought with longing of the simple, lightweight riding habits she'd fashioned herself and worn in America. Aunt Joanna had taken one look at them and nearly swooned. "Totally unsuitable, my dear," Aunt Joanna had declared. "We must do something about your wardrobe *immediately*."

Adjusting her heavy skirts around her as best she could, Elizabeth started off. At the end of the short path leading from the stable, she paused and looked back. Mortlin was crouched down on his haunches, his weathered face wreathed in tenderness as he gently petted George's swollen belly. He clearly thought she was out of earshot for he said, "We'll 'ave to come up with some dignified

names for yer new set of babies. Can't have any more of
them called Double Damnation."

Smiling to herself, she headed toward the forest. She
traveled along the bank of the stream, enjoying the fresh
clean air and the sunshine warming her face. She was not,
however, enjoying the sidesaddle or the blasted riding
habit that imprisoned her legs.

When she reached the area where the stream widened
and spilled into the lake, she pulled Rosamunde to a halt.
She was wriggling her bottom around, desperate to untangle her legs from the yards of ungainly material binding
them, when she felt herself slipping from the saddle. A
startled yelp of dismay escaped her. She grabbed for the
pommel, but wasn't quick enough. She fell ignominiously
from the horse, landing on her backside.

Unfortunately she landed right in the mud.

Even worse, she landed on a slippery steep incline.
She slid down the slimy, wet embankment, screaming all
the way, and landed in the stream with a loud splash. She
sat stock-still, speechless with shock. Her legs stuck
straight out in front of her, her boots completely sub-
merged under the muddy water. Cold water lapped at her
waist.

"Have an accident?" a familiar voice asked from behind her.

She gritted her teeth. Clearly he was unharmed, thank
goodness, but she did not care for him happening along to
witness her humiliation. "No, thank you. I've already had
one." Perhaps if she ignored him he'd go away.

Her hope was in vain.

"Dear me," the duke said, *tsk*ing his tongue in a sympathetic fashion. She heard him dismount and make his way
down to the water's edge. "You seem to have gotten yourself into a bit of a predicament here."

Turning her head, she glared at him over her shoulder.

"I am *not* in a predicament, your grace. I'm merely a bit damp."

"You're also horseless."

"Nonsense. My mount is . . ." Her voice trailed off as she scanned the area. Her mare was nowhere in sight.

"Probably halfway back to the stables by now. Must have been all that screaming you did on your way down. Makes some horses very skittish. Apparently Rosamunde is such a horse. Pity." His smoky eyes gleamed at her, clearly indicating his amusement. "I'd ask if you are all right, but I seem to recall that you possess a most robust constitution."

"That is correct."

"Are you hurt?"

She tried to lift her legs and failed. "I'm not sure. My riding habit is soaked and so heavy, I can barely move." Her irritation tripled when she realized she did indeed need help. "Do you suppose I could trouble you for some assistance?"

He stroked his chin as if seriously pondering her question. "I'm not certain if I should aid you. I'd hate to risk getting all wet and dirty. Perhaps I should leave you there and go back for some help. I could return in, oh, about an hour or so." He looked at her, brows raised. "What do you think about that?"

She didn't think much of it at all. In fact, she was pretty well sick and tired of his amusement at her expense. She'd spent a sleepless night worrying about him and now he stood before her, perfectly fit and healthy, and all but chortling at her. The arrogant man deserved to have that smug look wiped off his face. But she could barely move.

He turned as if to walk away and truly leave her stranded, and her temper snapped. Picking up a handful of mud, she slung it, meaning to make a splash and gain his attention.

Unfortunately he chose that exact instant to turn around.

Worse, she threw the mud with more force than she'd intended.

The large gooey blob landed smack in the middle of his chest, splattering his pristine white shirt. The goop slid down his body, smudging his immaculate buff breeches, landing with a soft thud on the toe of one of his highly polished riding boots.

Elizabeth froze. She hadn't meant to hit him . . . had she? Good lord, he did not look pleased. A horrified giggle bubbled up in her throat and she fought to contain it. His expression clearly indicated that laughing would not be in her best interests.

He didn't move. His eyes followed the ruinous downward path the mud had streaked on his clothing, then he raised his gaze to hers.

Plastering a sunny smile on her face, she said, "You no longer need to worry about getting all wet and dirty, your grace. There appears to be a rather nasty stain on your attire."

"You're going to regret doing that." His voice held more than a small amount of menace and his eyes bored into hers in a threatening manner. "You'll be very sorry indeed."

"Pooh," she scoffed. "You don't scare me."

He advanced a step. "You should be scared."

"Why? What are you going to do? Throw me into the water?"

He advanced another step. "No. I believe I'll throw you over my knees and thrash the living daylights out of you."

She raised her brows. "Thrash me? Truly?"

"Truly."

"Oh, dear. Well, as long as I'm to be thrashed, I might as well really deserve it." She launched another handful of mud. This one landed with a wet splat against his belly.

Austin froze. He looked down at his ruined shirt in stunned amazement. Few *men* would dare push him this way. He couldn't believe she had the nerve to hit him once, let alone *twice* with mud. She was going to pay dearly for this. Very dearly indeed.

His musings were interrupted by a mud ball whizzing by his ear. It missed his face by less than a hair.

That did it. He splashed into the water, grabbed her by her arms, and hauled her to her feet. "You're aware, of course, that this means war," he ground out, his gaze raking her flushed *laughing* face.

"Of course. But keep in mind who won the last time the Americans and the British engaged in battle."

"I'm most confident of your defeat, Miss Matthews."

"I'm most confident of *your* defeat, your grace."

Austin halted at her words, his eyes narrowing on the mud splattered across her pert nose. Her gold-flecked gaze met his with sparkling challenge, but a smile tugged at the corners of her mouth, and her dimples peeked out. His attention riveted on her full, lush lips. A tingle ran through him, recalling the feel of those lips crushed beneath his mouth. He forced his gaze upward and met her eyes—golden brown orbs brimming with laughter.

She was utterly impossible. Impertinent beyond all measure. His clothing was ruined and he was *standing in the damn lake.* He was wet, uncomfortable and . . . furious.

Wasn't he furious?

A frown pinched his brow. Yes, of course he was. Furious. He absolutely was not amused. Not in the least. This was not at all funny. And he certainly was not enjoying himself. Not a bit.

"Prepare yourself to be thrashed," he warned. Turning toward the embankment, he pulled her along.

"You'll have to catch me first!"

She yanked herself free of his restraining hand, and

lifting her sodden skirts to her knees, treaded her way farther out into the lake.

"Come back here. Now."

"So you can thrash me? Ha! I think not!" She backed several more steps away, until the water came to her waist. Suddenly her musical laugh rang out. "Good heavens! You should see yourself! You look so funny!"

Austin looked down. His wet filthy shirt clung to his chest like a second skin, and black muddy stripes adorned his riding breeches. Several dead leaves clung to his ruined boots.

"I would wager you've never been so *disheveled* in your entire aristocratic life," she said, laughing. "I must say, you're looking most distinctly un-dukelike."

"Come here."

"No."

"Now."

She shook her head, her smile never faltering.

Austin stalked forward, plowing through the chilly water, filled with purpose and grim determination. And somehow managing to conceal his unexpected and unwanted amusement. Damn woman. She was nothing but a plague on a man's sanity. He'd expected her to try to flee, but she stood her ground and awaited his arrival with a bright smile on her lovely face. He stopped a foot from her and waited.

"I started out this morning feeling rather grim, but this episode has cheered me considerably," she said, her dimples winking at him. "You must admit that this is rather humorous."

"Must I?"

She squinted in an exaggerated fashion and peered at his face. In spite of himself, a grin tugged at his lips.

"Aha!" she exclaimed. "I saw that smile."

For the life of him, he couldn't explain why he found

this debacle amusing. The "Notorious Duke of Bradford, England's Most Eligible Bachelor"—covered in mud, lake water lapping at his hips, conversing with a woman whose beaming smile held not a bit of remorse, only amusement. The esteemed members of the *ton* would take to their beds in shock if they could see him now, utterly filthy and bedraggled, accompanied by an equally filthy and bedraggled American.

Her gaze dipped to his wet shirt. "This was a lovely shirt. I'm sorry it's ruined, your grace, truly I am." Reaching out, she brushed her hand over his wet sleeve, then raised her gaze to his. "It was not my original intention to hit you with the mud, but once I had, well, it seemed a pity not to take advantage of the opportunity. To be perfectly candid, I think you needed something to make you laugh. And as for me, this adventure is the most fun I've had in months."

Austin's muscles jumped reflexively under her light touch. He searched her eyes for any signs of deceit or falseness and saw nothing but innocence and warmth. This was the most fun she'd had in months. Hell, he certainly could say the same. Of course, it wasn't necessary to tell her that.

Heaving a resigned sigh, he asked, "Does calamity follow you everywhere, Miss Matthews? This is the second time you've fallen practically at my feet."

"I fear that falling in such a manner runs in my family."

"What do you mean?"

"It's how my mother and father met. Mother came out of a millinery shop and tripped and fell at Papa's feet. She twisted her ankle in the fall, and Papa tended to her wound."

"I see. At least you come by your unfortunate propensity to tumble honestly."

"Yes, but I wouldn't call it unfortunate."

"Really? Why is that?"

She hesitated and he found himself mesmerized by her suddenly serious brown eyes. "Because it's how I first met you." A tiny smile curved her lips. "Even though you are somewhat arrogant and more than a little pigheaded, I find that I . . . well, rather like you."

Austin stared at her in blank astonishment. "You *like* me?"

"Yes. You're a warm and caring man. Of course," she added in a dry tone, "you manage to hide that fact quite well sometimes."

"Warm and caring?" he repeated in a bemused voice. "How did you reach *that* conclusion?"

"I know because I touched you. But even if I hadn't, I would still be able to tell." Her gaze settled on his muddy shirt. "You've been an exceptionally good sport about all this. I'd wager you've never done anything like this, have you?"

"Never."

"I thought not. Yet you eventually managed to see the funny side of this episode, although your initial shock was quite evident." Her gaze turned speculative. "You keep people at arm's length, thus cultivating an aloof, cool air. However, you treat your sister with kind indulgence and your mother with warmth and courtesy. I've spent enough time with you and observed you with enough people to know what sort of man you really are . . . how good and decent you are."

Tightness invaded his chest, her words confusing him, throwing him off balance. He was further surprised when a heated flush of pleasure flooded his face. He had to forcibly jerk his thoughts away from the staggering notion that this woman considered him warm and caring. Decent. And good to his family. *If you knew how I failed William, you would realize how wrong you are.*

Before he could fashion a reply, she said, "I realize our meeting last evening ended on a strained note, but might we not start afresh?"

"Afresh?"

"Yes. It's an American word meaning 'all over again.' I thought, perhaps if we tried very, *very* hard, we might be . . . friends. And in the spirit of blossoming friendship, I'd like you to call me Elizabeth."

Blossoming *friendship*? Bloody hell, now he'd heard everything. Friends? With a woman? And this particular woman? Impossible. There were only a handful of *men* he called friends. Women could be mothers, sisters, aunts, or lovers, but not friends. Or could they?

He searched her face and it struck him just how different she was from any woman he'd ever met. How was it possible that, in spite of her strange claims of visions and the fact that she obviously had secrets, she made him feel she was trustworthy? Whatever it was, he couldn't deny, even to himself, that she attracted him like a moth to a flame.

If she wished to believe they were friends, he'd do nothing to disabuse her of the notion—at least not until he'd found out everything he needed to know from her.

But with each passing moment it was increasingly difficult to believe that she was involved in any way with blackmailers or schemes of any sort.

Clearing his throat, he said, "I would be delighted to call you Elizabeth. Thank you."

"You're welcome." Amusement twinkled in her eyes. *"Your grace."*

He nearly chuckled at her obvious tone and expectation for him to return the honor. Didn't she have any notion how impertinent it was for her to even imply that she call him something other than "your grace"? Such familiarity, such *intimacy*, was completely beyond the pale.

Intimacy. A sudden, overwhelming longing to hear his name pass her remarkable lips assailed him. "Some people call me Bradford."

"Bradford," she repeated slowly, drawing out the syllables in a soft, husky voice that had him clenching his teeth. What would hearing her say his Christian name do to him?

"A few people call me by my given name of Austin."

"Austin," she said softly, shooting a hot tingle straight through him. "It's a very fine name. Strong, commanding, noble. It suits you perfectly."

"Thank you," he said, taken aback not only by her compliment but by the pleasurable warmth it sent trickling down his spine. "My friends call me Austin. You may do so if you wish."

He inwardly groaned, astounded by his unprecedented offer. He must be losing his mind. What the hell would people think of her if they heard her call him Austin? He'd have to warn her not to say it in front of anyone—to call him that only when they were alone together.

Alone together. Bloody hell, he *was* losing his mind!

"Why, thank you . . . Austin. So, am I forgiven?"

He jerked his attention back. "Forgiven?"

"Yes. For, ummmm . . ." She glanced down at his ruined clothes.

He followed her gaze. "Ah, yes. The extremely sad state of my attire. Are you truly sorry?"

She nodded vigorously. "Oh, yes."

"Do you promise never to do such a dastardly thing again?"

"Hmmm. Do you mean *never*—as in *never* again in my *entire* life?"

"That was the general idea, yes."

"Oh, dear." She pursed her lips, but her eyes glowed,

alight with mischief. "I'm afraid I cannot make such a far-reaching promise."

"I see." He heaved a sigh of resignation. "Well, in that case, can you possibly endeavor to behave yourself long enough for us to make it back to the house?"

"Oh, yes," she agreed with a beaming smile. "I can promise that."

"Thank God. In that case, I suppose I'll have to forgive you. Let's get out of this water before we shrivel up." He turned and started back toward shore. "Are you coming?" he asked when she didn't follow him.

"I wish I could, but I can't," she said, struggling to move. "My feet have sunken in the mud and my skirts are too heavy to budge." Her dimples winked. "Do you suppose I could trouble you for some assistance?"

Austin looked heavenward. "The last time you asked me that I ended up receiving a mud bath." He glared at her. "I trust you'll recall your promise to behave yourself? I could leave you out there, you know."

She held her hand over her heart. "I promise."

He sloshed his way back to her, muttering uncomplimentary words about females in general. "Put your arms around my neck."

She did so and he swept her up into his arms, nearly staggering under the combined weight of her and her sodden clothing. Cold water poured from her garments, sluicing down his body, while mud oozed from her boots. She nestled her face on his shoulder and his body tightened in reaction to the feel of her wet body snuggled against his chest. He bent his head and breathed in the flowery fragrance of her hair. Damn it, even covered in mud, she still smelled like lilacs.

Once on the shore, he lowered her until her feet touched the ground, her body slowly dragging along his.

Her wet clothes clung to her, outlining her curvaceous shape, and he swallowed a groan. Her hardened nipples were clearly outlined against the damp material, and her legs appeared endless. God, she was incredible. Even slathered in mud, he wanted her.

His entire body pulsed to life, and when she tried to step back his hands tightened on her waist. God help him, he'd never wanted to kiss a woman more. Even as warning bells clanged in his head, he moved his mouth slowly toward hers. He had to taste her again . . . just one more time.

She slapped her palms against his chest. "What are you doing?"

"I was preparing to collect my payment."

"For what?"

"My ruined attire."

"By *kissing* me?"

"Of course. It's an old and noble custom here in England. One kiss for a muddy shirt and breeches. Did no one tell you?"

"I'm afraid it has not come up in conversation."

"Well, now that you know, you'd best pay up. Otherwise, it's debtors' prison for you."

She raised her brows. "*One* kiss?"

"I'd be happy to charge you two. In fact—"

"Oh, no," she said hastily. "One is fine."

"Well, since you insist . . ." He drew her closer, until her breasts brushed his chest, then covered her mouth with his own.

The instant their lips met, he was lost. Utterly and completely. Lost in the silky feel of her, the warm taste of her, the soft, flowery scent of her. Every rational thought slipped from his mind as his hands ran up her sides and cupped her full breasts. He teased her nipples into points and she gasped, dropping her head limply back. He took immediate advantage, running his lips down the long slender column of her throat, each touch dragging him deeper and deeper into a heated haze where nothing existed but the woman in his arms.

"Austin . . ." she breathed. "Please. We must stop."

Expending an effort that nearly killed him, he lifted his head and gazed into her dazed, desire-filled eyes. Lust smacked him so hard his knees nearly buckled. He wanted nothing more than to peel off her wet gown and make love to her. And if he didn't move away from her *now*, he might do just that.

He stepped back and immediately missed the feel of her pressed against him. Unable to resist the urge to touch her, he reached out, took her hands, and entwined their fingers.

Elizabeth pushed the hazy cobwebs from her mind. For the second time, this man had kissed her breathless. Mindless. Until nothing mattered but him.

But she'd had to stop. She'd allowed him more liberties than any decent woman would. But the effort had cost her. She'd wanted nothing more than to let him continue kissing her, touching her, igniting her skin, filling her senses with his heavenly taste and woodsy scent.

At that instant he squeezed her hands and his thoughts filled her mind with breathtaking clarity.

He wanted to make love to her.

Wanted to peel off her wet gown and touch her. Everywhere.

Making love. Love. Heat flooded her and her heart nearly jumped from her body. Is *that* what this feeling was? This bone-melting, can't-breathe, can't-stop-thinking-about-him, never-want-his-kiss-to-end feeling? This overpowering need to help and protect him?

Dear God, was she falling in love with Austin?

Chapter 7

The trip back to the house was made in silence. Elizabeth rode on Myst in front of Austin, wrapped in his strong arms, his warm body surrounding her.

Am I falling in love with him?

Her mind immediately rejected the possibility. No. To love this man would bring her nothing but heartache. Although he obviously found her attractive enough to kiss, he did not trust her or believe in her or her visions.

And even if he did, the situation was impossible. He wasn't just any man. He was a *duke*, and she'd be a fool to entertain the idea that he would ever have deep feelings for an unsophisticated woman like her. No doubt he had only to raise his finger and dozens of beautiful, wealthy women would dash to his side eager to do his bidding. His position would require him to marry a woman of high social standing—and she was not that woman.

A lump lodged in her throat and her insides ached. She desperately tried to convince herself that she was merely attracted to him, simply infatuated, but her heart stubbornly refused to listen. It didn't matter that he didn't, wouldn't, return her feelings. Nor did it matter that she hadn't known him long. After all, how long did it take to fall in love? A day? A month? A year? Her parents had fallen deeply in love at first sight and Papa had proposed within two weeks. Her mother had always said, "Somehow, the heart just *knows*." Now Elizabeth understood what she'd meant.

But the realization was bittersweet.

Heaving a sigh, she leaned back against Austin and once again his loneliness, the emptiness that haunted him, seeped into her mind. She clearly sensed that secrets troubled him, but she couldn't discern what they were. Her heart ached for him. She had to help him. Make him whole again.

And if a broken heart was the price she must pay, so be it.

They arrived at the stables several minutes later. Austin dismounted, then assisted Elizabeth down as Mortlin ran forward.

"Blimey! Are ye hurt, Miz Elizabeth? Rosamunde just this minute returned to the stables without ye. Scared me to the toes, it did."

"I'm quite all right, Mortlin. Just a bit dirty."

Mortlin's gaze wandered over her. "A *bit*? Why, ye look like . . ." His voice tapered off as his gaze moved to Austin. The groom's jaw dropped open. "God save us! Wot 'appened, yer grace? It's a bloody mess yer lookin' like!"

"We're both fine, Mortlin. We took a small spill in the lake, nothing more."

"*Ye fell* off Myst?" Mortlin clearly couldn't imagine such a thing.

"No." Austin fixed the bugged-eyed groom with a repressive stare and silently handed him Myst's reins. Mortlin clearly recognized the "no-more-questions" look and snapped his mouth shut so quickly both of his teeth rattled.

Tucking Elizabeth's dirty hand under his filthy arm, Austin escorted her back to the house. She seemed uncharacteristically quiet, and he wondered what she was thinking. He forced himself to keep his own thoughts carefully blank . . . just in case. Of course her talk of visions was ridiculous, but she *was* uncannily perceptive.

She inclined her head toward the terrace. "Good heavens, there's Caroline. She just caught sight of us and is staring in much the same manner that Mortlin did. Quick! Shoot her that icy glare you silenced Mortlin with," she suggested out of the side of her mouth in a laughing undertone.

"Caroline is unfortunately immune to even my most freezing stare," he whispered close to her ear.

"What a pity," she whispered back.

"Indeed. It seems I'm suddenly surrounded by females who find me less than intimidating. I must be losing my touch."

"Not at all. Your touch is . . ." Her voice trailed off and he paused, drawing her to a stop beside him. A becoming blush stained her cheeks.

"My touch is what?"

She cocked a brow at him. "Do you normally fish for compliments in such a shameless manner, your grace?"

"Only on days when I resemble something dragged from the lake."

On the terrace, Caroline couldn't decide what amazed her more—her brother's *unprecedented* filthy appearance, or the sight of him smiling and whispering in Elizabeth's ear. Elizabeth, Caroline noted with interest, had her arm linked through Austin's, and her face glowed with a becoming blush as she laughed at something he said.

The couple stopped walking and Caroline's pulse speeded up at the long, intense look that passed between them. She'd never seen Austin look at anyone quite that way.

Happiness swelled in her heart. How wonderful to see her brother smiling and enjoying himself! It was a sight she hadn't seen in much too long.

"Have an accident?" Caroline asked when they stepped onto the terrace.

"No, thank you. We've already had one," Austin replied in a bland tone and kept right on walking, escorting Elizabeth to the house, as if nothing were amiss. Caroline watched them enter the house and a smile curved her lips.

This was turning out to be a *very* interesting house party.

After leaving Elizabeth at her bedchamber door, Austin entered his own chamber and bit back a bark of laughter when his normally unflappable valet stared at his filthy attire in slack-jawed amazement.

"That is a look I'm growing quite accustomed to, Kingsbury," he remarked, shrugging out of his ruined shirt.

"I'll have a bath drawn *immediately*, your grace," Kingsbury said, gingerly holding Austin's muddy attire as far away from himself as possible.

Several minutes later, Austin eased himself into a huge tub of steaming water and closed his eyes with a contented sigh. His mind suddenly flashed to an image of Elizabeth, who was no doubt stepping into her own fragrant bath, her magnificent hair cascading down her back in a mass of glorious curls.

He imagined himself joining her in the tub, his wet hands gliding over her full breasts, teasing her nipples into hard peaks. *Austin . . .* she would groan in that heated, smoky voice. He saw himself lean forward and draw one ripe nipple between his lips and suckle until she moaned in pleasure.

"Are you all right, your grace?" Kingsbury called through the door.

Yanked from his sexual reverie, Austin realized with no small amount of chagrin that *he* had been the one moaning, a most annoying habit of late, it seemed.

"Yes, Kingsbury, I'm fine," he snapped.

Damn.

This was turning out to be a *very* irritating house party.

At dinner that evening, Austin sat at the head of the table and surreptitiously observed Elizabeth. She sat at the far end next to a young viscount whose gaze grew more admiring as the meal wore on. Austin couldn't decide whether to applaud Caroline or curse her fashion efforts on Elizabeth's behalf. By the fifth course, the damn viscount couldn't seem to stop staring at her.

And who could blame him? She looked breathtaking in a low-cut, coppery-colored gown that showcased her full breasts and creamy skin. Austin noted with ever-growing grimness how the viscount's admiring gaze often strayed to the tantalizing skin swelling above her bodice.

And her hair. God! A single clip held the loosely gathered mass of curls on top of her head. Wispy tendrils surrounded her face and shoulders, and the rest fell down her back in a shimmering curtain of satiny ringlets. No doubt the seductive coiffure was again the work of Caroline's abigail. He didn't know whether to fire the woman or triple her salary.

He'd made it a point to avoid Elizabeth in the drawing room before dinner, but he'd been intensely aware of her every single movement, a fact that irked him to no end. He had to stop this . . . this whatever it was he was doing with her. Kissing her, touching her were blatant errors in his normally fine-tuned better judgment. And they were errors he could not afford to repeat.

After spending most of the afternoon reflecting, he'd decided his only course of action was to wait. Wait for Miles to return from London. Wait to receive information from his Bow Street Runner. Wait to get further instructions from the blackmailer. He chafed at the necessity, but there was no alternative.

After their time together at the lake, it was nearly impossible to believe that she was working in cahoots with the blackmailer or indeed knew anything about the letter he'd received. In fact, the more he thought about it, the more it became clear that she simply possessed an uncanny intuition that she placed far too much credence in. *She* believed her visions were real and had told him about them to help him. She wasn't vicious or out to harm him. She was merely . . . misguided.

Misguided . . . and tempting beyond all endurance. She set his blood on fire and he could not seem to exorcise her from his thoughts. And that damned viscount sitting next to her was now openly ogling her.

With each passing course, Austin's mood grew grimmer and he found it increasingly difficult to concentrate on the inane conversations going on around him.

"I believe you're in a brown study, your grace," a female voice remarked in a throaty undertone. A gloved hand brushed over his and he forced his attention back to his immediate surroundings. Countess Millham, the woman seated on his left, sent him a coy smile. Since her elderly husband's convenient death two years ago, the countess had engaged in numerous affairs, but she'd yet to lure Austin to her bed. He had the distinct impression she hoped to change that tonight.

She leaned closer, affording him an unimpeded view of her breasts that spilled over her bodice in a show of cleavage that he knew stupefied most men. Her emerald gaze roamed his face, her eyes glowing with sexual promise— the exact sort of look from the exact sort of woman he should be concentrating on.

With her eyes steady on his, she discreetly slipped her hand under the table and boldly caressed his thigh. "There must be *something* a woman can do to gain your attention, your grace," she murmured in a husky whisper meant only for his ears.

He did nothing to stop her or to encourage her; he simply watched her and waited for his body to react to her touch. Her tongue peeked out and she slowly wet her upper lip, her eyes blatantly telling him what she'd rather be doing with her tongue. Her questing fingers moved higher on his leg.

But instead of lust for her, he felt nothing. Absolutely nothing. This beautiful woman, with her voluptuous body and promises of sexual delights, didn't ignite the slightest spark of desire in him. He moved his hand under the table to forcibly halt her caress. At that same instant his mother stood, signaling the end of the meal.

Clearly misunderstanding the reason why he'd placed his hand under the table, Countess Millham smiled wickedly, as she stood along with everyone else. "Until later," she whispered close to his ear as the women departed for the drawing room, leaving the men to their cigars.

Leaning back in his chair, he lit a cheroot and blew out a long stream of fragrant smoke. Countess Millham had provided him with a perfect and much-needed opportunity to ease the relentless ache clutching his loins. So why the hell wasn't he happy?

Because she's not the one you want. Thoroughly annoyed with himself, he signaled a footman for a brandy and tossed back the potent drink in a single gulp.

He suspected this was going to be an excruciatingly long evening.

Elizabeth entered her bedchamber and leaned back against the closed door, grateful to escape the drawing room and the chattering women. Aunt Joanna and Caroline had both expressed concern when she'd pleaded a headache and excused herself to retire early, but she couldn't remain with the guests any longer. There were too many people, too many disjointed images flashing through her mind. Her head felt as if a corps of drummers pounded on her brain.

And then there was *him*. It was painfully obvious Austin was avoiding her. He'd barely acknowledged her before dinner, and every time she'd glanced down the table at him, his attention seemed riveted on the beautiful woman with the large breasts sitting at his elbow.

She'd turned her attention to Viscount Farrington, with whom she'd discovered a common interest in drawing. To her surprise, he paid her several flowery compliments and professed a desire to sketch her. She'd tried to concentrate on him, but she was constantly distracted by the vague, unsettling images flashing in her mind and the presence of the man at the head of the table.

After changing into her night rail, she mixed a headache remedy and slid into bed. Indistinct images collided in her brain, teasing her, just out of reach. She closed her eyes, willing the thoughts to go away, but they persisted.

Austin's face popped into her mind, his mouth curving slowly upward into a devastating smile. She tried to push him from her thoughts but failed.

What was he doing right this minute? Was he with the woman who had claimed his attention all through dinner? Was he touching her? Kissing her?

A groan passed her lips. The thought of Austin touching another woman pierced her with a pain that stole her breath, a pain made all the more agonizing because there was nothing she could do about it. Her feelings for him were hopeless.

Utterly hopeless.

In spite of himself, Austin noticed Elizabeth's absence the moment he entered the drawing room. Even though some two dozen people milled about, her height made her extremely easy to pick out. Another scan of the room only confirmed she was not present. She must have excused herself to see to personal needs. He headed toward the decanters and managed to convince himself he was glad she was not in the room.

After she'd still failed to appear twenty minutes later, however, he grew concerned. He approached Caroline and casually asked about Elizabeth's whereabouts.

"She wasn't feeling well and retired immediately after dinner," Caroline said, her blue eyes studying him with interest. "Why do you ask?"

"I was merely curious. Is she ill?"

"She had the headache. I'm sure she'll be fine in the morning, although Viscount Farrington is crushed by her departure."

Austin's fingers tightened around his snifter. "Is he?"

"Yes. He's quite smitten. I understand he asked Lady Penbroke's permission to call on Elizabeth."

A muscle twitched in his jaw and he had to squelch a sudden, overwhelming desire to inflict bodily harm on Viscount Farrington.

Lively curiosity gleamed in Caroline's eyes. "I hope Elizabeth's headache isn't the result of whatever adventure you two shared this morning. You never did say what happened to you."

"I wouldn't dream of boring you with the details."

"Nonsense. I love details."

She made me laugh. I held her in my arms. I touched her. I kissed her. I want to do it again. Right now. "There's nothing to tell, Caroline."

"I wish Robert had been here to see you covered with mud."

Austin was heartily grateful that his younger brother had *not* been present. Robert no doubt would have split his breeches from laughing and then have asked a hundred teasing questions. "When is he expected to return from his travels?"

"Within the next several days," Caroline answered.

A footman approached and held out a silver salver with a wax-sealed note. "A message for you, your grace."

Grateful for the interruption, Austin took the note. When he saw the distinctive imprint on the wax, he stilled.

"Is something wrong, Austin?" Caroline asked.

He forced himself to offer her a smile. "Everything is fine. Just a small matter that requires my attention. Please excuse me."

Leaving the drawing room, he made his way to his study, closing the door behind him. His hands shook as he slipped his fingers beneath the easily recognizable seal of his Bow Street Runner. Had he found Gaspard?

Tipping back his head, he closed his eyes for a brief moment. What he was about to read might well give him the answers he'd sought for so long. With his jaw clenched to the point of pain, he opened the note and anxiously scanned the contents.

> *Your Grace:*
> *I have information for you. Per our prearranged agreement, I will await you at the ruins at the north border of your property.*
> *James Kinney*

Austin read the brief missive again, his fingers gripping the vellum so hard he was surprised it didn't crumble apart. Kinney was the finest Bow Street had to offer. He wouldn't have traveled to Bradford Hall at night if he didn't have something important to report.

Locking the note in his desk drawer, Austin left his study and hurried down the back staircase. Slipping from the house, he kept to the shadows and walked swiftly to the stables. When he instructed Mortlin to saddle Myst, the groom looked up at the sky and scratched his head. "Are ye certain ye want to ride, yer grace? It's fixin' to storm soon. Me achin' joints can always tell."

Austin looked up and saw only the bright full moon. If a storm was even in the offing, it had to be hours away. But no matter. Nothing would keep him from meeting Kinney. "I want to ride. There's no need to await my return. I'll take care of Myst when I get back."

"Yes, yer grace."

Moments later, Austin vaulted into the saddle. He applied his heels to Myst's sides and the gelding took off in the direction of the ruins.

Mortlin watched him go, absently rubbing his sore elbows. The stiffness in his joints had grown steadily worse over the evening and he knew that the brewing rain would be upon them soon. Probably in less than an hour. No doubt the duke was meeting a bit of fancy fluff at the ruins for a little late-night snoogle, although why he'd choose to carry on his affairs in such uncomfortable surroundings when he had the luxury of Bradford Hall at his disposal mystified Mortlin. Clearly the lady in question was the adventurous sort, and you never could predict the actions of the Quality. A chuckle escaped him as he silently wished his employer a merry romp.

Elizabeth awoke with a start, her heart pounding painfully.

Perspiration slicked her skin and the ragged hiss of her labored breathing echoed in the quiet bedchamber.

Danger. He's in danger.

She fought to untangle her sweaty limbs from the damp sheets. Urgency pumped through her and a deep sense of dread pricked her skin like a thousand stinging bees.

Austin. Hurt. Bleeding.

Panic sliced through her and she forced herself to draw deep, calming breaths. Sitting on the edge of the bed, she closed her eyes and concentrated, trying to form the vague images careening through her mind into something coherent.

A stone tower, surrounded by crumbling walls. A gunshot. A black horse rearing. Austin, falling, injured. Bleeding.

Death.

A deafening clap of thunder followed immediately by a flash of lightning jerked her from her thoughts. She had to find him. She sensed he was not too far away—but where? Yanking off her night rail with shaking hands, she dressed as quickly as possible. Grabbing her medical bag, she dashed down the back stairs and ran toward the stables.

*   *   *

James Kinney paced in the shadows near the crumbling ruins, awaiting the duke's arrival, anxious to tell him the incredible, staggering information he'd discovered. Footsteps crunched on the rocks directly behind him, and he spun around.

"Your grace, I—" He froze, frowning at the man emerging from the shadows. "Who are you?"

For an answer the stranger aimed a pistol at James's temple. "You are good at asking questions, especially about me, *monsieur*," the stranger said in an unmistakable French accent. "You've been asking them all over London. Now you will answer one of mine. What information are you bringing to the Duke of Bradford?"

"You're Gaspard."

The Frenchman advanced another step. "The duke is a fool. He should have known better than to hire a Runner to find me. I ask you again, *monsieur*. What information do you have? You will tell me, or you will die." He smiled and James saw madness in his eyes.

And James knew that even if he talked, his time on earth had come to an end.

Chapter 8

Thunder cracked as loudly and suddenly as a gunshot.

Breathless and close to panic, Elizabeth arrived at the stables just past midnight. Mortlin had obviously retired as he was nowhere to be found. Without hesitation, she lifted the first saddle she saw, grunting under its weight, and quickly outfitted Rosamunde. It wasn't until she'd led the mare outside that she realized she'd used a gentleman's saddle. Without a thought to the impropriety of her actions, she employed a move she hadn't used since arriving in England. Hitching her skirts up to her thighs, she mounted the horse, sitting astride. Her muscles creaked in protest, but she ignored the discomfort.

Turning Rosamunde, she studied the series of paths leading into the forest. Which one would lead her to Austin? Closing her eyes, she emptied her mind, forcing herself to concentrate. *Left. Take the left path.*

Without hesitation, she headed down the left path, her eyes searching the darkness, her pulse pounding. Rosamunde followed the dirt trail, and Elizabeth kept concentrating, forcing the image of Austin into her mind's eye. They were getting closer . . . she knew it. But would she be too late?

Another roar of thunder split the silence. A lightning bolt streaked across the black sky, briefly illuminating the gloomy surroundings.

And she saw it in the distance.

The stone tower she'd envisioned. Urging Rosamunde into a brisk gallop, she headed directly toward it. Twigs snapped at her arms, and a branch whipped against her shoulder, but the stinging pain barely registered. Raindrops began falling, gently at first, but within moments they turned into a cold, needlelike spray that pelted her unmercifully. She emerged from the fringes of the forest and galloped full bent across the meadow. The outline of the tower flashed before her with every slash of lightning.

When the tower loomed no more than thirty feet away, she reined Rosamunde to a halt and squinted into the darkness. *Where are you, Austin?* Lightning flashed. The tower rose before her. A riderless black horse grazed by a low stone wall.

A figure lay sprawled facedown on the ground.

"Austin!" Her heart leapt with both relief and fear. Thank God she'd found him . . . but was she too late?

She slid from the saddle and ran to him, stumbling across the slippery ground. Heedless of the mud, she dropped to her knees beside him. With her heart lodged in her throat and a prayer on her lips, she pressed her fingers to his neck.

His pulse throbbed against her fingertips.

A relieved sob bubbled inside her, but she firmly pushed it aside. Now was not the time to allow her emotions to get the better of her. She had to determine the extent of his injuries.

As gently as possible, she turned him over, shielding

him as best she could with her body from the driving rain. The metallic scent of blood filled her nostrils and her stomach knotted with fear. Blinking the rain from her eyes, she peered into his face. His eyes were closed and blood oozed from a nasty gash on his temple.

She ran her hands quickly down his body, searching for additional injuries, praying he hadn't fallen victim to the gunshot she'd heard in her vision. She soon determined that he hadn't been shot, but her fingers discovered an egg-sized lump on the back of his head.

She gently patted his face. "Austin, can you hear me?"

He remained perfectly still and frighteningly silent.

Lightning flashed again. Glancing up, she saw an arched opening in the base of the tower. She had to get him out of this weather to treat him. Rising, she grasped him under his arms and pulled. Dear God, the man weighed a veritable ton. Thank goodness she only had to move him a short distance.

Her heart pinched when he moaned. Although she tried desperately not to hurt him, she knew the sharp rocks scraped him. Her back ached from the heavy weight, and she slipped once, landing hard on her bottom. Gritting her teeth, she dragged him the last few feet into the shelter of the tower. Then she dashed back into the rain and snatched her medical bag from Rosamunde's saddle. Rosamunde and Myst had moved close to the tower. She didn't tether them in case they grew frightened and wanted to bolt, in which case she suspected they would simply head back toward the stables.

Back inside the tower, Elizabeth dropped to her knees next to Austin's inert form, then immediately opened her bag and set to work.

First she removed a small lantern and lit it. Holding it close to his head, she examined his wound. She could see at once that he required stitches, but she was more concerned by the fact that he hadn't regained consciousness. If he was bleeding inside—

She ruthlessly cut off the thought and concentrated on the matter at hand. Controlled calm settled over her. She knew exactly what needed to be done for his wound. And it needed to be done immediately.

Pulling two small wooden bowls from her bag, she ran outside and quickly filled them with rainwater. Again kneeling next to Austin, she mixed roots and herbs together with quiet concentration.

After washing the wound, she closed it with a series of tiny, precise stitches, then snugly wrapped his head with a long strip of fresh gauze.

Resting her hand on his face, she was relieved that his skin remained cool and his breathing was slow and steady, good signs that his lungs were clear and his ribs uninjured.

All she could do now was wait for him to awaken.

And pray that he did.

After carefully replacing her supplies, she stood to rub her tense, aching back muscles. Fatigue washed over her with a vengeance and she stretched her hands over her head to relieve the strain in her lower back.

"Elizabeth."

Austin's voice was barely more than a hoarse rasp, but her heart jumped when she heard it. *Thank God.* Her exhaustion instantly forgotten, she dropped to her knees beside him and smiled down at his pale, handsome face. "I'm right here, Austin."

He moved his head and winced. "My head hurts."

"I'm sure it does, but at least you're awake."

Austin wasn't sure he was glad to be awake. White hot pain sizzled through his skull and he sucked in a sharp breath. Damn, it felt as if someone had smashed a rock over his head. In fact, he'd be hard pressed to name a body part that didn't ache in one form or another. And why the hell was he wet?

His gaze settled on Elizabeth. She appeared in a state of dishevelment, a fact that didn't surprise him.

"Where are we?" he asked, his eyes slowly scanning the room.

"Some sort of ruins. On the bottom floor of a tower."

He stared at her, his mind a blank. "Why?"

"You don't recall what happened to you?"

He forced himself to concentrate and suddenly he *did* remember. A note from Kinney. Information. The ruins. But Kinney never came . . . no doubt because of the storm. Starting back to the house. Lightning striking close by. A crack of thunder. Myst rearing. Falling . . .

"Thunder and lightning spooked Myst. He reared, tossing me." He lifted his hand and winced when his fingers brushed a bandage on his forehead. "What is this?"

"You suffered a deep cut on your forehead that I cleaned, stitched, and dressed. There's also a sizable lump on the back of your head."

Bloody hell, no wonder his skull hurt so much. His head actually *had* collided with a rock. "Is Myst all right?"

"Yes. He's outside. With Rosamunde. Now that you're awake, I'll check on them. I'll be back in a moment."

She exited through the arched doorway and returned several minutes later leading both horses by their reins. She walked them to the far side of the room, then spent some time patting each animal, speaking to them in comforting tones. Austin closed his eyes, listening to her. He couldn't make out her words, but her voice sounded soft and soothing.

She returned to his side and knelt beside him. "They're both fine. How are you feeling?"

"Sore, and my head is pounding like a legion of devils

is hitting me with hammers. Other than that, I believe I'm all right." He attempted to sit up, but nauseating dizziness washed over him.

"Don't try to move, Austin," she said, laying a gently restraining hand on his shoulder. "It's too soon."

"Perhaps you're right." Closing his eyes, he swallowed and waited, hoped, for his equilibrium to return. After several deep breaths, the nausea passed and he risked opening his eyes.

She knelt next to him, watching him, and his gaze searched her face in the dim light. Her hair was a wet tangle of curls surrounding her shoulders. Her eyes were wide with unmistakable concern but suspicions intruded, niggling at him. How had she located him? Had she followed him? No one had known he was going to the ruins. The only person he'd seen had been Mortlin, and he'd dismissed him for the evening. Had he told her what direction he'd taken?

"How did you find me?"

She hesitated, then drew a deep breath. "I was awakened by a vision of you. I knew you were in danger. I saw you. Hurt. Bleeding. By some sort of stone tower. I dressed, saddled Rosamunde, and allowed my instincts to lead me . . . to you."

The bark of disbelief that would have, should have, risen to his lips, died in his throat. Honesty and concern glowed from her eyes like beacons in a storm. As mad as her words sounded, he found he couldn't discount them. But surely there had to be another explanation . . . a *logical* explanation.

"Did you see Mortlin at the stables?"

"No. It was after midnight. He must have retired."

After midnight? He'd left the house just before ten, and according to Caroline, Elizabeth had retired a half hour before that. If she'd remained in bed . . . how could she have known where he was? Or what had happened? If she actually had the ability to see things in her mind . . . but no, he simply couldn't credit such an outlandish idea. She was merely greatly intuitive, as his mother had been during his childhood, always sensing when her sons had fallen into mischief. And Rosamunde was familiar with the paths leading to the ruins . . .

But he'd have to consider that later, when he felt more himself. When his head wasn't threatening to detach itself from his shoulders. Still, one thing was certain.

Elizabeth had undoubtedly saved his life. Who knows how long he would have lain bleeding on the ground if she hadn't happened along? She'd not only somehow found him, but had treated his injuries as well.

"I owe you a debt of gratitude and my thanks, Elizabeth."

A frown creased her brow and what appeared to be anger sparked in her eyes. "You're welcome. However, if you'd heeded my warning about riding at night, this would not have happened."

He stilled. By God, she *had* warned him . . . told him there was danger. *Bloody hell, get hold of yourself, man. 'Tis nothing more than a coincidence. There's always a risk of injury riding in the dark.*

"What on earth possessed you to ride at night?" she asked.

He debated whether to tell her the truth, and decided to do so, to gauge her reaction. Watching her carefully, he said, "I hired a Bow Street Runner to find information about a Frenchman I saw with William shortly before he died. The Runner had discovered something and was supposed to meet me here at the ruins."

"*Supposed* to meet you?"

"He never showed up, no doubt delayed because of the storm, but I'm certain he'll contact me as soon as possible."

Surely if she had any knowledge of Gaspard or his connection to William, she would look anxious, guilt ridden, or in some way suspicious. Surely she wouldn't look irate.

"Heavens save us," she fumed. "Can you explain why it was necessary to meet this man *outside*? *On horseback? During a storm?* Have you never heard of a drawing room?" She waved her hands at him. "Never mind. Don't even try to explain. 'Tis just fortunate that your mulish head is so hard lest you might have been killed."

Damn it, he needed to bring this woman to task for her disrespect. He opened his mouth to do just that, but before he could utter a word, she said, "At least you weren't shot."

He stared at her. "Shot?"

"Yes. In my vision I was certain I heard a gunshot, but I suppose it was thunder . . . yet I sensed death. Very strongly." Her expression turned grave. "Are you certain it was thunder that spooked Myst? Could it have been a gunshot?"

An immediate "no" rose to his lips, but something in her expression made him pause and consider her question. "It happened so quickly. I remember lightning, crashing thunder . . . then falling. It seems highly unlikely someone was out and about shooting during a storm."

"Yes, I suppose so. Obviously I was mistaken."

"Obviously." He cleared his throat. "And I am not mulish."

She cocked a clearly disbelieving brow. "I think that the fact that you are lying here, injured, is proof that you are. However, if you prefer that I call you pigheaded, I'm happy to oblige."

"I do *not* prefer. In fact—"

"I refuse to argue with a wounded man," she interrupted in a brisk tone. "Are you cold?"

"Cold?"

"Yes. It is an American word meaning 'not warm.' You're soaked to the skin, but I have nothing to cover you with."

It took him several seconds to recall that he was indeed wet. His gaze swept over her and he realized that she, too, was wet, her plain gown molded to her lush body as if it were painted on. His attention riveted on her full breasts and her clearly visible erect nipples.

Heat streaked through him. "No, I'm not cold." In fact, he was growing warmer by the minute.

He watched, mesmerized, as her chest rose and fell with every breath she drew. Forcing his gaze upward, his breathing stalled at the sight of her. The subdued glow flickering from the lantern illuminated her glorious hair. The unbound mass of damp curls spilled over her shoulders and down her back like a satin curtain, the ends brushing the stone floor around her where she knelt. He instantly imagined her in his bed, wearing nothing but that incredible hair and a smile on her luscious mouth.

Her luscious mouth . . . His gaze riveted on her lips and in spite of his numerous aches and the relentless pounding in his head, a surge of lust and desire slammed into him. An agonized groan he couldn't squelch filled the silence.

"The pain is bad?"

He gritted his teeth and snapped his eyes closed. "You have no idea."

She shifted away and he heard her moving around nearby. He grasped the opportunity to try and will his throbbing erection away. He pretended she was ugly. He desperately tried to convince himself he hated lilacs.

But nothing worked. His arousal pulsed and he groaned again.

"I want you to drink this," she said.

He opened his eyes. She sat next to him, holding a wooden cup. "What is that?"

"Just a mixture of herbs, roots, and rainwater." She gently raised his head enough to drink. "It will relieve your pain. It is too dangerous to attempt returning to the house until the rain stops. In the meanwhile, you need to rest and regain your strength."

There was only one thing that would relieve his pain and it was not in that cup, but because her eyes made it plain she would tolerate no dissention and he was too tired to argue anyway, he drank.

"Yeck," he said, grimacing as she gently laid his head back down. "That's the worst-tasting stuff I've ever had."

"It's not supposed to taste good. It's supposed to make you feel good."

His entire body shuddered from the bitter elixir. "Nothing that foul could possibly make me feel good." But even as the words passed his lips, an odd languor stole through him, relaxing his tight muscles, easing his aches.

He looked up at her, riveted by the unmistakable warmth and concern in her eyes. He could not recall any woman, save Caroline or his mother, ever looking at him with such a tender expression. Unable to stop himself from touching her, he lifted his hand and sifted his fingers through her damp curls. The auburn skeins brushed over his skin like a silken caress. "You have beautiful hair."

Surprise flickered in her eyes, prompting him to say, "Surely many people have told you that."

"Actually, no. I'm afraid that *beautiful* and my name are two words that are rarely heard in the same sentence."

"Beautiful," he repeated. "Soft." He twirled a curl around his finger, brought it to his face, and inhaled. "Lilacs."

She drew in a quick breath and he wondered how she

would react if he touched more than her hair. If her breath would catch in that husky way if he trailed his hands down her body.

"I distill my own lilac water," she whispered, her eyes wide but steady on his.

He inhaled again, allowing her fragrance to infuse him. "An abundance of lilacs bloom in the gardens at Bradford Hall. Please feel free to pick as many as you wish for your water."

"Thank you. You're very kind."

No, I'm not. A kind man wouldn't be contemplating how long it would take to peel that wet gown from your body. A kind man wouldn't be imagining you naked, trembling for him.

He squeezed his eyes shut to banish his sensual thoughts. A kind man would force himself to arise and get them both back to the house before anyone discovered their absence. Before her reputation was destroyed. Before he gave in to the longings that licked at him like relentless flames.

No, he was not a kind man.

He gently tugged on the curl wrapped around his finger. "Come here."

She scooted nearer.

"Closer."

She inched closer, until her skirt-clad legs pressed against his side.

"Closer."

Amusement flashed in her eyes. "If I move any closer, Austin, I'll be on the other side of you."

He twined his hand deeply in her hair and slowly pulled her head toward him. "Your mouth. Closer. Now."

Her amusement vanished and her breath hitched. "You want to kiss me."

His hand stilled and he searched her eyes . . . eyes filled

with concern and longing. *I want to make love to you. Desperately.* "Yes, Elizabeth. I want to kiss you."

"You must rest. And I don't want to hurt you."

"Then come here." He again pulled her downward until their lips touched. His pulse galloped and he nearly laughed at his strong reaction. Damn it, he'd barely touched her and already his heart was hammering at thrice its normal speed. What the hell would he do if he ever saw her naked? *I'd make love to her, slowly, for hours, then make love to her again. And again.*

"Austin." Her warm breath whispered against his lips and he barely suppressed a groan. Sinking his fingers deeper into her luxuriant hair, he pressed her lips more firmly against his.

When his tongue sought entrance to her mouth, she parted her lips with a breathy sigh that filled him with the subtle taste of strawberries. He'd never kissed any woman who tasted so sweet, whose skin felt so soft beneath his fingers, who made him want to be only inches away from her so he wouldn't miss out on a single waft of the gentle fragrance clinging to her skin.

She rested her hands on his shoulders and touched her tongue to his, igniting him. Wrapping his free arm firmly around her waist, he tugged her downward, shifting her, until the upper half of her body lay on his. Her soft breasts flattened against his chest, enflaming his skin through the layers of their clothes.

The kiss became an endless blending of heated sighs and pleasure-filled moans. *Just one more . . . just one more will be enough . . . I'll have my fill of her.*

But it wasn't enough. He couldn't get her close enough, feel her enough, taste her enough. His hands wandered restlessly up and down her back, first tunneling through her silken hair, then spanning her waist and cupping her rounded bottom, pressing her closer to him. He wanted to shift, to roll over so he lay on top of her, but the languor easing through him grew more pronounced with each passing second, relaxing his limbs until he felt as weak as a newborn babe.

She moaned softly and eased back from him. His eyelids drooped and he fought to open them, but the battle was lost.

"I'm so tired," he whispered.

"Just rest. I'll be here when you wake up."

He tried to answer, but he could not seem to move his lips. Oblivion eased over him like a velvet blanket.

Elizabeth watched sleep overtake him. She knew his body needed the rest, but she needed to watch him and awaken him at intervals to make sure that his sleep remained natural and that he did not slip into unconsciousness due to his head injury. She listened to the deep, rhythmic rise and fall of his chest, and laying her hand on his forehead, noted that his skin was dry and cool, both good signs that he was merely sleeping.

Relieved, she gently trailed her fingertips down his face. His features were perfectly relaxed, his dark lashes casting shadows on his cheeks. With no hints of sadness or bitterness firming his lips, he looked completely worry free. Brushing back a strand of raven hair that fell over his bandaged forehead, he reminded her of a vulnerable boy.

Her eyes swept down the length of him and she nearly laughed at herself. There was nothing boy-like about this man.

His broad chest rose and fell in his sleep, drawing her eyes to the intriguing bit of dark hair visible at the opening of his shirt. The need to touch him was so overwhelming. So tempting . . .

Unable to stop herself, she parted his dirt-streaked shirt

and laid her palm on his chest. His heartbeat thumped against her fingers, sending a frisson of warmth down to her toes. A sudden flood of tears gushed into her eyes.

"Dear God, I almost failed again. I almost lost you." That frightening image of him, lying unconscious on the ground, flashed through her mind. "My visions . . . I've always considered them nothing more than a nuisance, something that kept me from being like everyone else. But tonight I thank God for them because they helped me find you. I'll not let anything hurt you again. I swear it."

While the storm continued outside, she sat vigil, watching him sleep, stroking his face every quarter hour until his eyes flickered open, assuring her he wasn't unconscious. Dawn was approaching when she was finally satisfied that his sleep was natural. Fatigue overcame her and she allowed herself to lie down . . . just for a moment. The cold stone floor offered little heat, so she snuggled next to Austin's side for warmth.

I'll only rest my eyes for a moment. But in less than a minute, she was dozing off. A frown knitted her brow, pulling her back from the edge of sleep. Something . . . something wasn't quite right . . . in her vision . . . she'd been so certain she'd heard a gunshot . . .

But her tired brain couldn't figure out what was niggling at her, and exhaustion overcame her.

Chapter 9

Caroline descended the stairs just after sunrise. Normally she did not arise so early, but the birds chattering outside her bedchamber window had awakened her and her thoughts were too full to go back to sleep. A long solitary walk was exactly what she needed to clear her mind. The instant she stepped outside onto the terrace leading to the gardens, however, a voice sounded behind her.

"Why, Caroline, what a surprise to see you up so early."

Caroline bit her tongue to suppress a groan. Dash it, it was one of those infernal Digby daughters—Penelope or Prudence, judging by the high-pitched whine. Gritting her teeth, she turned.

Good heavens, it was worse than she'd suspected. *Both* girls stood before her. Penelope squinted at her through thick-lensed spectacles that magnified her eyes. She reminded Caroline of a bug. A bug with large teeth, three dozen bouncing sausage curls, and wearing a frilly bonnet.

Prudence stood beside her sister, her thin face pinched into a frown. She was currently engaged in her annoying habit of opening and closing her mouth without speaking, an unfortunate action that lent her a distinctly carplike air.

"Good morning, Penelope, Prudence," Caroline said, forcing herself to smile.

"Are you going for a walk?" Penelope asked, tilting her head to one side, thus now resembling a lopsided bug.

"Yes." Caroline realized there was no point in not inviting them to accompany her, for they would simply invite themselves. Somehow managing not to sigh, she asked, "Would you care to join me?"

"We'd love to," Penelope said.

Prudence opened her mouth and the word "yes" popped out.

" 'Tis fortunate we are awake so early to join you," Penelope said, "as it appears you're without a companion."

"Indeed," Caroline mumbled. "*Fortunate* is just the word I was searching for."

They descended the steps and Caroline headed down a path leading toward the tower ruins. Penelope launched into an excruciatingly detailed description of her new wardrobe while Prudence remained thankfully silent. Caroline nodded occasionally and uttered noncommittal noises, but otherwise strove to pretend she was alone.

As the tower came into view, she recalled the many times she had climbed the crumbling stone steps, then pretended to be a damsel in distress so either William or Austin would rescue her. Sometimes Robert and Miles would join in their games as well, then she'd have four knights to save her from the perils of evil.

Miles. A breathy sigh puffed from her lips. It was better that she not think of Miles. He was the very reason she'd longed for a solitary walk—to try to force him from her mind. But it was an impossible task, even with Penelope's nonstop stream of chatter to distract her. The man filled every corner of her mind, and every time she found herself in the same room with him, her heart threatened to sputter to a stop.

She'd loved him since childhood, but there was a vast difference between loving him and *being in love* with him. And without a doubt she was in love with him.

She scolded herself, knowing it was hopeless to yearn for a man who regarded her only as his best friend's baby sister, but no matter how many times she branded herself a fool, her heart would not listen.

The trail emerged from the forest and the tower ruins loomed ahead. Carefully picking their way over the stones, they'd nearly reached the tower when she heard a horse's soft nicker.

Prudence opened her mouth and the word "horse" popped out.

"Yes," Penelope agreed. "It sounded like it came from inside the tower."

"Someone else is clearly out and about this morning," Caroline murmured, wondering why anyone would bring their mount into the tower.

"What fun!" Penelope said. "Ohhh . . . perhaps it's your *brother*, Caroline! Let's say hello!"

Caroline barely withheld a groan. Dear God, if Austin *was* inside the tower and she foisted the Digby daughters on him, he was apt to succumb to apoplexy. She started to call out that they should walk in another direction, but clearly the possibility of coming upon the duke had spurred the Digbys into action. They dashed over the rocks like seasoned mountain goats.

Hiking up her skirts in a manner that would have horrified her mother, Caroline sped after them, but they reached the doorway well before her. Even from ten feet away, she heard Penelope's gasp, and Prudence obviously opened and closed her mouth twice for she said, "Oh. My."

Jostling them out of her way, Caroline entered through

the open arched doorway. It took several seconds for her vision to adjust to the dim interior light. When it did, she, too, gasped.

Austin lay on the stone floor. His arms encircled Elizabeth, who lay on her side next to him, her head cushioned by his shoulder, her hand resting lightly on his chest.

Good Lord, they'd clearly stumbled upon an assignation between them. She should have been shocked. Outraged. On the verge of swooning.

Instead elation ran through her. She had no doubt that Elizabeth and Austin were perfect for each other, and judging by the scene before her, they'd discovered as much themselves.

Another soft nicker captured her attention. Tearing her gaze away from the sleeping couple, she saw Myst and Rosamunde standing in the shadows.

She stepped backward, determined to slip away unnoticed, and backed into a body.

"Ouch," said Prudence.

Dear God, she'd forgotten about the Digby daughters.

Penelope elbowed her way forward and pointed. "Is that a bandage wrapped around his grace's head? Why, I'd wager that the Colonial Upstart arranged this assignation, then coshed his grace in an attempt to make it appear he'd ruined her!" She muttered something else that sounded suspiciously like "Why didn't *I* think of that?" but Caroline's attention was riveted on Austin.

"Stay here," she instructed the sisters. On silent feet, she moved closer. Yes, there most certainly was a bandage wrapped around Austin's head. God in heaven, what had happened to him? Clearly he'd suffered an injury. Was Elizabeth hurt as well?

Pushing aside any possible embarrassment, she knelt beside Elizabeth and gently shook her shoulder. "Elizabeth, wake up."

Elizabeth came awake slowly, gradually becoming aware of a voice repeating her name in an urgent fashion. She forced her heavy eyelids open a tiny bit. Her muscles were stiff and it seemed as if stones poked into her skin.

Her confusion disappeared instantly when she became aware of two things at once. She was curled up against Austin's warm body, and a pair of surprise-widened blue eyes was staring at her.

Her eyes snapped open and she bolted upright, pushing her tangled hair from her face. "Caroline!"

"Elizabeth, what happened? Are you all right? Why is Austin's head bandaged?"

"He fell from Myst."

A derisive snort sounded from the doorway. Turning, Elizabeth saw two Digby daughters—she wasn't sure which ones—standing in the archway. One squinted at her, the other gaped.

Caroline touched her arm, reclaiming her attention. "How badly is he hurt?"

"He hit his head and sustained a cut that required several stitches. As far as I was able to determine, he did not break any bones."

Caroline's face visibly paled. "My God. Are *you* injured?"

"No." She reached out and touched Austin's forehead and was relieved that he showed no signs of fever.

Fear flickered through Caroline's expression. "He *is* going to be all right, isn't he?"

"Yes." In an attempt to calm Caroline's fears, Elizabeth smiled at her. "Your brother has an exceptionally hard head."

"Indeed he does." Caroline gathered her into her arms. "My God, Elizabeth. You saved Austin's life. I'll always be in your debt. Can I do anything to help?"

"You could start by removing your knee from my

fingers," came Austin's raspy voice. "The last thing I need is one more aching body part."

Caroline gasped and immediately moved back. "Austin. Are you all right?" Lifting his hand, she cradled it against her cheek.

"I'm a bit sore around the edges, but otherwise fine." His eyes settled on Elizabeth.

She offered him a gentle smile. "You're looking better."

"I'm feeling better. Thanks to you."

Their gazes met and held. Elizabeth longed to reach out and touch him, but controlled the impulse in front of Caroline and the Digby daughters. There was something in his eyes, something intense and compelling, but she couldn't read the expression. Tearing her gaze from his, she stood and attempted to brush the twigs and dirt from her rumpled gown.

"Do you feel well enough to travel back to the house?" Caroline asked. "Shall I return to the house and bring help?"

Austin forced himself to give Caroline his full attention. When he did, the significance of her question hit him squarely between the eyes. "Help? God, no." With an effort he pushed himself into a sitting position, then sat for a moment with his eyes closed, waiting for the waves of dizziness to pass. After a moment and a series of deep breaths, he felt considerably better.

"Surely you realize, Caroline, that you cannot bring anyone here. Elizabeth would be ruined. We need to get her back to the house before someone misses her or sees her looking so disheveled. Now. Before it's too late."

Caroline coughed into her hand, then inclined her head in a meaningful fashion toward the doorway.

With a sense of dread, Austin turned around. Two young women, one who resembled a bug wearing a bonnet and the other an open-mouthed carp, gaped at him.

He closed his eyes and groaned. In addition to their other faults, the Digby daughters had miserable timing.

He was getting married.

Austin sat in his private study and watched the door close behind his mother and Lady Penbroke. Lady Penbroke was ecstatic, her feathers dancing and quivering with her excitement. His mother's reaction to his news had been a bit more reserved, but he knew she understood his responsibility to marry Elizabeth and she respected his decision. She'd naturally hoped for him to marry a highborn English girl, but he had no doubt that she'd cope with the situation and do all she could to ease Elizabeth's entrance into her new position. She and Lady Penbroke had agreed to make the necessary arrangements for the wedding. His only request was that they not tell anyone of their plans until he'd spoken to Elizabeth and formally announced their betrothal.

He ran a hand over his face, then leaned back in his chair. Marriage. He'd known the instant he'd seen the Digby daughters at the tower that he would have to marry Elizabeth. She'd saved his life and ruined herself in the process. Of course, both Digby daughters had vowed, ad nauseam, that they wouldn't breathe a word of what they'd seen, and he supposed that was possible. After all, the idiotic chits didn't want him off the marriage mart—unless it was to leg-shackle himself to one of *them*, a prospect that brought a shudder and had him reaching for his brandy. But their promised silence was not something he trusted.

Marriage. He'd avoided it for years. Yet, for reasons he could not decipher, he wasn't distressed at the prospect. He realized a few eyebrows would be raised at his choice of an American for his duchess, but as she was the niece of an earl, he knew the ripple would quickly quiet.

In fact, he knew damn well that once the engagement was announced, the same people who now disparaged Miss Elizabeth Matthews, Colonial Upstart, would seek to gain the favor of the future Duchess of Bradford. Although the knowledge disgusted him, he couldn't squelch the grim satisfaction that flowed through him. No one would dare utter another unkind word against her without incurring his wrath.

A series of mental pictures of Elizabeth rose before him. Elizabeth tumbling out of the bushes. Sleeping under the huge oak tree. Sketching him. Sliding off her horse. Covered in mud. Smiling. Laughing. Teasing.

A smile tugged at his lips. Although there was no denying this was a marriage of convenience to save her from ruin, he suspected he wouldn't find married life boring.

And of course marriage would allow him to bed her. His pulse stirred at the very thought. He pictured her lying in his bed, her beautiful hair spread all around her, her arms reaching out for him. *That* part of his marriage would be very . . . pleasurable.

Now all he had to do was propose.

When Elizabeth entered his study late that afternoon in answer to his summons, Austin was amused by the thorough visual inspection she gave him.

"How are you feeling?" she asked, looking concerned. "You should be resting."

"I'm fine, thanks to you." He smiled at her and was rewarded with a delicate pink blush.

"Is your wound causing you any discomfort? I can mix you a remedy if it is."

He recalled the last foul-tasting tisane she'd given him and barely suppressed a shudder. "It hardly hurts at all. That salve you prepared worked wonders."

"I'm glad." Her gaze scanned his face, then rested on the bandage at his temple. "It is indeed fortunate that I possess such a robust constitution or you may have frightened me to death." Once again meeting his eyes, she said briskly, "But we've already argued about that. I understand you wish to discuss something with me?"

Austin hesitated, not quite sure how to proceed. He normally was never at a loss for words, especially with a woman, but then he'd never proposed before.

He cleared his throat. "I'm sure you're aware that what happened last evening and our being discovered together this morning essentially destroyed your reputation."

She raised her brows. "Have the Digby girls been gossiping in spite of their promises not to? Caroline all but held me prisoner in her bedchamber since we arrived back at the house this morning, and she's refused to discuss matters with me until you and I spoke. If a scandal is brewing, surely we can squelch any rumors. After all, nothing happened between us."

"Really?" Reaching out, he trailed a fingertip over the pale freckles gilding her nose. "We kissed." His voice dropped to a husky whisper. "We spent the night alone together. We were discovered wrapped in each other's arms."

Color stained her cheeks. "You were injured and I helped you. That we spent the night together is totally beside the point, and it was also unavoidable. Surely anyone would understand that."

"*No one* would understand that, Elizabeth. Most especially not your aunt."

"Oh, dear. *Has* a scandal erupted?"

"No."

"Then Aunt Joanna doesn't—"

"She knows."

"She does? How do you know that?"

"I told her."

She planted her hands on her hips and glared at him. "It appears it isn't the Digby girls' mouths we need to worry about running amok. What exactly did you tell her?"

"The truth. That my injuries, coupled with the storm, necessitated us spending the night together at the ruins. Unchaperoned."

"Was Aunt Joanna terribly upset?"

"Not after I assured her that no scandal would touch you. In fact, she was quite pleased with my solution."

"What solution?"

"You and I shall marry."

She appeared frozen in place, a study of blank amazement. She stared at him and a full minute of the most deafening silence he'd ever heard ensued. With each passing second, his heart beat in slower, harder thumps until his chest felt as if it would burst. Finally she cleared her throat and spoke.

"You must be joking."

It was Austin's turn to stare. He wasn't certain what he'd thought her response would be, but it hadn't occurred to him she would think he spoke in jest.

"I assure you I am quite serious," he said stiffly. "As my wife, no one would dare utter a word against you. Any dalliance we may have engaged in prior to the actual nuptials would be overlooked because a wedding was in the immediate offing."

She clasped her hands in front of her, twisting her fingers. "Austin, I greatly appreciate this noble gesture, but surely such drastic measures are unnecessary."

"Such measures are absolutely necessary. Even if you choose to shrug off the damage to your reputation, the scandal will attach itself to Lady Penbroke. Do you want to see her ostracized from Society?"

"Of course not! Aunt Joanna has been nothing but kind to me."

"And would you repay her kindness by risking her position amongst the *ton*?"

Her eyes widened into pools of distress. "No! But—"

"Then marriage is the only way to protect yourself and her," he stated, amazed—and damn it, annoyed—by her obvious reluctance to become his wife.

Her golden brown gaze was so filled with worry, he wondered if he'd proposed marriage or a tar and feathering. A thread of unexpected amusement worked its way through his irritation—not at her, but at himself and his own conceit. He'd never expected he'd actually need to *convince* a woman to be his bride.

One look at her face told him he'd have to do just that.

Adopting a mildly teasing tone, he said, "Your expression, which can only be described as troubled, indicates you haven't taken into account the fact that marriage to me would come along with certain benefits."

His pride took another slap at her confused look.

"Benefits?"

"Yes. It is an English word meaning 'good things.' For instance, you would be a duchess."

Every drop of color drained from her face. "I do not want to be a duchess!"

He would have staked his own life on the certainty that he'd never hear those words uttered from any woman's lips. Before he could fashion a reply, she started to pace in front of him.

"Surely you can see that I'm a social failure and would make a dreadful duchess," she said. "People snicker at me from behind potted palms. I'm awkward. I know nothing about fashion. I'm a miserable dancer. And in case you haven't noticed, I'm horribly tall."

Austin's jaw tightened. "No one will snicker at the Duchess of Bradford." *Not if they want to keep all their teeth in place.* "As for the other things, you can easily learn about fashion and dancing. Between your aunt, my mother, and Caroline, you'll know more than you ever wanted to."

She stopped pacing and faced him, a small smile tugging at her lips. "You're quite adept at solving problems, I see. How do you propose we cure my height?"

He stroked his chin and pretended to ponder the matter. "Personally, I rather like the easy access to your mouth, and in case it's missed your notice, I *am* taller than you."

Her eyes filled with tenderness. "Oh, Austin, you are indeed wonderful to offer to sacrifice yourself this way, but I simply cannot allow you to do so. I would never want to bring embarrassment or shame to you and your family."

He barely refrained from shaking his head in amazement. She wasn't thinking of herself—she was thinking of *him*. And how ironic that the things she believed were faults—her awkwardness, her lack of dancing ability and fashion sense, and her height—were just a few of the dozens of things he found so unique, refreshing, and fascinating about her. The fact that she would even consider not accepting an offer of marriage from the man dubbed "England's Most Eligible Bachelor" truly stunned him.

And made him all the more determined to have his way.

As for bringing shame to the Bradford name, there wasn't anything she could do that could be worse than the secrets he already lived with—secrets that would destroy his entire family.

"You don't want to embarrass me, yet refusing my proposal will do just that," he said. "Everyone will believe that I'm a dishonorable libertine who ruined you, then refused to offer you marriage." He pushed aside his guilt at manipulating her soft heart and forced himself to add, "I'd be summarily cast out of Society, no doubt forced to flee to the Continent like Brummell."

"Oh, Austin, I—"

He touched a single fingertip to her lips. "Marry me, Elizabeth." To his surprise, he realized he was holding his breath, anxiously awaiting her answer.

Elizabeth gazed at his impossibly handsome, incredibly serious face and her insides simply melted. His proposal reverberated over and over again in her mind. *Marry me. Marry me. Marry me.*

Dear God, how could she possibly say no? How could *any* woman say no to this man? Even if she didn't consider the possible social harm to him and Aunt Joanna, she couldn't deny her feelings for Austin. Although she wished she didn't, she loved him. She wanted to help him. Protect him. What if further danger befell him? Whether he realized it or not, he needed her.

But he didn't love her. He was simply offering to marry her to save her reputation, to preserve his honor.

Sadness washed over her, but even as it did, a tiny voice inside gave her hope. *He may not love me now, but if I can discover something about William to prove he's alive, or perhaps learn something about this Frenchman . . . if I can bring Austin peace, then maybe he will grow to love me. As I love him.*

Was it possible? Could he fall in love with her? Clearly he could have his choice of any of the beautiful, fashionable Society *femmes* that moved in his world. She was painfully aware that she did not measure up in any way.

But by offering to marry her, he was clearly willing to make a huge sacrifice for her sake. The sheer enormity of that sacrifice stole her breath. Dear God, he was willing to spend the *rest of his life* with her. Surely it wasn't an offer he made lightly. So surely he had to care for her, even if it was just the *tiniest* bit.

Didn't he?

It wasn't an ideal situation, but it was a start. She'd be a fool to refuse the proposal of the man she loved, and it was sophistication—not intelligence—she lacked. There was only one answer. Before she could open her mouth, however, he spoke, his tone distinctly dry.

"I must say, your continued silence is a bit . . . deflating. I've waited nine and twenty years to offer myself on the matrimonial altar, Elizabeth. Are you going to turn me down?"

Good heavens, he actually looked . . . *worried*. A grin tugged at her lips. She tried to suppress it, but wasn't entirely successful. "Well, it *has* always been a dream of mine to give a crushing set down to an overamorous suitor."

Austin saw her dimples peeking through, heard her teasing tone, and forced his tensed muscles to relax. He stepped closer to her, until no more than several inches separated them. Skimming his hands down her arms, he entwined their fingers, then lightly brushed his lips over her cheek.

"I see. And if I were to become overamorous?" He breathed in the soft fragrance of lilacs, then gently captured her earlobe between his teeth.

"Oh!" Her shudder of pleasure filled him with masculine satisfaction. "Well, in that case, I suppose I would . . ." Her voice trailed off into nothingness as he kissed his way down her slender neck. She tilted her head back to give him better access and he touched his tongue to the rapidly beating pulse at the base of her throat. Her skin was smooth as cream and she tasted like flowers and warm sunshine. Like no other woman.

He lifted his head and studied her lovely, flushed face. Her eyes were closed, her lips moist and slightly parted, her breath coming in uneven puffs. "In that case you would . . . ?" he prompted.

She dragged her eyelids open and stared directly into his eyes. The warmth and tenderness shimmering in her expressive golden-brown depths awed him. He searched his memory and realized that no one had ever looked at him that way before. Heat pumped through him and his body pulsed to life.

A hesitant smile trembled on her lips. "I would relent and marry you."

An incredible wave of what could only be described as relief swept through him. "Is that a yes?"

"Yes."

Thank God. The thought hit him with the force of a fist to his head. Refusing to examine it, he instead gathered her in his arms. His mouth descended and claimed hers in a searing kiss that left them both breathless. His lips caressed her hungrily, his tongue slipping into the velvety warmth of her mouth. Moaning softly, she pressed herself against him and returned his kiss with a fervor that all but shattered his powers of restraint. *God. I cannot wait until this woman is mine.*

Her name whispered past his lips and he sifted his fingers through her silky hair while his mouth ravished hers, his tongue dipping and plunging, tasting her sweet warmth, until he ached beyond reason. Bloody hell, he wanted her. Now. Wanted her under him, over him, wrapped around him—

"Am I interrupting?" an amused voice asked from the doorway.

Austin stilled and smothered a heartfelt curse. Damn it all, Robert had been away from home for two months. Surely his younger brother could have remained away for another two minutes.

Lifting his head, Austin stared at Elizabeth's stricken, beet-red face. And her kiss-swollen lips. Robert was going to pay for this interruption. Very dearly.

Elizabeth tried to wriggle from his embrace, but he tightened his arms around her. "It's all right," he whispered. "It's only my brother." Keeping one arm firmly wrapped around her waist, he turned and shot Robert a murderous look. "I suppose while you were frolicking on the Continent, you forgot what a closed door means."

"Not at all," Robert replied, his gaze settling on Elizabeth with avid curiosity. "I knocked. Several times, in fact. You were apparently too, um . . . *busy* to hear me. I was about to return to the drawing room when I heard an unmistakable moan from within. Naturally I was concerned for your safety, so I entered." A devilish grin curved his lips. "Clearly there was no cause for alarm." He cleared his throat. "So, are you going to introduce me to this lovely young lady?"

Austin wanted to introduce him to the privet hedges. Head first. Sanity prevailed however. "Elizabeth, may I present my brother Robert, a young man not noted for his tact or timing. Robert, this is Miss Elizabeth Matthews . . . my fiancée."

"Pleased to meet—" Robert's words ended as if they'd been sliced off with a knife. His brows shot upward. "Did you say *fiancée*? As in betrothed? As in marriage?"

Austin's simmering annoyance was tempered considerably by the comically dumbfounded look on Robert's face. "Your command of the language and powers of deduction have always been a great source of pride to the entire family, Robert."

Without a word, Robert crossed the carpet and dropped to one knee in front of Elizabeth. Clasping both hands over his heart, he said, "My dear lady. It is indeed an honor to meet you. And you shall forever have my undying gratitude for removing my brother from the marriage market. Now perhaps some other poor, unfortunate, untitled bloke, namely myself, will stand a chance to capture a beautiful woman's eye. I don't suppose there's another like you at home? A sister perhaps? Aunt? Cousin? Grandmama?"

With hellfires scorching her cheeks, Elizabeth looked down at the young man kneeling before her. Teasing dark blue eyes gazed back up at her from a face that bore a marked resemblance to Austin's. But where Austin's countenance was firm, guarded, and serious, his younger brother's was softer, open, and smiling. In spite of her stinging embarrassment, she couldn't help but return his infectious grin.

"A pleasure to meet you, Lord Robert," she said, performing an awkward curtsy made all the more difficult by Austin's unmoving arm wrapped around her waist.

He rose to his feet and made her a bow. "You must call me Robert. And the pleasure is all mine." Turning to Austin, he extended his hand. "Congratulations, Brother. I wish you much happiness."

Austin's grip around her waist relaxed. He shook Robert's hand. "Thank you, Robert. And as long as you are here, so *unexpectedly*, I'll take this opportunity to ask you to serve as my best man."

"Delighted to do so." Robert sent her a twinkling smile. "I've always known I was the best man. It's just gratifying to hear Austin finally admit it. Did you say you had a sister?"

Amused, she said, "I'm afraid I don't."

"Just my luck." Shaking his head in a woebegone fashion, he crossed the room and poured a brandy. "When is the wedding?"

Elizabeth was about to reply that she didn't know when Austin spoke.

"The day after tomorrow."

Her jaw dropped open and she forcibly snapped it shut. *"The day after tomorrow?"*

Robert sent Austin an arch look. "Your bride-to-be seems a bit, er, surprised by the news. I don't know much about these things, but I believe it is customary to let the lady know when the nuptials will take place."

"I was about to discuss it with her when you barged in."

Mischief sparkled in Robert's eyes. "Really? Is that what you were about to do? It looked more like—"

"Robert." There was no mistaking the ice in that single word.

Robert set down his brandy snifter, then held up his hands. "Say no more. As much as I know you're perishing for me to stay and regale you with tales of my adventures abroad, I really must be off. I've barely spoken to Mother since I arrived an hour ago and I promised to meet her in the drawing room before dinner."

"I haven't announced the engagement yet, Robert."

"My lips are sealed." Crossing the room, he took Elizabeth's hand and pressed a kiss to her fingers. An image flashed through her mind and for an instant it was as if she'd looked into his soul. "I look forward to seeing you at dinner," he said, his eyes filled with friendly warmth.

"Thank you."

He walked to the door with an easy, unhurried grace, much in contrast to Austin's purposeful strides. Before closing the door behind him, he sent her a broad wink that warmed her cheeks.

She waited for Austin to speak, but he simply stared at the closed door with enough heat to burn a hole through the wood. Finally she said, "Your brother is very entertaining."

"He's a cursed pest."

"He loves you."

"He—" Austin turned and stared at her. "I beg your pardon?"

"He loves you. He's all but bursting with curiosity and concern about your decision to marry me."

"Concern? What makes you say that?"

He touched me. I felt it. "In spite of his teasing, it is obvious he's concerned that you're making the right decision. It was quite illuminating to watch the two of you together. I wonder if you realize how much you're alike."

Her words clearly surprised him. "Alike? Robert and I are nothing alike."

Oh, but you are. Inside. In your souls. Where it counts. Instead of arguing, she inclined her head. "Perhaps you're correct. After all, you are a serious man, and Robert is quite buoyant."

"I'm not certain *buoyant* is the word I'd use to describe him at the moment, but no matter. We've other things to discuss."

"Yes, we do. Austin, what on earth did you mean when you said the wedding would take place the day after tomorrow?"

"Just that. I spent most of the day contacting my solicitors and procuring a special license, which I shall have tomorrow afternoon. I suppose we could schedule the ceremony for tomorrow evening, but I thought you might want the extra day to make the necessary arrangements."

"But surely that's not enough time to plan a wedding!"

"My mother could arrange a coronation in half that time. Throw your aunt and Caroline into the mix, and we could be married before breakfast." Cupping her face between his hands, he regarded her with a frown. "I trust you're not changing your mind?"

A lump lodged in her throat. Changing her mind? *Not bloody likely, as the Brits would say.* "Of course not." His frown eased and she smiled at him. "But in deference to your mother's and Aunt Joanna's hearts, I agree we'd best plan on the day after tomorrow." She placed her hands on his forearms and felt the tension beneath her fingertips. "May I ask why you want the ceremony to take place so quickly?"

If she'd hoped romantic notions were behind his decision, his words dashed her. "A simple matter of logistics. I need to be in London by July first, and I plan to remain there for an undetermined period. By having the wedding take place before I leave, you can simply accompany me to London and I'll be saved from a journey back here or to Lady Penbroke's estate to fetch you."

She tried to hide her disappointment behind a smile. "Fetch me? You make me sound like a pair of slippers."

"Hardly slippers." His gaze settled on her mouth and her heart skipped a beat, hoping he was going to kiss her. Again she was disappointed, for he stepped away from her and crossed to the brandy decanters. "I have several matters to take care of before we make our announcement."

Realizing he was dismissing her, Elizabeth nodded. "Of course. If you'll excuse me, I must ready myself for dinner." She walked to the door. Before closing it behind her, she looked back. Austin was regarding her with an intense, enigmatic expression that somehow chilled and heated her at the same time.

Chapter 10

Elizabeth had just finished dressing for dinner when a knock sounded on her bedchamber door.

"Come in."

Aunt Joanna entered amidst a flurry of bobbing feathers and rustling purple silk. "My dear child," she said, her plump face wreathed in smiles. She enveloped Elizabeth in a plume-filled hug. "Did I not tell you?"

"Tell me what?"

Her aunt stepped back and regarded her with wide eyes. "Why, that it was only a matter of time until some nice young man took notice of you." She snapped open her fan and waved it vigorously, setting her feathers in motion. "I *knew* that we would find you a husband, but even *I* could not have predicted that we would land a *duke*! La, when Bradford told me that he wished to marry you, I nearly swooned. Not that he shouldn't *want* to marry you, of course. Any man would be blessed to have a lovely girl like you. But a *duke*! And such a young, handsome duke."

She leaned forward and confided, "Most of them are quite old and decrepit, you know."

Before Elizabeth could reply, her aunt plunged on, "Your parents would be so proud of you, as I am, my dear. So proud and happy for you." A dreamy expression entered her eyes and she heaved a rapturous sigh. "Why, I believe this is even more romantic than when your mother eloped with your father. They were so much in love . . ." She looked at Elizabeth, then frowned. "Whatever is wrong, child? You look quite stricken."

Elizabeth blinked back the tears suddenly stinging her eyes. "I was just thinking about Papa and Mother . . . how much they loved each other. How much they wanted me to have a happy marriage like theirs."

"And you will! Look who you are marrying! Can you doubt for a moment that you will be deliriously happy?" Her aunt studied her for several heartbeats. Elizabeth tried her best to look deliriously happy, but clearly she failed because her aunt said, "Yes, I can see that you do doubt it." Snapping her fan closed, she led Elizabeth to the brocade settee near the fire. After they were seated, Aunt Joanna said, "Tell me what is troubling you, Elizabeth."

Elizabeth looked into her aunt's concerned blue eyes, eyes that reminded her so much of her beloved mother's. She had no wish to dampen Aunt Joanna's enthusiasm, but she could not pretend that her upcoming marriage was a love match. "Surely you realize, Aunt Joanna, that the only reason the duke is marrying me is because he believes he *has* to."

Aunt Joanna *harrumph*ed loudly. "And surely *you* realize that no one could force Bradford to do anything he didn't wish to do."

"He is honorable and wishes to save my reputation—"

"Pish posh. If he were truly opposed to marrying you, he would simply refuse to do so, and because of who he is, he could get away with it. Clearly you do not understand his exalted position in Society . . . a position that you will share as his wife." She squeezed Elizabeth's hand. "Be happy, my dear. You will never want for anything."

Sadness tugged at Elizabeth's heart. "Except perhaps my husband's love."

Aunt Joanna wagged a gloved finger. "Darling, don't doubt for an instant that Bradford is well and truly besotted. If he weren't, wild horses could not have dragged a proposal from him. And once a man is besotted, he is nothing more than a fish on a hook."

"I beg your pardon?"

"You've hooked the largest fish in England, my dear. He's already infatuated with you. Now all you need to do is pull your line into shore."

Elizabeth suppressed a giggle at the impossible comparison of Austin to a fish. "And how do I do that?"

"By being your wonderfully unique self. And by engaging his interest *you-know-where*." Her aunt's eyebrows bobbed up and down several times.

Good heavens, surely Aunt Joanna wasn't going to embark on a discussion of Austin's *anatomy*. "Um, I afraid I don't know exactly where *you-know-where* is."

Aunt Joanna leaned forward, forcing Elizabeth to dodge a peacock feather. "The bedchamber," she intoned in a low voice, and Elizabeth sagged with relief. "If you keep your husband happy in the bedchamber, his infatuation will grow into love. It worked for me with my darling Penbroke. Your uncle was faithful to me until the day he died. A husband who has a warm marriage bed will not seek out a mistress."

Fire burned in Elizabeth's cheeks, but her aunt went on, "As your mother is not here, God rest her soul, I shall instruct you as I believe she would want. Now, tell me, dear, do you know where babies come from?"

Elizabeth fought a sudden urge to laugh. Her aunt looked so earnest and fiercely determined to do her duty. "Aunt Joanna, I am a physician's daughter and was raised around animals. I am well acquainted with the workings of the body."

"Excellent. Then you know everything you need to know."

"I do?"

"Yes." Reaching out, she patted Elizabeth's cheek. "Just remember everything I've just told you and you'll do splendidly."

Elizabeth stared, trying to recall *anything* her aunt had just told her.

"And if you have any other questions," Aunt Joanna said, "don't hesitate to ask. I'm delighted to help." With that, she rose and tossed her boa over her shoulder. "Come, dear. It's time to go downstairs. I want to make sure I have a clear view of Lady Digby and her horse-faced brood when Bradford announces your betrothal. Small and petty of me, I know, but it isn't every day that one's niece captures 'England's Most Eligible Bachelor.'"

Elizabeth decided that the betrothal announcement in the drawing room before dinner produced the greatest range of facial expressions she'd ever seen. Caroline and Aunt Joanna beamed. Austin's mother smiled regally while Robert simultaneously grinned and winked. Most of the other guests looked anywhere from surprised to stunned, while Lady Digby looked as if she'd swallowed an insect. The Digby daughters looked as if they'd all bitten into the same sour lemon. After the initial surprise, however, the guests gathered around her and Austin, offering their congratulations.

Dinner was a gala affair, with everyone raising their

glasses to toast the future bride and groom. Several guests who had planned to depart first thing in the morning hastily changed their itineraries to remain at Bradford Hall for the whirlwind wedding ceremony.

Elizabeth noticed that the Digby daughters were already turning their attention toward the other available gentlemen guests. She smothered a grin when she saw Robert seated between two Digby girls, both of them vying for his attention with cold-eyed determination. Robert caught her looking at him from across the table and rolled his eyes toward the ceiling. She had to cough into her hand to cover her laughter.

Her merriment faded, however, as the meal progressed. She realized with growing discomfort that everyone at the food-laden mahogany table was looking at her. Some of the guests were not as obvious as others, but she felt the weight of two dozen stares flicking over her. Assessing her.

Whereas before she'd been the object of sneers, now she observed speculation. Curiosity. And while she clearly felt skepticism veiled behind many of the smiles, as Austin had predicted, no one uttered an unkind word to her. Indeed, the gentleman seated next to her, instead of talking around her, hung on her every word as if gems of brilliance dripped from her lips. Penelope and Prudence, neither of whom had deigned to exchange more than a dozen words with her before, now made it a point to engage her in a conversation regarding fashion. Luckily they did most of the talking.

While the gentleman next to her droned on about a recent fox hunt, she glanced toward the head of the table at Austin. He was about to drink from his wineglass when their eyes met. And held.

Elizabeth gazed at him, his hand arrested halfway to his lips, his eyes intent on hers. Heat rushed through her and she fought a sudden urge to fan herself with her linen napkin. The way he looked at her, with that dark intensity that seemed to see inside her, unnerved her. And excited her in a way she could not put a name to.

With great difficulty, she returned her attention to her dinner companions, but her skin continued to tingle from the heat of Austin's gaze.

When the meal ended, the ladies retired to the drawing room for coffee. Elizabeth immediately found herself surrounded by half a dozen chattering women.

"Of course you must call upon us at your earliest convenience, my dear," Lady Dibgy said, elbowing her way to Elizabeth's side.

Before Elizabeth could open her mouth to reply, Lady Digby went on, "In fact, I should like to host a dinner party in your honor." She turned to her daughters. "Wouldn't that be lovely, girls?"

"Lovely, Mother," the Digby daughters chorused.

With a determined and proprietary air, Lady Digby linked her arm through Elizabeth's elbow. "Come, my dear. Let us sit down and discuss the plans."

A deep, masculine voice halted Lady Digby. "If you don't mind, Lady Digby," Austin said smoothly, "I need to have a word with my fiancée."

Lady Digby relinquished her hold on Elizabeth with obvious reluctance. "We were just about to discuss my plans for hosting a party in her honor."

"Indeed? Perhaps you should discuss the arrangements with my mother and Lady Penbroke. They will be helping Elizabeth organize her social engagements for the next several months, until she is settled with her new duties."

"Of course. Come along, girls." Lady Digby strode across the room like a ship under full sail, her fleet of offspring bobbing along in her wake.

Austin smiled at her. "You looked like you needed rescuing."

"I believe I did, although I'm not sure your mother or my aunt will thank you for it."

He waved his hand in a dismissive fashion. "Mother is very adept at these matters. She'll maneuver Lady Digby with an ease that I'd find downright frightening if I didn't admire it so much." His gaze roamed her face. "You look disturbed. Has anyone said something to upset you?"

"No. But I'm afraid that I feel somewhat . . . overwhelmed."

He extended his elbow. "Then come with me."

She didn't even consider refusing. Trying not to appear overeager, she took his arm and he led her from the room. "Where are we going?"

He cocked a brow at her. "Does it matter?"

"Not at all," she answered without hesitation. "I'm happy to escape all those people staring at me."

Austin felt the shudder that passed through her. He'd observed her all through dinner, saw how well she'd handled herself in the face of her newfound popularity. She'd been unfailingly polite to people who had once snickered at her, charming to those who had previously dismissed her, and smiled at everyone who had hurt her.

Bloody hell, he was proud of her.

When they reached his private study, he opened the door. A fire crackled in the grate, casting a soft glow over the room. Closing the door behind him, he leaned against it and watched her. She stood in the middle of the room, her hands clasped in front of her, looking more lovely than anyone he'd ever seen. Tenderness flooded him along with an overwhelming urge—no, a *need*—to kiss her. Before he could act on his impulse, however, she spoke.

"May I ask you something?"

"Of course."

A frown knitted her brow. "What happened to me at dinner . . . did that same thing happen to you?"

"I beg your pardon?"

"When you inherited your title and became the duke, did people *change* toward you? I'm the same person I was last week, last month, but everyone is treating me differently."

"Not unkindly, I trust."

"On the contrary, everyone seems quite *determined* to be my friend. Did that happen to you?"

"Yes, although before I was a duke, I was a marquess, so I was quite used to it already."

She studied him for a long moment, then shook her head sadly. "I'm so sorry. It must be very difficult for you, not knowing if someone likes *you* or your title."

He drew a deep breath. Would her words ever cease to amaze him? He walked across the floor, his footsteps silenced by the Axminster carpet, and stopped in front of her. She looked at him and his heart jumped. Tender warmth glowed from her beautiful eyes, sincere, honest, and unmistakable.

He simply had to touch her. Now.

Cupping her face between his hands, he brushed his lips across hers.

"Austin . . ." she breathed.

What was it about the sound of his name on her lips that moved him so? He'd only meant to give her a brief kiss. He'd brought her to the study for a different reason altogether. But now, with her soft curves so enticingly close, and her voice sighing his name, he promptly forgot his reason. Gathering her closer, he traced her full lower lip with the tip of his tongue. She needed no further urging to part her lips and welcome him. He half whispered, half groaned her name and deepened their kiss.

He slanted his mouth over hers and his senses caught fire. The warmth of her body, the strawberry sweetness of her mouth, her delicate lilac scent, all surrounded him, blanketing him from head to toe with a fierce heat that quickly turned into a burning, raging need. When he finally forced himself to lift his head, he was breathing hard and his heart rate had doubled. Possibly tripled.

"My goodness," she panted, clinging to his lapels. "You're quite good at that."

He pulled back slightly and took in her dazed expression with a swell of masculine satisfaction. "So are you." *Incredibly, indescribably good.*

"My mother once told me that Papa's kisses made her bones melt. I had no idea what she meant at the time."

A smile quirked his lips. "And now?"

A peach blush suffused her cheeks. "I understand. Exactly. It means you can no longer feel your knees. I must say, it's a delightful sensation."

"Indeed it is." And it would soon be more delightful—when they were in his bed, naked, making love.

A dozen erotic images popped into his mind, but he firmly pushed them aside. If he allowed his thoughts to dwell on *that*, she wouldn't make it out of the study with her virtue intact.

Reluctantly he released her and walked to his desk. "I want to give you something."

Her dimples flashed. "I thought you just did."

"Something else." He unlocked the bottom drawer, picked up what he wanted, then returned to her side. "For you," he said, handing her a small velvet box.

Her brows lifted in surprise. "What is this?"

"Open it and see."

She drew back the hinged lid and gasped. Nestled in a bed of snowy velvet sat an oval-cut topaz surrounded by diamonds. "It's a ring," she breathed, staring wide-eyed at the glittering gem. "Good heavens, it's extraordinary."

Just like you. The thought popped into his mind, startling him, but he couldn't deny its truth. She was extraordinary—and in ways that had nothing to do with her physical beauty. In ways that confused him and left him unsettled.

Removing the gem from its velvet perch, he slid it on the third finger of her left hand. "It's part of a collection that's been in the family for generations. I chose it because the color reminded me of your eyes." *The most beautiful eyes I've ever seen.*

Staring at the ring, she slowly moved her hand and stared at the glimmering shafts the stone threw off in the firelight. Then she raised those eyes to his. Tears shimmered on her lashes and he feared she was going to cry. Instead, she leaned forward and lightly kissed his cheek.

"Thank you, Austin. It's the most beautiful ring I've ever seen. I'll treasure it always."

His insides squeezed tightly together at the emotion in her voice. That now familiar warmth he always seemed to experience whenever she was near assailed him—a sensation he couldn't name other than to dub it the "Elizabeth feeling."

God. She possessed a sweetness, an innocence, he'd truly believed couldn't exist in a woman over the age of ten.

She was kindhearted. Generous and giving.

He was none of that. His failures regarding William proved it.

He stared at her for a long moment, imagining her as a bride. *His* bride. A disturbing thought hit him, and he frowned. She was going along with all his plans without question or complaint, and he'd never once considered that she might want the sort of lavish wedding women dreamed of. Shame filled him at his selfishness.

"Are you all right, Austin?"

"It has just occurred to me that this informal, whirlwind wedding may not be exactly what you've always dreamed of."

A gentle smile touched her lips. "All my wedding dreams have always revolved around the man I'd someday marry, not the pomp and circumstance of an elaborate ceremony. Two weeks after my parents met outside the millinery shop, they eloped and were married by a ship's captain at sea. It doesn't matter *how* you marry. What matters is *whom* you marry."

Not quite sure how to respond, he gathered her into his arms and buried his face in her fragrant hair, savoring her warmth for a moment. Then, after pressing a quick kiss on her forehead, he stepped away from her. "We should rejoin the others."

While they walked slowly back to the drawing room together, she said, "I suppose you realize that I'm quite unnerved about becoming a duchess."

"I'm afraid it's unavoidable given our intention to marry."

She sighed. "Things would have been much better, much simpler, if you'd just been a gardener. Or perhaps a merchant."

He halted and stared at her. "I beg your pardon?"

"Oh, I meant no offense. It's just that our lives would be much less . . . complicated, if you did not possess such a lofty title."

"You'd prefer to marry a merchant? Or a gardener?"

"No. I'd prefer to marry you. You'd just be *simpler* to marry if you were a gardener."

For the first time it really hit him that perhaps she

would be happier married to a merchant. While she was respectful of his title, she was clearly unimpressed by it. Yet the mere thought of her married to someone else, in another man's arms, pumped hot jealousy through him.

Forcing a lightness he didn't feel into his voice, he asked, "And if I were a merchant? You'd still marry me?"

Laying her palm against his cheek, she regarded him through serious eyes. "Yes, Austin. I'd still marry you."

Confusion assailed him. He'd half expected a teasing answer from her, but she'd surprised him—as she often did. Damn it, how did she consistently manage to throw him off center?

"Although your mother, Caroline, and Aunt Joanna have pledged to help me, I'm very unclear about exactly what a duchess does."

Gathering himself, he offered her a smile. "It's a very simple job. All she has to do is keep her duke happy."

She laughed. "How nice. For you. And how does she go about keeping her duke happy?"

His gaze wandered slowly down her long, lush body. "You won't have any trouble, I promise you." He intended to show her *exactly* how to keep her duke happy on their wedding night.

He wondered how the hell he would manage to wait that long.

While Elizabeth spent the next day ensconced or, he imagined, *trapped* in the sunny library with his mother, Caroline, Lady Penbroke, and the seamstresses, Austin labored over the accounts for his Surrey estate.

By late afternoon, the rows of numbers swam before his tired eyes, and when he heard the knock on his study door, he gratefully surrendered his quill.

"Come in."

Miles entered, closing the door behind him. "Well, I must say, Austin, you are full of surprises."

He pretended confusion. "Indeed? And here I thought I was rather dull and predictable."

"Anything but, old boy. First you send me off to London to gather information about Miss Matthews. Then you summon me back here to attend your *wedding* to the woman." Miles strolled over to the desk and made a great show of studying Austin. "Hmmm. You appear quite fit, no outward signs of insanity such as jumping uncontrollably about or screaming obscenities. Therefore I can only assume this whirlwind wedding indicates you've either fallen madly, passionately in love . . ." His voice trailed off and he raised his brows.

Unwelcome heat crept up Austin's neck. "The carriage ride clearly addled your brain."

"Or," Miles continued as if he hadn't spoken, "you ruined the girl." He paused, then nodded. "I see. Couldn't keep your hands off her, eh?"

"She saved my life."

Miles stilled. "Excuse me?"

Austin brought him up to date on the events of the past several days. When he finished, Miles shook his head.

"Good God, Austin. You're lucky to be in one piece." Reaching across the desk, Miles clasped his shoulder. "We all owe Miss Matthews a debt of gratitude."

"*I* certainly do."

A devilish gleam sparkled in Miles's eyes. "I'll wager you're thankful it wasn't a Digby daughter who found you injured."

A shudder passed through him. "God, yes."

"Which makes me wonder . . . how *did* Miss Matthews manage to find you?"

Before Austin could think up a plausible explanation for something that *had* no plausible explanation, Miles held out his hands. "Never mind. Clearly you'd planned an assignation. I do not need the details."

"Er, good." He cleared his throat. "Now tell me, what did you find out about Miss Matthews?"

Miles settled himself in the comfortable wing chair next to Austin's desk. Extracting a small leather notebook from his pocket, he consulted his notes. "My inquiries confirmed that she arrived in London on January third of this year aboard *The Starseeker*. As luck would have it, *The Starseeker* was in port for repairs and I spoke to her captain, Harold Beacham.

"According to Captain Beacham, Miss Matthews was a delightful passenger. She never complained, even when they encountered rough seas. Along with her companion, she often joined him on deck in the evenings to view the stars. She was very knowledgeable about astronomy, and he enjoyed her company."

He shot Austin a wink. "I believe he entertained some *romantic* notions toward your fiancée."

Austin's jaw tightened, but he ignored the teasing jab. "Did he know if this was her first trip to England?"

"She told him it was. He said that while she looked forward to arriving in England, there was a definite sadness about her. He assumed it was because she missed her home, but she never spoke of it." He flipped several pages in his notebook. "I also tracked down Mrs. Loretta Thomkins, the traveling companion."

Austin sat up straighter. "What did she say?"

Miles looked toward the ceiling. "What *didn't* she say? Hang it, the woman never stopped chattering from the moment she clapped her eyes on me." He tugged on his earlobes. "Good thing these are attached or she would have talked them off. I know more about that woman than anyone would ever care to know."

"And I'm certain you'll only share the pertinent details with me."

A deflated expression crossed Miles's face. "As you wish, but damned if I like it that *I'm* the only one who has to know her life history." Heaving a dramatic sigh, he consulted his book. "According to Mrs. Thomkins, Miss Matthews—whom she referred to as 'that dear, sweet child'—moved in with distant relations on her father's side named Longren after her father's death."

"Was she without funds?"

"Not destitute, but hardly wealthy. She was heartbroken after her father's sudden death. Miss Matthews told Mrs. Thomkins she hated living alone, so she sold the small house she'd shared with her father and moved in with her relatives. Apparently everything went along swimmingly until about nine months ago. That's when Miss Matthews packed her things and left."

"What happened?"

"Mrs. Thomkins didn't know for certain, but she suspected a falling-out with the relatives as Miss Matthews never spoke of them and she changed the subject whenever Mrs. Thomkins brought them up. Whatever the reason, it greatly saddened Miss Matthews and made her determined and, in Mrs. Thomkin's opinion, *desperate* to leave America."

"Desperate?"

"Desperate to leave with no intention of returning." Miles shrugged. "Mrs. Thomkins was nothing if not dramatic. She also said that 'that dear, sweet child' was like a lost soul for the first few weeks of their voyage and that her heart went out to her." He snapped his notebook shut and slipped it into his waistcoat pocket. "That was as far as I'd proceeded with my inquiries before you summoned me back here."

Austin pondered the information with surprise. What had made Elizabeth leave America so abruptly with no intention to return? Clearly there was more behind her trip to England than a simple visit with her aunt. Had there been a falling-out with her relatives? It seemed odd that she'd never mentioned them, but perhaps the memory was too painful to speak of—a concept he could well understand.

"Thank you, Miles. I appreciate your help."

"You're welcome. Will you require any further assistance?"

"I don't believe so. Why don't you stay on at Bradford Hall for a few days after the wedding? Robert has returned from the Continent, and Mother loves having you underfoot. Caroline also."

An odd expression flashed across Miles's face and Austin thought he was going to refuse the invitation. But Miles inclined his head. "I'd enjoy the visit. Thank you. And now you must satisfy my curiosity. I'm confused about all the secrecy surrounding your request for information. Miss Matthews isn't wealthy by any stretch, but you're certainly not in need of an heiress. And even though she's American, she is still an earl's niece. If you were harboring tender feelings toward her, you could have told me. Naturally I'd have understood your desire to discreetly investigate a potential bride."

Austin's brows collapsed into a frown. He was about to tell Miles that his inquiries had nothing to do with feelings, tender or otherwise, but it was simpler not to correct his assumptions. It certainly prevented him from making explanations he had no desire to make.

"Sorry about the secrecy," he said casually, "but you know how I'd have been hounded had anyone gotten wind of my plans. Thank you for your discreet help."

"Glad I could be of service." A devilish grin lit Miles's

face. "Doubly glad I didn't find out anything horrifying about your intended."

"As am I, although I suppose it would be a moot point. It is my duty to marry her."

Miles rose. With an amused smile playing around the corners of his mouth, he said, "Duty. Yes, I'm sure that's all there is to it."

Chapter 11

The wedding took place in the drawing room.

Fresh flowers adorned every surface, filling the air with their heady fragrance. The twentysome-odd guests sat in rows of chairs set up in the middle of the room facing the fireplace.

Austin stood between Robert and the local vicar who'd been called upon to perform the ceremony. When Elizabeth appeared in the doorway, all heads turned and a murmur of whispers ran through the guests.

Austin's breath caught in his throat. She was the most exquisite creature he'd ever seen. Her ivory satin gown fell from a scoop-necked bodice to her toes in a narrow, unadorned column. The soft material flared at her feet and ended with a small train in the back. Long white gloves, embroidered with pearls and gold thread, covered her arms to the dress's short, puffed sleeves.

Her hair was fashioned in a simple topknot, with hundreds of silky curls falling down her back to brush her waist. Her only jewelry was her betrothal ring and the ropes of diamonds twinkling in her hair. They were a wedding gift from his mother.

She walked slowly toward him, her luminous golden brown gaze fastened onto his. She sent him a tremulous, shy smile and the "Elizabeth feeling" washed over him.

"My God, Austin," Robert whispered in an awed tone. "She's incredible."

Austin, his attention riveted on Elizabeth, didn't reply.

Robert nudged him in the ribs. "It's not too late to change your mind, you know," he whispered. "I'm sure we could find someone willing to stand in your stead. Save you from the horrors of matrimony and all that. I might even consider volunteering myself."

Austin's eyes never left Elizabeth's face. "Another remark like that, little brother, and you'll find yourself in the rosebushes. Headfirst."

Robert chuckled and said no more.

The ceremony took less than fifteen minutes. After exchanging the vows that bound them for life, Austin brushed his lips lightly against Elizabeth's mouth and his pounding heart seemed to stall in his chest. *She is mine.* He could not even begin to fathom why he felt so . . . elated. While everyone extended their best wishes and congratulations to the bride and groom, he couldn't erase the smile of pleasure from his face.

An elaborate wedding feast followed the ceremony, and Austin chafed at the delay to depart for London. While supping on thinly sliced roast lamb and poached turbot, he repeatedly had to remind himself that the reason he was anxious to arrive in London was to await further word from the blackmailer. Tomorrow was July first. And as he still hadn't heard from James Kinney, a visit to Bow Street was in order. Yes, those were the reasons.

But then his gaze would settle on his wife . . . his beautiful, intriguing, fascinating *wife*, and all thoughts of investigations would somehow trickle from his mind like raindrops from the trees.

When the long meal finally ended, they changed into traveling clothes and, amid much waving and well-wishing, embarked on their trip to London.

Settled in the ducal coach, Austin watched, amused, as Elizabeth waved good-bye until everyone was a tiny speck. When she sat back on the luxurious burgundy velvet squabs, she smiled across at him.

"This is a splendid coach, Austin. So very comfortable. Why, you can barely feel a bump."

"I'm glad you approve."

"It was a lovely ceremony, don't you agree?"

"Lovely." He noticed a small bundle on her lap. "What is that package?"

"It's a gift."

"Gift?"

"Yes. It's an American word meaning 'something given to one person from another.'" She handed him the parcel. "It's for you."

"For *me*? You bought me a gift?"

"Not exactly. But you'll understand once you open it."

Curious, he untied the ribbon and carefully removed the wrapping. Inside lay the sketch she had drawn of him at the stream, when she'd asked him to reminisce. A beautiful cherrywood frame surrounded the picture.

He stared at it in silence, warm pleasure spreading through him. While it was customary for his family to exchange gifts on occasions such as birthdays, he couldn't recall the last time anyone had surprised him with a present.

It took a full minute to locate his voice. "I find myself at a loss for words, Elizabeth."

"Oh, dear. You don't have to say anything," she said in a small voice.

"But I do." He dragged his gaze from his gift and looked at her and was surprised to see she appeared distressed. "I suppose I should say thank you, but it certainly seems inadequate for such a thoughtful gift." He smiled at her. "Thank you."

"Oh! You're very welcome. When you didn't say anything I thought . . ."

"Thought what?"

"That my amateurish sketch was a foolish thing to give a man who has everything, including many priceless works of art."

"My silence meant nothing of the kind, I assure you. It's just that I cannot recall ever receiving such a lovely gift. I was momentarily at a loss for words." His candid admission surprised him. "Where did you get the frame?"

"Your mother graciously invited me to search about in Bradford Hall's vast storage room and I found it there." A wry grin pulled at her lips. "You would not believe the lengths I had to go to to escape the seamstress's clutches for even a few minutes. In spite of my time away from the pincushion, she fashioned a beautiful wedding gown."

"Yes, she did." He carefully rewrapped the sketch, then placed it on the seat next to her. "Would you care to sit beside me?" he invited, patting the cushion next to his thigh.

She moved alongside him without hesitation. As soon as she was settled, he leaned over and placed a light kiss on her lips. "Thank you, Elizabeth."

"You're welcome." She smiled at him and he fought the powerful urge to drag her onto his lap and kiss her senseless. Determined not to succumb to desires that would only leave him aching the entire journey, he pulled a deck of cards from his pocket.

"The trip to London will take nearly five hours," he said, shuffling the cards. "Do you play piquet?"

"No, but I'd love to learn."

It didn't take him long to realize his new bride possessed an uncanny aptitude for card games. It seemed he'd no sooner explained the rules to her than she was beating him. Soundly.

Although he'd suggested they play cards to keep his mind and hands occupied and off his bride, things were not going quite as he'd planned. He'd played quite well until she removed the spencer to her traveling ensemble. It was impossible not to notice how her full breasts pressed against the soft peach muslin of her gown as she studied her cards with frowning concentration.

Then, to make matters worse, she grew warm and discarded her fichu, allowing him a clear view of her creamy skin and an occasional teasing glimpse of cleavage. He found himself staring at her breasts, unable to concentrate, and down two tricks in no time.

"Are you all right, Austin? Is your head paining you?"

He snapped his gaze up to her face. "Actually, I feel a bit, er, overheated." He pulled aside the curtain and drew in a relieved breath. "We'll be stopping in a few minutes to change the horses." *Thank God. I need air.*

While the coachman changed the horses, Austin gratefully stretched his legs. He kept his eye on Elizabeth, whom he observed a short distance away, bending over some plants.

When she returned to his side, he helped her back into the coach and they resumed their journey.

"You'll never guess what I found," she said, settling her skirts around her.

"By your delighted smile I'd have to guess diamonds."

She shook her head and held out her bonnet. It was filled with bright red strawberries. "There were dozens of them. The coachman invited me to help myself." Reaching into the bonnet, she picked up a berry and handed it to him.

"Have you ever heard of the Origin of Strawberries?" she asked, popping one in her mouth and chewing rapturously.

"No. Is it an American story?"

"In a way. It's a Cherokee Indian myth. Papa told it to me. Would you like to hear it?"

Leaning back against the velvet squabs, he said, "Absolutely."

"A very long time ago, there was a couple who were very happy together. But after a time they began to argue. The wife left her husband and headed toward the Sun land, far away in the east. He followed her, but the woman never looked back.

"The Sun took pity on the man and asked if he were still angry with his wife. The man said no and that he wanted her back." She paused and popped another berry into her mouth.

"So what happened?" Austin asked, fascinated by her unusual tale.

"The Sun made a patch of succulent huckleberries rise up directly in front of the woman, but she paid them no heed. Later he put up blackberries, but she ignored them as well. He placed several other fruits along the way to tempt her, but still she walked.

"But then she saw the strawberries. Beautiful, ripe, luscious strawberries. The first ever known. When she ate one, her desire for her husband returned. She gathered the berries and returned to give them to him. They met on the path, smiled at each other, and went home together."

She smiled and offered him another berry. "Now you know the Origin of Strawberries."

"A very interesting story," he said, his eyes trained on

her lips, moist and stained pink with strawberry dew. The memory of kissing her berry-sweet mouth washed over him and he immediately commanded himself to think of something else. Bloody hell, why was that so difficult?

While they enjoyed the rest of the fruit, he wondered just what he was going to do to keep his hands off her for the remainder of the journey. His wife, however, solved that problem for him soon after finishing the last berry.

"My goodness," she said, stifling a yawn. "I'm so sleepy."

Her eyelids drooped and he breathed an inward sigh of relief. He could easily resist temptation if she fell asleep. Pulling her against him, he nestled her head on his shoulder. "Come here, Miss Robust," he teased, "before you slide to the floor and render yourself unconscious."

"I suppose that would be rather undignified," she said in a sleepy voice, snuggling closer against him.

"Behavior most unbecoming a duchess," he agreed, but she didn't hear him. She was already asleep.

Shifting gently so as not to awaken her, Austin stretched out and cradled her against him. With her lilac scent surrounding him, and her soft body pressed against him, all his senses leapt to life. Damn it, it appeared resisting temptation was not going to be as easy as he'd thought.

While he was throbbing, she was sleeping. He was hard and heavy with need, she was soft and languid with slumber. She sighed in her sleep and hugged him closer. A deep groan escaped him.

Damn it all, this was going to be one hell of a long ride.

Chapter 12

Elizabeth came awake slowly. The first thing she noticed was that it was dark inside the coach. The next thing she noticed was that she was stretched out full length on the soft velvet squabs.

Then she realized Austin was stretched out right next to her. And his arms were around her. And she was lying half on top of him and their legs were entangled. She tried to move, but his arms tightened, pinning her where she was.

"Where are you going?" he asked in a husky whisper near her ear, enticing a legion of chills to skid down her spine.

"I must be crushing you."

"Not at all. In fact, I'm very comfortable."

Thus reassured, she settled back, closed her eyes, and breathed in the wonderful smell of him. He smelled like . . . heaven. Like sandalwood and clean sunshine. Like Austin.

She breathed deeply again and sighed. "When will we arrive in London?"

"We'll be home in less than half an hour. In fact, as much as I'm enjoying lying here, we'd best sit up and repair ourselves before we arrive."

She sat up and shrugged her arms back into her spencer. "Where is your London home?"

"*Our* London home is on Park Lane, the same street as your aunt's Town residence. We're right next to Hyde Park in a section of London called Mayfair. We're also very close to Bond Street, so you may shop all you wish."

"Oh. Shopping. I cannot wait."

Clearly her unenthusiastic response gave her away. "You don't care for the shops?" he asked, his surprise evident.

"In truth, no. I view gadding about to dozens of shops, looking at items without a specific need to purchase them, as a total waste of time. However, if it is something that duchesses must do, I shall endeavor to force myself."

"Surely there will be baubles and personal items you'll wish to buy. After all, you need to do something with your allowance."

"Allowance?"

"Yes. It's an English word meaning 'a regular, periodic sum of money.' You'll receive a quarterly allowance that you may spend as you wish."

"How much of an allowance?" she asked, wondering what she would need to buy that he did not already own. He named a figure and her jaw dropped. "You're not serious." He couldn't possibly mean to give her that much money.

Even in the dim light, she saw his expression harden. "What's wrong? Is it not enough?"

She blinked at him, astounded. "Not enough! Good heavens, Austin. I assumed you were far from poverty stricken, but I had no idea you could afford to give me that much money every *ten years*, let alone every quarter."

Reaching out, she touched his sleeve. "I appreciate the offer, but it's truly not necessary. I already have everything I need."

Now it was Austin's turn to gape. She didn't know he could *afford* it? Had she really just stated it wasn't necessary for him to give her an allowance? She already had everything she needed? He thought of the many shallow, greedy, scheming, conniving women in the *ton* and tried to imagine even one of them saying the words Elizabeth had just said. He shook his head. Good God. Could this wife of his truly be *real*?

He continued to stare at her, to study her eyes, and his answer was clear. Yes. Yes, this woman—*his wife*—was absolutely real. She was everything good, kind, and unselfish. He hadn't even been looking, but he'd somehow found a treasure. *And I thought her reaction to the amount of the allowance was based on greed.* He shook his head at his own folly.

Her soft voice broke into his reverie. "I've upset you. I'm sorry."

"I'm not upset, Elizabeth. I'm . . . amazed."

"You are? Why?"

He brought her hand to his lips. "Because *you* are amazing." Just as he kissed the center of her palm, the coach came to a stop, marking their arrival. "To be continued," he promised in a husky drawl that brought a blush to her cheeks.

They alighted from the coach and he escorted her through the elaborate wrought-iron gate. Candles glowed from every window of the elegant brick town house, casting the house with warm, inviting, muted light. As they approached, the huge double doors were thrown open in welcome.

"Welcome home, your grace," the butler intoned, escorting them into the marble-tiled vestibule.

"Thank you, Carters. This is your new mistress, her grace, the Duchess of Bradford."

The butler bowed deeply. "The staff extends our heartfelt felicitations on your nuptials, your grace," he said to Elizabeth, his dour face sober.

"Thank you, Carters," she said with a smile.

Austin saw her gaze move beyond Carters to the group of servants standing in a line, waiting to greet them. Unmistakable pride bubbled up in his chest when she stepped forward and smiled at the group. One by one Carters introduced the staff to Elizabeth, and one by one each servant was charmed by their new mistress who repeated their names and favored each of them with a friendly, dimpling grin. What his wife lacked in polished sophistication, she more than made up for with warmth and natural charm.

"It's late, Carters. I suggest you and the staff retire," Austin instructed once the introductions were completed. "I'll escort the duchess to her rooms."

"Of course, your grace." Carters bowed again. He and the others filed out, leaving Austin alone in the huge foyer with his bride.

"Carters is rather intimidating," she whispered. "Does he ever smile?"

"Never, at least not that I can recall."

"Where on earth do you find such terribly *serious* people?"

Unable to keep from touching her, he tweaked one of her auburn curls. "Carters' family has been in service to the Duke of Bradford for three generations. He was *born* serious."

Tucking her hand beneath his arm, he led her up the curving staircase. Her head bobbed from left to right, taking in her new home.

"Goodness. This is fabulous. As is Bradford Hall. Are

all your homes this magnificent? Don't you own anything, well . . . *smaller*?"

He thought for a moment. "There's a modest cottage in Bath."

"How modest?"

"About twenty rooms, give or take a few."

She laughed. "Twenty rooms is hardly modest."

"I fear it's the best I can do. If you'd like, you can buy a hut or hovel with your allowance." He shot her a teasing wink. "Something with only ten rooms." Pausing, he opened a door. "Here we are."

She stepped over the threshold and gasped. The bed-chamber was decorated entirely in ivory and gold from the cream velvet drapes to the sumptuous Persian carpet beneath their feet. Several low, burning lamps bathed the entire room with a soft glow, and a cozy fire danced in the marble hearth.

"What a beautiful room," she said, clearly delighted. She ran her fingers lightly over the gold brocade settee and matching wing chairs. Throwing her arms out, she twirled around several times, her skirts billowing behind her. "What's in there?" she asked, pointing to a door on the far wall.

"A bathing chamber that adjoins my suite. It's part of the recently completed renovations I've done and is quite innovative. Your maid is drawing you a bath now. I'll await you in my suite." He touched her cheek, then left, closing the door behind him.

Elizabeth opened the door to the bathing room and was greeted by a shy young girl.

"Good evening, your grace. My name is Katie. I'm your abigail."

Thank goodness there wasn't anyone else in the room, or Elizabeth would have craned her neck around, looking about for "your grace," as she'd nearly done in the foyer when Carters had greeted her. The title was certainly going to take some getting used to.

Katie helped her undress and assisted her into the tub, which to Elizabeth's amazement was not only sunken into the floor, but easily large enough for two, possibly three people. Warm, lilac-scented water washed over her, and a blissful sigh escaped her. When she emerged fifteen minutes later, her skin tingled with pleasure.

"I've laid out your lovely peignoir, your grace," Katie said.

"Oh, thank you. It's a gift from my aunt. I cannot wait to see it."

" 'Tis unbelievably beautiful."

Elizabeth decided that *unbelievable* was certainly an apt word. Oh, the garment was beautiful enough, a diaphanous creation in the palest shade of blue, but it clung to her every curve in a way that could only be described as indecent.

"Gracious! What on earth was Aunt Joanna thinking?" she exclaimed, dismayed by the expanse of flesh the deeply plunging neckline left bare. The material barely covered her nipples. The back of the gown was no better, the scoop there was so low her entire back was bare to her hips. "I cannot possibly wear this."

"You look stunning, your grace," Katie assured her.

"Perhaps the robe will help," Elizabeth muttered. But it didn't help at all. The matching robe was nothing more than long sleeves with a back made of yards of material that hung to the floor. It was edged with cream-colored lace that only served to accentuate rather than hide her exposed flesh.

"I've never *seen* a robe like this," Elizabeth gasped, trying in vain to pull the two sides together in order to cover herself. It was hopeless. "What on earth am I going to do? And more important, what will my husband say?"

"Somehow, I believe his grace will be pleased," Katie said.

His grace was indeed pleased when he opened the door to his suite in answer to a quiet knock. In fact, he felt as if his breath had been knocked from his body.

Before him stood a vision in ice blue silk. An auburn-haired vision whose creamy skin glowed beneath a tantalizing gown that left her just barely covered. His gaze strolled down from her flushed face, taking in the daring décolletage of her gown and the provocative way it clung to all her curves. His groin instantly tightened.

"You look exquisite," he said softly, bringing her hand to his lips.

She cleared her throat. "I feel rather . . . *bare*. I cannot fathom what my aunt was thinking when she gave me such an ensemble."

Austin forced himself not to laugh and led her into his spacious bedchamber. He knew exactly what Lady Penbroke had been thinking and he sent her a mental note of thanks.

"Exquisite," he assured her again.

"Then the duke is pleased?"

"The duke is *very* pleased."

"Then I suppose I'm doing my job as duchess."

"See there? I told you it was simple." He indicated a small, beautifully set table near the fireplace. "Are you hungry?"

"No."

"Thirsty?"

"No."

"Nervous?"

"N—" A rueful smile curved her lips. "Yes. But I was trying so hard not to show it."

"I'm afraid those expressive eyes of yours give you away—as well as the crimson blush staining your cheeks and the fact your fingers are twisted into knots."

Her gaze dropped to her hands and she disentangled her fingers.

"Do you know what is going to happen between us, Elizabeth?" he asked, running a single fingertip down her soft cheek.

Her gaze lifted back up to meet his. "Oh, yes," she said, surprising him with her matter-of-fact tone. "I'm well acquainted with the studies of animal husbandry and human anatomy."

"I . . . see." Stepping closer to her, he gently laid his hands on her shoulders. "Well, if it makes you feel any better, I'm nervous, too."

Her eyes widened. "Do you mean to say you've never done this either?"

He choked back his laughter. "No, that is not what I meant."

"My apprehension springs from a fear of experiencing the unknown. As that is not the case for you, then why are you nervous?"

Because I want this night to be perfect for you. In every way. I hadn't dreamed it would be so vital that you be pleased. Plus he was damned uncertain about seducing an innocent. He'd always avoided virgins like a bad rash, yet now he stood faced with the suddenly unnerving prospect of deflowering his wife.

"There's always a bit of awkwardness the first time two people make love," he said. "I do not want to hurt you."

"And I do not want to disappoint you."

His gaze roamed over her. *Not much chance of that.*

She looked lovely and unbelievably soft. And so innocent. And appealing. And her gown was as provocative as hell. His gaze dropped to the daringly low neckline and he saw the pink tops of her nipples peeping over the edge. His sex swelled in immediate response, and it required a great deal of willpower for him not to groan out loud.

She shifted under his hands. "You're frowning. Is something troubling you? I'd be happy to discuss your problems with you."

"Would you indeed?"

"Of course. It's a wife's duty to relieve her husband of worries, is it not?"

God Almighty, he couldn't wait for her to relieve him of his worries. "In that case, I shall tell you what I am thinking." *And I'll show you.*

He gently drew her forward until only several inches separated them. She raised her chin and looked at him with questioning eyes.

"I was thinking," he began, "that I'd like your hair down." Reaching up, he removed the pearl-encrusted clip that held her hair up on top of her head. Hundreds of long, soft curls spilled over his hands and rippled down her back, their ends brushing just past her hips. He filled his hands with the silky tresses and brought them to his face.

"Your hair is incredible," he whispered, breathing in the flowery fragrance of her auburn locks. "I've wanted to touch it, run my hands through it, since the first time I saw you."

She stared at him, motionless, her eyes wide.

"I was also thinking how soft your skin looks," he continued, his fingers trailing down her cheeks to her neck, then to the delicate hollow of her collarbone. A soft gasp escaped her when his fingers dipped lower and brushed the swells of her nearly exposed breasts.

Placing his hands on her shoulders, he gently pushed

her robe down her limp arms until the material pooled at her feet. Words deserted him, and he could not stop staring at her, at her understated beauty and the onset of desire kindling in her eyes.

"What are you thinking now?" she asked in a breathless whisper when he continued to simply gaze at her in silence.

"I'd prefer to show you." He framed her face between his palms and saw her pulse beating wildly at the base of her throat—beating almost as fast as his own. He lowered his head and kissed her, his lips moving gently at first, then with increasing demand over hers. When his tongue sought entrance to her mouth, she welcomed it with her own. A moan escaped him, and he pulled her closer, his hands roaming up and down her smooth back that the daring gown left bare.

Slipping his hands down to her buttocks, he cupped her rounded bottom in his palms and lifted her, pressing her tight against his arousal. She gasped, but her gasp turned to a throaty groan when he gently rubbed himself against her.

"God, you feel so good," he whispered in her ear. She shivered in his arms . . . a delicate, pleasure-induced shudder that ran all the way down her body to her toes. "So damn good . . ."

His hands left the tempting enticement of her bottom and moved up, exploring her curves, then her rib cage, until the sides of her full breasts pressed against his palms. She gasped his name when his thumbs drew slow circles around her silk-covered nipples.

He filled his hands with her breasts, gently caressing their aroused tips through the filmy material of her gown, watching her face all the while. Her cheeks darkened and her eyes drifted closed when he slipped his fingers inside the scoop neck of her nightgown and touched her sensitive skin.

"Look at me, Elizabeth," he ordered softly, his fingers lightly playing over her nipples. "I want to see your eyes."

She dragged her lids open and gazed at him with a glazed, slumberous expression. Slipping his fingers beneath the thin straps of her gown, he slowly lowered it down her body.

Inch by inch she was revealed to him, a slow, sensual torture as his desire for her grew. High, full breasts, aroused rosy nipples thrusting forward, begging for his touch. A small waist gave way to gently rounded hips. The gown slipped from his fingers and fell to her ankles, revealing a tempting nest of auburn curls at the juncture of her thighs and long slender legs that seemed to go on forever. He instantly imagined those legs wrapped around his waist and desire exploded in him.

"Elizabeth . . . you're beautiful . . . perfect." He'd known she would be lovely, but she literally knocked the air from his lungs. Bending, he scooped her up in his arms and carried her to the bed and gently laid her down. He removed his clothes as quickly as his unsteady hands would allow, then stretched out next to her.

She immediately propped herself up on her elbows, her avid gaze wandering down the length of him. He forced himself to remain still and allow her to look her fill.

"I've never seen a naked man before," she said, her gaze touching him everywhere, scorching his flesh.

"I'm glad to hear it."

She stared at his arousal, which swelled to the point of pain at her scrutiny. "Tell me, are all men as . . . impressive as you?"

"I'm afraid I couldn't say," he ground out, although he couldn't imagine that any man had ever been as hard as he was at this moment. And she hadn't even touched him.

He needed to feel her, taste her. In his arms, in his mouth. Now.

Gently pushing her back on the pillows, he lowered his head and drew a plump nipple between his lips. Gasping, she twined her fingers through his hair and arched her back, offering more of herself to his questing mouth. He answered her silent plea, lavishing his attention on one breast then the other with his lips and tongue.

"Oh, my," she breathed. "I feel so . . ." Her voice trailed off into a vaporous sigh.

He raised his head. "So . . . what?" The vision of her, with her magnificent hair spread all around, her nipples damp and erect from his tongue, her eyes dark with passion, nearly undid him.

"So warm. And quivery. And wanting . . ." She moved restlessly, and he clenched his teeth when her soft belly brushed against his manhood.

God, yes, he understood those feelings, only he was burning. And shaking. And desperate. Never had he wanted a woman this much—so much that his hands trembled. So much he couldn't think straight.

His hands drifted over her abdomen and a long sigh escaped her. "Spread your legs for me," he whispered in her ear. She complied, opening her thighs to allow him access to the most private part of her.

The instant he touched her, they both groaned. With infinite care, he aroused her with a light, circular motion until her hips began to undulate beneath his hand, stoking a growing fire within him that soon threatened to overcome his resolve to go slowly.

Very gently he eased a finger into her. Velvety warmth clutched him. She was so tight . . . so hot and wet. His arousal jerked in response and a fine sheen of perspiration broke out on his forehead.

Their eyes met and held. Reaching up, she tenderly touched his face. "Austin . . ."

He'd imagined that hearing her breathe his name in that husky, passion-filled voice would excite him, but the reality stole his remaining control. Positioning himself between her thighs, he slowly, reverently entered her until he reached her maidenhead. He tried to ease through the barrier without causing her pain, but it was impossible. Knowing what had to be done, and unable to wait any longer, he grasped her hips between his hands and thrust, burying himself deep inside her.

Her gasp slashed straight through his heart. "I'm so sorry, darling," he whispered, somehow finding the strength to remain perfectly still. "Did I hurt you?"

"Only for a second. Mostly, you surprised me." A small smile played around her lips. "Wonderfully surprised me. Please don't stop."

He needed no second invitation. Propping his weight on his hands, he slid slowly in and out of her wet heat, withdrawing until he almost left her, only to plunge deeply back into her warmth. Her gaze remained riveted on his, and he watched every nuance of pleasure flicker in her golden brown depths. Her hips moved in rhythm with his and he gritted his teeth, fighting for control, determined to bring her to pleasure before he found his own release. But for the first time in his life he found that to be a nearly impossible task. Sweat beaded on his skin and his shoulders ached with the strain expended to delay his climax.

When she tightened around him, he watched, mesmerized. She arched her back and gave herself over totally to her passion. Her uninhibited reaction was so incredible, so erotic to watch, he lost his battle for control. Incapable of further restraint, he plunged into her, pulsing for an endless, mindless moment, spilling himself into her warmth.

When his throbbing finally subsided, he gathered her into his arms and rolled them onto their sides. They molded together in a perfect, breathtaking fit. She hugged him and nestled her head under his chin, pressing her lips to the damp skin of his throat.

Her tender kiss caressed him and his insides constricted with the "Elizabeth feeling." His breathing was still ragged and he forced himself to take slow, deep breaths. She laid her hand over his thudding heart and snuggled more securely against him.

God. She felt so damn good. And she was *his*. All his. A satisfied smile curved his lips. Smoothing his hand up and down her back, he waited for his pulse to return to normal.

It took quite some time for his heart rate to resume its regular speed, and since she was so uncharacteristically quiet, he thought she'd fallen asleep. He leaned back a bit, to look down at her, and was surprised when she raised her chin and looked directly into his eyes. Her golden brown gaze was serious and unflinching.

"I must tell you, Austin, that nothing in my studies of anatomy prepared me for the wondrous sensations we just shared."

Nothing in my previous experiences prepared me, either. He gently brushed a wayward curl from her brow, not sure what to say. Truth be told, his wife had rendered him quite speechless.

She captured his hand, pressing his palm against her cheek, then kissing it. "It was as if I were on fire, and you'd lit the match. Like I'd fallen off a cliff and drifted slowly back to earth surrounded by soft clouds. It felt as if our souls had joined." She shook her head and furrowed her brow. "Does that make any sense?"

He'd never felt anything that remotely resembled what he'd felt while making love to this woman. Never before had he been consumed by this wave of fierce possessiveness. Or this incredible feeling of tenderness.

"It makes perfect sense," he said. "And it gets even better."

She looked startled, then intrigued by his words. "*Better?* Heavens, how much better can it possibly get?"

"I'd be delighted to show you."

Elizabeth gasped in surprise when he rolled onto his back and she suddenly found herself sitting astride his muscular thighs. Looking down at him, her heart stalled. Dear God, he was the most beautiful man she'd ever seen.

"It would appear that you have the upper hand, wife," he said with a wicked half smile. "I wonder what you plan to do about it?" Linking his hands together behind his head, he watched her with glittering, smoky eyes.

Her gaze traveled slowly downward, studying his fascinating male body. The whirls of dark hair covering his chest narrowed to a thin line that ran down his abdomen, then spread again as it continued lower.

Gazing upon that part of him, her breath caught in her throat. His arousal rose hard and erect, the sight utterly captivating and intriguing. She longed to touch him . . . touch that part of him . . . touch all of him. She slowly brought her gaze back to his heated stare.

"Touch me," he invited, his voice a soft, raspy caress. "I'm completely at your disposal. Explore all you like."

She needed no further urging. Leaning forward, she placed her hands on the undersides of his raised arms and dragged her fingers slowly down his body. Fascinated, she watched his muscles flex beneath her touch. He groaned and gazed at her through half-closed lids, his eyes stormy and dark.

"Do you like that?" she whispered.

"Hmmm . . ."

Thus encouraged, she allowed her curiosity to take over. Running her fingers through the crisp hair on his wide chest, she marveled at the combination of textures. Springy hair on warm skin over hard muscle. With each ripple of his muscles and each moan he emitted, her confidence grew.

Eager to bring him as much pleasure as he'd brought her, she imitated his earlier actions. Leaning forward, she kissed his chest and was rewarded with a sound that resembled a growl. Flicking out her tongue, she lightly caressed one of his small, flat, brown nipples. His groan let her know he liked that. Her tongue grew bolder, laving first one nipple then the other, drawing each one into her mouth and circling them slowly with her tongue. As his groans grew more lengthy, a surge of feminine satisfaction swept over her that she could affect this powerful man so.

Austin clenched his jaw and prayed for strength. When he'd invited Elizabeth to explore his body, he hadn't realized what sweet torture he'd suffer. His painfully aroused body ached to be buried inside her, begged for release, but if he gave in to his raging need, he'd no doubt scare her. And he'd definitely disrupt her wide-eyed exploration of his body, a double-edged sword to be sure. He didn't know how much more he could stand, but he bloody well didn't want her to stop either.

He somehow managed to keep his hands linked behind his head, but his fingers were numb from gripping them together so tightly. Until tonight he'd considered himself a man of extreme self-control—his mind ruled his body, not the other way around. He was always able to defer his gratification for as long as he pleased.

But not tonight.

Not with Elizabeth's gentle hands running over him. Not with her soft tongue caressing him. Not with his arousal straining, rock hard and about ready to burst. Not with—

Her fingertips brushed over the head of his arousal and a sizzling bolt of desire shot through him.

He gritted his teeth and clamped his eyes shut as her hands softly caressed him, moving up and down over that part of him that ached and throbbed for her. Desire washed over him in ceaseless waves, drowning him in a sea of sensations. If she didn't stop soon, he was going to explode in her hands. Seconds later she wrapped her fingers around his shaft and gently squeezed and he knew he was done. A man could only take so much.

He could take no more.

Emitting an agonized groan, he flipped her onto her back and buried himself in her with one deep, powerful stroke.

"Austin!"

"God, I'm sorry." He couldn't believe that he'd just plunged into her with all the finesse of a green boy. And all because he couldn't help himself. Couldn't control himself. Holding back was beyond him. But, he realized with deep chagrin, if he'd waited any longer to sheath himself within her, he would have disgraced himself in a way he hadn't since he was a lad. Some force he couldn't control and didn't understand had him firmly in its grip. Dropping his forehead onto her brow, he fought to control the uncontrollable.

She surrounded his face with gentle hands. "Did I . . . displease you in some way?" Her voice held confusion and worry and Austin would have laughed at her ludicrous question if he'd had the breath to do so.

"No. You pleased me greatly. Too much," he whispered, his voice a hoarse rasp he didn't recognize. He began moving within her, his strokes long and forceful. "Elizabeth . . . wrap your legs around me."

She brought her long limbs up and clasped her ankles

together behind him. She matched him stroke for stroke as he drove into her, faster and faster, harder and higher until he was lost in a vortex of sensation. He heard her murmuring his name over and over again, felt her pulsing around him, squeezing him in her velvet warmth.

Completely lost, he drove himself into her again and again, his heart slamming against his ribs. His climax pounded through him, so strong that the force of his final thrust nearly drove her into the headboard. He collapsed on top of her, his head falling limply into the crook of her shoulder. Perspiration dampened his skin, and his ragged breathing burned his lungs. He couldn't have moved if his life depended upon it.

After several moments she shifted beneath him and he somehow managed to lift his head. He looked down into her beautiful eyes—eyes soft with tenderness that reached inside and touched his heart.

She brushed her fingertips across his lips. "You're wonderful," she whispered.

Her words flowed over him, surrounding him, and his heart rolled over. *You're wonderful.* Words he'd heard before from the lips of a satisfied lover, but this time he somehow knew they were different. Because of who said them. And because he sensed she wasn't talking about his lovemaking skills.

You're wonderful. No other woman had ever spoken them to him and meant *him.* That *he* was wonderful. Hell, he knew he wasn't, but pleasure rushed through him just the same.

A sense of . . . what was it? . . . enveloped him. Well-being? Yes, but something else. Some other feeling he couldn't quite place enveloped him, leaving him warm and content. It took him a moment to realize what that feeling was. It had been so long since he'd felt it, he didn't recognize it at first.

It was happiness.

She made him happy.

But he forcibly reminded himself that there were still unanswered questions about his wife. There were secrets about her past that she hadn't shared with him. And their marriage was only one of convenience.

But it would be so easy to believe otherwise.

Chapter 13

Robert stood in the drawing room at Bradford Hall, his ears still ringing with the shocking news the magistrate had brought. *Half his face was blown off, impossible to identify, but he was clearly a Runner. Wore the red vest of Bow Street. Looks like a robbery, but we'll have to conduct an inquest. Gave your groom quite a turn, finding the body like that. We'll need to notify his grace immediately.*

"I cannot imagine why a Runner would be at the ruins," Robert said to Miles, who stood near the mantel. "But whatever the reason, the entire episode has given me a bad feeling."

"Perhaps Austin knows the man," Miles said. "We'll find out tomorrow when we arrive in London."

"Yes. I've arranged for the coach to be brought around at first light. I didn't tell Mother or Caroline why we're going, but they are always eager for a trip to Town, thank God." Robert dragged his hands through his hair. "I couldn't very well tell them Mortlin discovered a dead body in the bushes and there may be a murderer on the loose. Of course, Mother balked at interrupting Austin and Elizabeth's wedding trip, so I appreciate your inviting us to stay at your town house."

"My pleasure," Miles said, tossing back his brandy.

"I'm relieved that the last of the guests, including Lady Penbroke, departed this morning," Robert continued, "so it wasn't necessary to make awkward excuses to them."

"Indeed," Miles said, pouring himself another brandy and downing it.

Robert stared at him. "Are you all right?"

"Fine. Why do you ask?"

"Because you've practically emptied the brandy decanter in the last five minutes."

"Just a bit unnerved, I suppose."

Robert nodded. "I understand perfectly." He glanced toward the mantel clock. "It's almost midnight. I'm going to retire. I suggest you do the same."

"I'll be along shortly. Good night."

The instant Robert left the room, Miles poured himself another hefty brandy. Leaning against the mantel, he stared into the flames, trying to figure out what a Runner was doing at Bradford Hall and why someone killed him. Nothing was clear other than the fact that Robert, his mother, and Caroline had to leave here until the mystery was solved. His stomach turned over. If anything happened to Caroline—

He swallowed half his drink and squeezed his eyes shut. No. No harm would come to Caroline. He would personally see to it. But first he would have to survive the five-hour journey facing him tomorrow.

Five hours in a coach with Caroline. Five hours of her sitting close enough to touch, five hours of breathing in her delicate fragrance.

Five hours of pure torture.

His guts tightened at the very thought. It was one thing

to avoid her in a crowd, but how the hell could he hope to pretend indifference in a carriage? And with her brother and mother looking on, no less.

Damnation, when the hell had she grown up? He'd looked at her a thousand times and had never seen her. She'd always been "Little Caroline," until that night two months ago when he'd waltzed with her. Since then it seemed he could not *stop* looking at her. She'd fit in his arms as if she were made for him alone and no matter how hard he tried, he'd been unable to erase the feel of her, the scent of her from his memory.

He closed his eyes, picturing her in his mind. What would her beautiful mouth feel like? Taste like?

His eyes snapped open and he gulped his brandy. *Hang it! What the hell am I thinking?* If Austin even suspected he was entertaining carnal thoughts about Caroline, he would snap his fingers and decree, "Off with his head!"

He simply had to push these insane urges aside. Caroline was not a woman to trifle with, and the "trifle" sort was what he liked best. Caroline would have a husband— and as he had no intention of being one, he simply needed to forget this madness. No wife for him, no indeed. He had no intention of being leg-shackled as his father had been to his second wife, a nagging harpy who'd made his life miserable until the day he died.

He would endure the carriage ride tomorrow and Caroline's presence in his home for several days, and then he wouldn't have to see her again until the start of the next Season, thank God. And even then, he could easily avoid her.

A knock sounded at the door.

"Come in."

Caroline entered, closing the door behind her.

It felt as if all the air had been sucked from the room.

"Good evening," she said, joining him by the fireplace

and offering him a tentative smile. "I was looking for Robert."

"He's gone to bed." He tried to force his gaze away from her, but failed completely. The fire's glow highlighted her delicate features and shiny golden hair. The memory of the feel of her in his arms washed over him again, bringing with it a heated rush of desire.

"Don't let me keep you from retiring, Caroline," he said, inclining his head in a meaningful fashion toward the door.

"Are you angry about something, Miles?"

He tore his gaze away from her and stared into the fire. Yes, he was angry. Angry for being unable to talk himself out of this unwanted, insane desire for her. Yes, he was very angry indeed.

"No, Caroline. I'm not angry."

"I don't believe you."

His gaze snapped over to glare at her. Looking at her proved a big mistake. Her blue eyes probed his, studying him with tender concern. Her breasts curved above her bodice and tendrils of golden hair curled in a beguiling fashion around her face. His loins clenched, and he swelled against his trousers. She was so damn beautiful. And he wanted her. God, how he wanted her.

"Are you calling me a liar?"

"No, of course not. I was just concerned that I'd done something to anger you."

"You haven't." He swallowed the rest of his brandy and continued to stare at her, helpless to stop himself. He knew he should stop drinking with such haste. He was beginning to feel light-headed.

Caroline watched him, her heart thumping against her ribs. On the outside she strove to appear calm, but on the inside her nerves jangled with tension and uncertainty. She'd known Robert had retired. She'd been waiting for an opportunity to be alone with Miles, hoping that he might make an encouraging move toward her, but his fierce scowl made hope of *that* outcome die a slow, withering death in her breast.

Well, she was prepared to take matters into her own hands. She'd loved him her entire life. It was time to show him she wasn't a little girl anymore. She had nothing to lose except her pride, and she would happily sacrifice that if it meant having Miles.

"I'm relieved you're not angry with me," she remarked with what she hoped sounded like a carefree laugh, "because I wish to ask your advice about something, if you don't mind."

He didn't answer her.

"It's a rather delicate matter," she went on doggedly.

"Ask your mother," he suggested, his tone anything but friendly.

"Oh, I couldn't ask Mother about *this*."

"Then ask Austin. Or Robert."

"Impossible," she decreed with a wave of her hand. She leaned forward and spoke confidentially. "They're *men*, you see."

He turned his head and stared at her. "And just what the hell am I?"

"Oh! Well, you're a man, of course," she replied, not even batting an eye at his use of an obscenity. "But you're different. You're not my *brother*, you see."

Miles didn't see. Not at all. He knew he wasn't her brother, damn it. He knew it all too well. "What do you need advice about, Caroline?" he asked in a tired voice. Maybe if he humored her she'd go away and leave him in peace. Then he could concentrate on something other than her.

"I need to know about kissing."

He gaped at her in amazement. "*What* did you say?"

"I said I need to know about kissing. As you know, Lord Blankenship was one of our houseguests this past week. I have reason to believe he holds me in some affection and may offer for me."

"Blankenship? Charles Blankenship?"

"Yes."

"Has he spoken to Austin about this?"

"No. At least I don't think so."

"Then what makes you think he plans to offer for you?"

"He kissed me."

"He *what*?"

"He kissed me."

"Where?"

Caroline blinked. "In the library."

Miles barely held his temper in check. "I meant *where* did he kiss you—as in on the hand or on your cheek?"

"Oh. Neither. He kissed me on my lips."

"He *what*?"

"You seem to have a decided problem understanding me. Is your hearing afflicted?"

"Certainly not," Miles answered, indignant. "I just simply cannot believe you'd allow him to kiss you in such a fashion."

She cocked her head to one side. "Indeed? Why? Lord Blankenship is titled, wealthy, kind, and fair of countenance."

"Isn't he rather *old* for you?"

"He's only two years older than you. But that isn't what I want to talk about."

"Really?" His voice resembled a growl.

"No. What I need to know is why I didn't *feel* anything when Charles kissed me. Except perhaps boredom."

Much to his disgust, a wave of relief washed over Miles. "Boredom? Really? What a pity."

"From conversations I've had with several friends, I

understand it's not necessary to feel bored when a gentleman kisses you. Apparently *some* gentlemen's kisses aren't boring at all." She looked directly into his eyes. "Is that true?"

"How the hell would I know?" He fought an urge to tug at his suddenly constrictive cravat. His damn valet had obviously tied his neckcloth too tight. And hang it, when had it become so *hot* in here?

"Are *your* kisses boring, Miles?" she asked, taking a step closer to him.

"I haven't the vaguest notion. I've never kissed myself." He took a wary step backward. His shoulders bumped into the mantel, effectively stopping him from retreating any farther.

She advanced another step, then another, stopping within a foot of him. Gazing up at him with luminous eyes, she said, "Well, then, why not kiss *me*, and I'll let you know."

"That is a most improper suggestion, Caroline," he said, grimly aware that he wanted nothing more than to oblige her.

She placed her hands on his shirtfront. "What's wrong, Miles? Are you afraid you'll discover your kisses induce boredom?"

He valiantly fought for control. The touch of her hands was driving him to distraction.

"Look at me," Caroline whispered.

He stared over her shoulder, silent and tight lipped.

"Kiss me," she breathed.

"No."

"Hold me."

"Absolutely not." He gritted his teeth and prayed for strength. He had to get away from her. He raised his hands and grasped her wrists, planning to forcibly move her away from him. But then he looked at her.

It proved his undoing.

Her eyes glistened with unshed tears, and the vulnerable longing on her beautiful face all but sliced him in half. He grasped her shoulders, intending to push her away, determined to be noble, but she raised herself onto her tiptoes and flattened herself against him.

"Please, Miles. Please . . ." She placed her soft lips against his jaw, the only part of his face she could reach without his cooperation.

Her plea and her tears pierced his heart like arrows. His control snapped and with an agonized groan he lowered his mouth to hers.

God help him. Had any woman ever tasted this sweet? Felt this good? She softly moaned his name and wrapped her arms tightly around his neck. The sound of his name coming from her lips on a breathy sigh made him tingle all over.

With unhurried languor he introduced her to the art of kissing. She was inexperienced, but very eager and a fast learner. When he ran the tip of his tongue along her lower lip, she did the same to him. She gasped in surprise when his tongue invaded the velvety warmth of her mouth, but within seconds she rubbed her own tongue against his, causing him to clasp her to him fiercely.

Again and again he slanted his mouth over hers, alternating between a lazy, coaxing touching of lips and a hard, demanding melding of mouths and tongues.

When he finally raised his head, she clung to him and buried her face against his shirtfront. "My goodness," she whispered. "That was—"

"A mistake, Caroline. A big mistake." His voice shook and his heart raced at triple speed. Dropping his head back, he squeezed his eyes shut and again prayed for strength. His arms still held her tightly against him, and he knew she must feel his arousal pressing against her, but she made no move to stand away from him. Instead she clung to him all the tighter. He wished he could blame the liquor for what had just occurred, but he couldn't.

He'd wanted to kiss Caroline more than he'd ever wanted anything before. He just thanked God he'd found the control to stop himself from taking any further liberties with her. He shuddered to think what Austin would do if he ever found out about the way his most trusted friend had just kissed his innocent sister. Pistols at dawn weren't beyond the realm of possibility.

She raised her head. "How can you possibly say it was a mistake? It was wonderful."

Miles forced himself to step away from her. "It shouldn't have happened. If I hadn't had so much to drink, it never would have." *Liar.*

"You didn't enjoy it?" she asked, her eyes clouding over with hurt bewilderment. "How can that be? It was the most wonderful moment of my entire life. Did you not feel what I felt?"

Dear God, how could he deny it? Their kiss had nearly brought him to his knees, but he could not, *must* not, tell her that. "It was just a meaningless kiss, nothing more." He pushed the lie past his lips and his insides cringed when her eyes filled with tears.

"Meaningless?" she whispered in a broken voice. She turned her back to him in an obvious struggle to compose herself.

He longed to take her in his arms, to take back his hurtful words, but he forced his hands to remain at his sides and he kept his mouth shut. He had to be firm. She was too young. Too innocent. Definitely not the woman for him. The only way he could ever have Caroline would be to marry her. And he wasn't about to get married simply to quell a lustful urge. He'd bring his lustful urges to a mistress and remain a carefree bachelor, thank you very much.

"So, did you glean your answer about kissing?" he asked in a light tone, trying to gloss over the last several cataclysmic moments.

Caroline drew an audible breath and whirled around. She faced him squarely, her eyes still damp, but shooting daggers nonetheless. "Yes. You'll be happy to know that your kiss isn't in the least bit boring," she informed him in a voice that shook with emotion. "But calling what happened between us meaningless is dishonest in the extreme." She raised her chin a notch. "A falsehood of the first order."

His eyes narrowed on her flushed face. "Are you calling me a liar?" he asked for the second time that evening.

"Yes, Miles. I'm calling you a liar." She stalked to the door, then shot his still-bulging manhood a scathing glance. "And a very poor liar at that." She swept from the room, and he gaped at the empty doorway.

Good God. What a crushing set down.

What an incredible woman.

And just what the hell was he going to do about it?

Chapter 14

Austin awoke slowly, drowsily becoming aware of gentle hands roaming his chest. He pried one sleepy eye open and was rewarded with a view of a perfectly round breast topped with a plump rosy nipple. Deciding this required further investigation, he slid his other eye open and delighted in the sight and feel of his naked bride sitting astride his thighs, running her hands slowly up and down his torso.

Her glorious hair surrounded her like an auburn cloud, cascading over her shoulders to touch her full breasts and caress her hips, the curling ends gliding behind her to rest on his legs.

The fact that he was aroused did not surprise him a bit. Indeed, he'd been in a constant state of arousal for the past three days.

But today things would change. He'd sent a message to Bow Street and had been informed that as of last evening, no one had yet heard from James Kinney.

And late last night another blackmail letter had been

delivered, demanding that Austin gather the incredible sum of five thousand pounds and await further instructions. He'd questioned the lad who brought the missive and learned that a "Frenchie" had offered him a bob to deliver the note. After paying the ragged youth a crown, he'd further learned that the "Frenchie" had frequented several establishments by the riverfront. The description the boy had provided of the man left no doubt in his mind that it was Gaspard. Austin planned to visit those places this afternoon in the hope of confronting the bastard face to face.

So, as delightful as this brief interlude with his bride had been, it was time to turn his attention to other matters.

"Good morning, your grace," she greeted him. She leaned down and kissed his lips. "Or perhaps I should say good afternoon?" Her fingers trailed down his chest to lightly tickle his belly. His muscles contracted with pleasurable spasms wherever she touched him. Yes, it was going to be a shame for this interlude to end.

She wrapped her fingers around his arousal and gently stroked him. "Are you going back to sleep?"

Instead of answering, he grabbed her hips, lifted her, and impaled her on his erection. "I'm wide awake and you have my *full* attention," he assured her, his voice ending on a husky groan when she squeezed him in her silky, wet passage.

Reaching up, he wound his fist in her hair and dragged her mouth down to his. His tongue slipped into her mouth while his other hand nestled between her thighs. When his fingers caressed her, she moaned deeply. Her climax came quickly, consuming her totally. Burying her face against his shoulder, she cried out his name over and over while she spasmed around him and melted in his arms.

The moment she relaxed against him, he rolled them over until she lay on her back beneath him. He settled himself between her splayed thighs and moved slowly within

her, withdrawing nearly all the way only to glide deep
once again.

Supporting his weight on his hands, he watched her
beautiful face as he stroked inside her, slowly and steadily,
until she writhed beneath him. She held absolutely nothing
back in her responses to him. There was nothing shy or retiring about his bride in the bedchamber. Elizabeth in the
throes of passion, with her long shining hair spread around
her, was one of the most erotic sights he'd ever seen. A
heartfelt groan escaped him when she wrapped her long
legs around him and her fingers grasped his straining
biceps.

"Austin," she moaned, arching beneath him. Her or-
gasm clenched him, and he sank into her one last time,
spilling his seed deep within her. Clasping her to him, he
rolled them onto their sides, and buried his face in her fragrant hair.

"That was a very nice way to wake up," he murmured
when he was able to speak again. He stroked the small of
her back and her rounded buttocks with a light, circular
motion.

"Very nice for me as well," she said with a sassy wink
that made him smile.

Yes indeed, the last three days had been the happiest
he'd ever known. They'd ventured out only once, yesterday, for a leisurely carriage ride through Hyde Park, then
window shopping along Bond Street. Austin had admired
a pair of diamond and pearl ear bobs at a fashionable jeweler's and purchased them for his bride in spite of her
protests. Elizabeth then discovered a small bookshop on a
cobbled side street and dragged him inside.

"I thought you said you didn't like to shop," he'd teased
as she browsed the shelves.

"I don't care for shopping for *things*. These are *books*."
He wasn't sure he understood the distinction, but he

was more than happy to indulge her. He bought her over a dozen volumes, and, he noted with amusement, she was more thrilled with them than the fabulously expensive ear bobs.

Aside from their outing yesterday, their time had been spent almost exclusively in his bedchamber. Naked. Touching. Learning. Exploring. Enjoying each other. Sharing their bodies. They even took most of their meals there, emerging only for dinner in the formal dining room. But once that was over, they escaped into their own private world where he taught his bride about passion, and in the process discovered that while he'd had many lovers, he'd never experienced the heartfelt tenderness he felt with Elizabeth.

They'd made one midnight excursion down to Austin's private study on their second night together. Saying he had a surprise for her, he made her close her eyes while he led her by the hand into his study. A fire glowed in the grate, bathing the room with gentle warmth. She looked around the room and spotted the framed sketch she'd given him hung in a place of honor on the wall opposite his desk.

He came up behind her and wrapped his arms around her waist. "Every time I look up I'll see it and think of you," he said quietly. He'd then spent the next hour teaching her to waltz, only to learn that the dance was much more sensuous than he'd ever believed. While Elizabeth may not have been the most graceful dancer he'd ever partnered, he'd never enjoyed himself more.

They ended up making slow, leisurely love on the thick carpet in front of the fire, and Austin knew he would never again enter his study without envisioning Elizabeth on the rug, her eyes filled with desire, her arms reaching out to him.

Now, her lips brushed the side of his neck. God, this woman made him happy, a fact that simultaneously unsettled, confused, and elated him. They'd spent many tender moments together over the past few days, laughing, talking, yet she hadn't confided her secrets about the sadness that had driven her from America. He'd broached the subject once, but she'd immediately turned the conversation to something else. To his surprise, her reluctance to discuss her past bothered him and he found himself waiting for her to tell him, hoping that she'd tell him.

"What would you like to do today?" he asked, his hands lightly caressing her soft skin.

"Hmmm . . . I'm doing it right now."

"Indeed? What's that?"

"Holding you. Feeling you next to me. Feeling you inside me." Tipping her head back, she looked at him with somber eyes that swam with emotion. She tenderly placed her hand against his face. "Touching you. Loving you."

Did she mean she loved him? Or simply "loving you" to equate "making love with you"? He didn't know, and although he'd never wanted a woman's love before, he suddenly found himself wanting to hear words of love for him pass Elizabeth's lips.

There was no denying his marriage of convenience was taking a very unexpected turn. And the vulnerable, confusing feelings hitting him were something he wasn't sure he liked at all.

She traced her fingertips over his brows. "What would *you* like to do today?"

"I'd *like* to stay right here with you and make love all afternoon, but I'm afraid there's some work that needs my attention."

"Is there anything I can do to help you?"

He smiled at the eagerness in her voice. "I'm afraid not. My work involves several errands and a great deal of boring correspondence."

"Perhaps I could accompany you on your errands?"

"I fear I must handle them alone." He was not about to bring her to the riverfront. "You'd be far too much of a distraction. My mind would be on you, not business."

She stilled and laid her hands against his face. "You're keeping something from me. You're going somewhere you don't want me to go." A sigh escaped her. "Austin. Let me help you."

Damn, could the woman see straight into his soul? An unsettling question at best. Could she see his growing affection for her?

Affection? He nearly rolled his eyes at the flavorless word that in no way adequately described what he felt for her. The idea that she might see or feel things he was not yet prepared to share disconcerted him, but she'd made no further mention of her visions or reading his thoughts.

He ran his finger down the bridge of her nose. As for taking her to the places he needed to go, it was out of the question. He couldn't expose her to danger or—

"You don't want to expose me to danger. I understand. But I'll be with *you*. I'll be perfectly safe."

"I cannot take you to these places, Elizabeth. They're seedy, to say the least. Not at all the sort of places a lady goes to."

"Exactly what are you planning?"

He considered not telling her, but he found he was oddly reluctant to lie to her.

"Do you recall my telling you at the ruins that I'd hired a Bow Street Runner to find information about a Frenchman I saw with William shortly before he died?"

"Yes. You'd planned to meet the Runner that night."

"Correct. Well, I've received information that the Frenchman I seek—a man I know only as Gaspard—was recently seen in a pub and gaming hell near the riverfront. I'm going there to find him."

"Why?"

Because the bastard is threatening everything I hold dear. He could destroy my family . . . which you are now a part of. In spite of his reluctance, he knew he'd have to lie. "I have reason to believe he stole several items from William. I want them back."

"Why not let your investigator find him?"

"I wish to follow up on this lead while it's still hot."

She regarded him steadily through serious eyes. "I want to accompany you."

"Absolutely not."

"Don't you realize that I could help you? Can you not at least *try* to believe that I could? I might sense something that could aid you in your search. If I touch something he touched or a person he spoke to, perhaps I could feel him . . . his whereabouts."

"Damn it, I know you want to help me, and while I cannot deny you possess a keen intuition, you're not a magician. There is simply no way you can assist me with this. And the idea of taking you to the slums of London is out of the question. I appreciate your concern, but—"

"But you won't allow me to come with you."

"No. The riverfront is dangerous. If any harm came to you, I'd never forgive himself."

"Yet you put yourself in danger."

"The risk is not nearly as great for a man."

Frustration simmered in her eyes. "What must I do to prove to you that I can help you?"

Prove that her so-called visions would lead him to Gaspard? A man Bow Street's finest talent could not find? He wished to hell he could believe that, but he'd given up on fairy tales long ago.

"There is nothing you can do," he said quietly, hating the hurt his words brought to her eyes, but he had no choice.

Elizabeth could not help him.

Of that he was certain.

Elizabeth walked down the stairs carrying a copy of *Sense and Sensibility*, one of the many books Austin had bought her yesterday. She had no desire to read, but with her stomach cramped with tension from worrying about Austin being at the riverfront, she was desperate for any diversion.

Standing in the marble-tiled foyer, she looked uncertainly from left to right. Perhaps she could first find the kitchens and pilfer a cup of cider?

"May I help you, your grace?" a deep voice intoned.

"Oh!" Her hand flew to her breast. "Carters! You startled me."

"Please forgive me, your grace." He bowed from the waist, then stood so stiffly erect she wondered if someone had stuck a plank down the back of his breeches.

"Think nothing of it, Carters," she said with a smile that went unanswered. "Can you please direct me to the kitchens?"

Carters stared at her, his face devoid of all expression. "The *kitchens*, your grace?"

A wave of dismay washed over her at the butler's forbidding tone. She drew herself up and smiled at him again. "Yes. I would like some cider."

"There's no need for you to *ever* enter the kitchens, your grace. I'll arrange at once for a footman to bring you some cider." He turned on his heel and started walking away, presumably to summon a footman.

She noticed his limp immediately. She was certain he hadn't been limping when she first met him. She studied his retreating form for several seconds, assessing his uneven gait. "Carters?"

The butler stopped and turned to face her. "Yes, your grace?"

"I hope you won't think me rude, but I couldn't help but notice your limp."

For a split second he looked startled. Then his mask of blandness fell back into place. "It's nothing, your grace."

"Nonsense. It's obviously something." She approached him, and when she stood directly before him, she suppressed a laugh. The top of his bald head came only to her nose. "Have you suffered an accident of some sort?"

"No, your grace. 'Tis merely my new footwear. The leather is quite stiff and not broken in yet."

"I see." She glanced down at his shiny black shoes and nodded in understanding. "You're suffering from a blister?"

"Yes, your grace. Several." He raised his chin. "But they'd never prevent me from fulfilling my duties."

"Heavens, I never thought they would. Anyone can see you're the soul of competence. I'm merely concerned that you're suffering." She smiled at the dour-faced man. "Has anyone treated your blisters? The doctor, perhaps?"

"Certainly not, your grace," he huffed, his shoulders thrown back so far Elizabeth marveled that he remained upright instead of falling over backward.

"I see. Where is the library, Carters?"

The butler pointed. "'Tis the third door on the left down this corridor, your grace."

"Fine. Meet me there in five minutes, please." She turned to go back up the stairs.

"In the library, your grace?"

"Yes. In five minutes." With that she swept up the stairs.

"Do you know what's become of my duchess?" Austin asked an under butler, striding into the foyer. He'd returned from the riverfront and had been looking for Elizabeth for nearly a quarter hour without success.

"She is in the library, your grace."

Austin gazed around the otherwise empty foyer. "Where is Carters?"

"I believe he's with the duchess in the library, your grace."

A moment later Austin strode into the library and stopped dead in his tracks. His wife was kneeling before his butler, who sat in Austin's favorite wing chair. Carters was barefoot, and the legs of his breeches had been rolled back several times, revealing skinny, hairy calves.

Austin watched from the doorway in stupefied disbelief as Elizabeth deftly placed Carters's bare foot upon her lap and proceeded to rub his heel and sole with some sort of cream. Just when Austin believed he could not possibly be more astonished, something happened that made his jaw drop.

He saw Carters smile. *Smile!*

A more proper, dour, *chillingly* correct butler than Carters didn't draw breath in all of England. In all the years Carters had served his family, Austin had never seen the man so much as crack a grin. Not even a tiny twitching of his lips. Until now.

But what happened next caused Austin's jaw to drop farther. He heard a deep-throated chuckle come from Carters's throat. The man was chuckling, for God's sake.

Austin shook his head to clear it. If he didn't know better, he'd swear the scene before him was the result of too much brandy. But he was stone cold sober. So it had to be real. Didn't it? Gathering his startled wits, he walked across the room.

"What's going on here?" he asked, approaching his wife who never ceased to amaze him and his butler whom he apparently didn't know at all. Elizabeth sent him a searching gaze, her eyes filled with concern. Carters looked absolutely stricken. Austin nodded to Elizabeth and sent her a reassuring look that drained the tension from her face.

"Your grace!" the butler exclaimed, his face flushing a mottled red. He attempted to stand, but Elizabeth shook her head.

"Stay seated, Carters," she ordered firmly. "I'm almost finished." Carters coughed and sank back into the chair. She lowered his one foot to the floor and picked up the other one, gently applying a small amount of salve from a wooden bowl. Her bag of medicines sat open on the floor beside her.

Austin cleared his throat. "What on earth are you doing to Carters, Elizabeth?" he asked, his eyes riveted to the extraordinary sight of his duchess tenderly administering to his formidable butler's feet.

"Poor Carters has terrible blisters from his new shoes," she explained, wrapping the foot with a clean bandage. "They were bleeding and stood a good chance of becoming infected, so I cleaned his wounds and prepared a healing salve to relieve his discomfort." She tucked the end of the bandage in and set Carters' trousers to rights. "There! All finished. You may replace your stockings and shoes now, Carters."

Carters hurriedly complied.

"How do your feet feel?" Elizabeth asked.

Carters stood, bounced several times on the balls of his feet, then took a few tentative steps. Pure amazement spread across his thin face. "Why, they don't hurt a bit, your grace." He walked back and forth in front of her several times.

"Excellent." She handed Carters the bowl. "Put this in your quarters and place a wet handkerchief over it to keep it moist. Apply the cream before you go to sleep and again in the morning. Your blisters will be gone in no time."

Carters accepted the bowl from Elizabeth and shot an uncertain glance at Austin. "Thank you, your grace. You've been most kind."

"It was my pleasure, Carters. If you need any help applying your bandages, let me know. And I'll have that poultice ready for you to bring to your mother tomorrow." Elizabeth smiled an angel's smile at him and Carters grinned back like a besotted schoolboy.

"That will be all, Carters," Austin said, cocking his head toward the door in a pointed fashion.

At the sound of his employer's voice, Carters apparently remembered himself. He straightened, jerked his jacket into place, and wiped his face clean of all expression. Turning smartly on his heel, he quit the room with barely a limp, closing the door behind him.

The instant the door clicked shut, Elizabeth jumped to her feet and asked, "Did you discover anything?"

"No. I was able to confirm that Gaspard has indeed been in the area, but I didn't find him."

"I'm sorry." Her gaze searched his face. "Are you all right?"

"I'm fine. Disappointed, but fine." Needing to touch her, he slid his arms around her waist and drew her to him. She felt so damn good in his arms, and he resolutely pushed away the memories of the filth he'd seen that afternoon. "I am also amazed. I've never seen Carters so much as crack a grin, and you had him *laughing*." He dropped a quick kiss onto her nose. "Unbelievable."

"He's not nearly as formidable as I thought," she remarked, resting her palms on his lapels. "He's actually rather sweet."

"Carters? Sweet? Good God, now I've heard

everything." He rolled his eyes heavenward and she laughed. "I must say, seeing you kneeling before my butler, doctoring his feet, surprised me."

"Why is that?"

"It's not something normally done by a duchess, Elizabeth. You shouldn't be so familiar with the servants. And you certainly shouldn't have their bare feet perched on your lap." He smiled to take some of the sting out of his rebuke, but she took immediate umbrage.

"Carters was in pain, Austin. You cannot expect me to allow someone to suffer simply because I'm a duchess and it is therefore deemed *improper* to help." She raised her chin a notch, her eyes shooting sparks of challenge. "I'm afraid I feel quite strongly about this."

A mixture of respect and irritation suffused him. He wasn't used to being defied, but it had been obvious since the moment they'd met, Elizabeth cared not a fig for his lofty title or position. The fact that she stood before him, eyes flashing, gaze unflinching, not backing away from his possible anger, filled him with pride and respect for her. She knew how to doctor people, and she was going to do it, by God, whether he liked it or not.

And who the hell was he to argue about her flouting propriety? God knows he'd done so himself on many occasions, most recently when he'd taken an American as his duchess. Bloody hell, he felt like hugging her. Of course, it wasn't necessary to let *her* know that. Instead he arranged his face into a suitably serious expression.

"Well, I suppose if helping those who suffer is *that* important to you—"

"I assure you it is."

"And it would please you to have my blessing and approval?"

"Very much."

"And if I refuse?"

She didn't hesitate for a second. "Then I shall be forced to help people without your blessing and approval."

"I see." She was so magnificent, he wanted to applaud her for her courage and spirit in spite of her defiance.

Cupping a gentle hand to his face, she said, "Please understand, Austin. I have no wish to defy you or anger you, but I simply cannot stand to see suffering. Neither can you, you know. You're far too kind and noble to allow others to be in pain."

Austin drew her closer to him, inordinately pleased that his wife thought him kind and noble.

"I'm so relieved that you're home," she whispered next to his ear. Her warm breath tickled him, sending a legion of pleasurable chills down his back. "I was so worried . . . I couldn't have borne it had anything happened to you."

The "Elizabeth" feeling rushed through him like the floodgates had opened. *She cared about him.* And if this extraordinary woman cared about him, perhaps he wasn't so bad after all.

Emotion welled in his throat. Leaning back, he framed her face between his hands and gently stroked his thumbs over her smooth cheeks. "I'm fine, Elizabeth." A teasing grin pulled at his lips. "Perhaps not so robust as you, but fine nonetheless. And you have my blessing and approval to heal anyone you wish. On one condition."

"That being?"

He lowered his mouth until it hovered just over hers. "I insist on receiving the bulk of your tender ministrations."

She wound her arms around his neck. "Of course, your grace." Leaning into him, she pressed against his very obvious arousal. "Oh, my," she whispered. "It appears you need some administering to right now. I believe we should begin. At once."

"An excellent suggestion," he agreed huskily as his lips claimed hers. She sighed his name and guilt wrapped around him like a noose.

He knew she would not be pleased when he told her he planned to return to the waterfront that evening.

Chapter 15

Robert, Caroline, Miles, and the dowager duchess stood in the foyer of Austin's London town house, surrendering their shawls, jackets, hats, and bonnets to Carters.

"Where are the duke and duchess?" Caroline asked the butler after he'd finished seeing to their outer garments.

"In the library, Lady Caroline. I shall announce you."

Robert watched Carters stride down the corridor. Stopping in front of the library door, he knocked discreetly. After nearly a minute passed, he knocked again.

When another full minute passed with no response, a knot of worry pulled Robert's insides. With Bow Street Runners turning up dead, and now Austin not answering the door . . . damn it all! Turning to Miles, he asked in an undertone, "Do you think something is wrong?"

A concerned frown knitted Miles's brow. "I don't know, but based on recent events, I'd say it's possible."

"Well, I'm not going to stand about in the foyer any longer," Robert whispered. He strode down the corridor,

Miles right behind him. Footsteps echoed behind them, indicating the others had followed as well.

"Is something amiss, Carters?" Robert asked.

Carters drew himself up straight as a stick. "Certainly not. I am merely waiting for his grace to bid me to enter."

"Are you certain he's in the library?" Miles asked.

"Positive." Carters knocked once more, again receiving no response.

Robert and Miles exchanged glances. "The hell with this," Robert muttered. He reached around Carters and opened the door, ignoring the butler's outraged gasp.

Stepping over the threshold, Robert halted so abruptly, Miles slammed into his back and nearly knocked him over.

He puffed out a relieved breath. Clearly his worries for his brother's well-being were unfounded, for Austin was obviously in fine form and unquestionably . . . healthy.

He held Elizabeth in a close embrace, kissing her passionately. Robert suspected Austin's broad back kept everyone from seeing whatever else they were up to. As it was, they all heard Elizabeth's unmistakable sigh of pleasure.

"Ahem!" Robert cleared his throat.

Austin and Elizabeth appeared not to notice.

"AHEM!" Robert tried again, louder.

Austin raised his head. "Not now, Carters," he growled, not bothering to turn around.

"Sorry to disappoint you, old man, but it's not Carters," Robert announced.

Austin stilled. The unwelcome sound of his brother's voice brought a vicious oath to his lips that he barely managed to smother. Emitting a startled gasp, Elizabeth tried to move from his embrace, but he kept her firmly clasped to him, reluctantly withdrawing his hand from inside her bodice. He looked at her and stifled a groan of longing. With her cheeks flushed with color, her lips moist and swollen from his kisses, and her coiffure not nearly so neat as it had been ten minutes earlier, she looked absolutely perfect.

He muttered a savage curse under his breath. He needed to do something about his brother. Throwing him into the Thames crossed his mind. Yes. That was an idea that definitely had merit. He turned to greet his unexpected guest only to discover that Robert was not alone. Miles, Caroline, his mother, and Carters all crowded in the doorway.

Carters stepped into the room, his normally blank face a picture of distress. "Forgive me, your grace. I knocked several times but—"

Austin cut off his words with a wave of his hand. "It's all right, Carters." Damn it, in all fairness, the man could have pounded on the door with a hammer and Austin doubted he would have heard him. "You may return to your duties."

"Yes, your grace." Jerking his jacket into place, Carters turned on his heel and quit the room, but not before leveling a sniff of disapproval in Robert's direction.

Austin's mother came forward and extended both hands. "Hello, darling, hello, Elizabeth. How are you?"

His mother was clearly so delighted to see them, some of Austin's annoyance evaporated. While Elizabeth greeted the others, he bent and kissed his mother's cheek. "I'm very well, Mother."

An elegant brow quirked in obvious amusement. "Yes, I can see that." She leaned close and said in an undertone, "Don't worry, dear. We're staying at Miles's town house."

He hoped his relief didn't show. After greeting Caroline, he nodded curtly at Miles, then glared at Robert. "What brings you all here?"

"Robert and Miles were traveling to Town," his mother said, "and invited Caroline and me to join them."

"It's a wonderful surprise," Elizabeth said. "We're delighted to see you."

Robert had the distinct impression Elizabeth spoke only for herself when she made that statement, as Austin looked anything *but* delighted. Now that he knew Austin and Elizabeth were all right, relief washed over him, easing the tension gripping his shoulders.

There were serious matters to discuss, but Robert couldn't speak of them in front of the women, and if he immediately asked Austin to leave the room, he knew his mother and Caroline, and no doubt Elizabeth as well, would be all a-twitter with curiosity. He had no desire to explain the real reason behind this visit to them.

While Elizabeth offered her guests seats and made arrangements for tea and refreshments, Robert approached his brother, who hadn't moved from his spot on the other side of the room. Austin greeted him with an arctic glare.

"I'm newly married, Robert. Perhaps you've forgotten?"

"Of course I haven't forgotten."

"Then what the hell could have possessed you to come here *uninvited*, dragging *them* along with you?" Austin jerked his head in the direction of the others, but his chilling gaze never left Robert's face.

Before Robert could reply, Austin continued, "So when are you leaving?"

"Leaving? Why, we've only just arrived." A devil inside him made him ask, "Aren't you happy to see us?"

"No."

"Pity. And here I thought to save you from the boredom you're no doubt starting to feel after three interminable days of marriage. Obviously you're dumbstruck with gratitude."

"Get out."

Robert made a *tsk*ing sound. "How incredibly ungracious you've become since you've wed."

Austin leaned his hips back against the huge mahogany desk, folded his arms across his chest, and crossed his ankles. "You have exactly two minutes to tell me everything you wish to say, then you will, regrettably, have to leave. Mother says you're all staying with Miles. Surely you wish to get settled."

Shooting a surreptitious glance across the room, Robert saw that the ladies were busy chatting. He raised his brows at Miles, who immediately excused himself from the women and joined Robert and Austin across the room.

Stepping closer to Austin, Robert said in an undertone, "There is actually a particular reason Miles and I are here."

"You mean other than to plague me?"

"Yes. But it's something we must discuss in private."

Austin narrowed his eyes on his brother's face. It was sometimes difficult to tell when Robert was teasing, but his grave expression seemed genuine. Miles, Austin noted, appeared equally intense.

"Perhaps we could retire to your study?" Miles suggested.

Austin alternated his glance between their serious expressions. "All right."

He had a strong suspicion that he was not going to like what Robert and Miles had to say.

He definitely hadn't liked what Robert and Miles had to say.

A dead body on his property. A Bow Street Runner.

Alone in his study, Austin paced the Axminster carpet,

his thoughts in turmoil, his gut churning with tension. There was no doubt in his mind that the dead man was James Kinney.

Bloody hell, no wonder Kinney hadn't shown up for their meeting. The poor fellow had been lying facedown in the bushes, half of his head blown away.

Robert's words echoed in his mind. *We thought it best to remove Caroline and Mother from the property, just in case there's a lunatic prowling about, although the magistrate said it was most likely a robbery.*

Robbery? Austin shook his head. No, Kinney had been bringing him information about Gaspard. And now Kinney was dead.

What had he discovered? Whatever it was, it was important enough to have been killed for. And there was no doubt in his mind who had killed him.

He raked a shaking hand through his hair. It was clear that Gaspard was not only a blackmailer, but a murderer as well. A murderer who claimed to have proof that William was a traitor. A murderer who could, at any moment, expose that information and ruin Austin's family.

I won't allow that to happen. What the hell would happen to Mother and Caroline? To Robert? To Elizabeth?

Damn it! What a mess. Kinney must have been killed the night they were supposed to meet . . . shot in the head, poor bastard. Probably the gunshot was what had spooked Myst—

He went completely still.

Elizabeth's words came back to him, drumming through his brain. *In my vision I was certain I heard a gunshot. I sensed death. Very strongly. I'm just so thankful you weren't shot.*

God Almighty. He grabbed the arm of the settee for balance and slowly lowered himself onto the cushion, the ramifications crashing over him like falling bricks.

There was only one possible explanation for her words—only one way she could have known.

She'd known there was danger at the ruins. She'd envisioned a gunshot—and death. Only instead of *him* being the victim as she'd thought, James Kinney was.

She didn't merely possess uncanny intuition, she could actually *see* events from the past. Events from the future. How could that be? It boggled his mind. There was no scientific or even logical explanation for her bewildering talent, but he could no longer deny it existed.

Elizabeth's visions were real.

And if her visions were real . . .

His heart and breath both stalled. That first night he'd met her . . . in the garden . . . she'd told him that she'd seen William.

And she'd claimed he was alive.

Jesus. Could his brother be alive?

Elizabeth answered the urgent tapping on her bedchamber door. Austin strode inside. "Are we alone?" he asked.

"Yes." She closed the door and looked at him. Her smile immediately faded. "What is wrong?"

"I need to speak with you."

"About what?"

He approached her, halting when only a foot separated them. "Touch me," he whispered. When she hesitated, he reached out and grabbed her wrists. "Put your hands on me." He flattened her palms against his shirt and laid his hands on top of hers. "What do you see?"

Confused by his request, but moved by the urgency in his voice, she splayed her fingers over the fine lawn. His heartbeat thumped against her palms. Myriad images flashed through her mind, and she closed her eyes, trying to make sense of them. And suddenly she did.

Her eyes flew open. "You discovered something about the gunshot I heard. Someone was shot."

He nodded slowly. "Yes. His name was James Kinney. He was the Bow Street Runner I'd hired to find Gaspard. He had information for me."

"And someone killed him."

"Yes."

"Gaspard?"

"I believe so." He drew a deep breath. "Elizabeth, the night we met you told me William was alive." He pressed her hands more firmly against him. "Are you certain? Can you see him? Can you tell me where he is?"

She went utterly still. For the space of several heartbeats, she stopped breathing and hot tears pushed at her eyes. "Dear God. You believe me. You believe I can see things."

His gaze burned into hers. "Yes, I believe you. There can be no other explanation for the things you know. Can you help me find William?"

"I . . . I want to, but I don't know if I can. I have little control over the visions. They're unpredictable. Sometimes when I most want to see things, I can't."

"Will you try?"

"Yes. Yes, of course." The quiet desperation in his voice galvanized her to action. Taking his hands, she clasped them between her palms and closed her eyes. She prayed she'd see the answers he sought, but she did not. Determined, she concentrated harder, stronger, until her head felt ready to burst. And then she saw it.

Opening her eyes, she looked at his grave face and wished she had better news.

"Did you see anything at all?"

"He's alive, Austin. But . . . he's in danger."

His face paled. "Where is he?"

"I don't know."

"Is he being held against his will?"

"I'm sorry . . . I cannot say."

He slipped a folded letter from his pocket and handed it to her. "Can you tell anything from this?"

She pressed the vellum between her palms and closed her eyes. "I feel evil. Menace. I feel a connection to William. Whoever wrote this is somehow connected to your brother." She opened her eyes and handed him the letter, which he tucked back into his pocket.

"Did you see anything else?"

"Only a vague impression that we shall soon have to travel somewhere." She studied his face, which appeared set in stone, and her breath caught. "Dear God, you're planning to go back to the riverfront."

"I have to. It is more imperative than ever that I find Gaspard."

She nodded slowly. "Very well. But I'm going with you."

"Absolutely not. Gaspard is even more dangerous than I'd thought. I cannot allow—"

"*I* cannot allow you to go without me. I may be able to sense his presence, and I simply refuse to argue with you. As for the problem of bringing a lady to the riverfront, there is an easy solution."

"There certainly is—leaving you at home."

"I shall disguise myself as a man," she continued as if he hadn't spoken. Taking advantage of his stunned silence, she rushed on, "Don't you see it's a perfect plan? I'm certainly tall enough to pass for a man. All we need to do is dress me appropriately and hide my hair under a hat."

"There is nothing appropriate about that suggestion, Elizabeth."

"It would be inappropriate only if one of us told someone. I have no intention of doing that. Do you?"

"What if someone saw through your disguise?" He

shook his head. "Bloody hell, did I actually ask that question? As if I were considering this madness?"

"Are these places well lit?"

"No, but—"

"Are they crowded?"

"Usually, but—"

"Then I see no cause for worry. I shall simply be another man in a semidark, crowded room." She lifted her chin a notch. "Now, how do you propose we go about getting me some gentleman's clothing?"

"I don't recall agreeing to this insane scheme of yours."

"Perhaps not, but I'm certain you meant to." She squeezed his hands. "This will work, Austin. I know it will. I can help you find Gaspard. I can help you find William."

Austin studied her earnest face. Without a doubt, he believed her. She could help him. But he didn't want her help at the price of her safety.

"Let me do this for you," she said quietly. "At least allow me to try. Just once."

He exhaled slowly, hating himself for considering her offer, but unable to disregard it. How could he contemplate turning down an opportunity to find William alive? And to stop Gaspard's schemes?

He fixed his gaze on her. "I suppose we could try—"

"Of course we can."

"You will remain by my side—"

"Every moment. I swear."

"I don't believe you've allowed me to finish a sentence in the last five minutes."

"Hmmm. You may be right. Of course, look at all the time I've saved us."

Slipping his hands from between hers, he cupped her face. "I won't allow any harm to come to you. I swear it."

A tender smile pulled at her lips. "I know, Austin. I feel perfectly safe with you."

Warmth spread through him at her simple statement. Her obvious faith and trust in him humbled him. And filled him with guilt. Damn it, he was using her, her abilities, to his own end, but he had to find Gaspard. And William. Dear God, William . . .

"What time do you want to leave this evening?" she asked, jerking his thoughts back to the matter at hand.

"My family and Miles are joining us for dinner, although I'm not certain how that came about, and then they are all going to the theater. We'll depart on our mission after they leave."

"Won't they wonder why we're not going to the theater?"

"I doubt it. We're newly married. I'm sure they'll assume we'd rather spend time here by ourselves."

Her cheeks flushed. "You mean they'll think we're . . ." Her voice trailed off into embarrassed silence.

Stepping closer, he drew her into his arms and pressed his lips to the sensitive skin just below her ear. "Yes, they'll think we're making love."

"How utterly . . . scandalous. What on earth will your mother think of me?"

"She'll be thrilled that we're getting on so well." He studied her flushed face. "Are you certain you're up to joining me this evening?"

"Of course. You know how robust I am."

"Indeed I do." He dropped a quick kiss on her forehead and stepped back. "Now I must go to Bow Street to report what I know about James Kinney. I'll see you in the drawing room at seven."

*   *   *

Austin sat through dinner that evening wishing his family would take their leave. He had much to think about, mainly the fact that William was probably alive. And in danger.

How the hell had the military authorities mistaken the matter of his death? Where was he? Was he still engaging in traitorous activities? *Ah, William . . . how did I fail you?*

But it was impossible to properly collect his thoughts with his family present. His normally self-contained mother was all but bouncing in her seat at the opposite end of the table, enthusiastically chatting with Elizabeth.

Caroline and Robert were engaged in a lively disagreement punctuated by lots of eye rolling and, when their mother wasn't looking, stuck-out tongues, a favorite childish gesture neither had outgrown. Austin noticed that Miles was the only silent member of the group, no doubt because the man couldn't wedge a word in anywhere.

The moment the meal ended, Austin stood and walked to the foot of the table where Elizabeth sat. "If you'll excuse us, I believe Elizabeth and I shall retire. Enjoy your evening." Holding out his hand, he assisted her to her feet, his fingers wrapping around her gloved hand.

Caroline's eyes widened. "*Retire?* At this hour?"

"Yes," Austin said calmly, purposely ignoring the smirks Miles and Robert weren't even attempting to hide.

"But it's so early! Don't you want—" Caroline's words snapped off and she glared across the table at Robert. "Did you just *kick* me?"

"Yes. But only because I can't reach you to stuff my napkin in your mouth." He waggled his fingers at Austin, then winked at Elizabeth. "Good night, Austin. Sweet dreams, Elizabeth."

Without further ado, Austin led Elizabeth from the dining room and up the stairs. He didn't pause until he'd closed his bedchamber door behind them. Leaning against it, he surveyed his wife's flaming face.

"Heavens above, I'll never be able to face them again," she said, pacing across the rug. "They all think we're doing *that*."

An overwhelming desire to do *that* slammed into him like a fist to his gut. He was restless and edgy and the mere thought of touching her ignited him. Pushing away from the door, he walked toward her. As she paced by him, he reached out, snagged her arm, and pulled her against him. Looking into her startled eyes, he murmured, "Well, as long as they all think so, we shouldn't disappoint them."

"I thought you wanted to leave as soon as they depart for the theater."

He reached behind her and began unbuttoning her bodice. "I do, but it will take them half an hour to ready themselves. Besides, you need to get into your costume, and as long as you'll be out of this gown, I suggest we make the most of the opportunity." Slipping the last button free, he eased the gown down her arms, then let go. It puddled at her feet.

"Heavens. No doubt I should develop the vapors at such a scandalous suggestion."

He trailed his fingertips over her breasts. "Vapors? Shall I ring for the hartshorn?"

"That won't be necessary. Fortunately I possess a most—"

"Robust constitution. Yes, that is indeed . . . fortunate."

"Oh, my. Your tone indicates a need for stamina. What did you have in mind? A race?"

"Well, I do want to leave in half an hour." Her chemise joined her gown at her ankles. The sight of her, naked and impossibly beautiful, a half shy, half devilish smile lighting her face, tightened his throat. Bloody hell, she moved him like no other woman ever had.

This *feeling* she inspired in him confused and confounded him. It was more than wanting. It was a *need*. A soul-wrenching need to touch her, feel her.

He drew her into his arms and kissed her deeply, endlessly, his muscles straining with the effort of bringing her closer, holding her tighter. Turning them, he backed her against the wall, pinning her in place while his mouth devoured hers and his hands skimmed down her sides.

She responded to his every touch, wrapping her arms around his neck and pressing herself against him until he could feel her heart slamming against his own.

"Austin . . . please . . ."

Her plea snapped something inside him. *Please.* God, yes, please. He was about to burst. He needed her. Now. *Now.*

Reaching between them, he all but tore his breeches open, then hauled her upward. "Wrap your legs around me," he ground out in a voice he didn't recognize.

With wide eyes, she obeyed and he slipped inside her. Her heat engulfed him, squeezing him in a velvety fist. Gripping her hips, he moved within her, his thrusts rough and fast. His brow beaded with sweat and his choppy breathing burned his lungs. With one final thrust, his climax battered him. Burying his head against her shoulder, he clenched his fingers into her hips, and for an endless moment, he pulsed inside her, spilling his seed and part of his soul into her.

It took a moment for sanity to return. When it did, he lifted his head and looked at her. Her eyes were closed, her face pale. Guilt hit him like a rock.

What the hell was wrong with him? He'd just taken his wife *against the wall*. As if she were some dockside whore. Without a thought to her feelings or pleasure. He'd probably hurt her. He looked down and saw the red marks his fingers had branded on her hips. She must think him a monster.

As gently as he could, he eased himself from her. Her legs unclasped from his waist and slid down. She would have sagged onto the floor if he hadn't grabbed her. *Damn* it! She couldn't even stand! How badly had he hurt her?

Holding her with one arm around her waist, he brushed a tangled auburn lock from her forehead. "Elizabeth. God. I'm sorry. Are you all right?"

Her eyelids fluttered and slowly opened. He braced himself for the condemnation he knew he'd see in her eyes, the angry words he deserved.

Her golden brown eyes focused on his. "I'm utterly marvelous. Who won?"

"Won?"

A small smiled played around her lips. "The race. I believe I won, but I'm willing to concede."

"I . . . didn't hurt you?"

"Certainly not. Of course, my knees feel like porridge, but that is an affliction that happens every time you touch me." Concern clouded her eyes. "Did I hurt *you*?"

Relief hit him so hard, his own knees nearly sagged. A lump lodged in his throat and he had to force the word around it. "No."

He needed to explain, to apologize, but how could he explain what he didn't understand himself? He *never* lost control like that. He didn't know the words, but he certainly owed it to her to try.

Before he could speak, however, she brushed her lips over his. "I believe we still have ten minutes left," she whispered against his mouth. "Do you really want to spend them talking?"

A half laugh, half groan escaped him. He should have

known to expect the unexpected from her. Bending, he scooped her up into his arms and headed toward the bed.

As long as she was willing, there were at least half a dozen things he wanted to do in the next ten minutes.

And talking was most definitely not one of them.

Chapter 16

Thirty minutes later, Elizabeth stood in front of the cheval glass and stared at her reflection. Even her own parents would not recognize her.

Snug black breeches hugged her legs. Scuffed boots, slightly too large, covered her feet. A billowing white man's shirt and cravat hid her wrapped bosom. With her hair firmly tucked under a sailor's cap pulled low over her eyes, she could easily pass for a tall, slim young man. Once she donned the black coat hanging on the bedpost, no one would ever realize she was a woman, let alone a duchess.

The bedchamber door opened and Austin walked in. "All right. Everyone has departed for the theater. Are you"—he caught sight of her and his footsteps faltered—"ready?"

She turned to face him. "Yes. What do you think?"

His gaze traveled from her head to her toes, then back again. Then he approached her, his expression downright grim.

Halting directly in front of her, he said between clearly clenched teeth, "You are not leaving the house dressed like that."

She planted her hands on her hips. "May I ask why not? This is a perfect disguise. No one will guess I'm not a man."

"The hell they won't. The way those breeches fit you . . ." He waved his hand around, his lips clamped into a flat line. "It's indecent."

"Indecent! *You* gave them to me!"

"I didn't know you'd look like *that* in them."

She tapped her booted foot. "Like what?"

"Like . . ." Again he waved his hand about, as if trying to conjure the word he was seeking from thin air. "Like *that*," he finally said.

A sigh escaped her. Clearly he was going to allow a misplaced sense of propriety to ruin their plan. Pulling the black coat from the bedpost, she slipped it on and buttoned it.

"Look," she said, turning in a slow circle before him. "I'm covered from chin to knee."

He continued to glower. After she'd turned before him twice, he all but growled, "That coat stays on every minute. On and buttoned. This pub we're going to where Gaspard was seen caters to a very rough crowd. The results could be disastrous should anyone there suspect you're a woman."

"I understand."

His gaze riveted on her cap. "How secure is that?"

"Like it was nailed to my head."

His expression didn't relax one iota and for a moment she feared he would truly refuse to bring her along. Arranging her features into what she hoped was studied calm, she simply stood and waited.

He finally spoke. "Let's go."

She followed him from the room, careful to hide her relief. And apprehension. She certainly didn't want to be left at home.

For she knew something important would happen tonight.

A half hour later, when the hired hack drew to a stop in front of a dilapidated building, Elizabeth drew the curtain aside several inches and peered into the darkness. Although she didn't know exactly where they were, the stench of rotting fish indicated their proximity to the riverfront. Her nostrils twitched in protest.

"Are you ready, Elizabeth?"

She jerked her attention away from the window and looked across at Austin. Even in the dim light she could see his frown. Tension was all but emanating from him in dark waves. Hoping to dispel his obvious disquiet, she forced a smile. "Yes, I'm ready."

He did not return her smile. "Do you understand exactly what I want you to do?"

"Of course. If I sense anything, I'll inform you immediately."

Although she would have thought it impossible, his frown grew grimmer. "Thank you, but that is not what I meant."

A frown pinched her own brow. "I don't understand. I thought you wanted me to tell you if I felt anything."

"I do. But you must not leave my side."

"I won't. I—"

He reached out and grabbed both her hands in his, cutting off her words. His intense stare sent shivers tingling across her skin. "Promise me," he said in an urgent whisper.

"I promise, but—"

"No buts. This is an exceedingly dangerous place. I cannot protect you if you wander away from me. Is my meaning clear?"

"Perfectly. Consider me sewn to your sleeve."

He blew out a breath. "Damn it, this a not a good idea. A thousand things could go wrong."

"A thousand things could go right."

"I'm placing you in danger."

"I'm in no more danger than you."

He released her and shoved his hands through his hair. "The more I think on this whole matter, the more I'm convinced this is not a wise idea. I'm instructing the driver to take you home." He made a move to open the door.

She slapped his wrist. "No."

He quirked an ebony brow at her.

"If you make me go home, I'll simply hire another hack and return here."

His gaze bore into hers like a spear of fire. She'd never seen him this angry and although she knew he wouldn't hurt her, a chill edged down her spine at the banked fury in his eyes.

"You'll do nothing of the kind," he said very slowly and distinctly.

"I will if I must." Before he could voice another objection, she cradled his frowning face between her palms. "Do you believe I can help you?"

He studied her for a long moment and she wondered if he had any idea how the shadows in his eyes hurt her. She sensed he withheld something from her—some dark, terrible secret that ate at his soul, and she suspected he deliberately held back his feelings and thoughts from her so she'd have no chance to "see" them.

Dear God, his torment was painful to see. If only he would trust her with his secrets . . . and see how much she wanted, *needed*, to help him.

How much she loved him.

She'd never said the words, not quite ready to voice the depth of her feelings out loud, and also not convinced he'd want to hear them, but dear God, couldn't he see it in her eyes?

Finally he said, "If I didn't believe William was alive and that you could help me find him, I never would have brought you here."

"Then let me help you. Please. I don't want you in pain any longer. Let me help you find the answers you seek. I'll stay so close to you, you'll be able to feel my every heart-beat."

She'd hoped to coax a smile from him, but his gaze remained serious. Reaching up, he slid her palms from his cheeks and intertwined their fingers, holding her hands so tightly her fingertips tingled. She could not clearly read his thoughts, but there was no mistaking his turmoil.

Just when she felt sure he was going to send her home, he raised her hand to his lips and pressed a heated kiss against her fingers.

"Let's go in," he said.

The sign hanging outside the pub read THE FILTHY SWINE.

The instant Elizabeth entered she decided the establishment was aptly named. The stench of sour liquor and unwashed bodies enveloped her like a noxious cloud. She fought the urge to gag brought on by the smell combined with the pungent smoke hanging heavily in the air.

Through the dimly lit interior she discerned coarse-looking men sitting at small wooden tables, hunched over grimy glasses. When she and Austin appeared in the doorway, the din of conversation ceased and everyone stared at the newcomers with suspicious, hostile eyes.

In spite of her earlier bravado, trepidation skittered

through her and she inched closer to Austin. This group looked like they wouldn't hesitate to stick a knife in them if given the least provocation, but clearly the downright dangerous look in Austin's eyes kept anyone from approaching them.

"Keep your eyes downcast and don't speak," Austin said quietly. He led her to a scarred table in the farthest corner. The weight of the patrons' stares bore into her back, but conversation began humming again once they were seated.

A woman wearing a filthy, grease-splattered gown sidled up to their table. "Wot will you gentlemen be wantin'?"

Elizabeth peeked up from under the brim of her cap and pity suffused her. The woman was painfully thin and her skin was badly bruised. Daring to peek up farther, she saw that the woman's lips were swollen and a yellowish bruise marred her cheek. She stared at them through the deadest eyes Elizabeth had ever seen.

"Whiskey," Austin said. "Two."

The woman straightened and winced, pressing a hand to the small of her back. "Two whiskeys it is. If you gents are lookin' fer a bit more than liquor, me name's Molly."

Elizabeth drew a deep breath. Dear God, how awful that anyone would be forced to exist in such wretched surroundings. Her heart pinched in sympathy for Molly, and she wondered if the poor woman had ever known happiness.

"Are you all right?" Austin whispered.

"That woman. She's . . ." She shook her head and bit her lip, unable to describe such despair.

"A whore." He leaned forward. "Did you sense something from her?"

Hot tears pushed at the backs of Elizabeth's eyes. Casting surreptitious glances across the room, she saw Molly making her way through the throngs of men. Nearly every man groped her as she passed, grabbing her breasts or squeezing her buttocks, but she barely reacted and her eyes remained flat.

"I felt only despair," Elizabeth whispered. "I've never seen such utter hopelessness."

"She would no doubt rob you in an instant if she thought she could. In fact, I'd wager that before we leave here she'll attempt to pick your pocket."

"If I had any coins with me, I'd gladly give them to the poor creature. Dear God, Austin, she's been beaten and it looks as if she hasn't eaten a decent meal in weeks."

Just then Molly appeared and set down two grimy glasses of whiskey. Austin reached into his pocket, withdrew several coins, and laid them on the table. Not a whisper of reaction flickered in Molly's eyes.

"All right," she said in an emotionless voice. "Which one of yer is first?" Her bruised eyes suddenly narrowed to slits. "Don't be thinkin' I'll take both of yers at once, 'cause I don't do that."

Elizabeth pressed her lips together, hoping her shock at such a suggestion didn't show. She couldn't begin to know the horrors that faced this poor woman on a daily basis. Pity overwhelmed her and she blinked back the tears that pooled in her eyes.

"I only want information," Austin said in an undertone. "About a man named Gaspard." He described the Frenchman. "Have you seen him?"

Molly thought for a moment, then slowly shook her head. "Can't say fer sure. Too many men in and out of this sty every night, and to be truthful, I try me best not to look at their faces. Only thing I know is they all smell bad and they've all got big, mean hands." Her gaze flickered to the coins on the table. "You need anythin' else?"

"No, Molly. Thank you." Picking up the coins, Austin handed them to her. He then reached into his pocket and withdrew several gold coins that he gave her as well.

Molly's eyes widened to saucers. She shot a stunned, questioning glance at Austin. "All this?" she asked. "Just fer a bit o' talkin'?"

Austin nodded once. Tucking the coins into her bodice, Molly moved quickly away, as if fearing he'd ask for them back.

"How much money did you give her?" Elizabeth asked.

"Enough to feed her."

"For how long?"

He hesitated for an instant, as if uncomfortable to say, then he shrugged. "For at least six months. Have you felt anything yet?"

"No. It's often difficult in a crowd. Too many sensations hit me all at once, resulting in a muddle. I need to close my eyes and relax."

"Very well. You do that and I'll look about to see if I recognize anyone."

She nodded and closed her eyes. Austin took careful note of every patron, but none looked familiar to him.

After several moments Elizabeth opened her eyes. "I'm sorry, Austin, but I cannot discern anything that could help us."

"Then let's go," he said, standing. "There are other places to investigate."

They left the pub without incident and entered the waiting hack. Austin gave an address to the driver and settled himself across from Elizabeth. In the dim light, with her masculine clothing, she could indeed pass for a young man, a notion he found oddly disturbing as he knew she was all woman.

"I'm sorry I was not able to sense anything in the pub,"

she said. "Perhaps we shall have more success in the next place. Where are we going now?"

"A gaming hell. According to my information, Gaspard was recently sighted there."

"I see." She hesitated, and he noticed that she was twisting her fingers together. "I'd like to thank you for your generous gesture toward Molly."

His conscience pricked him, urging him to tell her that he wouldn't have glanced at that whore if not for her, but before he could speak, she reached out and laid her hand on his sleeve.

"You're an extraordinary man, Austin. A remarkable and wonderful man."

His throat tightened. Bloody hell, there she went again, all but turning him into porridge with a single touch. A gentle word. A warm glance. She melted him like snow tossed into a fire.

And instead of being appalled by the admission, instead of wanting to flee or push her away, he ached to take her into his arms. Hold her. Love her. Try to somehow explain these unsettling feelings she evoked in him.

Taking her hand, he pressed a heated, almost desperate kiss to her gloved palm. "Elizabeth. I—"

The hack jerked to a halt, cutting off his words. Peering out the window, he saw that they'd arrived at their destination. Helping Elizabeth from the hack, he led her into a narrow alleyway between two seedy, crumbling brick buildings. They made their way down a set of steps littered with trash and entered the gaming hell.

The room was noisy, dimly lit, and dingy. Men from many different walks of life sat at the tables playing cards and throwing dice. Rough-talking sailors, a group of London dandies out on an adventure, members of the *demi-monde*; anyone with money to gamble was admitted.

Again requesting that she keep her hat pulled low and eyes downcast, Austin led her slowly around the circumference of the room. She paused near the end of the scarred wooden bar.

Blocking her from the room with his back, he whispered, "What is it?"

She frowned and shook her head. Without a word, she peeled off her dark gloves and slipped them into her pocket. She then placed her hands on the bar. Her eyes slid closed.

Austin watched her closely, keeping her hidden from the rest of the room. Her breathing deepened and just when he didn't think he could stand her silence another moment, she opened her eyes.

"Gaspard has been here," she said.

His stomach clenched. "When?"

Her eyes grew troubled. "Tonight, Austin. He was here tonight."

Chapter 17

Squeezing her eyes shut, Elizabeth held on to the bar, trying to assimilate the barrage of images flashing through her mind. The man Austin sought had been in this very place, and only several hours earlier. She was sure of it.

A clear picture blinked in her mind. "He's carrying a pistol." Her knees went weak. "He's used it to kill. More than once."

He gripped her hand and immediately more images materialized behind her closed eyes, flashing like lightning bolts. Her heart thumped painfully and the base of her neck throbbed as the disjointed impressions slowly took form. A clear vision swam through her brain and perspiration broke out on her brow. Light-headedness invaded her system, rendering her weak.

"Elizabeth, what's wrong?"

Austin's urgent whisper seemed to come from very far away. She struggled to open her eyes, but the images bombarding her sapped her strength. She was vaguely aware of a commotion, of being lifted up and carried, but she was too weak to protest. Blackness engulfed her and she slipped into oblivion.

Austin had never been so frightened in his life. Damn it, she was *unconscious*. Her face was pale as wax, her skin damp, her breathing labored. Ignoring the curious glances from several gambling patrons, he picked her up and strode from the building. Once outside, he barked out his direction to the hackney with orders to get them home posthaste. He closed the hack door behind them and tenderly laid her across his lap.

"Elizabeth," he said urgently, his body tense with fear. "Speak to me. Darling, please, say something."

He patted her cheeks and alarm raced through him at the clammy texture of her skin. The frightening atmosphere and noxious fumes must have gotten to her, but damn it, why didn't she wake up now that they were outside? He never should have brought her here. If anything happened to her—

Her eyelids fluttered open and she looked directly into his eyes. Relief hit him like a punch to the head. Laying his palm against her pale cheek, he tried to smile at her, but his facial muscles wouldn't cooperate. Bloody hell, he felt as weak as a newborn babe.

She attempted to sit up, but he kept her in place with a gentle hand on her shoulder. "Relax," he managed to say.

Her eyes panned around. "Where are we?"

"In the hack, on our way home."

A frown furrowed her brow. "Home? But why?"

"I'm afraid you succumbed to the vapors."

"Vapors? Nonsense." She again tried to sit up and he again restrained her.

"Vapors," he repeated, running his fingertips over her pale cheek, unable to keep from touching her. "For a robust girl, you went down like a tenpin."

She shook her head. "No, it wasn't the vapors. I had a vision. I saw it, Austin. I saw the entire thing. William. The Frenchman Gaspard."

That horrific night, that haunting scene that was forever burned in his mind, bombarded him, attacking his defenses from all sides. She grasped his hand, squeezing it, and her eyes widened.

Before he could utter a word, she whispered, "Dear God, you were there. You saw them together, loading crates of weapons onto a ship." He tried to rein in his thoughts, but there was no stopping them. Gripping his hand tighter, she said, "William saw you in the shadows. He went to you and you argued bitterly. You tried to stop him, but he wouldn't listen. Then you watched your brother sail away . . . with an enemy to your country."

Pain whipped through him, lashing him with guilt. "He was handing over weapons," he whispered, barely aware he was speaking. "He saw me and left the ship. He pulled me into an alleyway, away from Gaspard's eyes. I asked him how he could do this, but he refused to answer me. Told me to mind my own business and leave. We quarreled. I threatened to turn him in . . . I told him he was no longer my brother."

"You've never told anyone?"

"No." He leaned his head back and squeezed his eyes shut. "If it ever got out that William was a traitor, my family would be destroyed. I had to protect Caroline and Robert. My mother. I cannot believe that William would betray England, but I know what I saw, and he did not deny it. The question is why. *Why* would he do it?"

He knew he had to look at her, to read her reaction, but he couldn't yet bring himself to gaze into her eyes. What would he do if he read condemnation there? There was every chance she would reject him, his family, now that she knew the truth. And because she was his wife, she, too, would now be forced to suffer any shame brought upon the family.

Bracing himself, he opened his eyes and looked at her, and his breath hitched in his throat. A dozen emotions swam in her eyes, none of them condemnation. Only warmth, caring, and concern flowed from her gaze.

She reached up and cradled his face between her palms. "God in heaven, Austin. How you must have suffered, keeping this secret, trying to protect your family. I'm so very sorry for your pain. But you're not alone any longer."

That heartfelt look radiating from her eyes, the soothing, gentle touch of her hands, her softly spoken words, combined with the barrage of emotions attacking him from all sides, shattered the bleakness engulfing him. *You're not alone any longer.*

Gathering her close, he pressed his face into the warm curve of her shoulder. A long shudder passed through him, and he held her tighter, so tight her bones must have ached, but she never complained. She hugged him to her, running her hands soothingly through his hair, over his back, while the guilt that had festered inside him broke loose and poured forth in a torrent he was helpless to stop.

Long moments passed before his shudders subsided. When they did, he remained in Elizabeth's arms and tried to assemble his thoughts.

He would always bitterly regret his last moments with William, but now there was hope for a second chance. William was alive. He needed to find him, talk with him, discover why he'd done what he'd done.

Elizabeth claimed William was in danger. Why? Was someone seeking retribution for his wartime activities? Or was some other danger hounding his brother, holding him captive? Could William be trying to escape whatever evil had convinced him to commit treason? Regardless of the past, if William needed his help, he would give it.

Grim determination filled Austin. He would find William. And Gaspard. No matter what.

For the first time since that horrible night over a year ago, he drew an easy breath. The relief that surged through him at unburdening his soul left him all but light-headed. He'd been alone for so long, locked in the solitary confinement of his secret. But no longer. Now he had someone to share it with. Elizabeth. She knew his darkest secret.

This beautiful woman who held him against her heart, absorbing his pain and replacing it with her own goodness. She'd freed him and given him back his life. She'd given him hope for the future.

God, how he needed her.

He lifted his head and gazed into her eyes. There were so many things he needed to say to her, wanted her to know, but his throat was so clogged with emotion, he couldn't utter a sound.

The hack jerked to a halt. Forcing his gaze away from her, he saw they'd arrived at the town house. Without a word, he helped her alight and paid the hackney.

Holding tightly to her arm, he opened the oak door. The foyer was empty, as Carters had clearly retired hours ago. Without pausing even to remove their coats, he led her up the stairs and into his bedchamber, closing and locking the door behind them.

A need like he'd never before experienced rose up inside him. He had to touch her. Hold her. Skin to skin. Heart to heart. An affirmation of life after feeling dead inside for so long.

He longed to tell her what he was feeling, but he didn't know the words, and words were beyond him. He needed to *feel* her. Against him. Around him. Under him. To show her how he felt where words couldn't reach.

His gaze never strayed from her face as he began removing his clothes. His coat then his jacket hit the floor, carelessly falling from his impatient fingers. Cravat, waistcoat, and linen shirt followed, joining the heap at his feet. Bared to the waist, he approached her, unable to wait another instant to feel her hands on him.

She made a move to unfasten her coat, but he stilled her hands and performed the task himself. Layer by layer, he removed her clothes, then the remainder of his, until they stood before each other naked.

He'd never felt so needful or vulnerable in his entire life.

Reaching out, he cupped her face between his hands and brushed his thumbs over her cheeks. So many words to say, so many things to tell her, but he couldn't seem to find his voice.

"Elizabeth," he whispered in a husky voice.

It was the only word he was able to manage. What he couldn't say, he'd show her. Drawing her into his arms, he touched his lips softly to hers, aching with a tenderness completely at odds with the inferno burning inside him.

She breathed his name and slid her arms around him.

And the dam burst.

He crushed her to him, overwhelmed with the need to touch her everywhere at once. His lips claimed hers, his kiss growing increasingly hot and demanding. His tongue explored the soft interior of her mouth, withdrawing and then plundering again.

But kissing her wasn't enough. Pulling back, he studied her face, his heart doubling its already breakneck pace at the passion and desire shimmering in her eyes. "Elizabeth, my God, what you do to me . . ." he moaned, his voice thick and unsteady. Sinking to his knees, he pressed his mouth to the creamy skin of her belly.

"So soft," he murmured, his lips trailing across her ab-

domen. "So beautiful." His tongue dipped into her navel
before his mouth continued its downward journey. He
slowly kissed and licked his way down one long leg and
back up the other, while his fingers lightly ran up and
down the back of her thighs and calves. When he reached
the juncture of her thighs, he raised his head.

"Look at me, Elizabeth."

Opening her eyes, she looked down at him, showing
golden depths darkened with passion.

"Spread your legs for me," he commanded in a raw
voice against the smooth skin of her belly. When she did
as he bid, he ran one hand down her body, from her neck to
the dark red curls that hid her womanly flesh, then stroked
between her thighs. Her eyelids slid shut, and a long moan
purred in her throat.

"You're so beautiful . . . so wet . . . so hot," he groaned,
burying his lips against her navel. His lips drifted lower,
lower, until his tongue caressed her as his fingers had. She
grasped his shoulders and gasped.

Cupping her bottom in his hands, he worshipped her
with his lips and tongue, breathing in her feminine musk,
tasting her delicate essence, loving her until she shattered
against him. Digging her fingers into his shoulders, she
cried out as her climax washed over her. When the spasms
subsided, he picked her up and carried her to his bed, settling her gently on the counterpane. Positioning himself
between her thighs, he looked down into her beautiful,
passion-flushed face.

"Look at me."

Her eyelids fluttered open and he entered her with one
long, hard thrust, embedding himself in her slick heat. A
throaty groan escaped her, and she ran her hands restlessly
over his back. Moving slowly within her, he watched every
emotion passing over her expressive face, his strokes
growing longer, harder, and faster. She met him all the

way, moving her hips in rhythm with his until he felt her pleasure overtake her once again.

The instant her body clenched him, he lost any semblance of control. His world narrowed to the place where his body was joined to hers. Nothing mattered except her. Him inside her. Her around him. He thrust into her again and again, helpless to stop, mindless with passion. With one final thrust, he spilled himself into her, for an endless moment he whispered her name over and over again like a prayer.

When the earth righted itself again, he collapsed and rolled onto his side, bringing her with him. He wanted to stroke her back, but he couldn't move. He couldn't so much as make a fist. Truth be known, he could barely breathe. He'd never experienced such intense lovemaking in his entire life, and an inner warmth more wonderful than anything he'd ever felt pervaded his entire system.

He loved her.

By God, he loved her.

Loved her so much he ached.

He stilled. But what if she didn't return his feelings? What if—

He ruthlessly cut off the thought. She simply had to love him, and that's all there was to it. And if she didn't now, he'd just find some way to make her love him. As much as he loved her.

The words he'd never spoken to anyone welled up inside him. He needed to tell her. Had to tell her. He wondered if she already knew. Had she read his mind? Discerned his feelings? Possibly, but she'd never said so. But even if she had divined his feelings, she deserved the words.

Turning his head, he brushed his lips over her temple, then leaned back, determined to look in her eyes when he told her he loved her.

With his heart pounding, he opened his mouth to speak, then shut it.

His wife, his robust, energetic wife, was fast asleep.

"Elizabeth?"

A soft snore was his only response.

Well, bloody hell.

Shame filled him. How selfish of him to worry about his own needs when she'd had such an exhausting evening. By damn, she'd fainted in his arms only an hour ago. If he wanted to win this woman's love, he needed to banish his selfishness to the devil. His Elizabeth wouldn't be bought with baubles, titles, and jewels. But he could win her with kindness. And love.

Love. A smile tugged one corner of his mouth.

He'd finally put a name to the "Elizabeth feeling."

Careful not to wake her, he pulled the counterpane over them and settled her comfortably against him. After listening to her even breathing for several minutes, he pressed his lips to her forehead.

"I love you," he whispered. "I love you."

Chapter 18

The vision slipped into Elizabeth's slumber with the stealth of a master thief.

Images weaved through the shadowy recesses of her mind, curling like vaporous plumes of smoke only to dance just out of reach.

A child. A beautiful little girl with shiny ebony curls and bright, gray eyes. Running, laughing, calling, "Mama!"

Then the vision changed. Laughter turned to fear. The child's terrified screams filled Elizabeth's mind, reverberating through her, filling her with dread.

The child's angelic face turned to a pale mask of fright. Womanly hands reached out to her, but the child seemed to glide farther out of reach, until she disappeared completely from sight, leaving only the echo of her sobs.

Then Austin, torn apart with such grief, such desolation and guilt, that Elizabeth barely recognized him. His voice was a ragged whisper, *I cannot live without her . . . please God, don't tell me I've killed her by bringing her here.*

Elizabeth awoke with a startled gasp. Her heart slammed against her ribs and her lungs burned as if she'd run for miles. Yet she felt chilled down to her very soul.

Her eyes sought out Austin, who lay in peaceful slumber next to her. Thank goodness he was asleep, for she was incapable of speaking.

But dear God, she would have to tell him.

He had to know that she'd seen the death of a child.

A child whose death he would blame himself for.

A child with his ebony hair and gray eyes.

His child.

Their child.

Austin opened one eye. From the sliver of pale light peeking through the burgundy velvet curtains, he judged it was just after dawn—a perfectly respectable time to awaken his bride with soft kisses, gentle lovemaking, and tender confessions of love.

Turning his head, he discovered his bride on the other side of his massive bed, lying curled on her side, facing away from him. Too far away to touch.

Acute disappointment flooded him, and he nearly laughed aloud at himself. Bloody hell, what a besotted, lovesick individual he'd become. And in an appallingly short period of time. *No doubt I'll be spouting poetry by dinner. Sonnets by sundown.* A chuckle rumbled in his chest. Yes, indeed, he could all but picture himself, down on one knee, passionately reciting "Ode to Elizabeth."

He had only to shift closer to be able to wrap his arms around her, feel her warmth, but he knew once he did that, there would be no more slumber for her. *Don't be selfish. Let her sleep.* Clasping his hands behind his head, he forced himself to remain where he was and not disturb her rest, at least for a few more minutes. Yes, he'd simply lie here and marvel at how this woman had so drastically changed his life. And all of it for the better.

He imagined the ribbing he was going to receive from both Miles and Robert when they realized the "Notorious Duke of Bradford" had fallen under his own wife's spell. And they absolutely would realize it because it would be impossible for him to hide his love for Elizabeth.

And he didn't even want to try. Of course, it was highly unfashionable to be in love with one's own wife, but he couldn't have cared less.

A grin he couldn't suppress eased across his face. Yes, Robert and Miles would needle him unmercifully. *But I'll have my revenge when love bites them on their unsuspecting arses. And it will. If it can happen to me, it can happen to anyone.*

He couldn't wait another minute to touch her.

He wouldn't wake her . . . he'd simply hold her. Moving carefully, he slid across the bed until he lay behind her, then eased his arm around her waist.

The instant he touched her, she gasped.

"Good morning, love," he said, pressing a kiss to her shoulder. "I didn't mean to wake you."

"I . . . I thought you were asleep."

"I was. But now I'm awake. And so are you. Hmmm." He buried his face in her hair and breathed in her lilac scent. Slipping his arm more snugly around her, he eased her closer, molding her back to his front.

He stilled when she stiffened in his embrace. "Don't," she whispered. Before he could ask her what was wrong, she pulled from his embrace and sat up, covering herself with the counterpane.

He quickly sat up. "Elizabeth? Are you all right?"

When she didn't answer, he cupped her chin, gently turning her averted face until she looked at him.

She was crying. Her eyes looked like huge, golden

brown wells of hurt. The usual warmth that shimmered in her gaze was gone, replaced by an utterly bleak expression that broke his heart.

He let go of her chin and gripped her arms. "What's wrong? Are you hurt?"

Instead of answering his question, she simply looked at him with those pain-filled eyes. Something akin to panic slithered down his back.

He gave her a tiny shake. "Tell me what's wrong."

"I . . . I have something to tell you."

"About William?"

"No. About me."

Ah. So that's what this was about. Clearly she was finally going to share her secrets with him . . . explain why she'd left America so suddenly.

Relief edged aside his alarm and he relaxed his hold on her arms. Obviously she trusted him enough to bare her soul. And if she trusted him . . . wasn't it logical that love would soon follow?

God, was she going to tell him she loved him? And if so, she was no doubt agonizing over the decision because she didn't know how he felt about her. Because she'd never heard him tell her. She was probably afraid that he'd reject her love.

But that was a fear he could place to rest with three simple words.

"Elizabeth, I l—"

"I lied to you."

Definitely not the words he'd hoped, or expected, to hear. "I beg your pardon?"

Instead of answering, she eased herself from his grasp and picked up his shirt from the floor. Slipping on the garment, she gathered the edges together, then passed him his silk robe. He shrugged into it and knotted the sash, watching her inch away from him. Only when several feet separated them did she speak again. "I lied to you about why I'm here in England."

"Indeed? You did not come to visit your aunt?"

"No. I came here to *live* with her."

"Darling, I'd hardly call that a lie." He reached for her, but she shook her head and stepped away from him.

"You don't understand. I *had* to come here. I didn't want to, but I had nowhere else to go."

"What do you mean?"

She drew a deep breath. "After my father's death, I couldn't bear living alone in our house. An unmarried woman living alone bordered on impropriety, and in truth I was horribly lonely. Distant cousins on my father's side, the Longrens, resided in the same town and they invited me to live with them. It seemed a perfect solution as I loved them dearly and their daughter Alberta was my closest friend, so I sold my house and moved in with them."

He recognized the name Longren as the one that Miles had reported to him. "Go on."

"I loved being part of their family, and the younger children, rascals all three of them, were delights. For almost two years everything was wonderful." She twisted her fingers together and looked at the carpet. "Then Alberta met David."

He watched her, forcing himself to remain silent, to allow her to tell him her tale.

"David moved to town from Boston where he'd worked at a livery. He was wonderful with horses and a talented farrier, and Mr. Longren immediately hired him on at his livery. David was a very attractive young man, and all the ladies were quite smitten with him."

Austin's hands clenched. "Including you?"

"I must admit, the first time I met him, I thought him handsome and charming." She paused, then added in a quiet voice, "But then I touched him."

"What did you see?"

"Lies. Deceit. Nothing specific, but I knew he was not as he seemed. I forced myself to shrug it off. After all, as long as he worked hard for Mr. Longren, it was not my business if he'd lied in the past. I convinced myself he was making a fresh start and deserved a second chance. But several weeks later, Alberta told me that she was in love. With David."

She began pacing. "I was very concerned. I gently told her that she didn't know him very well, but she wouldn't listen to me. No one in the town, including Alberta, knew anything about my visions. I experienced them infrequently, and as you yourself know, they are not easy to believe in or accept. I therefore hesitated to tell her, especially when what I'd felt had been so vague. And I certainly did not want to destroy Alberta's happiness if I was wrong.

"I needed to know more, to find out if he was indeed dishonorable. I needed to touch him again, or at least something that belonged to him." She drew a shaky breath then continued in an agitated voice. "The next day I visited the livery and spoke to David. I touched his tools and even managed to hold his hand under the guise of examining a cut on his finger. And my suspicions were confirmed."

"What had he done?"

"I didn't know exactly, but I knew he'd left Boston in disgrace. I knew he was a liar and a cheat. I knew he needed money and the Longrens were financially well off. But worst of all, I knew he was going to break Alberta's heart. I prayed her feelings toward him would change, but two weeks later she and David announced they planned to marry. In one month."

Her voice dropped to a whisper. "I didn't know what to do. She was so in love with him, but she was making a

terrible mistake. Again I tried to warn her gently but to no
avail. Finally, the day before the wedding, I told her . . . not
that I'd had a vision . . . but that I had reason to believe
David was dishonest and not the man for her. That he
would bring her nothing but heartache."

The anguish in her voice ripped at him. "What did she
say?"

A humorless sound erupted from her throat. "She flatly
refused to listen. She then accused me of being jealous, of
wanting David for myself. He'd told her how I'd visited
him at the livery and he'd apparently convinced her that
I'd gone there in the hopes of winning him for myself. I
could not believe that she would think that of me, but
she did."

"Did you tell her about your visions?"

"I tried, but she wouldn't listen to another word. She
was so angry with me for trying to ruin her happiness and
wanting the man she loved. She told me she didn't want
me at her wedding. Didn't want me in her life." Stopping
directly in front of him, she stared at him with tear-filled
eyes that twisted his insides. "She told me to pack my
things and leave her family's house."

"Elizabeth." He reached for her, but she stepped farther
away from him.

"Maybe if I'd told her about the vision from the start,
she would have believed me. I don't know. But I vowed
right then and there that I would never remain silent about
another one—not if it involved someone's happiness." She
spread her arms in a defeated, helpless gesture. "I did not
experience another vision until the night I met you. That is
why I told you about seeing William."

After squeezing her eyes shut for a brief moment, she
continued, "Mr. and Mrs. Longren were surprised I was
leaving, but their allegiance was to Alberta and she was

adamant that I go. I knew deep down she was hurting, too. She loved me, but she loved David more. I packed my things and departed that same afternoon. I left Patch with them. He was too old to travel and the younger children loved him as much as I did."

Her voice cracked, and he imagined her leaving, alone and filled with despair. Bloody hell, his chest ached and his heart simply broke for her. "What did you do?"

"I walked to town and withdrew my savings from the bank. I had nowhere to go, and I wanted to get away, as far away as possible. I arranged transportation to the coast. When I arrived, I booked passage on *The Starseeker* and hired a traveling companion. I sent a letter to Aunt Joanna advising her of my arrival. I am fortunate and forever grateful that she was willing to take me in."

"Do you know what happened to Alberta and David?"

"No. I pray every day for their happiness, but I know it is only a matter of time before Alberta's heart is broken."

He had no idea what to say to her, how to comfort her, but he knew he had to try. The torment in her eyes was killing him. "I'm so sorry you were hurt like that, darling," he said, "but as sad as leaving your home was, it did bring *us* together." He held out his hand to her.

She stared at it blankly for a moment, then raised her gaze to his. Her expression actually frightened him. It looked as if all the life, all the energy and vitality, had been drained from her, leaving unspeakable anguish and guilt in its wake.

"There's more, Austin. I had another vision. Last night."

He slowly lowered his hand. "What did you see?"

"I saw someone dying."

Her agony was so palpable, he could all but see it flowing off her in waves. "Who?"

"It was our child, Austin."

He actually felt the blood drain from his head. "*Our* child? How do you know?"

"A little girl. She looked just like you, with ebony curls and beautiful gray eyes." Walking forward with jerky steps, she grasped his arms, her fingers digging into his skin. "Do you understand what I'm saying? I saw the future. We had a child. She was about two years old. And she died."

His mind reeled from the impact of her words. "Surely you're mistaken."

"No. I saw it. And I cannot allow it to happen. I cannot allow our child to die."

Drawing a deep breath, he tried to think clearly, but it didn't even occur to him to doubt her premonition. "All right. We won't allow it to happen. You've forewarned us, so we'll be prepared. She'll be watched every moment of every day. Nothing will happen to her."

"Don't you see? I cannot take that risk. I've already lost my parents, the Longrens, and Alberta. I cannot bear to lose someone else I love—our *child*. Nor can I bear to watch you suffer her death." She stared at him for several heartbeats. "There is only one way to ensure that our child does not die . . . and that is to not have a child."

Not have a child? Of course they would have a child. Many children. Sons with her keen intelligence and beautiful daughters with their mother's hair. "What are you saying?"

Letting go of his arms, she turned toward the window. He stared at her profile and listened to her flat-voiced words. "I cannot have a child with you. I *refuse* to have a child with you. The only way to ensure that I don't is to cease being a wife to you. Naturally, I do not expect you to live with such an untenable arrangement. I realize the importance of an heir to a man in your position." She raised her chin a notch, but her voice fell to a shaky whisper. "I therefore wish to end our marriage."

He froze, unable to comprehend her words for a full minute. Finally, he found his voice.

"Such drastic measures are not necessary, Elizabeth."

"I'm afraid they are. I cannot ask you to accept a wife who will not share your bed."

His hands fisted at his sides, but he managed to keep his voice calm. "There is no reason for me to accept a wife who will not share my bed. There are ways to prevent pregnancy—if that is ultimately what we decide to do."

"You are not listening to me, Austin. I have *already decided*. I will not risk becoming pregnant."

"I promise you we can find a way—"

"You cannot possibly hope to keep such a promise *for a lifetime*." She turned to look at him and the cold determination in her eyes chilled him. "Why can you not simply accept my decision?"

A bark of disbelief erupted from him. "Simply accept that you want to end our marriage? I'm stunned that you would even consider such a thing . . . giving up like this. Surely our marriage means more to you than that."

"We both know you married me only because you believed you had to."

"And we both know that nothing could have forced me to marry you had I not wanted to." Closing the distance between them, he gently took her by the shoulders. "Elizabeth. It doesn't matter why we married. What matters is how we feel about each other and what we make of our life together. We can make this marriage strong enough to survive anything."

"But surely you want to have children."

"Yes. I do. Very much." He gazed at her steadily. "With you."

She inhaled sharply. "I'm sorry. I cannot. I will not."

Silence stretched between them. He tried to reconcile this coldly resolute, distant woman with his warm, loving Elizabeth, and could not. Forcing words through his tight throat, he said, "I understand you're upset about this vision, but you can't let it destroy what we have together. I won't allow it." He cupped her face between his palms. "I love you, Elizabeth. I *love* you. And I won't let you go."

Every drop of color seeped from her face. He searched her eyes, and for an instant stark, raw pain emanated from their depths. She turned away from him, and it appeared as if she were choking back tears. But when she faced him again, her expression had hardened. Grim determination replaced the pain and she pulled away from him.

"I'm sorry, Austin. Your love isn't enough."

Those words slapped him right in the heart. Left him bleeding. God Almighty, if he'd been able to draw a deep enough breath, he would have laughed at the irony of this. After waiting a lifetime to give a woman his love, she'd tossed it aside like an unwanted trinket. *Your love isn't enough.*

"Even if *you* are willing to live with such an arrangement," she continued in that same flat voice, "*I* am not. I want children in my life."

He somehow found his voice. "You just said you didn't."

"No. I said I cannot have children with *you* . . . but I could with someone else. It was my child with *you* who died."

Everything inside him went rigid. Surely he'd heard her incorrectly. "Elizabeth, you don't know what you're saying. You cannot possibly mean—"

"I know exactly what I'm saying." Lifting her chin a notch, she regarded him with uncharacteristic coolness. "While I fancied being a duchess, I never dreamed that the title would cost me having children. It's not a price I'm willing to pay."

"What the hell are you talking about?" he bit out. "You had no wish to become a duchess."

She raised her brows. "I'm not a fool, Austin. What woman wouldn't want to be a duchess?"

Her words settled on him like a blanket of ice, freezing him to the bone. He didn't want to believe what she was saying, but she was clearly serious.

He was stunned. Numb. Bringing his hand to his chest, he rubbed where his heart should be. And felt nothing. All his newfound hopes and dreams slipped away, blowing like ashes in the wind. She didn't love him. Didn't want him. Didn't want his children. Or their marriage. She wanted to share her life with someone else . . . *anyone* else. Just not him.

The numbness suddenly fled and warring emotions pummeled him. Disillusionment. Anger. And a hurt that cut so deep he felt sliced in two. *Jesus. What a fool I've been.*

He forced himself to push the hurt aside, to concentrate on the anger, letting it pump through him, heating his frozen veins.

"I believe I'm beginning to understand," he said in a voice so raw he barely recognized it. "In spite of your protestations to the contrary, you actually had designs on gaining a title. Now you wish to end our marriage, seemingly out of concern for me, but in truth *you* want to be free to marry someone else so you can bear children. *His* children."

Her face paled at his tone, but her gaze remained steady on his. "Yes. I want our marriage annulled."

Fury and gut-wrenching hurt collided in him, rocking his foundation. God damn it, what a superb actress his wife was! Her concern, her caring . . . it was all a facade. All this time he'd thought her sincere and trustworthy, innocent and guileless, and most laughable of all, unselfish. She was no better than the fortune-hunting females who had dogged his heels for years. He could not believe she had the nerve, the *gall*, to stand in front of him and claim she wanted to end their marriage for *his* happiness when what she really wanted was another husband for *herself*.

But what fueled his rage to the boiling point was the thought of her with another man. That image filled him with such violence, he nearly choked. Yet he welcomed the rage, for without it, the raw hurt would simply overwhelm him.

"Look at me," he ordered in a voice that dripped ice.

When she continued to stare toward the window, he grabbed her chin and forced her head around. "Look at me, damn it." She met his gaze with a cool detachment that infuriated him. There was nothing in her expression to indicate she was the woman he'd made love with only hours ago. How had she hidden this side of herself from him? How the hell had she fooled him so completely? It took every ounce of restraint he possessed not to shake her.

"You missed your calling, my dear. You could have been superb on the stage. You certainly had me convinced that you were all things good and decent. But clearly you are nothing more than a common schemer and accomplished liar. Your refusal to be a proper wife to me is certainly ample grounds for me to rid myself of you." He dropped her chin as if she'd scorched him.

Her face turned to chalk. "You'll agree to an annulment?"

"No, Elizabeth. I shall *demand* an annulment—as soon as I've ascertained that you are not already carrying my child. For the next two months you shall reside at my estate just outside London. That should be sufficient time to determine if you are pregnant or not."

Stark fear slashed across her features. She obviously hadn't considered that the damage might have already been done. "And if I'm not?"

"Then our marriage will end."

"What if I am . . . with child?"

"Then we'll be forced to endure this sham marriage. Whether you choose to stay or leave after the baby's birth—"

"I could never abandon my child."

A bitter laugh escaped him. "Really? You're certainly willing to abandon your commitment to our marriage. Given that fact, I'm not sure what you are capable of."

Something flashed in her eyes, and for a moment he thought she meant to argue, but she merely pressed her lips together.

"One more thing," he said. "I shall expect you to behave with the utmost propriety during the next two months. You will speak of this to no one and you will do *nothing* to bring shame upon me or my family. Do you understand? I'll not have my wife bearing some other man's child."

Again he thought he detected a flash of raw pain in her eyes, but she merely lifted her chin and said, "I will not be unfaithful."

"You're damned right, you won't. And now, if you'll excuse me, I'd like to get dressed. I'll make the necessary arrangements for your stay in the country."

"What about me helping you find William?"

"If you see anything else, send me a message. I shall conduct my own investigation from here. Without you."

Striding across the room, he opened the adjoining door to her bedchamber. She stood still for several heartbeats, her gaze riveted on his, her expression unreadable. Then she swiftly crossed the room and walked into her chamber. Austin closed the door after her and very deliberately turned the lock into place. The click reverberated through the sudden silence.

Alone in his chamber, he braced his fists against the door and closed his eyes against the emotions battling inside him, stabbing him, consuming him, overwhelming him until he wanted to scream. Half of him was furious. Coldly, darkly furious.

The other half of him hurt so badly he nearly fell to his knees. There was an empty hole in his chest where his heart had beaten only minutes before. Before Elizabeth had torn it out with her bare hands and sliced it in two.

Before he'd met her, he'd been only half a man, existing yet not living. She'd made him whole with her sweetness and innocence, laughter and love . . . but they didn't really exist. He'd never thought a woman would want him for himself, but he'd believed Elizabeth had. He'd never thought he'd fall in love, but he had, with a heart and soul he'd thought gone forever.

Walking to the window, he pulled the curtain aside, and looked with unseeing eyes out the window at a world suddenly gone bleak.

She'd made him love her.

And it was all an illusion.

Until Elizabeth, he'd never carried around hopes and dreams for his future. He'd been consumed by the secrets he carried inside and had moved from one meaningless affair to another, from one club to the next, from one boring party to another.

But she'd changed him. She'd turned him from that cynical, detached, lonely man into someone with hope for the future . . . a future filled with happiness, a loving wife, and fine, healthy children.

And now all his newly found hopes and dreams were gone. Vanished. Shattered. She'd said she couldn't bear to lose someone else she loved—yet she was willing to lose him. And that left no doubt what her feelings toward him were.

God Almighty, if he didn't hurt so damn bad, if he wasn't so racked with pain and anguish, he could almost laugh. The "incomparable, invulnerable" Duke of Bradford brought to his knees by a woman . . . a woman he'd thought was the answer to all his dreams. Dreams he hadn't even known he had.

Instead she'd turned out to be his worst nightmare.

Elizabeth stared numbly at the door Austin had just closed and listened to the lock fall into place with a click that echoed in her mind like a death knell.

Just as she wondered if she'd ever feel anything again, pain ripped through her, exploding everywhere, searing her very skin. Clapping her hands over her mouth to contain a cry of anguish, she sank to her knees on the floor.

Never, ever, would she forget the look on his face, the gentle tenderness her words had turned into bitterness; the warmth changed into icy indifference; the caring into loathing.

Dear God, she loved him so much. So much that she couldn't bear to give him a child who would die. She'd never make him understand that he would blame himself for their daughter's death, and that his guilt and anguish would destroy him. That he would never recover.

She'd paid with her soul to offer him his freedom. But the cost to her did not matter. An honorable man like Austin would balk at ending their union, would have consigned himself to enduring a lifetime with her and a childless marriage. A celibate marriage. He deserved happiness, a proper wife, children to love. She would have said anything to convince him.

And she had.

A bitter laugh erupted from her throat as she recalled her words. *I fancied being a duchess . . . I cannot have children with you . . . but I could with someone else. It was my child with* you *who died.*

Those lies had cost her everything. The man she loved. Children. She could never, *would* never, be with any other man. She'd nearly choked on the words *I fancied being a duchess.* She'd said them as a last resort, when it became clear that he wasn't going to accept her decision unless she extinguished every bit of caring he had for her. And now he believed her to be nothing more than a scheming fortune hunter and a liar. The effort of keeping her anguish hidden, of making him believe she'd wanted a title, wanted a life without him, had nearly killed her.

But then he'd made it so much worse with his declaration of love. *I love you, Elizabeth.* She couldn't contain the tortured sob that rose from her chest. How much more pain could she bear before she simply shattered? To have longed for the precious gift of his love, to have been given that gift, then to have had to destroy it . . . to see that love fade from his eyes, replaced by hurt, then anger and disgust . . . Dear God, how was she going to survive this?

And what if it was all for naught?

What if she were already pregnant?

Chapter 19

Elizabeth snipped fragrant lilac blooms from a leafy bush along the perimeter of the formal garden at Wesley Manor, the country estate just outside London that had been her home for the past three weeks. She tried to concentrate on the task at hand so as not to cut her fingers, but it was nearly impossible.

Three weeks had passed since her confrontation with Austin.

Three weeks since he'd sent her here, sent her away from him with nothing more than a terse note: *You will send a message immediately should you see something or when you know if you're with child.*

But after three weeks she hadn't had a single vision . . . hadn't felt anything but heartache. And she still didn't know if she was with child. Every night she lay in her lonely bed, filled with anxiety, her hands resting on her stomach, trying to sense if a child grew within her, but all she saw was darkness. Unrelenting darkness.

These had been the longest, loneliest three weeks of her life.

Yet the alternative, living in the same house as Austin, facing him every day, trying to hide her misery and live the lie she'd created, would have proven impossible. She was much better off here.

Even so, the anguish that was her constant companion showed no signs of abating. She tried to keep herself busy, to keep her thoughts occupied so as not to torture herself wondering what he was doing. Or whom he was doing it with.

But no matter how many flowers she picked, how much lilac water she distilled, how many hours she spent reading or roaming the grounds, nothing eased the ache in her heart. She tried to console herself with the knowledge that her actions had spared Austin the torment of losing a child and the emptiness of a cold marriage bed, but nothing could erase the agony that clawed at her every time she pictured his face.

A memory of him filled her mind and turned her blood cold. Him staring at her, as he had in those final moments, with loathing in his eyes.

Hot tears spilled from her eyes and she impatiently wiped at them with her gloved fingers. She'd promised herself that she wouldn't cry today. How long would it take before she could make it through an entire day without crying? She almost laughed. Dear God, how long before she could make it through an entire *hour* without crying?

"There you are," came Robert's jolly voice from behind her. "Caroline and I had nearly given you up for lost."

Dismay filled her and she quickly swiped at her eyes. Adopting what she hoped was a cheerful expression, she turned and smiled at her approaching brother-in-law.

Robert saw her face and his footsteps nearly faltered.

By damn, she'd been crying again. In spite of her smile, there was no hiding the red-rimmed eyes that spoke so eloquently of sleepless nights and profound sadness.

A spurt of anger shot through him. What the devil was wrong with his brother? Couldn't Austin see how miserable she was? No, of course he couldn't—he was in London. Three weeks ago, Austin had asked him to accompany Elizabeth, Caroline, and their mother to Wesley Manor, explaining that he didn't want them to return to Bradford Hall until the case of the Runner's death was solved.

But Robert knew something was seriously wrong between his brother and Elizabeth. He'd visited Austin yesterday, and based on their time together, Robert knew his brother was just as miserable as Elizabeth, if not more so. He'd never seen Austin in such a holy foul mood.

As for Elizabeth, he'd simply never encountered such a dispirited, brokenhearted individual as his sister-in-law. She reminded him of a lovely flower that someone had forgotten to water, so it simply wilted and withered away. Well, he'd had enough of it. Whatever was keeping Austin and Elizabeth apart was about to end.

Pretending he didn't see the tears still shimmering in her eyes, he made her an exaggerated, formal bow. "How lovely you look, Elizabeth." Without giving her a chance to reply, he slipped her hand through his elbow and propelled her down the path. "We must hurry, the coach is leaving in"—he quickly calculated how much time Caroline and his mother would need to pack their things—"two hours." He knew both women would be frantic when he told them, but desperate times called for drastic measures. "We don't want to hold up the party."

"Coach? Party? What are you talking about?"

"Why, our excursion to London. Did Caroline not tell you?"

He glanced at her and saw she'd visibly paled. "No. I . . . I do not wish to go to London."

"Pshaw. Of course you do. Too many solitary days spent in the country is stifling. We'll attend the theater, go to the shops, visit the museums—"

"Robert." She halted, then pulled her hand from his arm.

"Yes?"

"Although I appreciate the invitation, I'm afraid I cannot join you. I hope you enjoy yourself."

He wondered if she had any idea how heartbreaking her palpable sadness was. And he guessed why she didn't want to go. His idiot of a brother.

Heaving a sigh, he shook his head. "A pity you won't join us. That big, empty town house certainly won't seem the same without you."

She frowned. "Empty?"

"Well, yes, what with Austin visiting his Surrey estate for the, er, annual inspection of the crops. Surely he told you." *Annual inspection of the crops?* He nearly rolled his eyes heavenward at his outrageous fabrication.

"I'm afraid he didn't mention it to me."

Shaking his head, he uttered a disgusted sound. "How like my big brother. Always forgetting these things."

"How long will he be in Surrey?"

"Oh, at least a fortnight," Robert lied with a perfectly straight face. "We'll have a wonderful time. Besides, Caroline will fly into the boughs if you refuse to join us. She desperately needs you as a shopping companion as Mother's tastes are far too staid. And you'll be saving me the dreary prospect of having no one to converse with except my *mother and sister*." He screwed his face into a horrified expression. "So you see? You simply must come."

He could almost see her mind working, and relief swept

through him when she offered what appeared to be a genuine smile . . . a *small* smile, but genuine nonetheless. "All right. Perhaps a trip to London *would* be a nice change. Thank you, Robert."

"My pleasure."

"I suppose I'd best be off to pack."

"An excellent idea. You go on ahead. I'll be along shortly."

He watched her retreating back, waiting until she disappeared into the maze. When he was sure she couldn't see him, he vaulted over a hedge in an un-lordlike manner that would have sent his mother into a swoon, and dashed pell-mell toward the side entrance of the manor.

He had to inform Caroline and his mother of their imminent trip to London.

Was she pregnant?

Austin sat in his study, staring into the fire, nursing his fourth brandy, trying without success to banish the question that had haunted him for three weeks. Miles stood by the mantel, relating something regarding the latest *on dit* he'd heard at White's, but Austin had no idea what his friend was saying. After another several brandies, he would no doubt cease to hear Miles altogether. Perhaps he would cease to feel as well.

He'd spent the last three weeks tracking down two soldiers who had served with William, but as they had a year ago, both men stated that they saw him, like so many others that day, go down in battle. He'd also waited, in vain, to receive further instructions from the blackmailer, but none came. Why hadn't he sought to collect the five thousand pounds he'd demanded? If Elizabeth were here, perhaps she could—

He sliced off the thought, but it was too late. She was

embedded in his mind, and no matter how he tried to banish it, the question reverberated through him—was she pregnant? He both longed for and dreaded the answer. If she was, they'd have a child . . . a child destined to die before she'd really had a chance to live. If she wasn't pregnant, his marriage was over. A bitter laugh rose in his throat like bile. Hell, either way, his marriage was over.

Tossing back the contents in his snifter, he rose and walked to the crystal decanters by the windows overlooking the street. He poured himself a double, then pushed the curtain aside.

The expansive lawns of Hyde Park lay just across the street, and a line of fine carriages promenaded through the lanes. Fashionably dressed lords and ladies strolled in the late afternoon sunshine, their faces wreathed in what appeared to be happy smiles.

Happy smiles. An image of Elizabeth, laughing and smiling, rose before his eyes, and he swallowed half his drink in one gulp. Bloody hell, how long would it take before she didn't occupy every corner of his mind? Before his anger, and damn it, his hurt, would abate? Before he could draw a breath without his chest aching with loss? Before he would stop hating her for tearing his heart out, and hating himself for letting her? Damn it, how long before he stopped loving her?

He didn't know, but by God, another brandy would hopefully speed the process along. He raised his snifter to drain the contents down his throat, but paused as a shiny black carriage pulled by four exquisite matched bays rolled into view. *By damn, that looks like one of my coaches.* Leaning closer to the window, he saw the distinctive Bradford crest emblazoned on the ebony lacquered door.

Bloody hell! It was no doubt Robert, come back to

plague him. He'd suffered through his brother's company only yesterday and he had no desire for a repeat visit.

"What has captured your attention?" Miles asked, joining him at the decanters. Miles craned his neck. "Isn't that one of your coaches?"

"Yes, I'm afraid so. Apparently my brother has decided to return for but yet another unannounced visit."

The coach halted in front of the town house and a footman opened the door. Austin's mother alighted.

"What is *she* doing here?" Austin asked. No doubt another shopping excursion. He suddenly stilled, his stomach clenching into a hard knot.

Could his mother or Robert have a message from Elizabeth? The disturbing thought had no sooner crossed his mind than Elizabeth alighted from the coach. His fingers tightened around his snifter and the elaborately cut glass dug into his skin.

"Bloody hell, what is *she* doing here?" But even as Austin growled the words, his mind whirled. Did she know if she carried his child? Only three weeks had passed. If she knew this quickly, she most likely wasn't pregnant—or was she? Or maybe she'd come because she'd had another vision of William? He looked out the window and fought the urge to press his nose to the glass like a boy at a sweet shop, eager for a glimpse of her.

She was dressed in a peacock blue traveling suit, with a matching bonnet. Loose auburn tendrils framed her face and he immediately recalled the feel of her soft hair sifting through his fingers. Even at a distance he could see the circles shadowing her eyes, a telltale sign of sleepless nights.

The footman reached a hand into the coach and helped Caroline alight.

Miles drew a sharp breath. "What the hell is *she* doing here?" he asked, elbowing past Austin to get a better view.

Austin contemplated his friend with surprise. "She's my sister. Why the hell *shouldn't* she be here? Besides, you know my family. They travel in packs. Like bloody wolves. I'd wager any sum that my brother is about to make an appearance."

As if on cue, Robert emerged from the coach, a huge grin lighting his face. *Damn it!* What was Robert up to now? And why had Elizabeth come here instead of sending a message? Turning away from the window, Austin slammed his snifter onto his desk and stalked toward the door.

"Austin! How wonderful to see you!"

Her mother-in-law's words jerked Elizabeth's head around. Striding down the corridor toward the foyer, anger evident in every taut line of his body, was her husband.

Dismay washed over her. Good heavens, what was *he* doing here? Why wasn't he in Surrey?

She stood frozen in place, her eyes riveted on him, and tried to hold back the swell of love and longing that hit her, but it was a hopeless task. Dear God, she'd missed him so much!

But it was clear from his expression that he had not missed her. In fact, as he strode into the foyer, he completely ignored her.

He bent down and accepted a kiss from his mother. "This is unexpected," he said in a tight voice. "I trust all is well?"

"Oh, yes," the dowager said with a smile. "Caroline, Elizabeth, and I had a hankering for the shops. Robert kindly offered to escort us to Town."

Austin turned a narrow-eyed glare on his brother. "How dutiful of you, Robert."

Robert's smile could have lit the entire room. "No trouble at all. Always happy to accompany a coach filled with lovely ladies."

Austin cocked a brow at Caroline. "Didn't you shop enough when you were here several weeks ago?"

A gay laugh trilled from Caroline. "Oh, Austin, how amusing you are! You should know that a woman can *never* spend enough time in the shops."

Elizabeth stood in an agony of embarrassment. Her husband had yet to so much as acknowledge her presence. An awkward silence ensued. Heat crept up her neck and she wished she could simply sink through the floor. Just when she thought he meant to walk away without greeting her, he turned and stared directly at her.

The icy fury shooting from his gray eyes chilled her to the bone. And although he stared directly at her, it seemed as if he were looking through her, as if she weren't really there.

Any hopes she may have secretly harbored that time would soften him toward her died with that single look. How on earth was she going to survive this visit? Not being with him, agonizing over what she'd lost, was a pain she could barely stand.

But *seeing* him look at her like this, with all the warmth and caring extinguished from his eyes, inflicted a piercing ache that weakened her knees.

But she'd done what she'd had to do. For him.

Determined not to let him see her inner torment, she forced herself to offer him a smile. "Hello, Austin."

A muscle ticked in his clenched jaw. "Elizabeth."

She tried to moisten her parched lips, but her mouth had gone dry. "I . . . I thought you were in Surrey."

His glacial expression could have frozen fire. *"Surrey?"*

"Yes. For the annual inspection of the crops . . ." Her voice trailed off into an agonizing embarrassed silence as he simply stared at her.

"Do you have something to tell me?" His clipped question hung in the air between them.

She felt the weight of everyone's eyes on them, watching their tense exchange. Humiliation washed over her, and if she'd thought her legs would cooperate, she would have run from the house. "No," she whispered. "Nothing."

She was saved from enduring further attempts at conversation when Miles joined them. He greeted everyone, but Elizabeth noticed that his bow to Caroline was stiff and that Caroline steadfastly looked at a place over his shoulder.

"I'd like a word with you in my study, Robert," Austin said in a voice that resembled a growl.

"Of course," Robert said. "The moment I'm settled in—"

"Now." Without another word, Austin turned on his heel and strode down the corridor.

A deafening silence ensued. Finally, the dowager cleared her throat. "Well! Isn't that . . . nice? Robert, it appears Austin wishes to speak with you."

Robert's brows almost disappeared into his hairline. "Indeed? I hadn't particularly noticed." With a jaunty salute, he ambled down the corridor Austin had just stalked down.

The dowager turned back to the silent group with a smile that could only be described as desperate. "They're going to talk. Isn't that . . . nice? I'm sure this is going to be a wonderful visit."

"Wonderful," Caroline echoed, looking everywhere but at Miles.

"Delightful," Miles agreed in a gloomy voice.

"Marvelous," Elizabeth said in a weak voice.

She hoped she lived through it.

The instant Robert closed the study door, Austin bit out, "What the *hell* do you think you're doing?"

"Following your orders, brother dear. You said you wanted to speak to me *now*, so here I am. Speak away."

Austin forced himself to retain his casual posture: hips leaning against his desk, legs outstretched, arms folded across his chest. If he didn't, he would be across the room in two strides, picking Robert up by his cravat.

"Why did you bring them here?"

Robert's face bore a mask of utter innocence. "Me? I didn't bring them here. You know how women love the shops. I—"

"Elizabeth *hates* the shops."

Robert's nonplussed stare clearly indicated that this was news to him. Austin studied his brother through narrowed eyes and tried to contain his anger. "Can you explain why Elizabeth thought I was in Surrey? And then perhaps you'd enlighten me regarding what the *annual inspection of the crops* entails."

"Surrey? Crops? I—"

"Enough, Robert. I'll ask you one more time. Why did you bring Elizabeth here? Don't lie to me."

Apparently the glacial fury in his tone served as a warning Robert decided not to ignore. Dropping all pretense of innocence, Robert said, "I brought her because it was painfully obvious to me when I saw you yesterday that you're miserable without her. And a blind man could see that she is equally miserable without you."

"If I'd wanted her here, I would have sent for her myself."

Temper flared in Robert's blue eyes. "Then I cannot fathom why you didn't do so, because it's clear you want her here, and even clearer that you *need* her here. You're just too stubborn to admit it. Whatever problems you're having, you cannot solve them if you're apart."

"Indeed?" Austin said in a deadly calm tone. "And when did you become an expert in marital relations—mine specifically?"

"I'm not. But I know you. I saw how you were with her. I saw how you looked at her. Whether you want to admit it or not, I know you care about her. Hell, let's just say it. You love her. And you're ill-tempered, unhappy, and damn near impossible to be around without her."

Pain and anger scissored through Austin, but he forced his features to remain blank. "You've clearly mistaken my feelings and mood, Robert. I am not unhappy, I am *busy*. I'm responsible for six estates and there is a great deal of work that requires my attention."

Robert made a disgusted sound. "Then you clearly don't know the difference between busy and unhappy."

Austin turned a frosty glare on his brother. "I know the difference." *Believe me, I know.* "I will not tolerate this interference in my marriage. Is that clear?"

"Perfectly." He went on as if Austin hadn't spoken. "What has Elizabeth done to anger you so? Surely, whatever it is, you can forgive her for it. I cannot believe she would intentionally hurt you."

She intentionally ripped out my heart and showed herself for a calculating schemer. Pushing himself away from his desk, Austin said in a deceptively mild tone, "I think it would be best, and certainly much smarter, if you ceased expressing opinions on subjects you know nothing about."

"Elizabeth is wretchedly unhappy."

His insides involuntarily pinched, but he ruthlessly

pushed his sympathy aside. "I cannot imagine why. She is, after all, a duchess. She lacks for nothing."

"Except for a relationship with her husband."

"You forget that our marriage was one of convenience."

"Perhaps it started out that way, but you fell in love with her. And she with you."

If only that were true. "Enough. Stop worrying about Elizabeth and me and turn your energies toward more productive endeavors. Why don't you find yourself a mistress? Concentrate on your own life instead of plaguing mine."

Robert's brows raised. "Is that what *you've* done? Found yourself a mistress?"

Austin barely managed to swallow the bitter laugh pushing at the back of his throat. He couldn't imagine touching another woman. Before he could issue a retort, Robert continued, "Because if you have, then you're a bigger fool than I thought. Why you would want another woman when you could have Elizabeth is beyond me."

"Has it not occurred to you that perhaps Elizabeth does not want my attentions?" He forced the question past his lips.

A bark of incredulous laughter escaped Robert. "Is *that* what this is about? You think Elizabeth doesn't want you? Good God, Austin, you're either an idiot or you've gone daft. The woman adores you. A blind man could see that."

"You're wrong."

Robert's eyes turned troubled. "You're throwing away happiness with both hands, Austin. I hate to see you do that."

"Your concern has been duly noted. Now, this discussion is over." When it appeared Robert was about to argue, Austin added, "*Permanently* over. Is that understood?"

Robert huffed out a clearly frustrated breath. "Yes."

"Good. I cannot ask you to leave *now*, but I shall expect

you and this houseful of company you brought here to depart by tomorrow afternoon. And until then, you will keep
them occupied and out of my way."

Without another word, Austin quit the room, resisting
an almost violent urge to slam the door.

She was here. In his house.

He didn't want her here. He didn't want to see her.

God help him, how was he going to manage to stay
away from her for the next twenty-four hours?

Chapter 20

Late that afternoon, Austin stood alone in his private study, staring out the window, seeing nothing. When a knock sounded on the door, his hands clenched. If it was her—

He cut off the thought. "Come in."

Caroline entered the room. "May I speak with you?"

He forced himself to offer her a smile. "Of course. Please sit down."

"I'd prefer to stand."

He raised his brows at her militant tone. "All right. What did you wish to speak to me about?"

Clasping her hands in front of her, she drew a deep breath. "I'll start by saying that as my brother, I hold you in the greatest esteem and affection."

A tired smile tugged at his lips. "Thank you, Caroline. I—"

"But you're a complete nincompoop."

Annoyance wiped the smile from his lips. "I beg your pardon?"

"Did you not hear me? I said you're a—"

"I heard you."

"Excellent. Would you like to hear *why* you're a nincompoop?"

"Not particularly, but I'm certain you're going to tell me anyway."

"Yes, I am. I am referring to this situation with Elizabeth."

His jaw clenched. "Situation?"

Blue eyes flashing, she said, "Don't pretend you don't know what I'm talking about. What have you done to her?"

"What makes you think I've done anything to her?"

"She's miserable."

"So everyone is determined to tell me."

She sent him a searching gaze. "I cannot fathom this icy indifference. I thought you two were so well suited, but she is clearly unhappy, and you're stalking about like a bear with a thorn in its paw. I've never known you to treat a woman, even the most annoying woman, with anything but the most respectful manner. Yet you're treating your wife as if she doesn't exist."

She doesn't. The woman I fell in love with doesn't really exist.

"Austin." Reaching up, she laid her palm against his cheek, tenderness replacing all vestiges of anger in her eyes. "You cannot allow this unhappiness to continue. It is obvious to me that you care deeply for her, and she for you. Please, search your heart and find a way to solve whatever problems you and Elizabeth are having. Now. Before it's too late. I want you to be happy, and the pain I see in your eyes tells me you're not. But you were. And it was because of Elizabeth."

Her tender words curled around his heart and squeezed like a vise. Yes, he'd been happy. For a very brief time. But it had been based on an illusion. And while he appreciated Caroline's concern, he'd had more than enough of first Robert, and now her, interfering in his life.

They were not aware of the circumstances, and he'd be damned if he'd tell them, or anyone else, that his wife wished to dissolve their marriage. Not until it became absolutely necessary. If it turned out that Elizabeth was pregnant, they would have to make the best of their marriage.

A knock sounded. "Come in."

His mother entered. "Am I interrupting?"

"Not at all." He stared pointedly at the door. "Caroline was just leaving."

"Excellent. The coach is awaiting us for our ride through the park, Caroline. I'll join you in just a moment. I need to speak with Austin."

Caroline closed the door softly behind her. Austin propped one hip on his desk and regarded his mother. "Are you here to call me names, too?"

Her eyes widened. "Names?"

"My siblings have seen fit to call me a fool, an idiot, and my favorite, a nincompoop."

"I see."

"I'm gratified that at least my mother is above name-calling."

"Naturally. Of course, if you weren't already laid so low, I *might* be tempted to label you a pinheaded dolt, but under the circumstances, I'd prefer merely to tell you that it hurts me to see you, and Elizabeth, so unhappy." She took his hand between her own and squeezed it. "Is there anything I can do to help?"

Bloody hell, he preferred the name-calling to this tender, warm concern.

"I'm fine, Mother."

"You're not," she corrected in a tone that belied further arguments. "I knew something was amiss when you sent

Elizabeth to Wesley Manor so abruptly. The poor girl's misery is palpable. As is yours. I've never seen you so angry and distraught." Her gentle blue eyes rested on his. "Your father and I suffered through many misunderstandings when we first wed—"

"This is not a misunderstanding, Mother."

He hadn't meant his tone to sound so harsh. She studied him for a moment before speaking. "I see. Well, I can only tell you that with great love comes other powerful emotions. When you love hard, you fight hard." A sad smile curved her lips. "Your father and I did both."

Sympathy pinched him and he squeezed her hand. His father's sudden death had devastated them all, but particularly her.

"She is your wife, Austin. For the *rest of your life*. For your sake, and for hers, try to solve whatever troubles are facing you and make a happy marriage. Don't let pride stand in your way."

He lifted his brows. "It sounds as if you think that I am to blame for the problems in my marriage."

"I didn't say that. But you are experienced and worldly whereas Elizabeth is not. She is going to make mistakes, some serious, some not, until she gains her footing in the world she's now in. Be patient with her. And with yourself." She pressed a soft kiss onto the back of his hand. "She is the right woman for you, Austin."

"Indeed? Are you the same mother who was apprehensive about my marrying an American?"

"I cannot deny I had some reservations at first, but I've spent the last three weeks getting to know my daughter-in-law. She is a lovely, intelligent young woman and has the makings of a fine duchess. And she loves you. And I suspect you feel the same way about her."

She offered him a gentle smile, then left the room. Austin stared at the closed door and exhaled a breath. His family was going to render him a candidate for Bedlam. He needed to get out of this house. Immediately.

Before he could take one step, however, his mother's words crashed over him. *She loves you.* Pain and anger combined with a bone-weary sadness, slumping his shoulders. His mother, Caroline, Robert—none of them knew how wrong they were about Elizabeth's feelings. She'd managed to fool every member of his family.

And I suspect you feel the same way about her.

Groaning, he raked his fingers through his hair. Yes, damn it, he loved her.

But he'd gladly give up everything he owned to make the damn feeling go away.

Austin strode into his private study at ten the next morning and halted at the unwelcome sight of Miles lounging in a wing chair. Damn it, if Miles had it in his mind to take up where his family had left off yesterday, Austin was bloody well going to plant him a facer. The urge to hit something was strong, and with very little provocation that something could be Miles.

Miles looked him up and down then slanted a pointed glance at the mantel clock. "Ten A.M. is a bit early for dressing in formal wear . . . or am I simply not privy to the latest fashion trend?"

"I'm not on my way out," Austin said, barely keeping his impatience in check.

"Ah. Then you must be on your way *in*. From where, I wonder? You're looking a bit ragged about the edges."

"I was at my club, if you must know." Austin made an exaggerated show of looking about the room. "Where is the rest of my esteemed family? Hiding behind the draperies?"

"Your mother and Caroline are visiting the jeweler.

Robert and Elizabeth are also out—where, I do not know."

Austin strode across the study floor, paused at the decanters, then moved on. He'd had more than enough brandy at White's last night. And instead of finding the oblivion he'd sought, all he'd gotten was a wretched, throbbing headache . . . and a loss of several hundred pounds at the faro table.

"You seem nervous," Miles remarked from his chair.

He halted, and realized with no small amount of irritation that he'd been pacing. "I'm not nervous."

"Really? I've seen gentlemen poised on the brink of imminent fatherhood who were more relaxed than you."

Imminent fatherhood. The casual remark stung like salt on an open wound. Smothering a vicious curse, Austin walked to the window and pulled back the curtain. Staring through the glass with unseeing eyes, he concentrated on bludgeoning back the torturous images conjured up by the words *imminent fatherhood*.

He'd almost succeeded when his attention was snagged by a hired hack stopping in front of his town house. The door swung opened and Robert stepped out, his lips pressed into a grim line. He reached in and offered a hand, and Elizabeth alighted. Her face appeared pale, her eyes huge.

Austin's fingers gripped the heavy velvet draperies. Where the hell had they gone? And why the hell had they taken a hack?

As he watched, Robert again offered a hand, assisting another woman down. She was small and thin, a dull brown bonnet covering her hair. When she turned, Austin saw her face.

Black bruises surrounded her eyes, and her bottom lip was swollen and cracked. Recognition hit him like a plank to the head.

It was Molly, the serving wench, the *whore*, from the

Filthy Swine. God Almighty, what the hell was going on? Did she have information about Gaspard? Why were Elizabeth and Robert with her?

Dropping the curtain back into place, he strode from the room, ignoring Miles's questioning look. He arrived in the foyer just as the trio walked through the door. Elizabeth and Robert supported Molly on either side. The ragged woman looked about ready to drop to the floor.

"Don't worry, Molly," Elizabeth was saying. "Just a few more steps and you'll be settled in a comfortable bed. Then we'll take a look at your injuries."

"What the hell is going on?" Austin asked, his gaze alternating among the three of them.

Molly visibly recoiled at his harsh tone and cowered closer to Elizabeth.

"It's all right, Molly," Elizabeth said. She looked at Robert. "Will you escort Molly to the yellow guest chamber and instruct Katie to prepare a bath? I'll join you in a few moments."

"Of course." Easily supporting the frail woman's weight, Robert led her toward the stairs.

Elizabeth turned her attention to Austin. "May I speak with you? Privately?"

"I was about to make the same request," Austin said in a tight voice. Recalling he'd left Miles in his study, he led the way to the library and closed the door behind them. He watched Elizabeth cross to the center of the room, then turn to face him. Her face was completely devoid of color, and her eyes appeared like haunted circles against the stark background. The need to draw her into his arms nearly overwhelmed him, angering him at his own weakness for her.

He approached her slowly, deliberately. He'd half expected her to retreat, but she stood in place, her hands folded in front of her, her eyes steady on his.

When only two feet separated them, he halted. God, how he missed her. Her warmth and smile. The sound of her laughter. *Forget that! It's over. Gone. She doesn't want you.*

Hurt and anger pumped through him, but he schooled his features into a cold mask and simply waited for her to speak.

Elizabeth stared at her husband's icy expression and her already cramped stomach tightened further. His glacial demeanor indicated she faced a battle with him, and it was one she was determined to win.

Lifting her chin a notch, she said, "I suppose you're wondering why Molly is here."

He cocked a single brow. "How astute you are. Yes, I would like an explanation, not only as to *why* a whore is in my town house, but also *how* she came to be here."

Elizabeth's temper flared. "I don't want you to call her that . . . word."

"Why? That's what she is."

"Not any longer."

"Indeed? What is she now?"

She had so many things to tell him, and time was short. She had to examine Molly, and then she had to prepare for a trip. There simply wasn't time for elaborate explanations. Searching for a suitable answer to his question, one popped into her mind and she seized it. "She's now a lady's maid. *My* lady's maid."

If the situation had been the least bit amusing, she would have laughed at his shocked expression.

"I beg your pardon?"

"I've hired Molly to assist Katie with my, er, vast wardrobe."

His hand shot out, fast as lightning, and gripped her upper arm. "What nonsense is this?"

She tried to jerk her arm from his grasp, but he tightened his hold, fueling her temper. "This morning I happened to touch the jacket I wore the night we went to the *Filthy Swine,* and I had a vision. I saw Molly being beaten and I had to stop it. I convinced Robert to take me to the docks—"

"Robert took you *to the docks*?"

"Yes." Fury flashed in his eyes and she quickly added, "Please don't be angry with him. After I pleaded and explained the dire circumstances to him—that a friend was in terrible danger—he agreed to help me, but not until I'd promised to remain in the safety of the carriage. When we arrived, we discovered Molly huddled in an alley, beaten and robbed."

She drew a deep breath. "She'd left the Filthy Swine the night we met her and taken a small room above a warehouse. The men who robbed her took everything she'd managed to save in the hopes of starting a new life." A shudder shook through her. "Dear God, Austin, the reason she even had enough coins for someone to steal was because we gave them to her that night." Drawing herself up to her full height she said, "I intend to help her."

"Yes, that much is clear." His fingers tightened like a vise around her arm. The chill had melted from his eyes, replaced by white hot anger. "However, did you even once consider the danger you placed yourself in by going there?"

"I did not go alone."

"Do you honestly believe that meant you were safe? You could have easily been beaten and robbed yourself. Or worse."

Under other circumstances, his anger, the heat in his gaze, might have led her to believe that he cared what happened to her.

But of course, he wouldn't want her harmed if she carried his child.

"Not only did you place yourself *and* my clearly idiotic brother in danger," he continued, his voice a low growl, "but you obviously didn't consider how scandalous it is that you went to the docks *and* that you brought her here."

"Scandalous? To help a beaten woman? Well, I don't care. And if it's her *former* occupation that concerns you, I have no intention of sharing that information with anyone. Molly certainly is not going to boast about it, and I trust Robert to keep it a secret." She raised her brows. "Do you intend to tell anyone?"

"No." He let go of her arm and tunneled his fingers through his hair. "But servants gossip. Word is certain to get out."

"Then I'll simply deny it. You seem to think I'm an accomplished liar, so perhaps I should be. Who would dare doubt the word of the Duchess of Bradford?"

A humorless laugh escaped him. "Only me."

His words hit her like a slap, and she bit her lip to contain her distressed gasp. She searched his cold eyes for a long moment, mourning the loss of the warm caring she'd once seen there.

"I understand that you'd find this situation shocking, but dear God, Austin, think of that poor woman. I haven't had the chance to fully examine her, but I'm certain she has several broken ribs, and she cannot hear from her left ear." Although she risked a scathing rejection, she reached out and touched his hand. "I know you're angry with me, but you have a kind heart. I cannot believe that you would turn away this helpless woman who has nothing."

A muscle ticked in his clenched jaw. "We can find a post for her on one of the estates. But you must understand that she cannot stay with *you*. If you will not think of the scandal to yourself, consider my mother's and sister's feelings."

She nodded, relieved. "All right. And if it turns out I am

not with child, you won't need to worry about Molly anyway."

The ice seeped back into his gaze. "Indeed? Why is that?"

"Because if I'm not pregnant, I plan to return to America as soon as our annulment is finalized. Molly can accompany me. She and I will both be free to make a fresh start."

"I see."

The tension in the air all but strangled her. She needed to see to Molly, and she longed to escape the stifling atmosphere surrounding her, but she couldn't leave the room just yet. Clearing her throat, she said, "There's something else I must tell you."

He dragged a weary hand over his face. "Hopefully it isn't that you revisited the gaming hell and rescued half a dozen debt-ridden drunks."

In spite of his dark tone, a tiny smile tugged at her lips. "No, although that is an idea that has some merit."

His eyes narrowed to slits. "No, that is an idea that has *no merit whatsoever*."

Relieved that she appeared to have won the first battle with relative ease, she conceded the point. "Very well. But now I must tell you my other news. It concerns your brother."

His eyes glittered with menace. "Indeed? Well, I certainly shall discuss with Robert this visit to the slums of London."

"Not Robert. This news concerns William."

He went perfectly still. "What is it?"

"I know where we can find Gaspard."

Chapter 21

Austin's entire existence narrowed down to those few words spinning through his mind. *I know where we can find Gaspard.*

He grabbed her shoulders. "Where is he?"

"I'm not certain—but I discovered someone who knows."

"How? Where?"

"At the docks. While Robert assisted Molly into the carriage, I saw a man enter a pub. Even though I didn't touch him, I sensed very strongly that he has some connection to Gaspard."

His grip involuntarily tightened. By God, if Robert had allowed her to go into that place in pursuit of this man, his brother would suffer. "You didn't attempt to speak to him, did you?"

"No. We left immediately." She laid her hands on his forearms. "But he's still there, Austin. I feel it. He's a large bald man wearing sailor's garb. He walked with a decided limp and sported a gold hoop earring in his right ear." She described the building's location.

"I'll find him." He released her shoulders and her hands fell away from his arms. For a long moment they stared at each other. He swore he detected a flash in her eyes of the warm, loving Elizabeth he'd thought he'd known and he fought the flood of feelings that swamped him. Damn it, those huge golden brown orbs pierced through his guard. But then it was as if a veil lowered over her and steely determination replaced any traces of warmth.

But that look that had flared in her eyes . . . hell, if he didn't know better, he'd swear she cared. Why was she helping him? Surely it wasn't because she'd promised to do so. He'd found out in the most hurtful way possible that she didn't keep her promises.

So perhaps she did care a little bit. But not enough. Not enough to find a way for them to share a life.

And he had to remember that.

Stepping away from her, he said, "I must go."

"I know. Austin . . . be careful."

The quiet plea in her voice formed a lump in his throat that he could not speak around. Offering her a stiff nod, he quit the room.

Elizabeth watched him go, staring at the doorway he'd just departed through. She knew he stood on the brink of finding the answers he sought.

She prayed that he'd be safe.

And that he might find it in his heart to someday forgive her.

Austin entered the dilapidated dockside tavern and allowed his eyes to adjust to the dim interior. His gaze panned quickly over the half-dozen patrons, then riveted on a man sitting alone in the corner, his large shoulders hunched protectively around his glass. He was bald and Austin caught a glint of gold shining in his right earlobe. He was the only man fitting the description Elizabeth had given him.

Austin approached the table and slid into the chair opposite the man. The sailor glared at him through narrowed, mud-colored eyes. "Who the 'ell are you?"

Instead of answering, Austin placed his fist on the table between them. Opening his hand, he revealed a leather pouch. "There's fifty gold sovereigns in there. You have information I want. Give it to me, and the money is yours."

The man's gaze flicked to the pouch. A nasty grin split his rawboned face, revealing rotting teeth. With the flick of his wrist, he slipped a lethal-looking knife from his sleeve. Leaning forward, he said, "Maybe I'll just take yer coins and keep me information to meself."

"You could try," Austin replied in a deadly voice, "but I'd advise against it."

A bark of laughter erupted from the sailor. "Would ye, now? And why's that?"

"Because there's a pistol pointing at your gut under the table."

He watched the sailor's gaze lower to where Austin's other hand was concealed by the table.

Doubt flashed in the sailor's eyes, but he quickly covered it with derision. "Yer expectin' me to believe a fancy toff like yerself would shoot me in front of a roomful of people? Ye'd hang."

"On the contrary, the magistrate would probably reward me for ridding London of the likes of you. And the silence of your so-called witnesses could easily be bought." Leaning back, Austin moved his hand from under the table long enough to afford his companion a glimpse of his pistol.

"You can leave here a rich man or a dead man. The choice is yours."

The sailor studied him for several seconds. Austin stared right back, his hand gripping the pistol, but knowing that greed would win out.

Avarice glittered in the sailor's beady eyes. "I'd rather be rich. Richer than fifty quid'll make me."

"If I find your information useful, I'll give you an additional fifty."

"And if ye don't find it useful?"

Austin allowed an icy smile to touch his lips. "Then I don't believe you'll be of any use to me. And I don't believe you'll recover from the hole I'll shoot in your gut."

Fear flickered in the sailor's eyes, but he quickly covered it with a shrug. "Wot do ye want to know?"

"You know a Frenchman named Gaspard. I want to know where I can find him." He purposely jangled the pouch filled with coins. "Tell me and the money is yours."

The sailor tossed back a gulp of whiskey, then wiped his mouth with the back of a meaty hand. "Bertrand Gaspard?"

Austin fought to remain calm. *Bertrand Gaspard.* He finally knew the full name of the man he sought. "Where is he?"

The sailor shrugged. " 'E was 'ere in London for awhile, but then 'e rushed 'ome. To France."

"Where does he live?"

"Some village near Calais."

Austin leaned forward. "Which village?"

The sailor eyed him cautiously. "Can't recall the exact name. Sounds like a bloke's name."

Austin thought for a moment. "Marck?"

Recognition widened the sailor's eyes. "That's it."

"Why was he in London?"

"Said 'e 'ad some business. Was lookin' fer someone. Didn't say who. Bragged some 'bout comin' into some big money."

His gaze narrowed on Austin's. "That's all I know. I kept up me end of the bargain. Now give me the blunt."

Austin placed two pouches on the scarred table and slipped his pistol into his pocket. The sailor opened the pouches to verify the contents and Austin seized the man's distraction to slip out the door.

Keeping to the shadows, Austin walked quickly through the labyrinth of alleyways to his waiting hack. Grim elation pumped through his veins.

Bertrand Gaspard.

His knew his enemy's name. And where he lived.

He knew where to find the answers he sought. And he hoped to God those answers included William.

I'm coming for you, you bastard.

When Austin entered his town house, he found Elizabeth pacing the foyer. She halted the instant she saw him, her gaze running down the length of him as if to assure herself he was still in one piece.

Handing his hat to Carters, he said quietly, "I'm fine."

An audible sigh of relief escaped her. Her gaze darted to Carters, then returned to him. "Can we speak privately?"

He hesitated. God knew he didn't want to be alone with her, but he certainly couldn't discuss his meeting with the sailor here in the foyer. Inclining his head to indicate she should follow him, he walked down the corridor to his private study. Once inside, he closed the door, enveloping them in silence.

She stood in the center of the room, her hands clasped in front of her, her eyes steady on his, and a flood of memories washed over him. Elizabeth smiling at him. Elizabeth opening her arms to him. Lifting her face for his kiss. Lying beneath him, trembling with need. Asleep in his arms.

He tried to bludgeon the unwanted images back, but they assaulted him, attacking him with relentless accuracy. His gaze strayed to the carpet beneath her feet. They'd made love exactly where she now stood, the night he'd taught her the waltz and shown her where he'd hung the sketch she'd drawn of him.

He forced himself to look at that now empty space on the paneled wall opposite his desk. He'd removed the drawing because he couldn't bear to see it, to relive the memories it evoked every time he entered his study.

Returning his attention to her, he saw that her gaze was fixed upon the blank space where her sketch had hung. He fancied he saw hurt flash in her eyes, but he forced himself to harden his heart to it. She'd made her choice. And she had not chosen him.

"You wished to speak with me privately?" he asked.

She pulled her gaze from the paneled wall and faced him with a cool expression that ignited his temper.

"What happened at the docks?" she asked.

He cocked a brow. "You don't know?"

She blanched at his sarcastic question, then shook her head. "I feel that you found the answers you sought, but that is all."

Hoping a drink would ease the tension knotting his shoulders, he crossed to the decanters. After a hefty swallow of brandy, he related the information the sailor had given him.

She listened intently, her brow furrowed with concentration. When he finished, she said, "I assume you're planning to go to France."

"Yes. In fact, if you'll excuse me, I must instruct Kingsbury to pack my things."

"You're leaving soon?"

"Within the hour. The journey to Dover will take nearly five hours. I'll sail for Calais with the morning tide." He stood, unable to tear his gaze away from her, knowing he could not leave without saying what needed to be said.

"Elizabeth." He coughed to clear his tight throat. "I owe you my thanks for your assistance in finding Gaspard. I shall always be grateful. Thank you."

"You're welcome." Elizabeth looked at his handsome, serious face and her heart broke into tiny pieces. Dear God, she loved him so much. "I . . . I would do anything for you."

The unguarded words slipped past her lips and she cringed as the budding warmth she'd detected in his expression iced over.

"Anything?" A humorless laugh escaped him. "If that weren't such a blatant lie, it would be positively amusing." He crossed to the door and opened it. He hesitated, as if deciding whether to say something more, but after several seconds, he simply walked into the corridor, closing the door behind him.

Elizabeth drew a deep breath and pressed her hands to her churning stomach. Her husband clearly thought he'd dismissed her.

Her chin lifted with determination.

Her husband clearly didn't know everything.

Austin strode from the town house, mentally congratulating himself on his hasty departure. He'd scribbled quick notes to his mother and Miles stating he'd been unavoidably called away to France. Regret pricked him at the way he'd left Elizabeth, but he hadn't had a choice. If he'd stayed in that room with her for another moment he would

have said or done something he'd regret. *Like dropped to
my knees and begged her to love me.*

An impatient sound escaped him and he forced himself
to push thoughts of her aside. He had to concentrate on the
task at hand. On his trip to France. On finding Gaspard.
And hopefully William. He had to stop thinking about
Elizabeth.

The footman opened the coach door for him. Austin
placed his foot on the step and froze.

Elizabeth, garbed in her peacock traveling suit, sat in
the coach.

"What the hell are you doing here?" he asked.

She raised her brows. "I'm waiting for you."

"If you wish to speak with me, you'll have to wait until
I return. I'm leaving immediately."

"Yes, I know. And the sooner you settle yourself, the
sooner we can depart."

"We?" A bark of incredulous laughter escaped him.
"We are not going anywhere."

Her chin raised an inch. "I beg to differ. *We* are going to
France."

Anger shot through him. With a curt nod he dismissed
the hovering footman. Leaning into the carriage, he said in
a tightly controlled voice, "The only place *you* are going is
back into the house. Now."

"Do you truly think that is for the best?"

"Yes."

She nodded thoughtfully. "It seems like a dreadful
waste of time to me. You see, if you make me leave this
coach, you will be further delayed by having to remove my
luggage. And then I shall have to arrange other transportation to Dover."

His lips collapsed into a tight line. "You will do nothing
of the kind."

Determination fired in her eyes. "Yes, I will."

"The hell you will. I forbid it."

"I shall go just the same."

He barely smothered the vicious oath that rose to his lips. Damn stubborn woman. "Elizabeth, you are *not*—"

"How is your French?"

That gave him pause. "My French?"

"According to Caroline, you understand the language but can't speak it well enough for anyone to comprehend."

Even while he mentally consigned his sister to perdition, he couldn't deny the truth of her words. His French was atrocious.

His lip curled. "And I suppose you're fluent?"

She shot him a beaming smile. *"Oui. Naturellement."*

"And who taught you French?"

"My English mother, who studied the language as all English young ladies do." Her smile faded, and her eyes turned imploring and determined at the same time. "Please understand. I cannot let you go alone. I promised to help you, and help you I shall. If you refuse to take me with you, I shall be forced to travel to Calais on my own."

He could tell by the tilt of her chin and the fierce resolve in her expression that she would do as she threatened, unless he planned to tie her forcibly to a chair. And even if he did, he didn't doubt that Robert, Miles, Caroline, or even his own mother would untie her. Damn it, the entire bloody family would no doubt accompany her to France.

Knowing he was defeated, but not liking it one bit, he climbed into the carriage. Without waiting for the footman, he slammed the door shut himself, then signaled the driver to depart.

Chapter 22

The damn woman was impossible to ignore.

He wouldn't have been able to ignore her if they'd been in a huge ballroom. The confines of his coach nearly undid him.

All his senses were intensely aware of her. Every time he inhaled, her gentle lilac scent filled his head.

In desperation, he closed his eyes, praying he'd fall asleep, but his prayers were in vain. Instead images of her danced behind his eyes. Images that nothing could erase.

What would it take to wipe her from his thoughts? From his heart? His soul?

He opened one eye a slit. She sat across from him, reading a book, and appeared cool and composed, a fact that rankled him. Clearly he was the only one who was suffering.

He slammed his eye shut and held in a grunt.

By damn, he was determined to suffer in silence.

Even if the effort killed him.

*   *   *

The coach ride nearly killed her.

Elizabeth exited the coach in Dover and stretched her cramped muscles. The journey had been sheer torture. Five hours of pretending to read a book she could not even name the title of. And all the while Austin had sat across from her, sleeping.

She would have gladly welcomed sleep, but she could barely sit still, let alone close her eyes. She spent the entire journey staring at her book, her heart desperately trying to convince her mind to accept the offer Austin had made weeks ago—to be lovers in ways that would not result in the conception of a child.

But as much as her heart begged, her mind refused to listen. *It would only take one slip in control—control that somehow eludes me when he takes me in his arms—and I could find myself with child. And I know that child's fate.*

An icy shudder ripped through her. As much as her decision hurt, she could not subject Austin to the torment of their daughter's death.

Austin stared at the innkeeper. "I beg your pardon?"

"There's only one room, your grace," the elderly man repeated.

He truly had to fight the urge to pound his fists upon the stone walls. Damn it, what else could go wrong? But even as the question entered his mind, he banished it. Better not to ask.

And no point taking his frustrations out on the innkeeper. It wasn't the elderly man's fault that his inn was full. After issuing instructions to the footman to deliver the necessary baggage to the available room, he allowed the innkeeper to lead him and Elizabeth up the stairs.

The room was small but cheerful, the space nearly

wholly occupied by a comfortable-looking bed covered with an intricately embroidered cream coverlet.

"There's fresh water in the pitcher, your grace," the innkeeper said. "Will you need anything else?"

Austin pried his attention from the bed and the wealth of thoughts it inspired. "Nothing else, thank you."

The innkeeper left, closing the door behind him. Austin watched Elizabeth fiddle with the ties on her bonnet. She looked at him and offered an uncertain half smile.

"This is a . . . tad awkward," she said.

He approached her, his eyes riveted on hers. "Awkward? Why is that? We're man and wife."

Crimson stained her cheeks. "I cannot share a bed with you."

"So you've said. But unfortunately there is only one bed. And two of us."

"I shall sleep on the floor," she said in what he believed she intended as a confident voice, but the slight tremor gave a clear indication that she was rattled.

Good. She was not as calm as she appeared. He'd just spent five miserable hours, and the notion that she might be miserable as well cheered him considerably.

He took another step toward her. Her eyes widened a bit, but she stood her ground. Another step closer and he detected her sharp intake of breath. Two more strides and he stood directly in front of her. Her golden brown eyes flickered with apprehension, but he grudgingly had to admire her spirit in not backing away from him. But damn it, he longed to shake her composure. As she'd shaken his.

Lowering his gaze to her mouth, he whispered, "It isn't necessary for you to sleep on the floor, Elizabeth."

"I'm afraid it is."

"Because you don't trust me not to seduce you?"

"I trust you," she whispered. "It's myself I cannot trust."

The ache in her voice snapped his gaze back to hers. He

studied her, the vulnerability glimmering in her eyes, the
need and desire shadowing their golden depths, and his
breath stalled. He sensed she was trying desperately to
hide it, but the evidence was there in her eyes. She wanted
him. Desire shimmered from her like warm sun rays,
beckoning him.

He lifted his hand to touch her, but curled his fingers
into a fist and resisted the powerful urge. Her eyes told
him he could seduce her, but he couldn't endure the pain
of having to let her go again. Of hearing her say afterward
that she planned to leave him. As much as he wanted her,
her betrayal still hurt too much.

Turning from her, he walked to the window and
dragged his hands down his face. It occurred to him that
Elizabeth's visions were a double-edged sword. On the one
side, they'd helped lead him to Gaspard, who would in turn
hopefully lead him to William.

But her premonitions had robbed him of his marriage.
His wife. The chance for a future filled with happiness.
And children. They'd left him with nothing but anger,
pain, betrayal, and a heartache so deep he didn't know if
he'd ever stop hurting.

He heard her crossing the room and he turned around,
freezing when he found her standing no more than a foot
away from him. She appeared equally startled by this sudden nearness, and equally riveted in place. He had only to
reach out to touch her . . . to take one step forward to hold
her in his arms. His brain ordered him to move away, but
his feet remained rooted to the spot as if someone had
nailed his shoes to the floor.

He could see every pale gold freckle on her nose, every
soot-colored eyelash surrounding her beautiful eyes . . .
eyes he didn't want to look into because they'd fooled him
too many times. His gaze dropped to her mouth and he immediately recalled the sensation of her soft lips crushed

beneath his, parting to accept the thrust of his tongue. Desire slammed into him and he clenched his hands, forcing them not to reach out. Damn it, he had to get out of this room.

"You sleep in the bed," he said, sidestepping around her. "I'm going downstairs for a drink. I'll find somewhere else to sleep."

She flinched, then stared at him. "It is not necessary to flaunt your . . . sleeping arrangements in my face."

He paused with his hand gripped on the doorknob. "I beg your pardon?"

"Naturally I don't expect you to remain celibate for the remainder of our marital union, but I'd appreciate your discretion."

An emotion he could not decipher glittered in her eyes. He made her an exaggerated formal bow. "I see. Your generous willingness to share me overwhelms me, and should the occasion arise, I shall endeavor to be discreet. However, for tonight it is my intention to sleep in that chair"— he inclined his head toward the wing chair in the corner—"but first I want a brandy." *Or two. Three was not outside the realm of possibility.*

He left the room, closing the door behind him, then drew a ragged breath into his lungs.

Bloody hell, he suspected an entire bottle would probably be necessary.

The packet docked in Calais late in the afternoon and Austin and Elizabeth were the first to disembark. He set out to arrange transportation to Marck and immediately realized what an asset Elizabeth was. She conversed in flawless French with the stable owner and ten minutes later they were presented with a handsome curricle pulled by two matched bays. God only knows what would have been brought had *he* been the one to order the transportation.

At once grateful and irked, Austin climbed onto the leather seat. Before he could reach down to assist Elizabeth, the stable owner helped her climb onto the seat. Austin noted the admiring warmth in the man's eyes and sizzled a glare at him. Bloody hell, he needed to master the French phrase "stop staring at my wife, you bastard." Clearly unfazed, the man merely grinned, then sauntered away.

Grabbing the reins, Austin set the curricle in motion and turned his thoughts to the mission that lay ahead. They would arrive in Marck in approximately an hour. If all went well, he'd locate Gaspard and finally get answers to the questions plaguing him—about the blackmail notes and perhaps even William's whereabouts.

They hit a rut in the road and his shoulder bumped Elizabeth's. Stealing a sideways glance at her, he noted that she appeared pale and her hands were clenched. There was no way in hell he was going to bring her along on his meeting with Gaspard. The man was dangerous. He'd have to find an inn at which to leave her. He suspected she wouldn't like it, but—

She grabbed his arm. "Austin."

Turning, he saw genuine fear in her eyes. "What is it?"

"We must hurry."

Alarm edged down his spine at the urgency in her tone. "Why?"

Pressing her fingers to her temples, she shook her head. "I'm not sure. It's not clear. But he's close by. And I know we must hurry." Her face turned chalky pale. "Please. It's a matter of life and death."

Austin flicked the reins, setting the horses off at a gallop.

Elizabeth held on tightly to her seat as the curricle

raced down the path. Fleeting images flashed in her mind, none of them clear, but all of them dark and menacing.

"When we reach the village, I'm leaving you at an inn," Austin said, his face tense from concentrating on driving the speeding curricle.

She opened her mouth to protest, but before she could speak, he reined the horses to a halt. They stopped before a fork in the road. Trees lined both paths. They looked identical.

"Damn it." Austin raked a hand through his hair. "Which way?"

Elizabeth stared alternately at both paths, but felt nothing. "Help me down."

He looked at her for the space of two heartbeats, then jumped to the ground to assist her. The instant her feet touched the ground, she ran to the fork. Drawing a deep breath, she knelt, closed her eyes, then placed her hands on the ground.

Images slashed through her mind, and she forced herself to relax, to try to get a clear picture. It took several minutes, but when the vision appeared, it was crystal clear.

And devastating.

She saw herself. Bleeding. Losing consciousness.

Dying.

Dear God, what was she going to do? If she told him what she'd seen, he would never allow her to go with him. He would insist upon bringing her to the village—and the time spent doing that would mean they'd be too late.

She knew someone was going to die.

But she also knew that if she went with him, she probably would not come back alive.

Opening her eyes, she stood and turned to face him. "We need to take the left fork."

Chapter 23

Austin closed the distance between them in a single stride and grabbed her shoulders. "What's wrong?"

"Nothing. I—"

He gave her a hard shake. "Don't lie to me. Your face is deathly white. You're frightened. What did you see?"

"We must take the left fork. We'll find him there."

"I'm not bringing you—"

"If we don't leave *now*, we'll be too late." She pulled herself from his grasp and ran toward the curricle. "Please. Hurry."

He caught up with her and grabbed her shoulder. "Too late for what?"

She fought the urge to panic. "Someone is going to die. I don't know who. I only know we're wasting time. Time we don't have." Realizing she needed somehow to reassure him of her safety, she said, "I'll remain in the curricle, or I'll hide in the woods. I'll do whatever you think best, but we must go *now*."

He didn't hesitate any longer. He quickly assisted her, then jumped into the driver's position. With a sharp flick of his wrists, he set the curricle in motion down the left path.

A quarter hour passed before Elizabeth saw it. Grabbing Austin's arm, she pointed. "Look."

He brought the curricle to a halt. In the distance, a thin plume of gray smoke floated above the trees. "Looks like it's from a chimney."

Elizabeth closed her eyes. "Yes. A stone chimney. It's a cottage." She opened her eyes and looked directly into his. "It's Gaspard's, Austin. He's there."

His face hardened. Without a word, he jumped from the vehicle. When she made a move to follow, he pinned her in place with an icy stare. "Don't move."

Snatching the reins, he led the horses and curricle off the road and into the woods, positioning them so that they were fairly well out of sight, yet facing the road.

He came alongside the vehicle and looked up at her. "You're to remain hidden here. If I haven't returned in an hour, I want you to drive to the village and check into an inn. I'll find you."

Fear gripped her. "Are you mad? I won't leave—"

"You said you would do whatever I asked."

"This man is dangerous."

Steel glinted in his eyes. "So am I."

"He's armed."

"So am I."

Fear turned her skin clammy. Her alarm must have shown on her face, because he reached up his hand to her. Without hesitation she clasped it between both of her own. And prayed.

He squeezed her hand. "I'll be fine, Elizabeth."

She couldn't speak around the dread clutching her

throat, so she merely nodded. Withdrawing his hand from between hers, he left, running between the trees toward the plume of smoke.

She pressed her palms together to retain the warmth his skin had left on hers and watched him disappear from view.

I'll be fine, Elizabeth.

"Yes, you will," she whispered. "I intend to see to it."

The instant he was out of sight, she climbed down from the curricle. She had no weapon, but perhaps . . .

Reaching up, she pulled her medical bag from the seat. Opening it, she withdrew a pouch and slipped it into her pocket. If she could get close enough to Gaspard to throw the peppery herb mixture into his eyes, he would be temporarily blinded. It wasn't much, but she couldn't let that stop her. If she didn't act, and act *now*, someone would die.

Drawing a resolute breath, she clutched her medical bag and followed the path Austin had taken into the forest. Her gown hampered her progress over the uneven ground. A thorny vine tangled in her hair, and stars swam before her eyes when she yanked free. Twice she stumbled, the second time skinning her palms when she landed hard on the rocky path. Tears pooled in her eyes at the heat stinging her hands, but without pausing, she pushed herself to her feet and pressed on.

Panting from exertion, she finally caught sight of the cottage in the distance. Fear skittered through her and her skin prickled with apprehension. Pushing her trepidation aside, she moved onward, using the trees and the shadows cast by the late afternoon sun to conceal herself, all her thoughts and energies centered on helping Austin.

Where are you, Austin? Dear God, where are you?

And then she heard a woman scream.

* * *

Austin heard a woman scream.

His heart thudding in heavy beats, he stole closer to the ramshackle cabin until he crouched on the ground directly beneath a window. A deep, muffled voice, obviously male, reached his ears. Rising cautiously, he peered over the window ledge.

He watched in horror as the man he'd been searching for raised his hand and struck a small child across her face. A woman's scream filled the cabin. The small girl crumpled into a heap on the floor, her hair falling over her face so he could not see how badly she was injured. Gaspard pushed the child aside with his foot as if she were trash and approached the woman.

Austin saw that the woman was bound to a chair. Bruises marred her face, and her dark hair lay matted around her head. She struggled against her bonds, sobbing.

"Bastard!" she screamed. "Keep your hands off her!"

Gaspard turned toward the window and Austin quickly ducked down. Pressing his back against the cottage, he controlled his breathing, forcing himself to bury his fury and concentrate. He had to get the woman and child out of there. He hadn't wanted to kill Gaspard, at least not until after he'd questioned him, but he had to stop him. Slipping his pistol from his pocket, he checked to make sure it was ready to fire. *One shot. I have one shot to stop this bastard. I cannot miss.*

His best chance was to shoot him through the window. He'd remain unseen and be able to line up an accurate shot. That decided, he rose and looked in the window. Gaspard was stuffing a rag in the woman's mouth. Austin held his pistol in steady hands, waiting for the bastard to move away from the woman.

At that moment, the front door burst open. Gaspard whipped around.

The ground beneath Austin shifted and his heart stopped.

Elizabeth stood in the doorway.

Elizabeth's gaze riveted on the bound woman and the child lying in a heap near the scarred wooden table. The woman was still alive. But the child . . . Elizabeth's breath stalled. She couldn't see the child's face, but she could make out the faint rise and fall of her shoulders. She was breathing.

Terror and relief collided in her. She wasn't too late. They were still alive.

But for how long?

"Who the hell are you?" Gaspard asked in guttural French. He crossed the room in two angry strides. Slamming the door, he slid the lock into place, then grabbed her upper arms. His fingers bit into her flesh and she couldn't control her gasp as pain shot through her.

Elizabeth looked into his eyes and fear skittered down her back. Pure menace emanated from his gaze. She tried to reach into her pocket for the herbs, but his grip tightened and she feared her bones would break from the intense pressure. Austin was somewhere nearby. She had to stall for time, to keep this madman from killing the woman and child. And herself.

"Answer me," he growled. He shook her so hard her teeth rattled and her medical bag slipped from her grasp. "Who are you?"

She swallowed and forced an outward calm. She simply needed to stall for time. At least Gaspard's attention was focused on her, away from the woman and child. *Hurry, Austin.*

"My name is Elizabeth."

His eyes narrowed to slits. "What are you doing here?"

"I . . ." Her words drifted off as a series of images flashed through her mind. She gazed at the bound woman whose terrified eyes pleaded with Elizabeth for help. Turning back to Gaspard she said in an accusing tone, "She's your sister."

An ugly laugh erupted from him. "What do you care?" Releasing one of her arms, he reached behind him. When his hand reappeared, he gripped a pistol. He shoved her away from him and she nearly stumbled. "Move closer to the wall," he ordered.

Righting herself, she inched backward, her eyes riveted on his weapon. Heaven help her, she was too far away to use her herbs.

"My sister was about to meet with an untimely demise, *Elizabeth*. Your ill-timed arrival means you'll be joining her."

He pointed the pistol at her heart.

Austin stood outside the window, battling the panic racing through him. Elizabeth stood directly in front of the window, her back toward him. Gaspard stood about twelve feet in front of her, a pistol aimed at her. Unless Elizabeth moved, Austin didn't have a prayer of getting a shot off at Gaspard without hitting her. He'd seen Gaspard lock the front door. This was the only window.

She had to move. He had to make her get out of the way. But how?

Chapter 24

Elizabeth had to distract Gaspard. And she had to do it quickly.

"I know about William," she said, relieved that her voice sounded so steady.

Gaspard went completely still. "Who?"

"William. The Englishman you bought weapons from in London last year."

A muffled moan sounded from the woman. Gaspard glared at her. "Silence, *putain*." He whipped his attention back to Elizabeth. "I don't know what you're talking about."

She raised her brows. "But you do. You were seen at the docks." Shaking her head, she made a *tsk*ing sound. "A very amateurish, sloppy job of smuggling."

"*Taisez-vous!* Shut your stupid mouth! It was perfect. Except that *bâtard Anglais* double-crossed me." He spit on the wooden floor. "But he will get exactly what he deserves. He will die. Slowly."

His words curled around Elizabeth, chilling her. "You know where he is."

Menace glittered in his eyes. "*Oui*. He was supposed to be dead, but a friend saw him. Just weeks ago. Not ten miles from here. I knew then Claudine was nearby. And I knew once I had her, he would come for her. And he did."

"Where is he?"

A sinister grin twisted his lips. "Close enough to hear her screams. I want him wondering what I am doing to his *pute*. I will enjoy showing him her dead body . . . then killing him."

Another moan came from the woman and Gaspard jerked his head in her direction. "Shut up!"

Scenes burst in Elizabeth's mind, colliding so quickly she could barely assimilate them. William. Bound and gagged. Struggling to free himself. Dear God, she had to keep Gaspard talking. An image clicked in her mind. "Claudine . . . she is William's wife."

Color mottled his fleshy face. "She is nothing but a traitorous *pute*. While the English pigs were killing our countrymen, our friends and neighbors, our own brother, *she* was rescuing the *bâtard Anglais*, spreading her legs for him. It took me over a year to find her, but now that I have, she will pay, as will he."

Elizabeth looked at Claudine. Tears ran from the woman's eyes. "William was wounded," Elizabeth said. "She nursed him and they fell in love."

"Love." Gaspard again spit on the floor, then settled a hate-filled glare upon his sister. "You forgot what they did to us, to our family. The English bastards stole everything from us. And that whoreson killed Julien." His voice rose to a near scream. "Our brother died in the battle that wounded your English pig. You betrayed us all, rescuing him, marrying him. How many of our countrymen's lives did you sacrifice for having that bastard between your thighs?"

His lips curled in a sneer and his gaze raked the bound woman. "When I found out what you'd done, how you'd betrayed us, I went to find him. When I did, he convinced me that because of you, he was sympathetic to our cause. Fool that I was, I gave him a chance to prove it." His eyes narrowed to slits. "He sold me English weapons. I tested a half dozen and they were good. I couldn't wait to kill English pigs with their own pistols! But he was lying. Only the top few weapons worked. When my men used them, they were massacred. Because of you. *You!*"

He returned his attention to Elizabeth. Madness glittered in his eyes. "His regiment killed Julien. He ruined my sister, turned her into a traitor." His voice went flat. "The blood of my compatriots is on her hands. The blood of my brother. And I shall see that she pays. It is my duty."

His gaze flickered to the pistol in his hand, and Elizabeth immediately sensed that her time was almost up. Desperate to divert him, she opened her mouth to speak, but her words were cut off by a sound filling her head. An urgent sound. Words.

Frowning, she tried to concentrate. Austin's voice suddenly filled her brain. *Move away from the window.*

It was as if he stood right next to her and had spoken aloud. *Move away from the window. Move away from the window.*

She took a tiny step sideways and Gaspard jerked his gaze back to her face. "Don't move or I'll shoot you."

Dear God, what was she going to do? Clearly Austin was behind her, at the window. He needed her to move to get a clear shot at Gaspard, but if she moved, Gaspard would kill her. He obviously planned to kill her anyway, but she didn't want to encourage him to do the deed sooner than he planned.

There was only one thing she could do.

Just as she contemplated it, Austin's voice echoed in her brain.

Drop to the floor!

She fell like a stone.

Glass shattered behind her and the deafening report of a pistol rent the air.

Austin looked through the shattered window. Gaspard was on his knees, his face a clenched mask of pain, his hands pressed against his stomach. Bright red blood oozed between his fingers, drenching his shirt. His pistol lay on the floor behind him.

Elizabeth. Was she hurt? The chilling thought had no sooner entered his mind than she jumped to her feet and stood before him. His knees nearly sagged. She was all right.

She was all right.

Swallowing the relief that threatened to liquefy his knees, he said quietly, "Unlock the door."

She immediately did as he requested. He entered the room, and shoving her behind him, he picked up Gaspard's pistol. Then he turned to her. "Are you hurt?"

Her eyes anxiously scanned his face. "No. Are you all right?"

He was anything but. He'd almost lost everything that mattered to him. But now was not the time to discuss it. "I'm fine." He tore his gaze from her pale face and fastened his attention on Gaspard, who was struggling to his feet. "Remain behind me," he whispered to Elizabeth.

Austin pointed Gaspard's pistol directly at the man's chest. "Stay where you are." One glance at the Frenchman's stomach wound told Austin that it was fatal.

Gaspard gained his feet and leaned heavily against the

table for support. He stared at Austin for a moment, then a wheezing laugh escaped him. "So we meet at last, *Monsieur le Duc*. It is amusing, *n'est-ce pas*? Your brother killed my brother. So many brothers. All dead."

Containing the rage boiling within him, Austin tightened his grip on the pistol handle. "So many dead," he agreed with icy calm. "And you're next."

Sly cunning glittered in Gaspard's eyes. "Perhaps. But at least I know that I rid the world of your bastard brother."

"I heard you through the window. He's alive."

"He won't be by the time you find him . . . if you find him."

"I'll find him as soon as I'm through with you. Why did you kill my Runner?"

Blood dripped from between Gaspard's fingers and he grimaced. "Another English pig. He was asking questions about me. When he suddenly wanted to meet with you, I knew he'd found something. I followed him. I couldn't risk him telling you whatever he'd found out, especially if it was where I was hiding or that I was sending you letters. He would have ruined everything." He hissed in a breath. "But the pig would tell me nothing. I shot him in the head."

Behind him, Elizabeth drew in a sharp breath. "Why did you wait a year to blackmail me?" Austin asked.

"I was wounded at Waterloo, because of the faulty weapons your brother supplied. It took many months to recover. I didn't know until recently that the *pute*'s husband came from such wealth." He narrowed his mad eyes. "But I had to be cautious . . . remain hidden. Just as I was ready to send you the next letter, I received word the *bâtard Anglais* was alive and had been seen in this part of France. I returned home to find him."

An image of William rose in Austin's mind, as he'd seen him that last night. Conversing in urgent tones to Gaspard, loading crates of weapons onto a ship. Not betraying his country, but risking his life to help the English cause by supplying this madman with faulty weapons. His hand tightened around the pistol. "You'll never hurt anyone again, Gaspard. I'll—"

A groan cut off his words. Looking across the room, he saw the child stirring, pushing herself onto her hands and knees.

Austin caught a movement from the corner of his eye and he whipped his attention around back to Gaspard. A knife glinted in the Frenchman's hand, and his hate-filled eyes were trained on the child.

"So you're still alive, eh?" Gaspard rasped. "No child of that *bâtard Anglais* will live."

Austin heard a gasp behind him. In the blink of an eye, Gaspard drew his hand back and let the knife fly. There was no way Austin could reach the child in time. He squeezed the trigger and Gaspard crumpled to the ground.

He turned toward the child and froze.

Elizabeth lay sprawled facedown on the floor, the knife protruding from her back.

Chapter 25

White hot pain ripped through her, so intense, it nauseated her. Warm wetness trickled down her collarbone and she inhaled the metallic smell of blood. Light-headedness swamped her.

The child. Was she all right? *Did I move in time?*

"Elizabeth!"

Austin's voice seemed to come from far away. An instant later, she felt herself being cradled in strong arms. Forcing her eyelids open, she looked up into Austin's face. Stark fright radiated from his gray eyes.

"Dear God, Elizabeth," he said, his voice a husky rasp.

She had to ask him, had to know, but her tongue was like a piece of thick leather in her mouth. Swallowing, she forced out, "The child."

"She's alive," Austin said, brushing a lock of hair off her brow. "You saved her."

Relief settled over her. She'd saved the child. Thank God. And Austin was all right. That was all that mattered.

She looked at him, confused that he appeared so stricken. He should be happy. The child was alive.

Yet even as relief afforded her some peace, regrets pushed at her. But now it was too late. A wave of dizziness and pain washed over her, forcibly reminding her how precious life is . . . especially when it's over and there's no time left to correct mistakes. And her biggest mistake had been not giving the gift of life to her daughter . . . Austin's daughter. They could have made the most of the short time they would have had together as a family, and she would have helped him through the pain. Somehow.

She longed to tell him, to explain, let him know how sorry she was, how much she loved him, but her tongue was too heavy to move and she could barely keep her eyes open.

Sleep. She was so tired. Pain rolled through her, stealing her breath. Everything hurt. So much. Her eyelids drifted shut and blackness engulfed her.

Austin watched her eyes close and sick panic roiled through him.

"Elizabeth!"

She remained perfectly still in his arms, her complexion waxy pale.

He had to get that knife out of her. Had to. She had to live. Had to. Had to. But he needed help.

With a herculean effort, he pushed back his terror and laid her gently on her stomach. It cost him to leave her side, but he had no choice. He crossed the room to Claudine. The child had just yanked the rag from her mother's mouth. While they spoke in rapid French to each other, Austin pulled his knife from his boot and quickly cut the ropes binding her.

The instant her arms were free, Claudine gathered the child to her. "Josette, *ma petite*. Thank God you are all right." With the child clinging to her Claudine raised her eyes to Austin. "How badly is the woman hurt?"

"She's alive, but we need a doctor. Immediately."

Claudine shook her head. "The village is far. But I am a good nurse." She stood and rubbed her stiff arms. "We must hurry to help her. Then we must free William."

"Jesus Christ. Where is he?"

"Locked in a shed hidden in the woods at the rear of the property. I know he is alive and can wait a few more moments. Your wife cannot." Jerking her head toward a metal pail near the fireplace, she said, "We need water. There is a stream just behind the house. Go! *Rapidement!*"

Snatching up the pail, Austin ran outside and quickly returned with the water. When he entered the cottage, Claudine was settling Josette on a pallet in the far corner.

Austin immediately went to Elizabeth and dropped to his knees, fighting back the turmoil that threatened to overwhelm him. If she didn't recover—

He refused to consider such a thing.

Claudine joined him and quickly examined Elizabeth. She then looked at him, her eyes grave. "The wound is severe and she has lost a lot of blood. When we remove the knife, she will lose more."

"She cannot die." If he said it enough, if he thought it enough, surely he could make it a fact.

"I hope not. But we must act quickly. We will need bandages. Remove her petticoat and cut it into strips. Hurry."

Forcing his mind to concentrate on the task at hand, he followed Claudine's terse instructions. His eyes strayed to the knife embedded in Elizabeth's shoulder and his stomach turned over with a combination of stark fear and helpless pain.

"Now I will remove the knife," she said. "Be ready to apply pressure to the wound with the bandages."

Austin nodded once, his eyes riveted on Elizabeth's shoulder. The instant Claudine pulled the weapon free, he began the grim task of staunching the blood flow. He focused on the chore, not allowing his mind to consider that the blood soaked through the bandages almost instantly.

She will not die. Grim, unrelenting determination filled him. He pressed bandage after bandage to her shoulder, applying pressure until his arms shook with the effort of holding back the blood flow.

Finally, after what seemed like hours but was actually less than a quarter hour, the bleeding tapered off to a mere weeping. He helped Claudine wash the wound, then wrap the shoulder with a clean bandage.

"How long before she wakes up?"

"I cannot say, *monsieur*. I can only pray to God that she does."

"She will. She has to." His voice dropped to a whisper. "I cannot live without her."

"We have done all we can for her," Claudine said. "Now I must free William." She ran to the mantel and snatched a key from the rough wood surface. "Bertrand kept the key within my sight to taunt me."

"Should I—"

"No, *monsieur*. You remain here with your wife. I ask that you watch over Josette as well. She is sleeping."

"Of course."

She ran from the cottage. He glanced at Josette and saw she lay on her side, her thumb stuck in her little bow mouth. A shudder passed through him at the thought of the horrors that the child had witnessed. Hopefully she wouldn't remember.

He knew he would never forget.

Turning back to Elizabeth, he gently caressed her face

and hair. She was ghostly pale, her lips chalky, her auburn curls matted, her gown splattered with her own blood. She hadn't so much as flickered an eyelid. He would have traded his very soul for her just to open her eyes.

He lost all track of time. Each minute that she remained unconscious seemed like an eternity. He had no idea how much time had passed when he heard voices. The door opened and he stood.

A man entered, a man who was immediately, hauntingly familiar, yet not at all the same. His face bore lines of suffering and he moved with a decided limp. But the eyes . . . those gray eyes so like his own. There was no mistaking them, even from across the room.

They stared at each other for an endless, stunned moment, while Austin struggled to draw air into his lungs, to comprehend the living, breathing miracle that stood before him. Even though he'd desperately hoped, believed, that William was alive, a grain of doubt had persisted, his logical mind telling him it wasn't really possible. But it was.

Wordlessly, he walked across the room until only a few feet separated them, his heart beating so loudly he wondered if William could hear it.

He watched his brother's eyes fill with tears and a thousand questions.

"Austin?" he whispered.

A sob rose in Austin's throat. Jerking his head in a nod, he opened his arms and spoke only one word.

"Brother."

Chapter 26

Austin knelt next to the cot, his gaze riveted on Elizabeth's face. Damn it, she was so frighteningly still. So pale.

William had left nearly an hour ago to get the doctor and the magistrate. How the hell long before he returned? His gaze flicked to the opposite side of the room where Claudine dozed, Josette wrapped in her arms. They were exhausted, but fine. If only he could say the same about Elizabeth . . .

He touched her cheek with a trembling hand. She was so soft. Like silk. And so beautiful. And brave. There was no doubt that she'd saved Josette's life.

God, he loved her. Totally. He was helpless to stop it, and he no longer wanted to. He wanted to love her. To tell her. Show her. Every day for the rest of their lives.

"Nothing else matters," he whispered, cupping her face against his palm. "What happened between us before . . . it isn't important anymore. I don't care why you married me, if you wanted to be a duchess. I don't care about having children. I only care about you. If you want, we'll adopt

children . . . as many as you like. Dozens of children . . ."
His voice broke and he swallowed hard, his gaze roaming
her face.

"You're so beautiful," he said around the lump in his
throat. "God, I love you. Since the first moment I saw you,
tumbling out of the bushes. You're in my heart, my soul.
You *are* my soul." His heart beat in hard, heavy beats, and
his chest ached. "Please open your eyes." Lowering his
head, he touched his forehead to hers. "Don't leave me,
Elizabeth. Please, darling. Please. I can't even think of being here without you. Don't leave me."

Elizabeth heard his voice from very far away, as if she
were in a cave. *Don't leave me . . .*

Austin. His name drifted through her mind. She struggled to open her eyes, but someone had attached heavy
sandbags to her lids. Weakness washed over her, in stunning contrast to the fire burning in her shoulder.

But she had to tell him. About her regrets. Had to let
him know how much she loved him and that she had said
those things to protect him. How the thought of leaving
him shattered her heart into a thousand pieces. He had to
know, but dear God, she didn't have the strength to tell him.
Her pain-racked body sought oblivion, to feel no more.

Focusing her strength, she forced her heavy eyelids
open. Austin's ravaged face loomed above her and sadness
washed through her at the bleak expression in his eyes.
Their gazes locked and he drew a sharp breath.

"Elizabeth. You're awake." Taking her hand, he pressed
his lips to her palm. "Thank God."

She tried to push the words past her dry lips, but dizziness invaded her, and his face wavered before her eyes,
ebbing and receding like waves upon the shore. Her eyelids drifted shut but she fought to keep them open, trained
on his face, fearing that once she closed her eyes, she'd
never see him again.

Summoning her strength, she pushed the word she most wanted to say past her lips. "Austin."

It was barely audible, but he heard her and gently squeezed her hand. "I'm right here, darling. Everything is going to be all right. Save your strength." His whispered words settled on her like a warm, velvety quilt.

So many things to tell you. But she was so tired. So sore. A spasm of pain rolled through her followed by a sickening wave of dizziness. She fought to remain conscious and focused on her thoughts, but blackness edged around the fringes of her vision. Relentless pain seeped through her aching body. Her eyes grew impossibly heavy and she realized she wasn't going to be able to tell him everything. But there was one thing he had to know.

Gazing at him, she tried to smile, but didn't know if she succeeded.

"Love you," she whispered.

Her eyes drifted shut. She heard him calling her name, over and over, pleading, but she couldn't fight the weakness, the pain, any longer.

She floated away toward a place where pain did not exist.

Austin sat on the steps leading to the cottage, his insides hollow, his heart filled with a crushing pain.

Lowering his head into his hands, he tried not to think the worst, but it was impossible. Desolation slammed into him. "Please, God," he whispered, "don't tell me I've killed her by bringing her here."

The doctor had been with her for nearly an hour, and each passing minute tightened the vise of misery strangling him.

The magistrate had arrived with several men who'd removed Gaspard's body. Austin, William, and Claudine had answered the magistrate's questions. With Claudine acting as interpreter, Austin had explained that Gaspard had sent him threatening letters, and that he'd hired a Bow Street Runner to find him. He allowed the magistrate to assume that the Runner had directed him to Gaspard's location. After the magistrate left, William had traveled back to the town to purchase food and supplies.

And still Elizabeth hadn't woken up.

Damn it, if that doctor didn't come out soon, he was simply going to barge in and grab him by the neck and force him to say that Elizabeth would recover.

The cottage door opened and he jumped to his feet. The doctor and Claudine emerged.

"How is she?" Austin demanded, his gaze flicking from one to the other. He knew they saw the stark fear he couldn't hide.

"Resting comfortably," the doctor said in heavily accented English.

Austin locked his knees to keep from falling down. "She's not going to . . . die?"

"On the contrary, I expect your wife to make a full recovery, although she is weak and experiencing a great deal of pain right now. I changed her bandage and administered a dosage of laudanum."

A full recovery. She was going to live. He braced his hand against the cottage to keep himself upright. "Did she wake up?"

"Yes. She asked for you, and I assured her you were right outside. I recommend she not be moved for at least a week, but once she's feeling up to it, she may travel back to England." The doctor removed his pince-nez and polished it on his sleeve. "Remarkable young woman. Very robust in nature."

Austin nearly laughed out loud, something he hadn't

thought he'd ever do again. "Yes, indeed, my wife is very robust." *Thank God.*

"You may see her now," the doctor said, and Austin didn't hesitate for an instant.

He entered the cottage and crossed the room, on decidedly wobbly legs. Elizabeth lay on the narrow bed in the corner, blankets neatly tucked around her.

He knelt next to her, his eyes anxiously scanning her face. Although she was pale, her skin no longer appeared waxy. Her chest rose and fell with slow, steady breaths. Reaching out, he brushed an auburn curl from her brow. A combination of relief and love suffused him, hitting him so hard, his breath stalled.

Elizabeth, his wonderful, unpredictable Elizabeth, was going to be all right. She'd said she loved him, and even if that were nothing more than delusional mutterings, he believed that it meant there was hope for them. He would make her love him. Somehow. By some miracle, they'd been given this second chance and by God, he was going to do everything in his power to convince her to put the past behind them and stay with him. He loved her too damn much and wasn't about to contemplate life without her. She was his, and he would spend the rest of his life trying to prove that to her.

Lowering his head, he rested his forehead against the blanket and whispered the only two words he could manage. "Love you."

Later that night, Austin sat at the scarred wooden table, warming his hands around a chipped mug of tea. A low fire burned in the grate, casting the small cottage with a shadowy glow.

Elizabeth had not awakened, but her breathing was

regular and she showed no signs of developing fever. Josette lay asleep on a pallet in the corner, William and Claudine kneeling beside her, talking in hushed tones.

Sipping his tea, Austin assessed Claudine. She was a very pretty woman, petite, with shiny sable hair and wide hazel eyes. An air of quiet competence surrounded her. He'd noticed that her hands bore calluses and she moved about the cottage with the ease of a woman accustomed to domestic duties. Certainly not a highborn lady or one of wealth.

He watched his brother lightly brush his fingers over the bruise marring Claudine's cheek, his lips thinning to a tight white line. Claudine captured William's hand and pressed a fervent kiss against his palm. There was no mistaking the love shining in their eyes.

William helped Claudine settle herself next to Josette, and once she was comfortable, he joined Austin at the table.

Austin looked at his brother, noting his marked limp and the changes in his appearance. His face was thinner and deep lines bracketed his mouth and creased his forehead. He saw no sign of the mischievous boy he'd known in this serious man and his heart ached for the hardships William had clearly suffered. There were so many things to say, to ask, he didn't know where to begin. Clearing his throat he finally said, "Josette looks just like you."

"Yes, she does."

"How old is she?"

"Two." William looked directly into his eyes. "Your wife saved her life. It is a debt I can never repay."

"Your wife helped save Elizabeth's life. That is a debt *I* can never repay." Reaching across the table, he grasped William's forearms and was gratified when William returned the gesture. "I cannot believe I'm sitting here with you, talking to you. That you're alive. My God, Mother, Robert, and Caroline will—"

"How are they?"

"Fine. They're going to be shocked . . . and ecstatic when they see you." He drew a deep breath. "I heard Gaspard talking to Elizabeth and I spoke to him myself, so I know most of what happened, but why did you let us believe all this time you were dead?"

"I had no choice. I couldn't risk Gaspard's finding Claudine and Josette. If I'd contacted you, told you I was alive, I would have exposed myself and them. And it might have placed you and the family in danger as well."

"There were soldiers in your regiment who witnessed you going down in battle."

"I did. My horse was shot and we went down together, but unlike so many others, I was not crushed by my mount. There was mass confusion following the battle at Waterloo, thousands of dead and wounded soldiers everywhere. I managed to escape, slipping my timepiece under the body of a dead soldier I knew no one would ever be able to identify."

He squeezed Austin's arms, then sat back. "I returned to Claudine and Josette. I knew Gaspard would be searching for them to take revenge for my double-cross . . . if he had survived. We had to go into hiding until I knew if Gaspard was still alive. I soon discovered he was."

"How did you meet Claudine?"

"She'd saved my life two years earlier. I'd taken a bayonette in the leg. The next thing I remember was waking up and looking into the kindest, gentlest eyes I'd ever seen. She said she'd found me in the woods, about two miles from the battle site. I suppose I must have dragged myself there, although I don't recall doing so. She nursed me back to health."

"Why would she help a British soldier?"

"She told me she'd just lost her younger brother to the war. Even though I was British, she didn't want to inflict the pain of losing a loved one on someone else and she didn't want my death on her conscience. She decided to do what she could to help me recover, then send me on my way."

He clasped his hands in front of him on the table. "We never intended to fall in love, but we did. After two weeks, I was healed enough to rejoin my regiment, but I couldn't leave her. She refused to marry me, fearing the danger I'd be placed in by having a French wife, but I was stubborn. We traveled to a village several hours away and were secretly married.

"After that, I settled her in another village, under a different name. I wanted her away from Gaspard, whose vicious hatred of the British had turned to madness after Julien's death. The need to keep her safe became even more crucial once I learned she was with child."

His gaze drifted briefly to where his wife and daughter slept peacefully. "Gaspard found the church where we'd been married and he came after me. He was going to kill me, then find Claudine and kill her. I managed to convince him I was sympathetic to the French—after all, I had a French wife—how loyal to the English could I be? To prove my loyalty, I promised to provide him and his men with weapons."

"Which is what you were doing that night on the docks," Austin said. "Only the weapons were useless."

"Yes, except for the top several in each crate in case he tested them, which he did." He dragged his hands down his face. "When I saw you there, I panicked. I couldn't explain things to you, and I couldn't let Gaspard see you. Both of our lives were at stake."

"I want you to know how much I regret that night,

William. Branding you a traitor, disavowing you as my brother—"

"You had no way of knowing, Austin."

"I should have trusted in you, known that you would never commit treason."

"You believed what I wanted you to believe. I could have confessed what was going on when we spoke, but I couldn't risk that someone might overhear, or question you. I would have said anything—*anything*—to protect Claudine and Josette, even if it meant pretending to my own brother that I was a traitor."

Austin looked over at Elizabeth. Yes, he could understand that depth of love.

"I'm sorry that I've had to allow you, Mother, Robert, and Caroline to mourn me this past year," William said in a quiet voice, "but until I took care of Gaspard, I couldn't risk returning to the family. By killing him, you've set me free."

A shudder passed through Austin. "That bastard almost killed my wife. I would kill him again if I could."

"She is very brave, your wife. Have you been married long?"

"No. But she's changed my life." He looked at William and understanding flowed between them. "You understand."

"Perfectly. Claudine changed mine."

Silence fell for several seconds, then Austin said, "The first night I met Elizabeth, she told me you were alive. I didn't believe her."

William frowned. "How could she possibly have known I was alive?"

Austin gazed at the cot by the fire, at the woman who held his heart and soul in her hands. He would not dishonor her and what she'd done for him and his family by hiding the gift of her visions . . . for that's exactly what they were. A gift. Returning his attention to William, he explained just how extraordinary his wife really was.

When he finished, William simply stared at him. "That's incredible."

Once again his gaze drifted to Elizabeth. "Yes, William. That's exactly what she is. Incredible."

And the moment she awoke, he would begin convincing her she was just that. And that she belonged with him.

Chapter 27

Elizabeth came awake slowly, gradually becoming aware of her surroundings. A dull, relentless ache throbbed in her shoulder, but it was a vast improvement over the inferno that she recalled burning there earlier. She breathed deeply and the savory aroma of something delicious cooking filled her nostrils. Her stomach instantly tightened with hunger.

She lifted her eyelids. Gentle shafts of sunlight lit the room, arcing over the beamed ceiling. Birdcalls twittered faintly in the distance.

"Elizabeth."

She slowly turned her head toward his voice, wincing at the pull on her shoulder. He sat next to where she lay, his elbows resting on his spread knees, his hands clasped between them.

Stubble shadowed his jaw, lending him the look of a dark angel. His hair was pushed haphazardly back from his forehead as if he'd raked his fingers through it a dozen times. He looked rumpled and tired, yet incredibly strong and solid.

And so very worried. Hoping to erase the concern in his eyes, she forced a tiny smile to her lips. "Austin."

A breath whooshed from his lungs and he closed his eyes for a brief second. Reaching out a visibly shaking hand, he gently touched her cheek. "How do you feel?"

She thought for a moment. "My shoulder hurts. I'm very thirsty, and whatever that delicious smell is has my stomach growling."

His tense features relaxed. "I'll get you something to eat and drink, then give you some laudanum for the pain." He stood and her gaze followed him around the room, watching him pour water from a metal pitcher into a thick cup.

Returning to her side, he very gently helped her sit partially up, stuffing several pillows behind her. Dear God, it felt so good to have his hands on her, even if the touch was given solely for caregiving purposes.

Once she was settled, he held the cup to her lips. She drained it three times before the dryness in her throat finally abated.

"More?" he asked.

"No, thank you."

"Would you like some broth? Claudine made it early this morning."

Her stomach rumbled, but she said, "Later. First I need to speak with you." *So many things to tell you . . . so much to hope for.*

"Of course."

He sat in the straight-backed wooden chair and she wondered if he'd spent the entire night sitting on its hard surface. She suspected he had for it looked as if he hadn't slept at all.

"How is the child?" she asked anxiously.

"She's fine, Elizabeth. Her name is Josette. She and Claudine are outside. William is with them."

"William? Then he's—"

"Here. Alive. And well."

"How—"

"I know you have questions, and I shall tell you everything you don't already know, but first there is something I must say to you."

Reaching out, he took her hand, pressing her palm between both of his. His expression was so grave, so intense, her insides cramped with apprehension.

"I've come to a decision, Elizabeth."

"Decision?"

He gazed into her eyes, then shook his head. "Bloody hell, I've been waiting so long for you to wake up, so I could talk to you, and now that the moment is here, I don't know the words."

Her throat constricted. As she well knew, there was no easy way to tell someone that you didn't want to remain married to them.

Releasing her hands, he leaned down. When he straightened, he held a dented bucket in his hands. "I brought you something," he said quietly. Reaching into the bucket, he pulled out a large, ripe strawberry.

Confused, she watched him hold the berry by its green stem.

"Do you remember our journey to London, after our wedding?" he asked, his gaze probing hers.

She nodded mutely.

"You told me a story about the origin of strawberries, about a couple who was wonderfully happy, but then they argued. The wife walked away from her husband, not stopping until she saw the red ripe strawberries. When she ate them, her desire for him returned, and she came back to him." He held the berry to her lips. "I want you to come back to me."

Her heart slammed against her ribs. Dazed, she bit the fruit, its sweetness surrounding her tongue. When she finished the strawberry, he placed the bucket on the floor.

Taking her hand, he pressed a heated, fervent kiss into her palm. "God, Elizabeth, when I thought you might die, everything inside me died right along with you. I realized at that moment that nothing, *nothing* else mattered but keeping you with me.

"I cannot let you go," he said, his warm breath beating against her fingertips. "I cannot allow you to return to America. If you leave, I'll simply follow you there. I won't annul our marriage. It doesn't matter if we don't have children. If you want, we'll adopt children. Dozens of them if that's what you want, but you will not bear another man's child. And I will not seek comfort in another woman's arms. If you do not want to share a bed with me, I shall accept your decision. The only thing that matters is that you stay with me. Do you understand?"

She couldn't have pushed a word past her bone-dry lips if her life depended upon it. She nodded.

"Good. Because there will be no further talk of ending our marriage." His gaze blazed into hers, heated, intense, and deadly serious. "I love you," he whispered. "Totally. And I'll take you on any terms. My heart is yours. Now and always."

She stared at him, rendered speechless by his words. He loved her. In spite of everything, he still wanted her as his wife. Dear God, what he was willing to give up . . . a real marriage, children. For her. Because he loved her. Hot tears flooded her eyes. How well she understood that depth of love, that willingness to give up everything for the person who held your heart in their hands.

It was exactly the way she felt about him.

"Austin," she said, her voice shaking. "You need to know, I never would have had a child with another man. Please, believe me. I desperately didn't want to end our marriage, but I couldn't ask you to accept me when I could no longer be a wife to you."

He stilled. "You lied to me?"

Trepidation skittered down her spine at his tone, but she plunged on. "Yes. I lied. I wanted you to be free to have the sort of marriage you deserved. With a woman who would give you children. Annulling our marriage, having a child with someone else, claiming designs on your title—they were all fabrications. But please understand, I would have said anything—*anything*—to convince you."

The muscles in his throat worked convulsively. "Those are almost the identical words William used last night about protecting Claudine." He drew a deep breath. "You're saying you said those things to force me to go on with my life. Without you."

"Yes."

"You lied to me."

She nodded. "It's the only time I ever have, and I swear on my soul, I never will again."

He appeared almost dazed for several seconds, then a slow smile spread over his face, a devastating smile that stopped her breath.

"You *lied* to me," he said again.

"You seem . . . *happy*?"

"My darling, under the circumstances, I'm ecstatic."

Relief, so intense it left her weak, flooded her. "There's something else I must tell you."

Her expression clearly mirrored her serious tone because the humor faded from his eyes. "I'm listening," he said.

"When I thought I was going to die, never see or touch you again, I felt such profound regrets. About you. And our child." Reaching up, she laid her palm against his stubbled jaw. "No more regrets," she whispered. "I want us to have a real marriage. I want to have our baby, regardless of what manner of hardships we will have to face together."

His eyes searched her face. "Elizabeth, are you certain?"

She nodded and swallowed the hard knot gripping her throat. "Life is too short, too precious. There's a beautiful child in our future, a child I don't want to deny life to— even if that life is destined to be short. I can be strong because I love you, because you love me." Drawing a deep breath, she studied his grave expression. "Do you want the same, Austin? Do you want our child? Knowing we'll lose her? Knowing the pain we'll have to face?"

He grasped her hand and squeezed it hard. "I always wanted her, even knowing we could lose her. And I swear on my soul that I will do everything in my power to see that we don't."

"But if we do?"

"Then I'll thank God for the time I had her, for the precious days she was ours to love."

Dear God, she was terrified to tell him the full extent of her vision, of his despair and guilt and self-blame, but she had to know. "Austin, what if something one of us does causes her death?"

He rubbed his thumbs over the backs of her hands, his eyes riveted to hers. "We would handle it. Together. Always." Leaning forward, he brushed his mouth across hers in a tender, bittersweet kiss. "Our love is strong enough to survive anything."

His quiet vow wrenched her heart and she blinked back the hot tears pooling in her eyes. Clutching his words to her heart, she prayed he wouldn't regret saying them after she told him the rest of her vision. And she had to tell him. It was only fair that she make him understand the depth of misery she knew awaited him.

"Austin, I saw you grieving. I felt your despair, your hopelessness and guilt. I heard you say, 'Please, God, don't tell me I've killed her by bringing her here' and 'I cannot live without her.'"

He stared at her with a puzzled frown. "But I said those very words. Yesterday. When I thought you were dying."

Before she could reply, voices sounded outside the door. Austin rose. "William, Claudine, and Josette have returned," he said. "They are anxious to meet you."

He crossed the room and opened the door. The woman whom Elizabeth had last seen bound to a chair walked in, her arm linked with a man who was undeniably Austin's brother. Elizabeth smiled. Before she could say hello, however, the child appeared in the doorway.

Elizabeth looked at the little girl with ebony hair and gray eyes.

And her entire world shifted on its axis.

Chapter 28

Only two days had passed since Austin had departed for France, and already Robert knew that he didn't have a prayer of keeping up with his brother's correspondence. He sat behind Austin's massive mahogany desk and groaned at the ever-growing mountain of letters piled in the center. Trying to keep his head above water until Austin and Elizabeth returned from the Continent was going to prove a daunting task.

A knock sounded at the door. Relieved to have something to contemplate other than the correspondence, he called, "Come in."

Miles entered. "You wished to see me?"

"Yes. There's something I need to discuss with you."

Miles settled himself in the chair opposite him. "I'm listening."

"This concerns Caroline, and I'll not mince words with you. My sister is in love with you." He sat back and regarded Miles through hooded eyes. "I'd like to know what you plan to do about it."

Miles grew very still. "Caroline told you she, er, cares for me?"

"No, she hasn't directly *said* so, but she was unable to deny it when I asked her point blank. Good God, Miles, even a blind man can see she loves you. I think you'd make an admirable husband for my sister, provided, of course, that you hold her in some affection."

Miles tapped his chin, clearly mulling over his words. "And if I don't wish to marry at this time?" he finally asked.

"In that case, I'm certain Austin will entertain other offers for her." He waved his hand over the letters covering the desk. "There's a note somewhere in this monstrous pile from Charles Blankenship. In it he strongly hints that he's considering offering for Caroline." Rising, he laid his hand on Miles's shoulder. "Think about it, my friend," he said, then left the room.

The instant he was alone, Miles paced the length of the room, plunging shaking fingers through his hair. Caroline was in love with him! The thought brought his agitated pacing to an abrupt halt. He recalled her melting in his arms, her eager lips seeking his, and his pulse took off at a brisk gallop. A thin film of perspiration broke out on his forehead. *Bloody hell!*

He wasn't ready to get married! *Married*, for God's sake. A lifelong commitment. *Hell no. Not me.* Caroline was lovely, but there were many lovely women in the world. *But none that makes me feel like she does.*

He tried to shake off the bothersome inner murmurings that threatened his sacred bachelorhood, but the voice simply would not cease. *Caroline would give me handsome and strong sons, and daughters as beautiful as their mother.*

Sons? Daughters? Hang it, he was going mad.

He almost ran to the decanters. Pouring himself a

generous amount of brandy, he swallowed the potent liquor in a single gulp. He immediately felt better.

Caroline wasn't really in love with him, she was merely infatuated. And he was attracted to her only because she was so unlike the other women he knew. Why, the only thing he needed was to leave this blasted house and engage in a good sexual romp. Slamming down his empty glass, he headed toward the door.

Just as he entered the foyer he heard Carters speaking to someone.

"I'm so sorry, Lord Blankenship, but his grace isn't in at the moment," Carters intoned in a deep monotone.

Miles skidded to a halt. *Blankenship*. He must be here to offer for Caroline. And Robert had said that Austin would entertain offers . . .

"I say, are you quite certain?" Lord Blankenship asked. "I sent a note around several days ago advising him of my arrival this afternoon. Surely he was expecting me."

"He was called away rather suddenly—"

"I'll handle this, Carters," Miles broke in, walking to the door. "His grace gave me a message to deliver to Lord Blankenship."

Carters bowed and left the two men alone. Miles turned to Lord Blankenship and gave him a frosty smile. "Blankenship."

"Always a pleasure to see you, Eddington."

Ten minutes later, Lord Blankenship no longer thought it was a pleasure to see Miles. With his handkerchief pressed to his bleeding nose, Lord Blankenship stalked angrily from the drawing room. He saw Caroline in the foyer and brushed past her without a word. Not waiting for Carters to open the door, he jerked it open himself and slammed it after him.

"Good heavens!" Caroline exclaimed to Miles, her eyes wide. "What on earth is wrong with Charles?"

"*Charles?* You call him *Charles?*"

"Yes, of course. Is he all right? It appeared as if his nose were bleeding." She looked out the window and watched Lord Blankenship's elegant coach pull away.

"His nose *was* bleeding," Miles confirmed with a great deal of satisfaction.

"How did that happen?"

"There was a bit of a collision, I'm afraid." Grabbing Caroline's arm, he led her down the corridor, all but dragging her along. She had to run to keep up with him.

"What sort of collision? And where are you taking me?"

Miles didn't answer. He just kept walking with grim determination, not pausing until they reached the privacy of Austin's study.

"My goodness, Miles!" she puffed when they finally stopped. Her eyes spit blue sparks at him and she jerked her arm from his grasp. "What on earth has come over you? You're pulling me around and—"

Her indignant words were cut off when his mouth crushed her lips into silence with a kiss.

Caroline wilted against him, her knees turning to water, her anger instantly forgotten as a flood of heat suffused her. She ran her hands up Miles's broad chest and over his shoulders until her fingers tangled in his hair. She didn't know why he was kissing her, but as long as he *was*, she didn't care about the reason.

"Caroline . . ." he whispered in an aching voice several minutes later. "Look at me."

Clinging to his shoulders for support, she dragged her eyelids open and stared at him, utterly dazed. "Why did you kiss me?" she asked in a shaky voice.

"Because I wanted to."

Her eyes narrowed with sudden suspicion. "You're acting very strangely. What happened to Charles? You mentioned a collision?"

"Yes. A most unfortunate collision occurred between his face and my fist."

"You *punched* Charles?"

He nodded.

"What would possess you to do such a thing?" she asked, completely staggered.

"The bastard is lucky that is all he got," he said in a voice that resembled a growl. "I should have called him out."

"*Called him out?* What on earth did he do?"

"He lied about kissing you. Flat out denied ever having done it, in essence calling you a liar. As if that weren't bad enough, he then had the gall to interrupt me as I defended your honor and tell me that *it was none of my business*."

Caroline swallowed. "Actually, it *is* none of your business."

Smoke all but sizzled from him. "The hell it's not. Not only did he kiss you, then lie about it, but he had the audacity to come here today to *offer* for you. Yes, I definitely should have called him out. He should know better than to offer for another man's woman."

"Charles wanted to offer for me?" she asked in a weak voice. A frown pinched her brows. "What do you mean Charles should know better than to offer for another man's woman? I'm no one's woman."

"You're *my* woman. I think you always have been . . . I was just too blind to see it." To her astonishment, he lowered himself to one knee and took her hands. "Marry me, Caroline."

She was robbed of speech. *Dear God, he's foxed.*

Or . . . he was making a cruel jest at her expense. Jerking away from his hands, she turned her back on him. A choked sob escaped her. "How can you possibly joke about something like this?"

He stood and grabbed her shoulders. Turning her

around, he gathered her into a tight embrace, burying his face in her hair. "Caroline, darling, this is no jest." He pushed her chin up with his fingers until her teary gaze met his. "I bloodied Blankenship's nose because he dared to touch you. The thought of you with him, or any man for that matter, is completely impossible. I simply cannot allow it. I want you too much for myself."

His solemn eyes regarded her steadily. "I love you, Caroline. I want you to be my wife. Say you'll marry me."

She stared up into his handsome, serious face. If he hadn't been holding on to her, she would have slithered into a boneless heap at his feet. "I'll marry you," she said softly.

"Thank God." He bent his head to kiss her lips, but she pulled back.

"Ummm, Miles?"

He kissed her neck instead. "Yes?"

"Now that you've asked for my hand, and I've accepted, you won't change your mind, will you?"

"Never," he vowed against her neck. He suddenly stilled, then raised his head and looked at her, a frown forming between his brows. "Why do you ask?"

She chewed on her lower lip. "Well . . ."

"Well what?"

She drew a deep breath, then blurted, "Charles Blankenship never kissed me."

Miles stared at her for long moment. "He never kissed you?"

She shook her head. "No."

"You mean you—"

"Made it up. To make you jealous." She stared up at him, waiting for his reaction. *Please, God, don't make me sorry I told him the truth. I just don't want a lie between us.*

He frowned. "It worked."

"It did? You were jealous?"

"I wanted to kill the bastard. Now I suppose I shall let him live—provided he never comes near you again."

"After that bloody nose you gave him, I'm sure he never will." She rested her palms against his chest. "Are you angry?"

He pulled her against him and cupped her face between his hands. "Angry? Hardly. You've accepted my proposal. Now, if you'd cease chattering long enough for me to kiss you, I'd be a very happy man indeed."

"I won't say another word."

"Excellent. But before you stop talking, you could tell me you love me."

"I love you," she whispered, rising up on tiptoes and pressing herself against him.

A groan rumbled in his throat. "I hope you don't want a long engagement."

Heaving a blissful sigh, Caroline wound her arms around his neck. "Not at all. In case you haven't noticed, whirlwind weddings run in the family."

Chapter 29

Elizabeth stared at the child. She tried to draw a breath into her lungs, but the room was bereft of air. The girl's dark hair, her gray eyes, her age registered in Elizabeth's mind with an instant click of recognition.

This was the child from her vision.

Realization slammed into her with such force she felt light-headed. Claudine was the child's mother, which meant William . . . *William* was her father. Not Austin.

The child in danger was *this* child. Josette. *Not my child.* And she'd saved her from the danger. *Austin's words in the vision . . . his desolation, they were because he'd thought he'd lost* me.

William and Claudine walked in and smiled at Elizabeth. Tugging lightly on the child's hand, they approached Elizabeth. "We're so happy you are awake," William said. "There is so much to talk about, but most important, we must thank you for saving our daughter Josette's life."

In a daze, Elizabeth held out her hand. Josette shyly placed her small palm on Elizabeth's. Joy instantly suffused Elizabeth. Nothing but joy radiated from this child. No danger. No death. The threat was over. The relief sweeping through her left her faint.

Austin knelt beside the bed. "Elizabeth, are you all right? You look pale."

She tore her gaze from the little girl and stared at him. With an effort, she dragged a ragged breath into her lungs and moistened her dust-dry lips. Reaching out, she grasped his hands. "Austin. Josette . . . *she* is the child I saw in my vision."

For several heartbeats he simply stared at her. In a low voice he asked, "You mean the child you saw dying—"

"Was Josette. But she didn't die. We saved her. And it was *William's* child. Not ours." Tears pooled in her eyes, spilling over to wet her cheeks. "Not ours."

"Not ours?" he repeated, his eyes dazed. But then he frowned and lowered his voice further. "Do you mean that Josette is in danger?"

"No. The danger is over. Josette is fine."

"She's fine. And there's no danger to *our* child?"

"None."

He briefly squeezed his eyes shut, then brought their joined hands to his lips. "My God, Elizabeth." He swallowed audibly. "Does that mean what I think it means?"

"It means we're free. Free to love and bear our children without that horrible fear hanging over us."

"Elizabeth . . ." Leaning forward, he kissed her with aching tenderness.

She squeezed his hand and images flooded her mind. She tried to push them away, desperate not to see anything bad, anything that might ruin this moment. But the picture that formed in her mind stole the breath from her lungs.

With crystal clarity she saw herself and Austin, standing close together in a field of wildflowers, their eyes filled with loving promise. He held his hand out to her. *I love you, Elizabeth.*

The image faded, leaving a well of warmth and bemused wonder in its wake.

He leaned back and studied her face. "What did you see?"

"You and me . . . it was a vision of love. And happiness."

"Happiness."

"Yes." A joyous smile rose from her heart. "It is an American word that means 'heavenly bliss.'"

He brought their clasped hands to his lips. "It is also an English word that means 'you and I loving each other for the rest of our lives.'"

She looked into his eyes and immediately knew he was right.

Epilogue

Austin paced the length of the drawing room, raking his fingers through his hair. The doctor had been with Elizabeth for over an hour. How the hell long did it take to remove the dressing on her shoulder and determine if she was fully recovered? They'd been home for a month. Surely that was enough time for her injury to have completely healed.

Laughter distracted his thoughts and he walked to the opened window. His entire family, minus Caroline and Miles who were honeymooning in Brighton, sat around the round table on the terrace. His mother was beaming at William, who bounced a squealing Josette on his knee. Claudine and Lady Penbroke were engaged in an animated discussion, and Robert was occupied removing the end of Lady Penbroke's boa from his teacup. Under the table, Gadzooks and his cohorts frolicked with the small white puppy Austin had recently purchased. He'd had to search nearly all of England to find a dog that looked exactly like the sketch of Patch Elizabeth had drawn, but he'd finally succeeded.

Elizabeth had laughed and cried at the same time when he'd placed the squirming furry bundle in her arms. The delight shining from her eyes had touched him . . . in that place deep inside him only she could reach.

A knock sounded on the door.

Turning from the window, he called, "Come in."

Elizabeth entered.

He reached her in two strides. "Are you all right?"

She smiled. "The doctor said I am fine."

A relieved breath whooshed from his lungs. "Thank God." He drew her into his arms and kissed her brow. Leaning back, he noticed she held a letter. "Is that from Caroline?"

"No. It's from my friend in America. Alberta."

"The young woman you warned not to marry?"

"Yes. Unfortunately my premonitions proved correct." She looked at him through sad eyes. "David was unfaithful to her. He was killed in a duel by his lover's husband."

"I'm sorry, Elizabeth."

"As am I. In her letter she begs for my forgiveness, which I shall gladly give her, along with an invitation to come visit us."

The sound of laughter drew their attention and Austin walked with her to the window. He watched a smile curve her lips when Robert spied them at the window and waved. She returned the greeting, then stilled, her gaze alternating between the letter she held and Robert's laughing face.

"Oh, no," Austin said. "What are you seeing now?"

She hesitated, then smiled. "I'm just thinking that I shall make it a point to write to Alberta today. I think a trip to England is *exactly* what she needs. And, um, Robert might enjoy it as well."

The significance of her words hit him and a smile tugged his lips. "I see. Should I warn my dear brother?"

Her dimples winked at him. "Oh, I don't think a warning will help." She slipped her letter into her pocket, then drew a deep breath. "I haven't told you everything the doctor said, Austin."

His smile collapsed. "You said you're fine—"

"Oh, I am. Most robust. I may resume my normal schedule, but he cautioned me against activities that he feels are too rigorous for one in my . . . delicate condition."

"Delicate?"

She nodded, her eyes shining with joy. "Yes. It is an American word that means 'I'm going to have a baby.'"

His heart skidded to a halt, then thumped back to life. She was going to have a baby. His child. Their child. He squeezed his eyes shut, absorbing the joy, savoring the miracle.

"Give me your hand," she whispered.

Opening his eyes, he held out his hand. She clasped it and brought it to her stomach, gently pressing his palm against her gown.

"Do you see anything?" he asked, watching her closely.

A slow smile lit her beautiful face. "Hmmm . . . you appear to have some plans that include you, me, and that sofa by the fire."

He laughed. "You're a difficult woman to surprise, my love."

Her eyes widened and his amusement instantly vanished. "What do you see now?"

"I see a baby . . . a beautiful baby boy," she said, her voice filled with wonder. "He's going to be just like you . . . with your dark hair, strong chin, and noble bearing."

"You're wrong," Austin corrected quietly. He looked into her eyes, eyes so full of love and warmth and goodness, and his heart, quite simply, rolled over. "He'll be just like you . . . just like his mother . . . a vision. A vision of love."

About the Author

Jacquie D'Alessandro grew up on Long Island and fell in love with romance at an early age. She dreamed of being swept away by a dashing rogue riding a spirited stallion. When her hero finally showed up, he was dressed in jeans and driving a Volkswagen, but she recognized him anyway. They married after they both graduated from Hofstra University, and are now living their happily-ever-afters in Atlanta, Georgia, along with their very bright and active nine-year-old son, who is a dashing rogue in the making. *Whirlwind Wedding* is Jacquie's second book for Bantam/Dell. Her first, *Red Roses Mean Love,* is an award-winning romantic comedy/murder mystery set in Regency England. She is currently working on her next historical romance and she would love to hear from readers. Visit her website at www.JacquieD.com or write to her at 875 Lawrenceville-Suwanee Road, Suite 310-PMB 131, Lawrenceville, GA 30043.